The Nidus:

Cradle of

Terror

The Nidus:

Cradle of

Terror

by

Bob Pearce

and

Nayereh Fallahi

BONNEVILLE BOOKS ™
Springville Utah

ISBN: 1-55517-563-5
v.1

Published by Bonneville Books
Imprint of Cedar Fort Inc.
www.cedarfort.com

Distributed by:

Typeset by Virginia Reeder
Cover design by Adam Ford
Cover design © 2001 by Lyle Mortimer

Printed in the United States of America
10 9 8 7 6 5 4 3 2 1

Printed on acid-free paper

Library of Congress Control Number: 2001095147

Dedication

To people everywhere who follow their
faith and tradition tenets that honor fellow human
beings, regardless of their gender, color of their
skin or economic status.

Chapter 1
Conference in St. Thomas—Days 1 & 2

At first, Jim Schriver, Pharm. D., had said no, but Ed and Claire kept insisting that he attend the infectious disease conference in St. Thomas with them. At the last moment before Jim decided, Ed had said, "Dammit, Jim, there comes a time when you should start going through the motions of living again. You're never going to complete your mourning process hiding in your shell."

If it were left up to him, he would just as soon have forgotten the whole thing. When he finally consented to go, he told Ed and Claire, "It's just to get you two to quit nagging me." But in actuality, two lectures really did interest him. The first was to be about a theoretical capability of a common influenza virus—a virus identified in Tehran, Iran, that Jim felt might possibly suggest some relationship to Jaynee's death in Utah. The second lecture he was interested in was one his friend Ed was to give.

Logic should have prevailed—he was a teaching professor and he shouldn't have dumped his lecture duties on his associates. But, he just hadn't been able to focus on much of anything since Jaynee's death many months ago. Escaping with their old friends might be the most therapeutic thing he could do for himself and for his students.

The chairperson of his department at the University of Utah, Art Kim knew that a leave-of-absence was the best thing for Jim and his students right now. "Maybe just the change of environment will help him." Dr. Kim gambled and authorized it.

They all had warm memories of sharing Jaynee's life, those picnics in the parks, weekly jogging and hiking, the great ski treks in the backcountry, exploring the wonders of Canyonlands. It gave them all a romantic fantasy that the "fearsome foursome" could conquer anything. Jim, Jaynee, Claire and Edward had been wrong.

Somehow his best friend seemed to express what was needed to finally motivate him. Jim simply could not say no, so now they were about to depart for Charlotte Amalie on St. Thomas in the Virgin Islands.

Through the kaleidoscopic drops of rain on the cabin window, Jim could feel himself being hypnotized by the rotating beacon on top of the plane next to them. His despondency was complete. He questioned, "How could a benevolent and omnipotent god have allowed his Jaynee to be taken from him? If the worldwide human instinct to seek out a creator was genetically encoded, perhaps we would all be better off if we removed it. Oh, if only it was that simple—a single gene; a single "nidus," a single nest.

It was 12:30 A.M. on Delta's bargain red-eye flight. He had been dozing off at the wrong times during the day and then he couldn't sleep at night. The chronic lack of meaningful sleep had plagued him ever since the memorial service months ago, and Jim feared chronic insomnia.

However, in just a few moments he plunged into a nightmare. Jaynee was gasping for breath . . . delirium, spasms, convulsions . . . frantic efforts to intubate and resuscitate . . . alarms and monitors screaming . . .

"SIR! SIR!" The flight attendant pleaded, "Your seat belt—we are about to depart from Salt Lake."

James Schriver was catapulted from unconsciousness, abandoning his bride in his repetitious nightmare.

"Sorry," he said, fumbling for his belt.

"Here, Jim, let me help you," Claire said sympathetically. She found his missing belt buckle resting in the middle seat.

In a contrived tone slightly suggestive of her southern black heritage, Claire added, "We cain't have that pretty flight attendant stressed out, now can we Jim?" Claire and Eddie looked at one another the way wives and husbands tacitly communicate.

Claire's ebony beauty and classic figure contrasted with Ed's bleached complexion, sandy hair, and stocky build on one side of her and Jim's undersized wrinkled white shirt stretched over his tall, strong frame on the other side. Except for Ed's red Chum cord securing half-lenses, the two studious men looked dull and reserved despite the fact that both had removed their conservative ties. The fellows were in their late thirties. Claire looked ten years younger— even though she wasn't.

Jim, somewhat embarrassed, completed the preflight ritual and again settled back for the non-stop flight to Atlanta. He looked for a distraction. He found it in the Salt Lake Gazette in the seat pocket, which carried all the exhausting stories of the candidates in the upcoming presidential election in November.

On page five of the national section, he found a story of Idaho's so-called patriot-group, STRIKE (Special Trained Response Individuals for Key Events). At one of their UN flag-burning parties, they cheered Nick Cabal. He was a retired Green Beret and former CIA agent who was pictured with them as a mentor of STRIKE, leading the militant arm of the extremist group. The report indicated Patrick Buchanan had been selected as their choice for president. They supported his posture concerning the KKK, right to bear arms, abortion, and his support for the Confederate Stars and Bars flag. It was all too much; Jim inhaled a bourbon-and-water he had been served and drifted into sleep again.

Ed and Claire could not ignore Jim's noisy sleep—he was probably dreaming again.

The concern was evident on the little black face of eight-year-old Jamal Brown as he looked into his teacher's eyes while he described what he had found. Near the "School With No Name," a humble one-room school for children staying in the homeless center, Jamal found something bad. On Union Pacific Railroad property, a short distance away, he had found "a drug thing."

Jaynee Schriver, his teacher, had the complete trust of most of the children. She always tried to protect her kids from the stereotyping drug-abuse label that most of society was prone to affix on any homeless child.

Jamal knew that he should show his teacher any strange-looking vials, syringes or bottles. He showed her the vial that had fallen out of the odd plastic container. Jaynee congratulated Jamal when she squatted down to his level and cradled his smiling face in her hands. "I am so proud of you, Jamal, you did the right thing. Now, hurry in to class. Kendra is holding the flag to raise for the Pledge of Allegiance."

Kendra Yazzie, the Navaho teacher's aide, held the door open and watched them from quite a distance. Jaynee and Jamal were outside the fence. Vindictively, Jaynee smashed the vial with the nearest rock that she could find. Some of the liquid contents squirted into the air in tiny droplets, causing her to blink and then sneeze.

"Yuck! I should've known better," she lamented as she swiped her face with the sleeve of her sweatshirt. "I don't have time to mess with this crap and I am not going to file any more bureaucratic bullshit reports." Only broken glass remained, still clinging to the label, a short way from the crushed box.

Jim had leaned over his dying wife as she whispered, "That's all I remember, Jim. . . . That's all I remember."

Jim dozed half awake and yet disturbed, and thought to himself, "Why do I always seem to ruminate, even in my dreams, over all the tiny details?" After all, a thorough study and consequent presentation at the hospital's Morbidity and Mortality Committee meeting had determined that all concerned with the case had done everything they could. "What is bugging me? I just can't put my finger on it."

As he crept closer to consciousness, he became aware of the smell of coffee, jet exhaust, and cologne . . .

"How was your little nap?" Claire inquired from her seat.

4

"Still full of disturbing memories, I'm sorry to say," Jim said.

"Like what?"

Jim described his dream to Claire and Ed.

Claire said, "I don't recall Jaynee mentioning a broken box of any kind, just a broken vial." Ed nodded his head to confirm her perspective. "What was that all about?"

"Oh . . . I guess that must have been something Jaynee told me that I spaced out until now. I guess I was too focused on the treatment to consider trying to find the nidus," Jim replied.

"Nidus?" Claire repeated inquiringly.

"Nidus literally means 'nest' in Latin. In health care we usually use the word when we mean the hidden location or source of an infection," Jim explained. "Jaynee's symptoms were indicative of some damned fulminating virus that had invaded her body and ravished her brain. I still can't understand how she caught the virus."

Claire nodded understandingly while she put her hand on his arm. "Everyone did all that could be done—you should work at trying to internalize that, Jim. As a clinical psychologist, I have seen people stall in their grief process if they don't face why they can't let go of certain things. Of course, it is normal for you to have some self-blame, repressed hostility and confusion. But having said that, you can't let it consume you." She paused then said, "I'm sorry—I won't preach anymore."

"It's O.K, Claire, I know what you say is true, but it's so hard! If only we could have found another intact vial or, for that matter, the styrofoam box that Jaynee talked about, I think it would have been easier. It may have had nothing to do with her illness, but I will never be convinced. After all of our experience with contaminated needles and other drug paraphernalia that go with transfer of diseases such as AIDS, I'm convinced the vial was the nidus—the source. As you know, we simply didn't look for it until it was too late. The vial debris was taken away by the FDA as possible drug evidence."

"Jim, if by some miracle you found out what the vial contained, it wouldn't bring her back," Ed responded. He had been reviewing the material that he was to present at the meeting and had only been partially aware of all that they had discussed.

"You are both right, I'm stuck in a rut. Even though I don't want to get it behind me, I'm going to try to focus on the beauty of the Caribbean as much as I can," Jim responded. In an attempt to show his conviction he asked, "What time does our flight from Atlanta get into Puerto Rico?"

"We should be in San Juan by 1:00 P.M. I booked us rooms for tonight in a quaint little hotel, the El Canario Inn," Ed answered. "We were hoping to go out to the old town and visit San Cristobal and the old fortress, El Morro. It's got walls 20 feet thick and 140 feet high. It will give us a chance to stretch our legs. There should be good fresh ocean air. We'll check in at the hotel first and then take a cab out there; does that sound okay?" Ed asked.

"That sounds fine, Ed."

"We are booked on an American flight tomorrow, arriving in the Virgin Islands at about 1:00 P.M.," Ed said, reading from his travel agent's memo. "I guess the airport is not too far from the 1829 Hotel in Charlotte Amalie." Ed peered up from his reading and said sarcastically, "Well, don't show so much enthusiasm, Jim."

"I'm already getting out my suntan cream and my sunglasses," smiled Jim.

A few hours later they were standing on the old fort wall contemplating the strategically placed cannons and piles of cannon balls, when a voice from Jim's past bellowed, "O-Mah-Hell! Is that you—Boots?"

Startled, Jim looked down the gray castle's stone rampart and parapet to confirm the voice.

"Boots! Jim Schriver—don't you know your old pharmacology buddy anymore?"

"Ben Carlson? Is that you?"

A sturdy, prematurely gray-haired man wearing an expensive-looking summer suit elbowed his way from a tour group, then with bounding steps quickly closed in on the three.

"Can you believe it? You don't see someone for years and then you practically bump into him thousands of miles from home! What are you doing here, Boots?"

"Ed and Claire Woodsman, I'd like you to meet my old College of Pharmacy classmate, Ben Carlson. Ben, these are my two closest friends in Salt Lake City." Then Jim said to Ed and Claire, "Ben and I suffered through higher education together, as you might have surmised."

"You folks don't call him Boots, do you? Well, I should explain. That was a label Dr. Dave Toll hung on him in those days because he would wear his Colorado cowboy boots into the lab, the clinics . . . everywhere. Dave had a great sense of humor. He once asked Jim in clinic, 'How would a patient on an exam table feel about the competency of his caregiver if he looked down to see him with dung on his cowboy boots?' The name stuck with him."

"Jim, I heard you got married a while back—where's your bride? I'd like to meet her."

"I wish you could," Jim said haltingly.

Ed and Claire strolled away with brochure in hand to allow Jim to explain how his life with Jaynee had ended so prematurely. Jim and Ben headed in the other direction as Jim briefly related the story of his married life. Ben expressed his condolences.

After an uncomfortable silence, Jim thought to inquire, "We're on our way to attend a conference in St. Thomas—is that what brings you here, Ben?"

"I'm director of marketing for Alpha Omega Pharmaceutical and we are indeed helping support Academic Learning Systems with an infectious disease conference out of Ft. Lauderdale aboard the *Royal Caribbean*. I'm going to meet the ship in St. Thomas. Damned management problems detained me until now."

"Serendipity," Jim responded. "We are attending the same

seminar! Ed is presenting a paper on the history of immunizations to a group of pharmacists, nurses, physicians and other infectious-disease professionals. However, the first lectures on board were going to be redundant for Ed, because he attended a conference last month where most of the data was presented, so we felt we could pick up the cruise in St. Thomas and meet his academic responsibilities. I'm along primarily as the group's comedian. Seriously, I just needed to get away, though I am interested in two lectures," said Jim.

"Oh-oh, I see I am losing my fellow tour partners, Jim. Let's say we will continue this reunion in St. Thomas," Ben said, scurrying after his group. "See ya there—where are y'all staying?" Ben called over his shoulder. Jim told him.

Back at the hotel Jim reflected as he sat on the veranda off his room. "It was a good day today. For once I didn't get choked up or teary-eyed telling Jaynee's story. I may make it yet." But he still felt uneasy. Suddenly he couldn't visualize Jaynee clearly. He hastily unzipped his bag. Panic almost set in as he unpacked his suitcase to locate her picture. "I can't find it! I can't find it! No! I left it on the dresser along with the razor," Jim cried. He finally called Claire and Ed to inquire, "Am I really losing it or not?"

They consoled him and assured him that his problem was quite common with grieving.

Ed insisted, "Jim, take fifty milligrams of diphenhydramine and get some sleep. That antihistamine will have just enough sedative effect for your needs now."

"You go on and do some sightseeing," Jim responded. "I'm going to eat light, take your advice and try to get some sleep."

The warm Caribbean breeze gave his black locks of hair a rough-hewn appearance. Coupled with his square-set jaw, his six-foot trim physique, two days growth of beard and then a few days' tan, he could almost pass for one of the many Latin American or Mediter-ranean visitors who saw this city during the year. After making his purchase at the little pharmacia, he decided to walk to the water's

8

edge with a snack.

The soft Reggae music in the distance complemented the smells wafting from the restaurants at seaside. Visual stimulation demanded his attention. For the first time in months, Jim was starting to be aware of the here and now. He even ogled the brightly colored bikinis of a trio of beautiful black women talking in a dialect that he didn't recognize. He guessed he had walked about three miles, when he realized how bone-tired he really was. He found his way back to the hotel and regretted that he would miss the balance of the beautiful evening in San Juan because of his exhaustion.

It was the first whole night's sleep he had in months, but near morning he experienced a dream that would forever seem real to him. Jaynee appeared next to him. He felt her touch and even dreamed he recognized a fragrance she wore. In the subdued light he could see her smiling face when she spoke to him.

Jim felt it was so brief—yet so poignant. "I am fine—everything is okay," she seemed to say. Then she was gone in the bright light of the new day. Jim awoke rested and reconciled that he could never return to their Camelot.

When they landed at St. Thomas' quaint airport Jim said, "this reminds me of the small towns in Utah. You've got to read the greeting on the terminal building to be certain where you are."

As they taxied down the runway, the drifting ocean mist evaporated and allowed a good view of the arid-looking terrain.

Ed attempted to hire a cab but was told, "It might be a while, because the cruise ships have just docked."

"Ni modo" *it doesn't matter* was the immediate response of one authority. "One will come." "Hey mon, doon wary—be hoppy," seemed to be the prevailing philosophy, spoken by one airport clerk.

They found some shade under a palm tree and parked their gear, but it was too hot and humid and the breeze disturbed the shade of the palm. Claire bought a local newspaper while waiting for their transportation, but Jim and Ed just sat and enjoyed people-watching—especially the pretty women.

Claire looked as though she belonged on the island; she seemed to look good in anything. She had done some smart shopping before leaving home, buying comfortable-looking shorts with a yellow blouse that flattered her athletic figure, and of course she didn't need to work on her tan.

While scanning the paper, Claire declared, "This is the last news I am going to read until we go home!"

"What's that all about, Spike?" inquired Ed. She had acquired her affectionate nickname, Spike, from her volleyball days in school. Claire called him Eddie, as did his family back home.

Claire read out loud. "When they consolidated the National Reconnaissance Office with the National Security Agency, it gave the director of the CIA, John Deutch, new power. That's the group that controls the spy satellites. Well, now he can move money from one foreign intelligence account to another without the approval of the account managers. This is the opportunity that Newt Gingrich, our House Speaker, lusted after. Newt wanted $18 million for covert action in Iran, just a crumb under the table of the $28 billion classified budget for the U.S. intelligence community. Now the skids are greased for who knows what? Perhaps they can rehire Robert Cleare, the spy they fired for sleeping with the secretary of an Arab ambassador and accepting bribes. You may recall, he took the fall for allowing Sheik Omar Abdel Rahman to enter the U.S. and bomb the World Trade Center in New York City in 1993," she said cynically.

Both Jim and Ed knew better than to pursue her "favorite villain crusade," any further. Foreign affairs had always been her favorite diversion when escaping the travail of psychotherapy with a difficult patient. She was intense in almost everything she focused on and really only needed an audience to vent her pent-up hostilities. Fortunately a cab circled into the area at that time and erased everyone's impatience. They left with all windows open, no seat belts visible and Novo-Reggae music roaring.

The cascading pink steps, palms and red hibiscus led up to the quaint entrance of Hotel 1829 on Government Hill in Charlotte Amalie, and provided the prelude to serendipity. Despite the travails of Hurricane Marilyn of September 1995, the Spanish architecture demonstrated that this hotel had been the center of ambiance for over one hundred years and was ready for the next one hundred. Dr. Laleh Bazargan and her sister Sonbol lounged on the porch, oblivious to the new arrivals. Laleh and Sonbol languished on rattan furniture in colorful filmy attire that revealed sensuous figures beneath layered veils. They were enjoying the view of the harbor as the gentle warm breeze off the Caribbean complemented the soft music coming from the antique Danish kitchen-turned-lounge.

The taxi, with its music competing with the atmosphere of the hotel, labored up the hill to the base of the long stairway. The steep pink steps leading up to the porch were built in an era that never acknowledged disabilities. The three athletic travelers from the U.S. denied assistance from "Hen-ray," the hotel's doorman, plumber, electrician and ombudsman. Even though each was encumbered with their own luggage, they seemed invigorated at the challenge. As they reached the porch summit, they relinquished their gear to Hen-ray who insisted that he be allowed to carry it to their rooms yet to be assigned. It was then that Ed thought he recognized one of the two women.

"Dr. Bazargan?"

"I'm sorry, I do not recognize you." she responded.

Ed's attention was still fixed on Dr. Bazargan. "I recognized you from your photo in the conference brochure. I am Dr. Edward Woodsman and this is my wife Dr. Claire Woodsman and our good friend Dr. Jim Schriver."

"Please call me Laleh. We can refrain from formalities here, we'll have enough of those tomorrow."

Jim seemed awe struck with Laleh's beauty and poise. Staring into her dark brown eyes he realized that she was almost as tall as he was. The chemistry was unmistakable to both Jim and this woman he had just met. Jim had a schoolboy grin on his face. Surreptitiously he became aware of her figure and that she was wearing very fashionable high heels, barely visible below her flowing garments. Her Hijab, Islamic women's attire, included a colorful translucent Roosarie or hair covering.

Awkwardly, Jim finally said, "I'm pleased to meet you. I'm looking forward to attending your lecture tomorrow." He finally released her hand, oblivious of violating any possible Islamic mores.

Dr. Bazargan reciprocated introductions. "My sister, Sonbol Bazargan."

Jim managed to focus his attention briefly on Sonbol, but returned his attention to Laleh.

Sonbol felt Laleh was exaggerating her accent to avoid the supercilious Americans congratulating her on her command of the English language. Laleh also spoke French, German and of course Farsi, her native Persian language.

Her sister seemed puzzled, as Laleh obviously experienced pleasure in this unexpected display of emotional chemistry from such a handsome man.

"I believe I detect a Mideast accent; where is your home?" Claire asked.

"Tehran, Iran," Sonbol responded.

Jim inquired, "Is it proper for two beautiful Iranian women to travel alone without being accompanied by a male family member? I read somewhere that your culture required that."

Laleh looked into Jim's eyes and smiled, "Oh yes, that is right. Unfortunately, my brother, Amir, had to stay in Iran because of some demanding family problems. He is younger than we are, but according to Iranian Islamic law, he has given us permission to leave the country since he is the only male in our family after our father died."

Jim, driven by the newly unleashed repressed desires said,

"Would you ladies like to join us this evening for dinner? I under-stand the restaurant here has been featured in a gourmet magazine as one of the major dining spots in the Caribbean."

Ed and Claire could not believe their ears. They had been emotionally nurturing Jim for over a year and a half and hadn't been able to initiate any social activity whatsoever.

"That would be so nice," Claire quickly added. "We would be honored if you would join us."

"We have no other plans," Laleh quickly responded, looking for the approving nod from her sister.

All seemed to sense the magnetism between Jim and Laleh and were surprised but happy. They agreed to meet at 7:00 P.M. for dinner.

Walking from the porch through the main entryway, Jim focused on a Latin-inscribed Spanish crest of a bygone era. It was fixed on the opposite wall of the large greenery-filled patio. The open area allowed a few birds to perch and inspect the new guests. When Jim looked from the courtyard up the rambling staircases to the fifteen suites three flights up, he was reminded of the famous artist, Escher, and his illusion of endless stairs. Each level was a separate building imbedded into the mountain. When he reached his eagle's nest accommodation at the top level of suites, he noticed an ancient, very small machine gun mounted on a tripod, tucked into a corner like a substitute flower vase. The paradox—beauty and peace versus war—served to pique his consciousness with its incongruous pres-ence.

Everything else was relaxed beauty. He found he could look south and see the entire harbor. One of two cruise ships was now leaving the area, evidently to get under way to another area in the British Virgin Islands. Jim mused to himself, "I would rather be going on any one of those small sailing boats tomorrow, instead of that posh cruise ship for the seminar. Oh, well." Because of his penchant to march to a different drummer, Jim fantasized visiting a desert island

and maybe swimming nude with Jaynee. "I'm doing it again," he said to himself, "I've got to quit living in the past and relating to things as a couple; I've got to think in 'single' status. Getting deeply depressed is too easy—still."

The huge split-leaf philodendron, reaching from the lower story to shade his suite's white wood-railed deck, grew higher than many trees in his native state of Colorado. The aroma of sweet fresh flowers greeted him as he unlocked his room. The bathroom notice reminded guests that fresh water on the island was not abundant, and one should not be wasteful. The little sign warned him that even paradise had limitations. Jim looked below to the inviting swimming pool. Soon he was doing laps in it. The exercise seemed to release some of the travel weariness he had accumulated. Just enough time remained to stretch out on his bed before going down to dinner. A tambourine and what Jim thought were oboes and bells awakened him from his short, dreamless nap. It sounded Middle-Eastern. From the shaded privacy of his window, he sought out the source of the music. It was coming from a room directly across the courtyard, also on his elevated level. Then he noticed flashing bodies of the Iranian sisters between the partially opened curtains of the large room. The undulating women were advancing and retreating in full costume— obviously talented dancers. Jim became aware that his voyeuristic mood had begun to excite him. He was reminded of his youth when he would steal looks at a ranch hand's daughter as she bathed in a creek. Those Bazargan sisters were certainly skillful and beautiful, he thought as he finally retreated to get dressed.

Jim changed clothes and timed his exit from his room to inter-cept Laleh and Sonbol as they descended the fragrant stairway to the restaurant. The aromas of flowers and cooking herbs complemented one another. The mood was festive and relaxed, the setting sun's reflection shimmered on the water, and everyone commented on the beauty of the bay below and the grand vista the hotel offered. Jim, Ed, and Claire spoke of analogies to the Great Salt Lake—views they enjoyed at various times from different vantage points. The Bazargans compared the view to the Caspian Sea in Iran, where they went on holiday. But all agreed that this vista was truly unique in the world. When the hors d'oeuvres were served and the wine list was offered, Claire noted, "The Mormon culture is like the Islamic culture with its religious restrictions against the use of alcoholic beverages."

"I believe we all tend to stereotype. There are some very demonstrative orthodox followers, and then there are the passive partisans and every variance in between," Laleh responded. "For instance," Ed added, some Christians use real wine in their Catholic communion observances and yet many Protestants, who have few religious reservations personally on the use of alcohol, still insist on using plain grape juice." The six proceeded to engage one another in lighthearted conversation about the local experiences each had already had in Charlotte Amalie. They seemed eager to seek common ground and find a human bond, even though their cultures were so different. The arrival of menus eventually gave rise to a discussion of the differences and similarities of typical meals to be found in the homes and restaurants of Iran and the U.S. Laleh described an Iranian wedding feast: "A traditional 'must' wedding feast starts with, sheerin polo, which includes cooked rice, slivered almonds, chopped or slivered pistachios, sliced carrots, raisins, barberries, cardamom, and dissolved saffron." Laleh looked to her sister for confirmation. Sonbol's smile suggested amusement with her sister's choice of the wedding topic. "We also use slivered orange peeling after the pulp is removed from the peelings—yes?" Sonbol added. Laleh nodded her approval. All the time Laleh was talking, she was aware that Jim seemed to be swimming in her eyes. As she finished speaking, she fixed her gaze on Jim's wedding band and then on his face. The tacit query was obvious to the sisters at the round table: "What is this married man doing?" Jim, however, seemed oblivious to anything but Laleh's aura, unaware of any possible question. Fortunately Claire, the matchmaker, caught the look and intuitively inquired, "That reminds me, Jim, do you recall the meal that you and Jaynee fixed us—something special—about a month or two before she died—when we got together on your patio? Those little chickens with the wild rice—remember?"

It was a wake-up call for Jim, "I—ah—oh yeah—Cornish game hens stuffed with wild rice." Suddenly Jim was obviously lost in memory and somewhat withdrawn.

Laleh seemed visually relieved, yet also compassionate. "Was Jaynee your wife?"

Jim nodded.

"How long has it been since she died?"

"About eighteen months. Sometimes it seems like yesterday—other times it seems like a decade. I'm still dealing with it," confessed Jim.

"We can, as you say, identify with your grief. Our father died about that long ago. It has been very difficult. Our brother has had to act as head of family. He had to stay in Iran, as you know. Even though he is younger than Sonbol and I, he still is in charge of our inheritance. In Shi'ite law, the male sibling receives one half; we sisters share equally the remaining half and our mother receives one eighth. So it was only natural that he must attend to our interests."

"Is Islamic law always so male-chauvinistic?" Jim innocently inquired.

"Cordially, I agree with you. But most Iranian people do not consider it chauvinistic. It was fatwa, a legal decision made by our Islamic Mullahs who interpret the sacred teachings of the Koran. According to their interpretation, it is done to protect the females, and yet recognizes that it is the males who usually must be responsible for managing the money," Laleh responded.

Jim's pious look said volumes.

Laleh felt indignantly obliged to continue. "However, we do not have many young unmarried women with children who are not financially cared for, like the U.S.A."

Jim was totally unprepared for such a quick backhand indictment of the United States. Ed and Claire looked to see how Jim was going to respond.

Jim sat back in his chair and confidently folded his hands on the edge of the table. He scrambled to compose his thoughts.

"Then, that is the main reason women want to get married in the Moslem World?" Jim responded jokingly to challenge Laleh. Then, looking into her eyes, he thought, "Oops, I might have lost her interest on that one."

"When Americans can only see the faults of other countries, it is predictable that they will not see clearly in a mirror," joined Sonbol.

Claire, sensing a need for a shift in diplomacy, calmly asked, "What about your new year; do all Moslems celebrate the New Year?"

"I think we all need the serkeh of Norooz. At the time of New Year or Norooz, every home sets a symbolic-table, haft-sin, with items to remind us of desirable things, like a mirror—to see ourselves as we really are. Also vinegar, serkeh. Vinegar represents patience and age," Sonbol responded.

Claire, relieved, said, "Tell us more about Norooz, Sonbol. I find this fascinating."

"Norooz is an ancient Iranian spring festival. 'No' means "new" and 'rooz' means 'day.' Norooz is the 'new day' of the new year. Every year on the first day of spring, March 20 or 21, Iranians will celebrate Norooz. It usually lasts thirteen days. Arabs do not celebrate Norooz."

Jim and Laleh realized what the others were trying to do for them and the expressions on their faces seemed to communicate better priorities for the two. They were now aware of a certain mutual chemistry between them, one that demanded exploring.

Sonbol, enjoying the attention, continued. "This Persian festival has been celebrated continuously for more than three thousand years by Iranians. It is a farewell to the cold of winter and a happy time for new life. For twenty-five days before Norooz, people clean their houses, buy new clothes and look forward to the holiday."

"The Persian New Year table reflects Sofreh-yehaft-sinn, a table set with seven items. The number seven is important, and all of the items on the table begin with *s*," Sonbol added.

Laleh seized the opportunity to contribute, "Sabzeh is one item on the table. It is green wheat or lentil—ah—sprouts. It represents new birth. Samenu, is a sweet creamy pudding—for life. Seeb is the apple for health and beauty. Senjed for sweet—for love. Seer, or garlic, is for medicine. Somaq, in English the Sumac, for color of sunrise and last Serkeh, again, or vinegar—yes."

"Don't forget, the Seven Sinn are not the only things on the table," Sonbol reminded. "We also have religious books of the Koran or maybe the Bible for Christian Iranians or the book of hafez, all kinds of spring flowers like tulip or laleh; narcissus or nargus and hiecine or sonbol. Rose water or Golab, oranges floating in the water like the earth in space, will also be included."

"Tokhmeh—morgh-e-ramgi, or painted eggs, are for each of the family members, or as a symbol of fertility. Also candles," she added.

"Finally the goldfish in the bowl for change of year and life," Laleh said. "And don't forget the Sabzee Khordan, herbs, Persian baklava, almond and walnut cookies, chickpeas with Shikar or sugar. Noghls, sugar almonds, are also at the table, placed there the week before spring. Also, a gold coin, Sekeh, is included. And something that is relative to our conversation earlier—a mirror . Then we can see ourselves as others see us."

Sonbol nervously regressed into another lecture, "You Americans, have Santa Claus, for Norooz we have Haji Firouz, or man-of-happiness.

"Many men dress this way—in red or orange satin. They sing and dance—parade in the city. Very—how you say—festive?

"Oh—I almost forgot, we celebrate the last Wednesday of the year with a bonfire, Chahar Shanbeh Sury. People jump over the flame and petition it, 'give me your beautiful red color and take my pallor.' Then they wear the chador and go door-to-door making much noise and asking for treats. If you don't give treats, you get bad luck all year.

"From the first day of Norooz until the twelfth day, it is visit and revisit parties. At first the young will visit the older family members, such as grandparents. On the day of the thirteenth, called seezde-be-dar, people picnic and single girls receive tied knots in grass or sprouted seeds for luck in finding a mate," Sonbol giggled. "If you are not so lucky, you get Ajil-e-Moshkel Gosha, or the problem-solving nuts." Everyone seemed relaxed when Sonbol finally ended her monologue.

After dinner the culture lecture evolved into a discussion about festive celebrations in America and the experiences to be enjoyed in various places around the world. As the diners decided to delay dessert, they stood and began talking in smaller groups. Jim some-how found himself next to Laleh and found out that her name meant "tulip" in English. Laleh learned that Jim had grown up on a ranch near Walden, a small town in Colorado.

The waiter quietly interrupted them with a FAX message for Laleh. She looked puzzled at the document. Her expression turned to concern as her brow wrinkled and her beautiful smile faded.

"I don't comprehend this," Laleh confided as she read the FAX to Jim in a manner soliciting help. "I have been arrested by the authority of the Revolutionary Council and confined to home. No charges have been revealed to me. I am afraid for you. Don't send messages. Don't come home until I send you our special childhood message. Amir."

"Do you know your special childhood message?" inquired Jim.

"No," replied Laleh, obviously disturbed, with tear-filled eyes. "I'm upset. I don't understand what could have happened. I'm sorry, but I must call my sister and retire—I must also prepare for my lecture tomorrow."

The two women talked briefly to one another. "Thank you for your concern," Laleh said to Jim. Then as they left, Laleh and Sonbol expressed to everyone their gratitude for a beautiful evening.

As the party abruptly ended and Jim was relating what little he knew to Ed and Claire, a heavy aroma of cigar smoke preceded the entry of Ben Carlson. On his arm was a blond woman who looked to Claire very much like a prostitute.

"Hi, we had dinner up at Blackbeard's Castle, where I'm staying—decided to come here for a nightcap. How are your accommodations here, Boots?" Ben inquired, exhaling another cloud of cigar smoke. It seemed pointed that he did not introduce the woman to Jim or Claire and Ed.

"Why don't you all join us in the lounge? Mother Alpha Omega is buying," said Ben.

Claire quickly declared that she wanted to walk down to see some of the illuminated sailing ships docked in the harbor and get some exercise before retiring. Jim thought he knew how the Woodsmans felt about Ben before this episode of poor taste—now he was positive. Ed and Claire Woodsman were an example of a married couple that "lived and let live." He knew how disgusted they felt about Ben's flaunting indiscretion. Jim then mumbled something about, "a rain check tomorrow" and complained, "I'm bone tired."

"I'll expect to see you tomorrow, then, at the seminar aboard ship at 8:00 A.M." Ben waved a preoccupied farewell as he ogled the blonde's plunging neckline.

Jim climbed the stairs in the starlit night, and looked back to see Ben herding his "date" with his hand low on her back. Jim reflected on their old college days, remembering when both Ben and he would go from bar to bar looking for available females who liked to party. That was before Jim met Jaynee at a 10K race.

He marveled how Jaynee had changed his life. He hadn't even considered going bar hopping since his frivolous youth spent with Ben. He couldn't understand why Ben hadn't found that one special woman yet.

Trudging up the stairs, he regretted not asking Laleh about her belly dancing. It had been a full day. He wondered what her brother's problem was all about.

Chapter 2
The *Royal Caribbean*—Day 3

Ed, Claire and Jim left quite early to walk from the Hotel 1829 to the *Royal Caribbean*. Normally they would have jogged together in the very early morning, but the holiday mindset allowed them to be more casual. Because Laleh was scheduled to be the first speaker of the day at 8:00 A.M., she also left early by taxi. Ed had his slides in a carousel under his arm, but other than that, they were unencumbered.

Like an impending earthquake, no one could forecast what startling information would be unleashed on such a beautiful day by Dr. Bazargan. The three American professionals assumed that they were going to attend just another scientific conference. They were totally unaware she would disclose the first disturbing clues that would eventually lead to events endangering their very lives.

It was Sunday, and a church in Charlotte Amalie was ringing its bell to remind all of the parishioners of their Sabbath. Ed and Claire had attended mass at a cathedral close to the hotel at 6:00 A.M. while Jim was still showering. Even though Jim had become more inclined to attend his Protestant church in Salt Lake since Jaynee's death, he never seemed to feel compelled to seek a worship service away from home.

On the way down Government Hill to the harbor, they saw a vendor sandwiched between two souvenir shops with nothing but a wooden box to support the newspapers he was selling. Politely smiling at the trio, he did not hawk in a loud voice, just a smile. Claire spoke to the man in Spanish and the two exchanged the greetings of the day as she paid for a paper.

Most of the shops down the street had their immense hurricane-proof doors of varnished wood securely locked. The trio swiftly angled toward the waterfront accompanied by the songs of birds in all of the trees announcing the new day. At the harbor the morning sun was so bright they could only squint at the panoply of boats and ships. A full palette of color demonstrated the diverse backgrounds of the people who were circulating early. The many hues of skin reflected the history of the Virgin Islands. Out of slavery, conquest, abuse and human suffering, love prevailed—and it was beautiful to the three newcomers who saw only the moment. The antique machine gun left in the shadows of the flora of the hotel held no significant impact on the lovers-of-life that morning.

When they arrived at the *Royal Caribbean,* a waiting steward ushered them up to the ballroom, where Dr. Bazargan stood poised to be introduced. The tropic breeze was intoxicating with the mixed aromas of flowers, fruit and either waffles or pancakes for the early risers on board the ship. Most of the seminar attendees were accustomed to even earlier schedules in their hospitals or other health care centers. Jim, Ed and Claire joined the others who had been sailing for four days. They felt compelled to explain to some people why they had not been seen until now.

Dr. Laleh Bazargan, often labeled a "control freak," was the epitome of readiness. After she had prepared her lecture, she had digitally compressed all of her presentation—slides, syllabus, graphs, charts and video clips of patients and microscopy—onto a single compact disk. She carried her own laptop computer and compact video projector including the tiny, new, powerful speakers. She even had her own lapel mike and a laser pointer the size of a ballpoint pen. All she needed was a screen or a blank wall plus some source of electric power. Of course, she also had her own extension cord.

When colleagues had inquired at past conferences why she felt so obsessive, she would explain with pride. "I come from a proud ancient culture in Iran with a tradition of excellence. Being female I feel an even greater need to be perfect. Besides, experience on the lecture circuit has taught me that AV and computer equipment are often lacking in one way or another."

Her dress for this lecture was quite western; she did not wear a chador. Her light-beige business suit, with a multicolored but somewhat conservative patterned scarf around her neck, contrasted nicely with jet-black hair drawn back into a modified bun. Her black-rimmed glasses accented her aura of authority, even if she didn't need much optical correction. She had practiced and was ready. Her only regret was that her supportive father was not there to hear and see her. His death still stood in the shadows of her mind, and she would dedicate this effort to him.

Dr. Don Wilkins of Academic Learning Systems was effusive in his introduction and description of her credentials. Perhaps it was his way of impressing his fellow revelers of the night before, that it was now time to center themselves on learning. It was always difficult to get people to change their frame of mind on the Sea Seminars, as the recreational distractions were always present.

Laleh began with the usual acknowledgments and expected light humor to give people a chance to settle in their seats.

She continued. "My observations of two special patients really launched me into the research that has caused me to title my talk, 'Causal Relationship of Parkinson's Disease and Influenza Type A–Induced Meningitis.' These two patients I will refer to as B. K. and N. K. B. K., a twenty-four-year-old black male born in southern Iran, who was a refugee to a small town, Jahrom Fars, near Shiraz, Iran. As a patient he was referred to us, along with his thirty-nine-year-old aunt. Both had symptoms of late stage Parkinson's Disease, even though they both had shown first signs and classic symptoms only two months previously. They were transferred from Namazi Hospital in Shiraz to Khomeini Hospital in Tehran."

Laleh assumed her audience knew that the coincidence of two patients concomitantly developing the symptoms of such a disease in the same household was a very questionable diagnosis. Add to this the fact that neither patient was over forty years old, and it defied all probability. Parkinson's is considered a disease of older people.

"It was also confirmed that neither patient violated the Islamic culture—neither patient had indulged in any drugs like one might see in the United States. For example, some patients ingest street heroin that can cause Secondary Parkinsonism. But, a complete neurological history and exam showed no evidence of carbon monoxide or manganese poisoning, nor other neuroleptic drugs such as halperidol or reserpine. Both patients rapidly deteriorated and died within a week of each other following their admission to our service."

Jim whispered to Claire as they sat in the audience, "Any one of those drugs might have caused a problem if either patient used one of them; she's just eliminated drug-induced causes."

Laleh continued her lecture. "An exhaustive study to identify structural lesions, tumors, infarcts involving the midbrain or basal ganglia, subdural hematoma, degenerative disorders including stria-tonigral degeneration and olivopontocerebellar degeneration was completed. Identical atrophy was found in both patients.

"We found very tiny blood clots in the center of the brain no bigger than a small grape." The MRI and CAT scan films were shown to the audience. "The patient interviews, very poignant videos of each patient, showed puzzling parallel symptoms: similar rigidity and slowness, bradykinesia, difficulty in initiating movement, akinesia, stooped posture, masklike face and open mouth with drooling, depression in both patients, and finally oculogyric crises—the forced, sustained deviation of the head and eyes."

Claire looked at Jim and whispered to him, "I don't know how you and Ed can stand to listen to this techno-jargon without going to sleep!"

"The historical data suggested Postencephalitic Parkinsonism, similar to that which occurred following the epidemic of Van Eco-nomo Encephalitis in 1918–24. A few of you may also recall the pandemic flu of 1918 that followed the First World War."

Jim again leaned over and whispered to Claire, "Now it might get more interesting! She's going to compare her virus to the world's worst pandemic virus ever known."

Laleh continued. "Based on speculation and previous patient interviews, I had the plasma which was previously drawn and frozen from the patients tested for the presence of multiple strains of different influenza viruses. These comparative slides you now see on the screen were taken in complete darkness to allow only the ultraviolet illumination to cause the positive samples to glow. As you can see, there is definite activity associated with the influenza A. It is brighter than the control sample in both patients.

"This data is conclusive; it suggests some unique new virus as a result of natural mutation or a molecularly manipulated flu virus. These two patients were de facto, both carriers of this virus. We returned to the exhaustive in-depth patient histories and videos that we obtained before they were mentally incapacitated."

"Wow," Jim said to Claire, almost audibly to others near them. "She's suggesting that someone may have messed with the virus to make it worse! No one else in the world has reported finding such a naturally mutated virus."

"Really?" Claire responded.

Laleh demonstrated that special care had been taken to inquire if both patients could remember having any bad fever or flu-like illness in the recent or distant past.

"Both patients finally recalled that they had experienced a severe fever that caused temporary delirium. This happened shortly after B. K. had arrived at his aunt N. K.'s home in Jahrom, Iran, almost sixteen years ago. The following anecdotal information had seemed abstract initially. In casual conversation, the young man revealed that he had been in Abadan, southern Iran, when he was ten years old. His first family was bombed by Iraqi forces. It was the Iran-Iraq War during 1980–88. He recalled finding one strange 'cactus-looking' bomb that dropped through that awful nightmare of a foggy

25

morning. It had spewed its own mist as it fell. It was not very big compared to most bombs, about the size of a large watermelon. The bomb was fastened to a small parachute that caught in the limbs of a tree and did not explode for some unknown reason.

"What he couldn't see was an explosive charge, big enough to destroy the evidence, in the base of the biological bomb. As the attack continued from the air, B. K. had sought shelter behind a ruin. As he crouched behind his wall, he saw a mist being expelled through the spines of the cactus bomb. When it had exhausted its contents, the curious child crept under the strange device to see what it was more closely. He could read on the object suspended just above his head some Arabic religious statement written in chalk. It also had the American manufacturer's name embedded in the steel. It had 'USA' imprinted on it."

"It can't be!" Jim exclaimed. "She's implicating the United States in assisting germ warfare on Iran." Claire's mouth dropped open. People in the audience started to buzz.

Laleh went on calmly. "He was then frightened away by more bombs which eventually exploded the 'cactus bomb.' He took refuge among the luggage on top of a bus going to Shiraz, Iran, because his home and family had vanished in the devastating shelling. The boy rode the bus until it stopped in Jahrom near Shiraz. It was here where his aunt, N. K., sheltered the young boy before both became ill with the severe new flu virus a few days after his arrival. They both had a severe course of the disease, including a high fever, headache and some delirium that suggested meningitis."

"Wait until the media gets hold of this news," Jim said to Claire.

"Do you believe this?" Claire inquired.

"Her credentials are good—I have to believe *she* believes it." Jim replied.

Laleh continued on as if nothing was disturbing. "The two patients had seemed unusually healthy since their single initial illness, until the recent Parkinsonism events, sixteen to seventeen years later. The diagnosis of a latent virus effect was then a possible conclusion."

There was now a general reaction by most of the scientists in the audience. Guarded whispers rustled throughout the large ballroom. The most disturbed listeners seemed to be the Americans, who felt that the scientific lecture had been used as a political backhand against the United States.

Laleh compared patient charts and retrospective data from B. K.'s original bombed home, Abadan, plus N. K.'s residence in Jahrom. The data supported her original laboratory findings and the patients' experiences. Her lecture came to a close with appreciated and prolonged applause.

Dr. Wilkins, with a relieved expression, opened the floor to questions. He recognized Dr. Ben Carlson. Most knew he was a financial supporter of the symposium and had never previously challenged any speaker because it wasn't "politically correct." Ben stood his tallest as he began.

"Dr. Bazargan, I would like to compliment you on your excellent slides, video clips and presentation. . . . However, I was hoping that your research might also have shown some sort of hard evidence in the form of pictures, army depositions, government records or other patient record sources—something to confirm a young child's recollection of a United States bomb in a tree in Iran. Can you add anything to that observation, clarifying the authenticity of such an ancient recollection?"

Dr. Bazargan quickly responded, "It is common knowledge that germ warfare was used on innocent civilians by the Iraqi forces during the war—it never occurred to me that it might be necessary to confirm, in my patient's record, that his traumatic experience was documented in every political detail. We were looking for a nidus of infection and nothing else."

She paused then continued, "I can't help but wonder why the original manufacturer of that particular biological weapon could not have been from the world's largest known source of biological warfare agents at that time. Certainly, no thinking person could assume that Iraq had developed such sophistication at that time—they had to have obtained it elsewhere. The coincidence of the failed invasion by U.S. armed forces sent to extricate the former U.S. embassy personnel held by Iran, coupled with Iraq's sudden intellectual ability to wield unique biological agents, suggested United States complicity. The motive and opportunity were there for them. Don't you agree?"

Ben sat down, saying nothing. It seemed odd to a few that he did not appear the least bit embarrassed that he had lashed out in righteous indignation only to be effectively neutralized. He had appeared to rebuke her for making this scientific symposium a vehicle for her tacit political agenda. He was now a man with reconsideration in mind.

Other participants asked specific questions, which were answered to the satisfaction of the majority, and she received an unusually spirited applause from most of the international attendees.

The next speaker was to be Edward Woodsman, M.D. During a short break, Ben Carlson, Jim Schriver, Claire Woodsman and someone called "Tex" discussed Dr. Bazargan's presentation in heated terms, all derogatory of Laleh's inference that the U.S.A. unleashed a horrible agent on the world and that she saw no ethical responsibility to substantiate it.

Ed was introduced as Head of Epidemiology at the University of Utah Health Care Center. He was also described as a member of a watchdog committee to oversee activities involving the U.S. Army's Biological Center and its research activities at Dugway, Utah. The potential for accidents required that the state of Utah, and Salt Lake City in particular, be advised and prepared to handle civilian exposure to various biological agents.

His topic was "History of Epidemiology" and Ed realized, as he talked, that many in the audience might wonder if he was going to mention the concepts raised in Laleh's allegation about the "unique" virus.

"I will start by briefly covering the history of some of the diseases such as typhoid, syphilis, TB, rabies, malaria, polio and the childhood diseases such as mumps, measles and rubella, and the fact that the U.S. government, in some way or another, had been mandated by the people to become involved in their protection. The Swine Flu vaccine was chosen as an example of government assuming liability for the resulting consequences of untoward reactions associated with a vaccine developed in a crash program. I hope you will come away with an understanding of government's role throughout history in providing protection for its citizens and the problems associated with it."

Ed could see his audience was drifting a bit as he meticulously followed his prepared slides without the benefit of the polished multimedia presentation Laleh had. He began to wish he could just escape to his favorite fishing stream, the Bear River. He hadn't bargained for all of the distractions of this seminar. Out of the corner of his eye he noticed that there was a hand extended in the audience; someone did not feel like waiting until the end of his presentation to get in a question. It was Ben, again. Ed stopped. "You have a question, Dr. Carlson?"

"Could you tell us when the United States Government ceased development of new biological agents for offensive biological use?" Ben inquired.

"Well, Dr. Carlson, I remember that fact only because my father died on that date in 1969. President Richard M. Nixon signed an executive order that outlawed the development of offensive biological weapons. It did not prohibit defensive research, however," Ed replied. He decided to deviate from his scripted message and seize the moment.

"While we are on the subject of threats from weapons, I would like to remind everyone that perhaps our biggest worldwide threat is from nature. Consider the infamous emerging viruses: HIV, Ebola and Marburg, all of which can kill 90 percent or more of the victims who become infected. Other viruses are Lassa, Rift Valley, Oropouche, Rocio, Q fever, Guanarito, VEE, Monkeypox, Dengue, Chikungunya, hanta viruses, Machupo, junin, The Kyasanur Forest brain virus and others that are related to rabies. Our country's defense, and the rest of the world's defense, needs to be welded together when we think of such threats. They could explode at any time in some remote place of the world. And with today's air travel, we are but hours away from an unpredictable pandemic calamity. The United States Army Medical Research Institute of Infectious Diseases, USAMRID, has a big responsibility relating to the defense of people from the ravages of nature without developing new problems with a genetically manipulated monster of our own making."

By that diversion Ed seemed to have recouped his audience and proceeded to finish his talk.

The academic portion of the seminar finished by 4:00 P.M. and the majority of conference-goers gravitated in small groups toward the various lounges and bars on board. The exceptions were the people whose religious background prevented them from imbibing, such as Moslems, Mormons, Seventh Day Adventists and certain Protestant Christian groups—and also a limited number of recovering alcoholics.

Jim waited patiently by the deck rail near where Dr. Laleh was being interviewed by two reporters. The reporters were from medical journals and they seemed to be asking hard questions about the disclosures of her unique patients.

When the reporters finally left, Jim quickly moved to her side along the rail. He caught her by surprise when he asked her, "Where do you expect to get your work published?"

"If you are implying that my work won't be published in any reputable journal, I'll have you know that I have already been approached by several international journal panels who will consider it!" Laleh retorted with fire in her eyes.

Jim backpedaled in confusion about what he had said and mumbled something about speculating what purpose the reporters might have. Laleh was obviously very stressed and her eyes filled with tears while her jaw set in anger.

Jim felt compelled to try to correct the misunderstanding. "I like to keep my mind open to various points of view when scientific thought is concerned. I might add that is the case even if they don't coincide with my political views. I must admit that my primary motivation for coming on this trip was to get a new perspective on the causative agent of my wife's death by listening to your lecture. You reinforced my concern that new viruses are always appearing for a variety of causes. Unfortunately, some may be man-caused. I would like to ask you a few things about this influenza A variant. My wife's disease seemed very similar to the disease you described, except her symptomatology was so compressed—it was just hours, not years, until she died. Yet the autopsy showed gross destruction in the substantia nigre."

"Do I understand you correctly, Dr. Schriver, that you feel that the virus your wife had was a naturally occurring virus and not the result of germ warfare? I am confused. Did they culture your wife's virus and identify it?"

Before Jim could respond, Ben appeared out of nowhere and interrupted by saying, "Can I ask you two to take a break a moment while I make you an offer? I have been talking to a captain of the sailing ship *Maverick*. She has had a cancellation and I would like to invite you, Dr. Bazargan, your sister, Sonbol, and Dr. Schriver to join me for a short cruise at my firm's expense. I've already asked Dr. Ed and Claire Woodsman. It will be just a short trip. We can escape this stuffy academic environment for a few days and see some of the British Virgin Islands up close. Maybe gain a better perspective. I'll fly on afterward to catch the *Royal Caribbean* Cruise again. Think about it, talk it over, and I will get back to you," he glanced at his watch, "in about an hour."

31

Jim was speechless. After listening to Ben briefly in the meeting breaks he couldn't believe what he had just heard. "That's a tempting offer, Ben. Dr. Bazargan and I will see you in an hour." Jim looked to her for confirmation. Lalaeh nodded consent to the delay of her decision.

She was obviously still waiting for an explanation from Jim about the virus, and Jim finally responded. "I'm sorry, I guess I just had hoped that if the virus could be identified as identical to the type my wife had, a vaccine could possibly be developed from your live virus cultures and my wife's death would have meaning. They didn't retain any frozen virus from my wife's disease. Just a report."

"Thank you for your honest explanation. I'm sorry I was so defensive," said Laleh.

They were still watching Ben depart when Laleh commented, "Perhaps his reconciliation offer has merit. I will talk to my sister. However, my brother has insisted that we return home immediately. I received a FAX very early this morning from a family friend who indicated that my brother would like the 'flowers' in the family garden to bloom on the mountain as soon as possible. When we were children, my father used to call us ' blossoms.' My name, Laleh, literally means tulip in English and Sonbol means Hiecine or Hyacinth. We had a special place on Mt. Damavand in the Alborz range where our family went on holiday. I know Amir needs us, but I also feel we need to discuss the lecture more."

Jim responded, "By all means, you should do what's best for your family. I wouldn't expect you to do anything else. I know the others would feel the same way. But from a selfish standpoint, we would all benefit if you could stay."

Laleh pondered Jim's observation and then confided, "Unfortunately, my brother is somewhat prone to exaggeration and at times has been known to overstate his problems. I just don't know if he is acting paranoid or if he really is in serious trouble. I'm afraid that his love life may have gotten him into trouble again. He has shown poor judgment in the past; a woman caused our whole family trouble with her charges some months ago. I suspect that this might be his problem again, so perhaps it will do him some good to consider his actions for a while. Ever since my father died, Amir has been acting like a person trying to compensate for his feelings."

She turned to face the sea. "I will talk to my sister; she relates more compassionately to our youngest sibling. We will both go for this short cruise on the *Maverick* and then return to Tehran—if she agrees. I believe she will agree with me."

"I can't help believing that this will work to everyone's benefit," answered Jim. "Its the one-on-one personal communication that gets real results. It is usually a few individuals on a committee that motivate the majority. This could allow cross-fertilization of ideas and some common goals."

"I shall go find my sister," said Laleh.

Jim replied, "And I will tell Claire and Ed. I feel certain they'll want to take this opportunity. However, I know they planned to walk back to the hotel previously. I'll go find them while you talk to your sister. Then we all had best communicate with Dr. Carlson, and make plans for the *Maverick*." The two went their separate ways.

Jim felt swept up by the previous events. He thought to himself, "I can't believe how impulsive I've been acting. No prolonged analyzing of every aspect. I've been making very quick decisions. My reactions seem to be out of character—I am uncomfortable about something that I can't verbalize. Perhaps it is guilt to Jaynee's memory, perhaps it's Ben's ability to spend vast amounts of company money for impromptu events. Or, is it guilt? Dr. Kim, my chairman at the U. of U., referred to pharmaceutical company's funds as—'patients' money.'"

He considered the possibility that his infatuation with Laleh was just a fantasy that was blinding his scientific judgment. The beautiful vision of being on a yacht with her in the Caribbean was overpowering. He would go.

Realizing that the sun was quite bright, Jim slid the sunglasses that had been resting on the top of his head into position on his nose. He toyed with the thought that Laleh might just be using them all as political pawns.

"Perhaps, perhaps, perhaps. . . . Hell, it's time for action!" He scolded himself. "I'm going to trust my instincts. Tomorrow morning we will all be aboard the *Maverick*!"

Chapter 3
Alpha Omega in Palo Alto—Day 4

Martin Reichstadt, M.D., Ph.D., had been Director of Research and Development at Alpha Omega Pharmaceutical ever since he had left Yale University in 1986. His corner office in the Alpha Omega Research Administration building was built in 1955 overlooking a sequestered wooded park with a small pond. His administration building was unique, the rest of the new concrete-and-glass buildings that housed the production facilities were only a few years old and none of those had a single window that would open. He could hear ducks outside when the weather would permit open windows. But it was not one of those mornings, and Martin was concentrating on his work when the phone rang.

"Hello, this is Dr. Reichstadt," Martin answered.

"Martin, this is Ben. I'm calling from the Caribbean Infectious Disease Conference, as you may be aware."

"Yes, I've been wondering how it was going down there," said Martin.

"I've got a problem," said Ben. "Do you know if we've ever produced live viruses for any agency of our government? Being the world's biggest producer of vaccines, it occurred to me that we are also capable of mass-producing live viruses. If not us, which of our competitors might have had a contract during the Iraq-Iran war in 1980–89?"

"Of course there were several manufacturers worldwide at that time who could have sold such viruses. But why do you specify the Iran-Iraq war? The U.S. wasn't involved," commented Martin.

"I should have specified U.S. manufacturers, because Dr. Laleh Bazargan of Iran has accused some unnamed U.S. firm of producing a bacteriological bomb for Iraq in that period," replied Ben.

"Even though you weren't with Alpha Omega at that time, Ben, I have the feeling you already believe that we were the manufacturer of viruses for such U.S. bombs, and if so, why are you asking the question of me at this point? This is all very mysterious," said Dr. Reichstadt.

"Dr. Bazargan said she had evidence of a unique variant of influenza A virus that might have originated in an Iraqi bomb with 'USA' printed on it. She said that her patients, who were exposed to it at that time, just recently exhibited Parkinson's Disease symptoms. Then, something you said a long time ago stuck in my memory. Didn't you mention that some mysterious influenza-A virus had been isolated from a few of your Parkinson's Disease patients when you were at Yale? You said you had grown it on cloned human brain embryo tissue. We have had a lot of vaccine contracts with various governmental agencies in the past. We had the connections," Ben challenged.

Dr. Reichstadt crushed the paper origami bird inscribed "to Daddy from Zelda" that he had been idly fondling in one hand while listening to Ben. Martin's face could have told Ben the truth if their call had two-way video. He was flushed and his eyes narrowed over the half glasses perched midway down on his nose. His position as director had conditioned him to summon his composure as he spoke with overly controlled tones.

"Ben, your quantum leaps in logic defy the imagination. I suppose I should congratulate you on your recall ability of old conversations, even if the subjects are not related. I hope that I misunderstood your implying that I might have been the person who could've inflicted innocent human beings with such a dreaded disease. Tell me exactly what you hope to determine."

"Martin, I didn't mean to infer that you personally instigated such a thing, I simply felt obliged to answer a challenge thrust at the American Pharmaceutical Industry. With your knowledge of the subject,

I thought you could shed some light. This afternoon I may have to respond to these allegations. As Director of Marketing for Alpha Omega, I need to know if we can be implicated in any way. We must separate ourselves from other possibly guilty manufacturers quickly to have any credibility. In order to convince others, I must be satisfied that I am on firm ground and that our history is not clouded. I must anticipate problems and preempt them," Ben explained with emotion.

"Ben, large multinational corporations have many conflicting priorities with different customers all over the globe—almost every day. You know that. I think that you should carefully consider your involvement in such old historic matters that won't be changed despite anything you might do now," Martin said evasively, then continued.

"You're not only dealing with Alpha Omega's reputation and possibly privileged information, but you might be bordering on revealing national security secrets. Have you really thought this through to a possible conclusion? When you're done, what will you have accomplished? Besides, I 'm unaware of any evidence that would support your worst fears. Ben, just take a deep breath and let some other member of our industry pick up the gauntlet and tilt at broken windmills," advised Martin.

"Just tell me one thing, Martin, what would you do if you were me at this moment? If we were not the ones who made the viruses for the bomb, should I try some P.R. damage control and point in some other manufacturer's direction, or try and convince them Iraq alone did it, or just deny everything? In any case, I sure don't like lying to an international audience," Ben said, piously raising his voice.

"Ben, I know that I have the CEO's support on this policy matter—we simply have no records of such an activity by this company at that time. You are going way out on a limb—for what?" Dr. Reichstadt inquired.

Ben countered, "I'm not inexperienced in diplomacy, Martin.

I feel I must respond to Dr. Bazargan's accusations with our image in mind and the industry in general. I have arranged to charter a sailing ship, the *Maverick,* to cruise with several of the key doctors for a few days so that we can discuss the issues privately, away from the media's influence."

For a few seconds the transmission was garbled with static. "So I'll call you when we get back to St. Thomas. Thanks for your counsel, Martin." More static and total silence. Ben could not hear any other response above the static. He ended his cell-phone call without getting a reply, and said to himself, "I hope he got the last few words. Oh, well!"

"Dat pompous, supercilious, pious dumkopf!" Martin exploded, his seldom-heard native German accent emerging. Punching his stubby index finger on his line to his secretary he shouted, "Marsha, would you please contact Ben's secretary and get his telephone number in St. Thomas of the Virgin Islands and his cellular number ASAP?

"What a putz! A loose cannon!" Martin fumed to himself. "And, Marsha, also get Mr. Granite on my private line. The CEO needs to be advised of this matter ASAP," Martin commanded. He should be at the corporate headquarters administration building this morning."

Marsha was accustomed to taking orders without question. As his administrative assistant ever since Dr. Reichstadt had come to Alpha Omega, she knew to drop everything when he was angry.

Dr. Martin Reichstadt ruminated as Marsha waited for him to conclude his diatribe. He felt that everyone should know he wouldn't accept a contract to produce live viruses to cause death. Those who knew him knew his penchant for making only lifesaving products. What was Ben thinking? He distinctly remembered Rock Granite, the CEO, telling him that his work would be used only to insure peace and defense; he couldn't believe that anything like this would have been allowed to happen without his knowledge. The only seed virus of influenza A the company ever supplied to the government was for its study to possibly order a vaccine if they determined it was a threat to the nation's health," he remembered. "I'll call Dr. Carlson on line three and Mr. Granite on line six, and I'll notify you when both are ready, sir." Marsha responded in a militant voice. Her past service in the country's WACs was often evident.

The bay breeze was blowing up a storm and the clouds were racing in from the Pacific. The smell of eucalyptus was unmistakable because of the wind blowing through the grove of trees around the west side of Alpha Omega's Palo Alto environs. The billowing mist made mystic images on Martin's windows. He moved to shut the window he often kept open despite the efficient air conditioning in the old building. He loved the aroma, but he knew his asthma would kick in if the wind continued to blow. Martin stood at parade rest, his five-foot-eight, trim, stocky frame "at the ready" for Marsha's telephone efforts.

His thoughts became paranoid. "All my life I've had to be vigilant; you never know when some fool will turn on you," he thought. "There is always some stupid swine," Martin mumbled to himself.

When he was a professor at Yale's School of Medicine, his research work with neuro-transplantation was terminated because the National Institutes of Health funding grants were abruptly canceled. Christian Pro-Life activists had objected to the use of aborted human brain tissue for experiments. Not only had his funding been canceled, but his tenure at the university had been compromised when he refused to cease his interest despite the political pressure. It had cost him his job at Yale. He had always been grateful to J. R. Granite for his support in bringing him to Alpha Omega. J. R. Granite's nickname "Rock," was consistent with his personality and his last name. Rock understood the importance of finding the possible source of Parkinson's Disease, and he saw to it that Martin had the autonomy and funding to pursue his pet research project while acting as Director of Research. They had investigated a host of suspect rogue viruses since that time, but no vaccine had yet been possible.

39

"With my experience," he mused, "I know that neither Iraq nor Iran had the expertise in the eighties to have developed a bacteriological bomb of any consequence without America's technology. I also know that Dugway and Tooele, Utah, had more bacteriological and chemical bombs stockpiled than anywhere else in the world at that time."

Martin's gray-streaked beard glistened with perspiration in the subdued light of his desk. The sky darkened with impending storm clouds. He was tense, sensing the unknown and unavoidable. The sudden rain was insistent as it pelted his large office window in staccato rhythm.

He stood stoically waiting for the phone to ring, too tense to sit in his plush executive chair. The cuckoo clocks in his office started simultaneously to announce that it was 8:00 A.M. in Palo Alto, probably noon in St. Thomas. The phone on his magnificent walnut desk remained unusually silent. There seemed to be a post-hypnotic effect by the multiple clocks on Martin Reichstadt. His eyes drifted to the pelting rain on his window.

His muted reflection on the darkened glass seemed to beckon him to his childhood in Pennsylvania. He could almost hear his anti-Semitic elementary school teacher speaking to him and the entire snickering class, when he erroneously answered a question she posed. "What else can you expect from a cuckoo bird?" she responded rhetorically.

The pain of that one event caused him to do the first research in his life. He became compulsive about learning everything he could about cuckoo birds. He learned that the parent cuckoo bird often laid her eggs in other birds' nests to hatch and be raised by surrogates. The analogy was all too fitting for Martin's history. He found out that he had been born to German-Jew parents in Nazi Germany who saved his life by sending him with visiting friends to live in America just two days before his yellow-starred parents were sent to Dachau and the gas chamber. His foster parents felt that it was important that

40

he should keep his tradition and original surname when they brought him to the states. Hence, his childhood label of "cuckoo bird."

Martin's hand rested on the heavy solid brass statue of a cuckoo bird. Then when the telephone sounded it was like a gunshot. He quickly lifted the phone.

"Dr. Reichstadt, I have not been able to reach Dr. Carlson, but I did find out that he left on a sailing vessel, the *Maverick,* from St. Thomas. They don't have a responsive shore-to-ship radio nor does his cellular work," announced Marsha.

"Sounds consistent with Ben's erratic behavior," commented Martin.

"Mr. Granite is on line six. I paged him from a meeting and he's impatient," said Marsha.

"Rock, sorry to keep you waiting, but I'm afraid we have a possible problem that you may need to become involved with," Martin said in a measured tone. "It seems that an Iranian physician, a Dr. Bazargan, presented a lecture in St.Thomas at an I.D. conference. She related her experience with patients infected with a strange variant of influenza A in the eighties that she thinks caused Parkinson's Disease in some patients much later. She contended that the virus came from a bacteriological warfare bomb dropped on an Iranian Village by Iraq, but labeled 'made in the U.S.A.' Our man, Ben Carlson, believes that only an American pharmaceutical company, possibly Alpha Omega, could have reliably mass-produced such viruses during that 1980–88 period. He is struggling with an ethics dilemma and feels that he alone must respond to such an allegation. He intends to effect some sort of damage control to the industry's and our image in particular," explained Martin.

"What?" asked Mr. Granite. "Who authorized him to do that?"

"No one," responded Martin.

"How could he come to such assumptions without your help, Martin? Tell me that! You can't tell me that this was some sort of knee-jerk reaction he suddenly came to," Mr. Granite accused.

"It seems that even though he wasn't here at that time, he recalls bits of old anecdotal data he read here that gave him a basis for an educated guess," Martin explained.

"I need to talk to him now!" snorted J. R. "Rock" Granite.

"I knew you would, but he left St.Thomas on a small sailing vessel called the *Maverick* with all of the concerned docs and won't be back for a few days."

"You've got to be joking—he's off sailing the Caribbean on a boat called the *Maverick*? This would be funny if it were not so serious. Call him now," Mr. Granite demanded.

"We can't. There is no ship-to-shore communication nor does his cellular phone respond," said Dr. Reichstadt.

"Perfect! Just perfect! He's out there ready to breach national security and involve Alpha Omega in an international conspiracy. He's a national traitor and I am supposed to just sit here and let him destroy us all. Well, Martin, what do you think I should do? Turn the other cheek or get an eye for an eye? Don't you dare tell me we should sit and study the subject until it's too late," Mr. Granite exclaimed.

"But what can we do now?" Martin inquired. "After all, new flu viruses spring up every year due to natural mutation. What conclusive proof could she possibly have that we were somehow responsible?"

"Don't you remember, we did sell the government an A virus several years ago for them to study at the Dugway, Utah, facility?" Mr. Granite reminded him. "Maybe we erroneously gave the government a seed culture of Alpha Omega's Parkinson's Disease–related influenza virus. You know, the one you obtained so very long ago when you worked at Yale." Mr. Granite's accusing tone struck home.

"I don't see how I could have inadvertently given them access to it." The color drained from Martin's face. "No! It couldn't be, that is too bizarre!" He tried to reassure himself as well as Rock of his innocence. He started ruminating out loud. "The government would've had to modify the original virus to make it adaptable for bombs. But maybe, just maybe, an error was made in the government lab at Dugway. . . . Perhaps this whole thing was an elaborate conspiracy of those Muslims to discredit the U.S. and is just a lie. . . . I'm not going to rush into judgment of our government's guilt or mine!" Martin defiantly stated.

"That's fine for you to say now, but if the international press gets hold of this story and starts interviewing this Iranian doctor and some of her newly developed disciples, who the crap are they going to believe, us or them?" Mr. Granite shouted.

"Well, what do you intend to do, anyway?" Martin challenged.

"I'm sure not going to contemplate philosophy. I'm going to take action, Martin! And, I want you to forget that we have had this discussion. I'll assume full responsibility from this moment on. Do you understand me, Martin?" Mr. Granite hung up.

Rock had maintained his college football physique, and Martin could visualize his massive frame hovering over him—he knew he was determined to influence the outcome somehow. Martin couldn't imagine what in the world Rock might have in mind to deal with these strange circumstances. As CEO, it was his right and responsibility to handle this. Martin certainly wasn't responsible for such a possibility. It made him feel a little impotent but he was also relieved that Rock was going to completely take this mess out of his hands. However, Martin still felt a need to do something, but he didn't know what. All of this was so alien to his sense of control. He was the kind of person who liked a place for everything and everything in its place.

At that moment, Rock located a number he kept in code on his secured computer file and called. A voice answered.

"STRIKE Patriot Seminars," a man answered.

Mr. Granite recognized the powerful voice. He had previously received paramilitary training from this man, Nick Cabal, a former Green Beret and retired CIA operative.

Nick had set up a paramilitary organization, the STRIKE— Specially Trained Reaction Individuals for Key Events—team. It was one of many such organizations in the western United States. Some militant groups had published their hate to more than twenty false patriot groups already listed in the state of Idaho by the Klanwatch/ Militia Task Force of the Southern Poverty Law Center in 1996. The Militia Task Force had identified 441 armed militias in all fifty states. Most of the groups had some religious affiliation, belonging to various fundamental Christian denominations.

"This is J. R. Granite of Alpha Omega Pharmaceuticals," announced Rock. He articulated carefully for the voice pattern identification. " My I.D. number is 88821762; my name is J. R. Granite."

"This is Colonel Cabal. Rock, I haven't talked to you since you shipped our special order to Salt Lake City a while back. I hope you're not calling to tell me of some delayed repercussions about that missing vial," pondered Nick Cabal.

"No, I wasn't calling about that, but how did that Afghanistan hostage problem get resolved? Was the special Salt Lake order useful?" inquired Rock.

"Yes, it worked well in Afghanistan and the missing Salt Lake vial was accounted for. An informant told us it was reported crushed in the railroad yard there following the cover-up robbery we staged to obtain the virus vials hidden in the computer cartons. No trace to us. I should have told you. Well, tell me what's happening at good old Alpha Omega?" Nick asked.

Rock explained why he was calling, adding a few embellishments to ensure that Colonel Cabal understood the threat to national security. He emphasized how all of the "interested parties" would be aboard a single small sailing ship, conspiring to divulge state secrets to the world. He noted that the original vague information implicating the U.S. was divulged only to a limited scientific audience.

"At this time, the data seems significant to only the group which is aboard the *Maverick*."

Colonel Cabal then inquired, "I don't understand why anyone in the scientific community would take this Iranian accusation seriously."

44

"Only those with a theoretical vent toward possible instead of probable cause for an unlikely coincidence would buy such an obvious plot to discredit the U.S.," responded Rock.

"So this Parkinson's Disease association with the influenza A virus is completely without scientific foundation?" queried Nick.

"Absolutely! If there was, we would be making a vaccine to prevent Parkinson's Disease," lied Rock.

After a long pause, Cabal told Rock, "I will take it from here." He then told Rock, "For security's sake, any future communication should refer to the matter with a code word—what would you suggest?"

After a moment's thought, Rock responded. "When I think of a successful campaign, I think of Desert Storm. What do you think of the name 'Alpha Storm' for our campaign?"

"Alpha Storm it is!" Cabal confirmed. "This problem will be terminated. You know, Rock, we have some very special contracts now with the CIA because of President Clinton's irrational sensitivity to covert operations that involve questionable solutions to difficult problems. This liberal administration has effectively tied the hands of the best operatives of the CIA, and for that matter, any other official U.S. agencies. Sometimes, you know, the only way to be effective is to have the balls necessary to do what must be done. Thank God we had Oliver North when we needed him. True patriots of our country must take some risks to insure that we will still have a republic," Colonel Cabal pontificated.

Rock Granite nodded agreement and said, "Amen to that!"

Colonel Cabal continued, "Unfortunately, we need funding to sustain our organization because Congress has tied the CIA's hands. They can't openly support our activities. But we are happy to be of service. It is our duty to our country in these strange times. I will inform you of our progress with Alpha Storm," he added cryptically.

"Colonel, I know that you have set the plans for next spring's training program, but I would like to offer my ranch near Hayden Lake, Idaho, as a possible site for maneuvers next time. I have a big bunkhouse and five cabins, and the 'great room' in the 6000-square-foot main building would make a perfect conference center. We also have six trailer hook-ups, lots of parking room for RVs plus endless tent space and lots of water," said Rock.

"That is a very generous offer, Rock, I'll plan on that."

"I knew we could count on you, Colonel. Incidentally, I personally want to thank you for that last patriot training program and I intend to do whatever I can to insure success in your next training session in Idaho next spring. For a 'retired' government employee, you are certainly an active role model for all true Americans. Thanks again. I will be sending my 'special contribution' to the STRIKE Patriots Seminar as before," concluded Mr. Granite.

Rock felt good about his inspired initiatives. He truly believed STRIKE had "a clear mission to do good for their God and country."

Colonel Nick Cabal was reminded how Rock and he had worked on Patrick Buchanan's presidential campaign together. It was good, but now the shared zeal to eliminate a common enemy and the camaraderie he felt was intoxicating. "Pity anyone who might get in our way," he thought. "All Americans should know that at least some of us have the balls to do what's necessary."

Chapter 4
The *Maverick* in the Caribbean—Days 4–7

They all gathered on the dock in Charlotte Amalie of St. Thomas Island. They were looking toward the yacht *Maverick,* anchored about one hundred yards off shore, waiting to be ferried to it.

The big copper-sheathed *Maverick,* an authentic copy of the famous English Brixham trawlers, was noted for its seaworthiness. It was truly built for the rough sea. Made from teakwood and fastened with copper rivets, it glistened in the evening sun from loving care, an example of a lost art. Three jibs, a main sail and a mizzen stood ready to be unfurled on the two large masts. The bowsprit's twenty feet added to make the overall length one hundred feet. The large, glassed-in deckhouse gave it an elegant uniqueness. The temporary blue canvas awning stretched over the nineteen-foot-wide forward deck to give shade and a festive flare for the anticipated passengers.

Dora Daly was made captain by the new owners, Dutch and Ann Ring. The ship's original owner was a retired British naval commander who sailed her to adventures off the wild coasts of Africa and down the Nile River. He and the *Maverick* were commissioned in World War II to survey German naval movements. He died at the helm off the coast of Scotland, strafed by bullets from a German plane.

The group on the dock observed Ben and the ship's Captain Daly departing the ship in a dinghy and starting in their direction. Dora's physique, with her long black hair pulled back into a ponytail and her tank-type blue swimsuit, gave them the feeling that she was capable of swimming the English Channel. Belying her calm exterior, Dora had her share of scrambling to prepare for this voyage.

Murphy's law had been in effect. Her radio had chosen today to conk out and she would not be able to get it repaired until she reached Tortola Island, in the British Virgin Islands, the next day.

The only CB and short-wave reconditioning service available was a free-lance rendezvous radio repair company, Sparks, which had a small power boat that roamed the ocean of the B.V.I. (British Virgin Islands) and American V.I. of the Caribbean. But, thanks to the use of Ben Carlson's cellular phone, Dora had contacted Sparks and attended to a host of logistics. She had been on the phone constantly. There had been food to expedite, sailing course agreements to generate for the passengers, notification to the *Maverick*'s insurance carrier of the manifest of passengers and crew. Fuel, necessary for entering and leaving ports, had to be obtained for the diesel engine. Even though most of the voyage would be powered by the wind, speed could best be controlled with the engine. Fresh water, eight hundred gallons of it, had to be loaded. Of course, the up-to-the-moment weather forecast had to be obtained. This time of year every tropical storm had the potential to escalate to a hurricane.

Barbara Barboli, the blond woman whom Ben had failed to introduce the night before, had boarded the ship much earlier and had settled in with him in his cabin. Ben then left Barbara on board to freshen up while he and Captain Daly boarded the inflatable tender and immediately put the fifteen-horsepower outboard motor full throttle to the dock. Ben was quite eager to greet the other passengers. He could see them all waiting with Paul'le, the charming *Maverick* assistant mate. Paul'le spoke with a Caribbean accent and, with his flashing white perfect teeth contrasting with his jet-black skin, he presented the image of a crewmember seen over a century ago.

Ed and Jim, busy with luggage, looked more like casino employees with their conservative golf shirts and long pants hiding their untanned bodies. However, with logos of their favorite baseball teams, their billed caps gave them away as tourists.

Doctors Michael Andrikopolis and his wife, Helen, from

48

Athens, Greece, looked more natural in their attire. Both had white shorts, white canvas deck shoes and pastel-colored short-sleeve shirts that tastefully fit their generous figures. They had been invited because he was Chief of Infectious Disease in the most prestigious hospital in Athens and was also a frequent author of articles concerning influenza diseases. Both moved as though they had arthritis in most of their weight-bearing joints. They would mainly enjoy just floating in the warm waters of the Caribbean.

Dr. Lu Wong and his associate, Dr. Sue Chow, were senior citizens from Taiwan, China. They had lectured about the history of new strains of influenza viruses that had originated in their part of the world. Both were quoted extensively in the medical literature and were very influential. And, because both were drawn to each other after the death of their respective spouses a few years previous, they found it convenient to travel together and share accommodations. Because of their advanced years, few questions were ever asked about the propriety of their cohabitation when they traveled together around the world. The captain speculated that these two probably wouldn't be among the guests that learned to help raise and lower the sails. She could picture both doing Tai Chi exercises on deck, the slow motion movements a curiosity to younger people.

Laleh and her sister, Sonbol, seemed to feel ill at ease waiting in their very casual and colorful attire on a public dock. The nine guests in waiting watched Ben and the captain as they secured the tender to the dock and prepared to ferry them all to the ship.

Once on board the *Maverick,* the guests quickly stowed their gear, then met on deck for the obligatory safety meeting. Barbara, who had been below deck was finally introduced by Ben. "Just call me 'Bubbles,' all of my friends call me that," she said.

If Claire, Laleh and Sonbol had previously been aware that this buxom blonde would be a fellow passenger, they might have worn their bikinis just to compete for the attention all of the men were giving her. Ben and Barbara were unmarried, and the trio felt they

49

violated social mores. Bubbles, who was well aware of the men staring at her red string bikini, seemed accustomed to the stares and yet somehow exhibited a childlike innocence. Perhaps it was genuine, but with her figure it was hard to be objective.

When they were headed out of the harbor, the passengers received the perfunctory monologue from Dora about the mechanics of the head—toilet—and the proper use of fresh water in the shower.

"There will be three meals served each day of our trip, and courtesy guidelines include a quiet time between 10:00 P.M. and 8:00 A.M. Those who wish to learn some of the basics of sailing can start just as soon as we have cleared the harbor," she advised.

Claire, Laleh, Sonbol, Ben, Ed and Jim volunteered to be working guests. Bubbles had to do her nails and looked as though she felt guilty that she had to decline. But, as she explained, "One just has to look at the rough ropes to realize the risk to one's manicure. Besides, I'm not very good at manual labor."

The six volunteers played out various fantasies from their childhood as they performed their sail tending duties. Jim pretended he was helping crew for the America's Cup and Laleh was the female pirate, Anne Bonny of 1720, who had prowled these waters.

Most took interest in the sailing chart Dora was displaying in the deck house. "We're headed for Frenchman's Cay on Tortola Island of the B.V.I. There, your passports will be checked and we will anchor until morning. We will then head for Norman Island, believed to be the Treasure Island of Robert Louis Stevenson's book. After that— Peter Island, Dead Chest Island, St. John and back to St. Thomas."

Ben smiled. It was just the tranquilizing therapy he had hoped for. Perhaps these overly concerned scientists could now casually discuss their concerns over a cold drink and rationally verbalize what they felt the lecture meant to them individually. Ben planned to isolate each person, and at just the right time, put some spin on each of their perceptions to change any conspiracy misconceptions. He would talk to Laleh first and then the others, one by one. Ben thought he was an expert manipulator, and he knew he could effect change in the group's attitude. Ben found Laleh facing the wind wearing a colorful full-length, almost transparent, multicolored scarf covering her yellow swimsuit.

"Dr. Bazargan, I see that our sail-raising efforts have allowed us to shut off the engine. Isn't this quiet wonderful?"

"The fresh air across the bow up here is indeed splendid." A moment passed while they both seemed to appreciate the serenity. "Once again I wish to thank you for this," answered Laleh. All the while she was looking over his shoulder at Bubbles stretched out on some cushions conspicuously taking a sunbath.

Ben could not help noticing Laleh's line of sight and felt obliged to explain his relationship with Bubbles.

"Barbara has a relaxed naturalness about her that is so refreshing. She really knows who she is. By that I mean she knows her own strengths and her weaknesses. I've noticed that besides having good looks, she has intellectual qualities I really admire and respect. She also has had a hard life, but has learned to make the best of it despite an abusive father and unfortunate relationships. I hope to help her as much as I can."

Laleh was trying to comprehend what all of Ben's monologue was about, as she peered first at Ben and then Barbara. She got the impression that he seemed to be rationalizing to himself why he had become so impulsive about his infatuation. She decided to ignore the whole relationship as a problem for Ben to work out with Bubbles. She did not need to judge her.

Laleh decided to change the subject. "I did not get to talk to you after my lecture. I'm curious, what was your overall impression? Did you feel that it was well received?" She avoided the specific unpleasant questioning that he had thrown at her from the audience during the lecture. At least for the time being she would be civil.

"The crowd loved it; I think you could tell by the applause," responded Ben. "You had excellent slides and videos."

"I was referring to your impression. I judged by your line of questions that you did not accept my observation, seen by my patient, that the maker of the biological bomb for Iraq was a United States manufacturer," said Laleh.

"I guess I was shocked and full of denial. I couldn't accept the supposition that my country could be a party to such a diabolical plot. I still can't believe that the intent was to inflict pain and suffering on innocent civilians in Iran. There must be some other explanation," Ben responded.

"Money," answered Dr. Bazargan.

Ben, struggling to control his temper, diplomatically responded. "I suppose that money is always a factor in any contract. But, I know many of the scientists that work for American industry, and I can't believe that they would develop a virus that would be intended for inflicting Parkinson's Disease. The idea of a possible pandemic plague being unleashed on mankind by such well meaning scientists—much like yourself—is unacceptable to me."

Dr. Laleh Bazargan studied Ben's eyes and face, as well as his body language, to detect any sign of a possible lack of sincerity. There was none. He seemed to be telling the truth, as he knew it.

She pondered what he had just said before she replied. "Dr. Carlson, I can understand your disbelief considering that you have lived in America all of your life. You did not see what the American oil companies and the CIA did during the reign of the Shah. You did not see firsthand what many of our citizens endured under the Shah's Secret Police, Savak, Sazman-eitelaat va Amniat-e Keshvar or The National Information and Security Organization. If you had, you might reconsider my report as quite plausible. Unfortunately, I doubt if I can ever get you documentation of such data."

"Dr. Bazargan, could you perceive of any scenario where perhaps Iraq wanted to implicate the U.S. by such action?" postulated Ben.

"Perhaps. I also suppose that they may have routinely used old

52

U.S. bomb casings for loading their deadly viruses. But, at that time in history, America was courting Iraq for favor. They needed a friend in our part of the world and the Shah in Iran was gone," she concluded.

"I could accept the 'empty bomb casing theory' and an unintended implication of a U.S. firm. It would all make sense," Ben said somewhat relieved.

"I guess the main thing we all must be concerned about now, is what do we need to do from this point forward? Do we need to monitor influenza-A outbreaks for specific subspecies to determine if it is spreading naturally? Or is any nation intentionally keeping it in their arsenal? I believe the virus should be given an internationally recognized designation—like the old Swine Flu and others," suggested Laleh.

"Perhaps Alpha Omega might be of help by developing a vaccine from the isolates that you have in your lab," Ben suggested, "As you know, making a protective vaccine from most influenza viruses is quite possible with today's technology."

"I think we need to involve all the nations with industries that make vaccines. The first step must be convincing the World Health Organization, the Centers for Disease Control and the National Institutes of Health in America, that this virus is truly a danger and that a vaccine should be made that is safe and effective. I am still suspicious that some single company in the U.S.A. may have a head start in this research that could save us all time and money, but, of course, that would imply an admission of original guilt!"

Laleh could read the strained expression on Ben's face. She intuitively thought that she could easily win this battle and lose the war with a line of veiled accusations. Ben, the smooth communicator, chartered the trip for everyone. Laleh wanted him to subtly know that she was not a fool to be manipulated or bought off. She knew that this was an opportunity to gain something for the potential patients of the world. If she could facilitate a life-saving vaccine by utilizing a rich pharmaceutical company's resources, she would!

She stayed focused. "With Alpha Omega's long-held world dominance in the production of vaccines, do you think your company would really be willing to help lead a cooperative research program to develop such a vaccine?" inquired Laleh.

"We've been involved in other humanitarian, nonproprietary and cooperative research ventures in the past. I personally feel that we have an obligation. But, it would be necessary to communicate with my company before I could commit them to anything," said Ben.

"It is so good to hear you say that. I am sure that your influence with your company will have a positive effect, and your company's influence among other industrial giants will help make a worldwide response possible. I just wish it would be as easy for me to convince my country to support the venture. This humanitarian joint effort could also go a long way in normalizing relations between our countries. There is nothing like the common enemy of disease to bring countries together. Will you help me convince the others on board of the need to work together to protect against this deadly flu? They are all influential in their different organizations worldwide," said Laleh.

Ben felt that he *was* going to make lemonade out of the lemons. Evidently, faultfinding was not the motivation of this Iranian doctor. She was a practical humanitarian. Ben quickly said, "It would be my pleasure—I would love to talk to everyone on board." He couldn't believe it—she had asked *him*!

No one, if they had been asked, would have recalled the strange-looking tourist filming them all, indiscriminately, while they waited in line to get their passports checked on Tortola Island that day. He had just seemed to be one of those tourists who would video fish swimming in a bowl if he didn't have anything else to do. They also did not notice the seaplane among the various vessels in port. The unusual seaplane was temporarily anchored well out of sight, away from the *Maverick*.

That evening Ben grabbed his phone and found a quiet corner to call Alpha Omega and give them his good news.

"What! Not now!" Ben mumbled. The captain had used the cellular phone so much that the battery apparently lost its charge. But since the emergency was defused, Ben decided to pack the phone away in his waterproof duffel bag for the rest of the trip. "It probably couldn't locate a cell site anyway," he thought. Besides, the Sparks radio repair guy had just finished fixing the boat's radio, and Ben figured he could try to contact Alpha Omega with it later. For the time being, he wanted to continue lobbying fellow passengers.

Laleh decided to share Ben's discussion with Jim, but only after she discussed the situation with Sonbol that night before retiring. The two sisters were on the ship's deck when Laleh said, "Look at the sky, it looks like a black satin bed, letting the stars and moon rest on it." Then she stood proudly when she looked at Sonbol and said, "Sonbol, I had a conversation about the deadly virus with Ben. I think I have convinced him that there is a need for an international recognition of this organism. I told him how his company could be in a position to lead a cooperative program to develop a protective vaccine from this virus. Isn't it great?" Laleh asked.

"That simple? Ha!" replied Sonbol. "Why are you trusting these people? Can't you see ? They take a vacation after each conference. They are so relaxed. Everything to them is just fun—even a deadly virus. Laleh, I don't have a good feeling about this trip." Sonbol did her best to increase her sister's suspicions.

Laleh was taken aback by Sonbol's reaction. "We have grown up in a suspicious culture. I have always tried to learn to stand on my humanitarian principles. In this way I could reach to a stronger logical position. I am certain that no matter how much politics there has been, there will be some hope. I know, Sonbol, that you feel uneasy, but I feel the vaccine will become a reality. I know that if I can get Alpha Omega involved, we will be half-way on the road to success. Do you understand what I am trying to accomplish?"

"I understand, but I'm just not as trusting of Americans as you."

All night Laleh wondered how she would share Ben's discussion with Jim. Her emotional feelings for Jim were somehow holding her back. Several times she wished her father were alive so that she could talk to him about Jim. She closed her eyes and thought about surrendering to Jim's embrace and kissing him. She knew it might be all too presumptuous. She wondered if he might not have the same feelings. She had very pleasant dreams.

Ben had schmoozed his way around to talk privately to half of the passengers before everyone retired after enjoying a wonderful meal and the beautiful sunset. Ben and Barbara were rocked to sleep by the gentle motion of the ship. The others also slept soundly, including Paul'le who slept in the widow's nest, a rope net below the bowsprit. Dora slept on a pad on the deck with the stars as a blanket. With virtually no insects and the warm temperature, it was perfect. . . .

Laleh was roused from sleep by Jim's knock on her cabin door. "Ready for breakfast?" asked Jim through the door.

It was a hope realized. Her heart started beating fast—she looked in the mirror. "Oh, of course, in a minute!" she replied. She quickly threw on some clothes and they left. He complimented her on her appearance as they climbed to the upper deck.

They took their coffee together at rail side basking in the warm gentle breeze. The sun shone in her hair. They both looked at the pink early morning hue on the edge of the clouds; the intense reds and purples of daybreak were almost gone. The gentle waves rocked the ship in slow motion.

"What a beautiful day!" Jim said.

"Just gorgeous. These waves remind me of my childhood cradle." Laleh answered. There was a faraway look in her eyes, a peaceful gaze.

Laleh then spoke after both had their first sips of coffee. "What do you think about Ben?"

"What about him?" Jim replied, somewhat startled by the question.

"Oh. I am sorry. I was so anxious to share Ben's and my discussion about the possibility of making a useful vaccine from the virus I lectured about yesterday. I am curious—did Ben talk to you? Anyway, I want to know just how serious he will be. He has already shown some interest in my proposal of obtaining an international recognition of the virus and his company's possible leadership for making the vaccine," Laleh explained.

Jim, still frustrated at being interrupted from "surging on the ocean wave's cradle" with her, mumbled, "I have known Ben for a long time. He is my old buddy and classmate from college. Always funny, but also always a good politician. . . . If he has shown some interest, I am sure that he is able to make some positive things happen at Alpha Omega. When you realize that he was made Director of Marketing at his young age, you know he must have talent. His prematurely graying hair, alone, wouldn't have gotten him there."

"Thanks Jim. I was just curious," replied Laleh.

By lunchtime at Virgin Gorda, Ben had managed to talk to everyone and he felt he had consensus that the influenza A Parkinson's Disease/Shiraz, Iran, strain should be investigated thoroughly and Dr. Bazargan's isolates be used as seed cultures. Ben was being charitable to those who objected to Alpha Omega being given any unfair advantage.

Ben believed that all countries should receive the approved seed cultures from Dr. Bazargan after the World Health Organization evaluated her data and presented its findings. Ben could afford to be generous because Alpha Omega would only need two months of lead-time and they could capture 60 percent of the whole market. He felt Alpha Omega had the best brains in the business and the most efficient organization to produce more vaccine, faster. He knew that Dr. Reichstadt could guarantee it. His only question now was, how was Dr. Bazargan going to convince her government that they should allow her to be equally cooperative so he could get his hands on a seed culture first.

Ben was amazed how this little microcommunity of scientists on the *Maverick* had concentrated on the idea of fixing the problem instead of the blame. They really weren't interested in expending their energies on the history of who had caused this virus, they simply wanted to get on with saving people from further morbidity and mortality. It had gone so well earlier; he wondered if he had been duped. Dr. Laleh Bazargan was brilliant and classy. He wasn't certain about anything, but his gut told him this was the right thing to do. He would cooperate fully with her and earn some leadtime to obtaining a seed virus first.

Everyone on board enjoyed the rest of the day relaxing after touring Virgin Gorda. Then they had sailed on to Peter Island in time to anchor and have dinner. They truly were vacationing tourists.

After dinner, Captain Daly tuned the newly repaired radio on to the Caribbean weather forecast. "A tropical storm is eight hundred miles away, southeast, and moving northwest about thirty-five miles per hour in the direction of Tortola, Norman and the U.S. Virgin Islands," the announcer said.

Dora figured that at that speed and distance they didn't need to be too concerned, just respectful. She knew that most often these storms either deteriorated or changed course. This storm, however, did have reported gusts of about 80 miles per hour which is as destructive as many hurricanes. "I must always be cautious," she reminded herself.

She contacted her sister ship, located further east of them, the *Latina,* and asked "How is the weather?" They were anchored near Spanish Town on Virgin Gorda where the *Maverick* had been that day.

"The weather is fine, beautiful with a slight breeze," the captain answered.

Dora relaxed and went to sleep, keeping her weather ear alert while she slept. The next morning she announced to the passengers, "We will sail to Norman Island today. You probably will remember it as Treasure Island, because of all of the folklore you have heard on this trip. We'll anchor the ship about one hundred yards offshore and ferry everyone in who wishes to go, via the tender. You may snorkel into the caves, but be aware of the currents. We'll anchor the tender only a few yards from the openings, but that'll still give everyone who snorkels enough exercise."

The wind was now becoming brisk from the East, and they tacked more than normal to get to a west-side anchor off Norman Island in proximity of the caves and out of the breeze. The diesel engines eventually had to be used and the sails furled. Paul'le was the tender pilot as Dora anchored and stayed on board the *Maverick*. Ben, Barbara, Jim, Laleh, Sonbol, Claire and Eddie were the only brave adventurers who felt like snorkeling in the caves.

Immediately upon entering the water, the swimmers saw fish of many colors—yellow butterflyfish, pink soldierfish, black-and-white-striped bannerfish and small red juvenile fish that hid in holes and darted in and out. A huge ray slid slowly, about forty feet beneath them, close to the bottom. The water was so clear one could see conch, the large conical-shaped snail-like creatures, resting on the bottom. They were spotted with a green seaweed camouflage that helped make them undetectable. Dora was diving close to the ship to recover a few of these sea delicacies to make a conch hors d'oeuvre for supper—an impossible task for almost anyone else to do with just a snorkel and face mask. The forty-foot dive to the bottom required a strong swimmer with good breath control. Dora had given Paul'le a package of frozen peas and he had given each swimmer a handful. Dora had discovered that peas were fish treats when she had scraped a former guest's plate overboard. Clouds of colored fish, first of one color and then another, swarmed around each swimmer as they dispersed food. Underwater cameras recorded people having the joy of a lifetime.

As Jim, Laleh, Sonbol, Claire and Ed swam toward the entrance of the caves on the west end of Norman Island near Treasure

Point, they saw Barbara and Ben turn back. Ben pointed toward Barbara's leg—she had been stung on the calf by a dark sea urchin when she had kicked it accidentally. Ben signaled that they were going back to the tender, as the noise of the surging surf into the caves made it impossible to be heard. Laleh, for the first time, saw a genuine concern and respect exhibited by Ben for Barbara. The fact that he chose to return to the ship with her, even though she could have easily made it back on her own, impressed Laleh favorably. Because all had been issued swim fins and masks by Dora to make the trek, swimming was easier than it might have been.

The rest swam on into the caves—a bit more cautious. But they also realized that their level of fitness would have enabled them to swim that distance easily without fins if there had been no wind. However, they did have to be careful, as the coral was beautiful but dangerous. They all had been cautioned that coral is a colony of living organisms that can slough off tiny one-cell fragments into an individual's open wound if they get cut. The transplanted cells then resume living in the new host—you. They are difficult to remove.

Jim was the first to reach the caves with openings above water of about ten to fifteen feet wide and perhaps six to ten feet high. Below water they varied from three to seven feet. Inside the opening, the caves expanded right and left for thirty to fifty feet. Some caves were interconnected.

Jim signaled for Claire and Ed to go right and Sonbol, Laleh and he would go left. Jim eventually reached the far end of the cave after exploring everything else, the others following his lead. A small ledge allowed them to slide out of the water and sit. As they marveled at this dark recess, their eyes adjusted to the semi-darkness. Here they could hear each other above the noise of the surf.

Jim said he felt a breeze behind his back, coming from the wall of the cave. With his fins on, he crawled over to see what was causing it. He located a small crack that almost seemed to breathe. It reminded him of moist rales, abnormal respiratory sounds of patients with lung disease. He reasoned that there had to be an airway on the other side of that wall or he wouldn't be able to detect such activity. He pressed his ear to the crack first and then positioned his eye to see something. The laughter he provoked in Laleh and Sonbol caused him to explain his peculiar behavior.

He said, "I have a theory. There must be another airway on the other side of this wall that is connected with this cave. It surges with the tide like this side, but must also have another source of air, because at times it blows into this cave."

With no further explanation, Jim slid off of the ledge and did a surface dive beneath it. Laleh and Sonbol sat in wonder, looking at each other. Jim stayed underwater long enough to concern the two women. He suddenly broke the surface, purged his snorkel like a whale, and popped up beside them. Jim was bursting with excitement, as he pulled off his face mask and removed his mouthpiece.

"You must come with me—the most marvelous shaft leads up to sunlight from a room just on the other side of this wall!" shouted Jim.

Sonbol immediately drew up her arms and legs, almost into a fetal position. She was speechless. Laleh knew that Sonbol was already having trouble dealing with her claustrophobia on this side of the wall, let alone becoming a spelunker.

"Sonbol, would you mind if I left just for a moment to see?" Laleh inquired.

Jim understood the body language completely and added his support. "We will just take a quick look and come right back," said Jim.

Sonbol unfolded her arms and got a better grip on the rock shelf. "You two go, I'll wait here," she said with a bit of trepidation in her voice.

Jim reached out his hand to Laleh as she apologetically glanced at Sonbol and slid into the water. After seating their masks and mouthpieces, Jim signaled for the simultaneous dive. It was hard to see; Jim felt the surface of the rock and coral with his diving gloves, one hand for the wall and one hand for Laleh. It reminded Jim of a three-point stance in rock climbing, one hand and two feet—or vice versa—on the rock for safety at all times.

Jim quickly led Laleh to the surface on the other side and they broke into the chamber together, hand in hand. Jim was reluctant to release her hand. They removed their masks and snorkels after perching on the small rock floor of the chamber. The feeling was mystic to them both. They looked up to see a sliver of indirect sun disappearing from sight. The glimpse of the undulating shaft reaching almost four hundred feet above them was breathtaking. In that moment they knew what they had to do, but how? They couldn't abandon Sonbol for the amount of time that it would take to climb the shaft. Each surge of air in the shaft seemed to tempt them—as though they could almost hear the mountain calling.

"Let's just go up for five minutes, she will be all right that long," coaxed Jim. "After all, she's with Claire and Ed."

"Only five minutes," cautioned Laleh, pointing at Jim's diving watch.

Much to their amazement, they found ancient iron rods that had been driven into the rock a very long time ago. They were strategically placed to accommodate some heavily burdened traffic that transversed this shaft in the more vertical areas. Jim realized that novices to rock climbing, like Laleh, often go up easily but have great difficulty coming down. Jim speculated that pirates were the only ones who might have gone to this trouble to stash some loot. It would have been better than digging a large hole in the rocky areas on the steep side of the island. At the first large resting place they came to, Jim said, "Laleh, we need to go back."

"I couldn't go much further anyway, Jim," Laleh agreed.

"Maybe we can come back if we can find some good rope and some flashlights on the *Maverick,* to do it safely," responded Jim.

Laleh looked up at the rapidly diminishing light source and

realized that they had witnessed the only fifteen-minute window of intense sunlight inside the shaft that was possible each day. It was like being at the bottom of a well—she could now almost see stars above.

They rejoined a very anxious Sonbol. "It is a good thing that you did not wait a second later. I had just made up my mind to go get help."

Back on board the *Maverick,* they were all eager to tell everyone of their discovery. At first Dora was skeptical and thought they were fabricating a tale for her benefit. She had been in the caves countless times before and had also talked to other captains and their crews. All had taken tourists there and none had ever spoken of seeing such a thing, but she reconsidered as they each verified each other's stories.

The others had seen magnificent beauty and sea life on the other side of the cave, but their experience was upstaged by the hidden-shaft story. As Jim told the story, he came to speculate that there had to be a perpendicular side-tunnel off the shaft one-quarter or one-half way up, or they would not have had the subdued light they needed to do what they did. Jim explained, "The interior of the shaft reminded me of a slot canyon in Utah. It is a mountain whose interior is almost solid rock that had fractured into two halves and barely separated. In some places we could see the gap was five feet and others only two feet apart with an occasional shelf. Most of the top seemed to be closed together with just the single small opening remaining. I guess that 'chimneying' might be practical." He explained, "That's rock climbing language for a technique that involves placing one's back and hands against one side and pushing against the other side with one's feet. It would be safe for beginners with the avail-ability of a rope to belay or secure individuals. The anchored rope would be secured on the old iron bars. It isn't like most caves with stalactites and stalagmites and mineral deposits. It is solid black rock."

It was happy hour, time for hors d'oeuvres and drinks. Those

63

BOB PEARCE AND NAYEREH FALLAHI

who stayed on board watched Paul'le use a claw hammer to puncture the top of the conches in just the right place to affect a coup de grace. Simply grasping and pulling the Conche's foot out of the large open end, the meat was easily removed. Conch meat was a delicacy when minced and mixed with spices and celery. It was served with crackers and wine and the hungry guests munched heartily. The aroma of broiling fish being prepared for their main entree enhanced everyone's appetite. The vapors swirled above and below deck to entice all.

Conversation was light and curiously untechnical for a group of scientists. Everywhere they looked and listened, beauty could not be denied. The setting sun, the cloud formations, the foliage on the island with red flowers contrasting with yellow among the guava and palm trees, the radiant faces, the ebullient voices and soft Caribbean music hypnotized everyone into tranquillity. The mixed aromas of natural flowers, different exotic perfumes hidden in various women's attire and the soft warm air helped soothe the senses of everyone on board.

An aura of Caribbean passion was contagious. Paul'le had climbed the ratlines to stretch his legs and perhaps dream of a woman he had met in some port. From his perch he could look below to couples pairing off for intimate conversations. He was aware of his loneliness this night, but not overcome, as he knew the next port of call would reward him for his patience. Tonight was for the guests. The stage was set for a very special evening.

Chapter 5
Norman Island—Days 7–8

Jim and Laleh found themselves together again at the bow of the boat which had drifted on anchor to face the setting sun. Their hands were close on the handrail.

"I don't think I'll ever forget this view," said Jim. "See, that's St. John's Island far to the west and Tortola to the north. And the music they have playing now—they certainly go together." *Jamaica Farewell* by the Cockspur Five Star Steel Orchestra was playing faintly. "There are times when I have felt that the beauty of a special moment is a religious experience. Have you ever felt that way?" he asked.

During a moment of silence, Laleh was afraid that the new sunshine in her life, Jim, might set and never again rise. She was painstakingly facetious: "Religious experience? For the beauty of a special moment, forty million people are experiencing religion right now in Iran—it should be heaven." Laleh was anxiously trying to change the subject. She felt her religious beliefs were private and personal.

Jim was confused and stifled. He was eager to understand her thinking, but he obviously did not understand her culture or her need to veil her emotions.

"Laleh, I've a confession to make. I haven't felt really happy since Jaynee's death—until now. I almost feel like God has given me license to be happy—finally. But, I must admit that somehow you have helped me feel this way and I want to thank you. It isn't something I can explain—nothing intellectual—I just feel good when we have time together to talk," Jim said, looking deeply into her eyes.

Laleh was speechless. Her heart beat faster. She was caught.

Jim's confession had caught her by surprise. She tried to control her trembling voice. "Thanks, Jim. I'm flattered. I hope I will not be the cause of your becoming an orthodox religious man," she said, again being facetious.

Jim refused be diverted. "Please be serious, Laleh, I'm of the opinion that you and I share a common feeling. I don't know why I assume that. . . . I've never felt that I've had a valid intuition about much of anything. I guess that's because my scientific discipline has restricted such fantasies. However, having said that, I must ask you if you also believe we have such chemistry, " Jim inquired.

Laleh smiled. "Jim, a minute ago you mentioned that you can't explain your feelings intellectually. Now, you're asking me if I believe there is such chemistry between us. I must confess that I do believe in such chemistry too, I felt it from the beginning when I looked at your wedding ring, remember? But—why not someone else?" she asked. "Why not Sonbol? Why not Ben, only you and I? And, what is it about us? Could it not be just physical interest? In that case—I am not a 'Bubbles'! If there is something else, love—beauty—spiritual—it is just too early to jump to any conclusions. Don't you agree, we should know each other better before we make any hasty judgments?"

Talk had drifted from beauty to religion and back to beauty. In fact, each was curious to know as much as possible what the other felt concerning anything and everything.

Jim continued to be intense. "What little I know about Islam is, that there are Shi'ite and Sunni factions. I seem to recall that they both accept the fact that Christ really lived. But, do both groups not accept the Christian concepts of the Trinity, the Father, Son, and Holy Spirit?" Jim couldn't remember at first why this was supposed to be such a defining question, but then vaguely he remembered. "The reason I ask, is because I had an American associate at the university who told me that she wouldn't marry her Iranian boyfriend because of this difference. She couldn't reject her belief in the Trinity to become a Muslim."

Immediately Laleh got the impression that Jim was alluding to their possible marriage! That was a complete surprise. This American is so confusing, she thought, too fast, so presumptuous, so direct and yet possibly honest.

Maybe he is just a young widower on a rebound. . . . His intent seems to be honorable even if it is so contrary to my culture, thought Laleh. She decided to risk being a bit more open and explore his question.

"That's interesting. How could this American woman have an Iranian boyfriend, and I assume have physical contact and perhaps sex, yet not marry him due to their religious differences? If that were me and I loved a person in such a way, it should be as Attar wrote in his poem, 'The Story of Shaikh San'aan.' He was a twelfth century Persian Sufi poet. In this poem, Shaikh San'aan fell in love with the Christian girl, Dokhtar-e-Tarsa. She asked him to do four things for her trust:

"Burn the holy book of Muslims, the Qur'an.

"Drink wine.

"Seal up Faith's eye.

"Bow down to images.

"Finally, Shaikh, due to his pure love for her, did it all. This is similar to what you mentioned earlier, 'the beauty of a special moment as a religious experience.' The purity of love for Shaikh San'aan was the moment of unity, as God only knows unity. Good and bad has no meaning for him! At any rate, at the end of the poem, Shaikh recruited the Christian girl into Islam. Jim, to me all religions are one, as God is the only one, and the purity of love is the only unity."

Jim pondered and tried to fully comprehend. He thought to himself, what did she say? With his limited understanding of Persian poetry, he wasn't sure. He wondered how much literal meaning he could project into what she said. But he was afraid he might offend or frighten her again, so he elected to be a diplomat and digress a bit.

"It's been a long time since I have had a comparative religion course, but I remember that western Christians seem to be different from eastern Christians. Western Christians often seem to believe that it's okay for God to remain external to man. People that I know tend to imagine three divine figures or else ignore the doctrine altogether, and identify God with the Father and make Jesus a divine friend and not the same. Certain orthodox Christians believe that God and man must be inseparable.

"Some especially adopt an exclusive notion that Jesus was the first and last Word of God to the human race, rendering future revelation unnecessary. This is unacceptable to my Mormon friends in Salt Lake City who believe Joseph Smith had direct revelations from God in the Nineteenth Century—like Muhammad did in Arabia during the Seventh Century. How do you feel about it?" inquired Jim.

Laleh answered with a look of openness he had not seen before. "Jim, I grew up in a Shi'ite Muslim family. I consider myself a 'Quasi Muslim.' I neither fast during Ramadan, nor do I pray five times a day. I certainly believe in God, but I don't believe in institutional religions. I like mysticism or Sufism, but I don't participate in their institutionalizations either. To me, God is love, unity and purity. Many religions, such as Zororastrianism, Judaism, Hinduism, Christianity and Islam, all try to teach love, unity and purity. But they've not been successful because they've also tried to teach ethics. Ethics is a learning process. Metaphysics is beyond what we learned. In every culture we learn ethics; we learn what is good and what is bad. I believe that for God, good and evil have no meaning. He knows only unity. Unity comes through love, and love is the only purity."

"I was raised to believe that 'God is Love.' It seems to me now that . . ."

Jim hesitated, as he thought he saw a searching look in Laleh's eyes. She seemed to be looking for some sort of affirmation from him. He perceived that she wanted some points of unity, but he felt inadequate to respond directly. He simply wasn't as well-educated in theology as Laleh on the various religions of the world. Even though the facade of calling each other by their respective titles had long disappeared, their discussion would have seemed anything but romantic to a passing eavesdropper.

"You know, the more we talk about religion, the more convinced I become that most people everywhere believe in God, a supreme being, an omnipotent force or power in their lives. Don't you?" Jim inquired.

"Yes I do, Jim. We need to learn more about unity, love and purity. I will be more than happy to be your classmate in this learning," replied Laleh.

Jim's eyes met hers and there was physical magnetism. He covered her hand with his in a slow deliberate movement that left no question. She forced herself to look away to the horizon, and the two focused their eyes on the sunset. The disappearing sun's brilliant orange was changing the color of the clouds to crimson and yellow, then the final hues of violet and purple slowly disappeared. Laleh's perfume distracted him. Jim struggled with his urge to engulf Laleh in a passionate embrace. The air felt heavy and intoxicating. He thrust his fingers slowly between hers. He felt her response. Her look reminded him, "Careful, not so fast." He managed to return to their previous dialog—barely.

"It sounds bizarre, but I have a theory that God has implanted a special gene in humans. It is an instinct gene as real as the migratory instinct in birds and animals, one designed to cause a people to seek communion with their maker. How else can you scientifically account for such intense universal behavior that makes people seek their maker, their God?" inquired Jim.

Laleh hesitated with her answer to contemplate what Jim was suggesting. It was obvious that Jim felt very strongly about all of this and she felt that he had shared this perspective with few other people. But he still couldn't comprehend her perspective.

Jim sensed the hesitation and quickly added, "Laleh, as an

infectious-disease physician, you might make an analogy to a nidus, a point of origin, the hidden source. Like in Michener's book, *The Source*."

"I have not read that book, Jim, but you remind me of the Shi'ite Muslim's argument to prove the existence of God and their analogy to electricity. They argue that we can't see the invisible hidden source which is the electron. The same can be said about life. We can't see life—but we know we are alive. We may use electricity in both positive and negative ways. We use it to warm ourselves and cook a meal or to burn and kill ourselves. In both ways the electron, the source, does not change."

Jim was touched—she understood. Then for some unknown reason Jim launched into a story from his youth. "Years ago on the ranch in Walden, Colorado, Uncle Andy interrupted me in my quest to seduce one of the ranchhand's daughters. Uncle Andy was handicapped by polio as a youth and was left with one leg about six inches shorter than the other. He walked with a compensating built-up sole on the shoe of that leg. It had been Andy's motivation to direct my life toward things not physical—like nature, religion, accounting, philosophy, literature and poetry. I had always listened to Uncle Andy, even when I was rebelling against my parents. Uncle Andy was my mentor and confidant.

"Instead of berating me for my lust for the girl, Uncle Andy took me on an unplanned Jeep tour of the ranch to view nature and to learn from it. He pointed out the huge Hereford bulls that they kept separated from the cows most of the year. Then we were lucky to see a buck deer alone at the edge of the forest bordering our property; no doe in sight. It was autumn and the geese were leaving to fly south. Uncle Andy asked me to tell him what I could deduce from all of these lessons of nature. Eventually I was guided to the logic that there is a time and place for everything.

"Uncle Andy could always point to evidence of God's work everywhere in our environment, watching the chickens hatch or helping a cow with a difficult labor to deliver a calf. Observing the spring bringing forth new life everywhere after an exceedingly difficult winter, instilled my confidence in a life after death. The natural instincts of birds, animals and even the tiniest insects to create new life was evidence, Uncle Andy pointed out. When I doubted God's infinite influence and power, Uncle Andy knew what to do. We would watch a lightning storm or gaze at the majestic mountains of Rocky Mountain National Park to the south, the Rawah mountains to the east or the Zirkel Wilderness to the west of North Park where our ranch centered. There has never been much of a question in my mind about the existence of God because of my uncle's teachings. I wish my Uncle Andy were still alive. . . ."

Laleh had become the consummate listener. "It is refreshing to hear a man able to talk about something else besides boasting about his macho achievements," she thought to herself.

As Jim wound down his story he thought about Jaynee, and how he never would want to forget her. How could an omnipotent God have allowed that to happen? And now . . . what about Laleh?

Sudden applause erupted on board. Claire and Ed had climbed up the ratlines and made dual swan dives off the yardarms into the sea on the port side. They made quite a handsome couple; some felt envious of their fit bodies. Jim and Laleh joined in the applause.

No sooner had Claire and Ed climbed back on board, when Paul'le shouted,

"HEY, MON! LOOK-A-DAT!"

The conch and other scraps from dinner that Paul'le had just thrown overboard were attracting some huge marlin. The floodlights they had hung over the sides of the boat for swimming illuminated huge marlin racing under the keel, their silver scales reflecting streaks and flashes. Quickly, nature's recyclers disappeared as miraculously as they had come.

"Maybe we should rejoin the others and see if anyone would like to take a midnight swim into the caves with flashlights. We'll be leaving early tomorrow and won't ever have another chance. It's tonight or never," said Jim.

Capt. Daly had just been in erratic radio contact with the Latina because of a short in a switch that Sparks had not completely fixed. She was frustrated, as she wanted to get their report on the pending weather. On the water where they were, it was it was almost calm, but Dora was mildly concerned because the high stratus clouds were thin and moving fast. She decided to get out the earphones to enhance her listening ability.

Suddenly, Barbara came to her with concerns about Ben. "Can you come help me? Ben has been violently vomiting. I'm scared."

Dora quizzed her about Ben's symptoms. She said, "Oh, he's probably had an allergic reaction to the conch. He isn't going to die, but he might feel like it for a while. Have him drink water to replace the fluid he loses, and by morning he'll be fine." Dora put some hydrocortisone cream on Barbara's leg where the sea urchin caused a large, bright red, hand-sized patch.

Dora speculated to herself that Bubbles must have managed to get her nickname from her excitable personality, because she babbled incessantly about their peril, like a teakettle. For a moment Dora felt as if she were back in the emergency department in Boston where she had practiced nursing. It had been like this all day on the *Maverick,* with first one guest needing ibuprofen for his arthritis, two with sunburn, one seasick. She thought she had escaped all of that when she became a captain of a windjammer. If it hadn't been for the folks that went to the caves, she thought she would have nothing but a floating infirmary.

She sent Bubbles off to care for Ben and went back up topside to hear everyone's account of the marlin.

No one seemed to notice the twin-engine seaplane as it banked out of view behind Norman Island, except Dora. Even she just barely noticed, because it did not have the red and green wing lights turned on in this night of a dark moon. "That's odd," she mumbled, but she

72

did not internalize the significance. No one saw the plane land on the other side of the island and taxi into Sabu Bay to anchor. Norman was an uninhabited island. Usually, only day tours came here, and yachts usually anchored in Bight Bay where small ruins and foot trails of a by-gone habitation offered more recreation. The white sand beach of Money Bay, toward the other end of the island and over a mile away, offered a second choice for most tour leaders. However, it was out of sight to the anchored plane.

Dora was about to return to her radio when Jim, Ed and Paul'le approached her. "We would like to take the tender back to the island for our 'midnight madness,'" as Jim called it.

When Dora voiced concern about disturbing the sleeping guests, they promised to use the oars instead of the outboard motor. If Paul'le would accompany them, she reluctantly gave them permission. Paul'le, Jim, Ed, Claire and Laleh were the only ones who would go.

"I need to stay up anyway," Dora said. "I want to get the earphones on and, if I can coax that defective switch to work on the radio, I'll secure a weather report." A moderate breeze was blowing from the southeast and the barometer was falling slowly.

After obtaining the two headband flashlights that Ed and Claire brought with them, and borrowing one of the ship's floatable flashlights, the midnight revelers loaded their gear into the small boat. A strong, heavy seventy-five-foot rope, three water bottles, Claire's small waterproof Canon Sure-Shot A-1 camera, light windbreakers and their snorkel gear were crammed into two daypacks that Paul'le and Ed carried. Jim and Ed manned the paddles. Paul'le guided the boat with the rudder. The two women, Claire and Laleh, sat toward the bow.

"This reminds me of our expeditions down the Colorado River on a raft," Jim observed.

The explorers had reached the caves in only ten minutes with the accomplished paddling of Jim and Ed. In another fifteen minutes all were inside the shaft and Jim was securing a hand-line for everyone to follow. He determined that a horizontal tunnel perpendicular to the shaft led out in a westerly direction. He figured seven iron bars led to this side tunnel and they might even be able to see the ship from there. They quickly abandoned any notions of going clear to the top of the four hundred and forty foot shaft.

Jim, carrying a flashlight, revealed a large room with a small opening at the other end. This explained the sunlight they had enjoyed the previous trip. It took another thirty or thirty-five minutes for all to use the climbing technique demonstrated to enter the room.

"This reminds me of the lava tubes in Craters of the Moon National Monument in Idaho," Claire commented.

They picked their way carefully across the rock-strewn floor. Then they saw the ship anchored out in the bay with very few lights—just enough to reveal its location.

There was a stiff breeze, so most positioned themselves out of the wind with their backs to the rock wall. The slope outside the cave mouth was too steep to descend without a longer rope. Glissading down the slippery undergrowth, as Jim had hoped they might do, was also impossible. They all sat down to rest and reflect on what they had just accomplished.

Laleh found three small coins of various metals, each with a small hole drilled in them and remnants of gold-looking thread. "My theory is that they belonged to a belly dancer who had sewn the coins to a belt on her hips, a symbol of her value in the society over one hundred years ago. I wonder how they got left in this cave? What happened? And when?"

The Legend of the Marooned Belly Dancer began to grow—each person adding something. Jim and Laleh were seated close together. For now, the topics of virus, sickness, death and vaccines had been shelved.

Back on board the *Maverick,* Dora was the only person awake, almost an hour after the revelers had left for their fantasies, when she

heard through her earphones, "Hurricane Lili has been named a category 1 storm. The wind is now sixty-five miles per hour and the pressure 988 millibars as determined by a weather plane tracking the
storm."

She struggled to determine exactly what direction it was
moving to determine when and if they would need to alter their plans.
She did not hear the strange, small black rubber raft come alongside
the *Maverick,* and two darkly dressed figures stealthily come aboard.
Darting quickly here and there on deck, they found no one. Quietly
they crept down below, prepared to use their knives like the professional killers that they were. Dora had no warning. She didn't suffer—
she died instantly with the headphones still on her head crackling and
popping with static. Then the two assassins slithered into each cabin
and simultaneously killed bunkmates. The previously peaceful
sounds of deep sleep and snoring had been quietly silenced. The
innocents had no warning of their impending doom.

The machiavellian scene was beginning when one dark figure
opened the valves to the stove in the galley. All that could be heard
was the ominous sound of the hissing propane filling the hold of the
ship. When the dark figures prepared to leave the ship, they could
hardly believe how easy it had been.

They noticed something was wrong when they finished their
quick search for survivors and five passengers were not even on
board! Frantic, hushed conversation ensued over a hand-held radio.
It was decided that the five had to be somewhere close by. More than
likely, they reasoned, they're scuba diving or swimming somewhere."
Then their leader observed, "Their rubber dinghy isn't secured to the
ship—it's gone! Maybe they're ashore." Quickly they boarded their
own black boat and headed toward the beach. The noise of the sea
continued to mask any of their activity, including the hissing sound
left back on board the ill-fated sailing ship.

None of the killers discovered the caves because of the inky
darkness. They searched the sandy shore with precision. Yet, no

lights or voices could be detected, only the wind and waves. They could not find them! This was not supposed to happen! Then, over their radio, they were informed that the plane's pilot was insisting that they must leave. "Very bad flying weather is upon us already," he protested.

They had already been over their time limit for the mission and still had no clue where next to search. The leader was exasperated. He reluctantly aborted their search and ordered, "Terminate the ship."

As a final action, when they were far enough away, one of the figures with a black face mask fired a short, incendiary volley from his submachine gun. Instantaneously a fireball erupted from the boat, sending the masts and rigging high into the air while the rest of the ship disintegrated into small pieces. The shockwave spread in all directions and the incandescent rain of debris fell over a wide area. Bodies that were partially intact floated for a brief time.

Fortunately, there was no moon to illuminate the feeding frenzy of the natural inhabitants of the sea that followed. An oil slick burned for a few minutes and small, unidentifiable smoldering objects floated and sustained a dim outline of the area. As winds began blowing up the surf, flames slowly died out, and the debris began to disperse with the wind. The ominous breath of Lili had just begun; the hurricane was headed directly toward Cuba with Norman Island in the way.

First there was the huge fireball. No one was looking directly at the ship when the blast went off. Heads snapped and then the shock wave and violent noise reached the cave opening. Laleh reacted by jumping into Jim's arms. Claire and Ed clutched each other instinctively. Paul'le dropped to the ground like someone who had been trained in the military.

"What was that? What happened? What should we do?" Laleh screamed, "Sonbol! Sonbol! Sonbol!"

Paul'le shouted. "The boat blow up—I must go down."

Laleh was about to jump straight down the slippery slope when

Jim restrained her and said, "Laleh . . . Laleh . . . that way is impossible! We must go back the way we came."

"I must go," said Paul'le.

"Sonbol! Sonbol!" wailed Laleh. Jim held her firmly.

"We can't all go, you must stay here," cautioned Jim. Jim looked to Ed and Claire for support. They consoled Laleh.

"I'll go with you, Paul'le," Jim pronounced.

"No! Nobody else. . . . My job."

"It takes two people to lift an unconscious person into the raft," Jim insisted.

He finally convinced Paul'le that it would be best for him to have a partner in the raft. "You, Jim, come. Others stay here. . . . Will need room for people in water," Paul'le said.

Jim didn't want to leave Laleh alone in the cave, but the people who were in the explosion needed his help now! Everyone left in the cave would be safe. They could watch from this vantage point.

Jim spoke quickly to Laleh. "You must wait here, I'll go and help Paul'le. I want you to know that I'll look for Sonbol as intently as you would if you were there in person. Trust me, I'll see you soon, Laleh . . . I love you." Jim embraced and kissed her, then he bounded down the shaft. It happened so fast neither had time to think. It was a bond Jim had made with Laleh and sealed with a kiss.

Paul'le had already left. Quickly, Jim was on his heals. Jim had Claire's headband flashlight and Paul'le had Ed's. They had agreed to use their lights sparingly. No one could predict when help would come . . .

Paul'le jerked the rope to start the outboard motor on the rubber boat. Nothing! He pulled again. Nothing! He pulled and pulled frantically.

"MON—IT NOT WORK!"

Jim demanded that he try. Nothing! Despite either man's efforts, the motor wouldn't start. They grabbed the paddles and started paddling, Jim on the bow and Paul'le in the stern, straddling the motor and raised rudder. Both flashlights were dimming dramatically, probably due to water that seeped in during their diving. The only other light came from the small fires on the surface. The whitecaps and waves increased in the open sea. They decided to stop and purge their lights of water so they would be more effective in looking for the injured. Jim fumbled with his flashlight and dropped its batteries into the brine at the bottom of the boat. Paul'le had to assist him with his dim light to search for the parts.

Suddenly a twin-engine seaplane with its landing lights on, roared out of nowhere and flew low over the waves. Startled, Paul'le dropped his light. The plane buzzed slowly over the accident scene. Jim and Paul'le instinctively jumped to their feet shouting and waving their arms—but with no lights, the dinghy was invisible to the plane's occupants, and they certainly couldn't hear them. To Jim and Paul'le's amazement, the plane eventually shut off its landing and wing lights and powered up to a cruising altitude. It vanished into the darkness.

Jim could not recall seeing either red or green wing lights or any other illumination after the landing lights were turned off. The confused pair could not make sense of what they had just witnessed.

The watchers in the cave above did not have the presence of mind to turn their flashlight on, much less try to signal the plane. It all happened too fast. Not until the plane was long gone did they turn it on and scream pathetically. Self-reproach was uniform for all of the survivors. If only this—if only that.

Jim and Paul'le realized that the wind was steady now, probably at forty miles per hour or higher. They decided to try the motor again after they fixed their flashlights. They knew they were no match for the wind, just paddling.

Jim then thought to turn on the ignition switch that neither man had remembered originally in their panic. The motor started with the first pull. As they left the protection of the rock and island, the swells grew in size and the wind became intense. The dark was like a black hole in space—it seemed to swallow their light beams like a magnet.

They were just about on top of the debris before they felt it. The piece of mast and bow hit them below the water line. They barely avoided falling overboard and tangling their prop in the sail and rope attached to the mast.

After five minutes of fruitless search, they became aware of how far they really were from the island. They realized that they were risking their own lives each additional minute they stayed on the water and decided to turn back toward the island.

Jim couldn't even make out the island, even though both had put their snorkel masks on. He was glad that Paul'le took the rudder. Jim started bailing water while watching with his headlamp for any signs of life. Paul'le spotted a floating gym bag; it was Ben's. Jim pulled it on board.

Because of the brisk wind, their shouts were pitiful. Still, they toiled back and forth picking up items that might be useful while looking for survivors. Four life preservers were found. They put two on without discussion. The weather tacitly spoke to the men's fear.

A total of six litre bottles of water were found grouped in a large plastic bag. A large yellow flashlight bobbing in the water was so elusive that they almost gave up trying to grab it. Assorted food containers were scooped up. It became evident to Paul'le that he had to concentrate on piloting the boat directly back to the caves; the swells and wind demanded it. Paul'le seemed to be struggling to stay on course. Suddenly the raft jerked to a stop.

Then Paul'le burst into tears screaming, " Dora! Dora! Dora!" He pointed in the general direction of a body he had just struck with the prop.

Jim immediately stumbled toward the stern as the boat gyrated from the lack of power and the rudder being raised by Paul'le. Jim again almost fell overboard just as he reached the stern. He could see Dora's body sinking into the deep; her eyes still open—grotesque lacerations evident on her abdomen. She faded from view. Paul'le was fixed in a catatonic stare—motionless. He was in shock, his eyes glassed over. A wave crashed over the boat. Jim removed Paul'le's limp hand off the rudder handle and managed to put the bow of the boat into the wind just as another wave swamped them.

Jim yelled at Paul'le. "You couldn't help it! You couldn't help it! Paul'le, she was already dead. It wasn't your fault." Paul'le wouldn't hear him.

Jim realized that he did not know where the island was! A wave of fear chilled him to the bone. Jim could not be sure where they were headed. Just then he thought he might have seen a light. So, with the motor at full throttle, he tried to head directly for the light and the island to save the two of them. The other possibly injured survivors had to be forgotten. He struggled to see an outline of the island or a light. Only occasionally did his steering instinct seem rational. The little outboard motor would race every time the swells would free the prop into the air. Alternately it returned to its frantic labor in the troubled waters.

Jim yelled at Paul'le, "Hang on Paul'le! Hang on!"

But Paul'le's mind was somewhere else. He was dead weight, swaying in his sitting position on the bottom of the boat. Jim put a foot on him to steady his motion. The rain started abruptly as a deluge—it was too much. Trying to bail with one hand on the tiller wasn't effective. They didn't seem to be making any progress. Jim still could see nothing. He didn't know where he was going, but he had to gamble. He knew how quickly hypothermia could set in with the rain and wind. His teeth were chattering and every muscle was trembling.

"I've got to concentrate. Got to stay alert."

He did not see the looming shore in the rainy darkness. "OH NO!!" was all Jim managed to scream as the raft slammed to a stop. He was instantly airborne. Flying head first, his chest and abdomen ricocheted off the rubber bow, knocking the wind out of him. He landed on his back with his head pointing to the boat. He struggled to gasp some air. He felt he was going to die because he was stunned and unable to do anything. He felt himself shake and release urine before he passed out. The wind, rain and surf were everywhere.

Paul'le had struck his head on the interior of the raft, and was knocked to the bottom. Unconscious only briefly, he awoke not remembering the most recent past. He staggered to his knees and climbed out of the raft to see Jim, his headlamp beam pointing to the sky.

"Hey, Mon—can't stay here!"

Instinctively he started dragging Jim's body by the feet until he found shelter behind some large boulders. Tree limbs, palm fronds and other vegetation had fallen to form a natural roof, of sorts, over the boulders. Paul'le had no idea where they were or how they got there. His head hurt and he was sick at his stomach. He vomited.

He sat beside Jim's unconscious body and tried to remember anything that had happened that day.

"Maybe on Norman Island—not sure. What day it is—don't know. Anything else? Nothing."

After an hour he recalled seeing various items in the boat before he had started dragging Jim. He was thirsty. Staggering from his injury, he forced himself to carry the contents of the raft to the shelter among the boulders. Gradually he became aware that the sun was shining through a hole in the clouds and there was an eerie silence.

Paul'le had lived in the Caribbean all of his life and he recognized this as an eye of a hurricane. He knew they were on borrowed time, as the full force would soon return. He had to abandon any attempt at securing the boat as it was still half full of water and the motor and prop were screwed into the sand. He resumed sitting by Jim. The nausea was overpowering; he vomited again.

The wind and rain returned with full vengeance. Paul'le looked up just in time to see the wind lift the front of the raft, empty the water and propel the little boat end over end into the sea upside down. Paul'le became aware of the mask with the tethered snorkel tube still dangling around his neck.

They had worn their masks while on the raft because the wind-born saltwater stung their eyes. He took it off. He was afraid to touch Jim again—who knew what his injuries were? He felt Jim's neck for a pulse. He thought he might have felt one but he wasn't sure. Jim lay with his feet pointing inside to the rear of their shelter and his head was still pointing toward the sea, just where Paul'le had dropped him. Paul'le could do no more—he collapsed from exhaustion. The storm continued.

The cave dwellers could not see the shore or disaster area even when they put their snorkel masks on. Darkness, flying leaves and mud seemed to fill the air outside. Ed and Claire pulled Laleh back out of the elements. She didn't sound coherent, possibly speaking Persian. Ed and Claire could only understand the word "Sonbol."

"Sonbol Rast Migoft, Hamash Naghsheh Bud. Beh Amicaiha Nabayad Etemad Kard. Eih kash beh Iran Barmigashtim. Sonbol, Sonbol, Kojai? Sonbol, you were right. It was all planned. We should not trust Americans. I wish we would have returned to Iran! Sonbol! *Sonbol*! Where are you?"

They had all been too busy and frightened to speculate on why the seaplane had been there the night before, or why it had not circled or kept its lights on after it left them—until now. It was almost 10:00 A.M. and still no sign of Jim or Paul'le.

The rain had been unbelievable and the wind as fierce as any of them had ever experienced. Subdued light was adequate to allow them to shut off their flashlights. Ed and Claire had tried making a mini water reservoir to save rain for drinking water. Laleh had been praying. The surrealistic wailing caused by the wind blowing through the cave had not allowed anyone to rest.

"It reminds me of a thousand Tibetan monks humming the same basic mantra, over and over again," Ed said. Then he had another theory. "Or like the noise made by a giant blowing over an equally large bottle."

Claire recalled visiting a spook alley at Halloween. "The amplifiers were turned to a maximum that approached one hundred decibels."

As the trio recalled individual stories, they busied themselves stacking large volcanic rocks from the interior of the cave to make a wall at the small opening, hoping the noise could be reduced.

Laleh shared what the explosion caused her to remember. "I just saw it flash past my memory last night. In August 1978, the Rex Cinema, at Abadan—five hundred people lost their lives. . . . I still have a problem sitting in any theater. I don't think anyone will have survived here either. Oh God! Sonbol, Please be alive!"

Claire was comforting Laleh when she saw it. "Look!—the sun is trying to shine through the clouds and the rain has stopped. I can't see any of the other islands, though."

Ed came to the opening where they had built a small wall about waist high. He exclaimed, "We're in the eye of a hurricane!"

For some reason no one had verbalized the word *hurricane* until Ed mentioned it. Then it had an emotional impact on all of them, but Laleh started to sob uncontrollably.

It was a statement of finality. It was the coup de grace. It meant that none of them would likely see their fellow travelers ever again. Not Sonbol, Paul'le or Jim. Claire dissolved into a river of tears next to Laleh. Ed slowly realized what he had said and why it caused the reaction. Tears swelled up in his eyes and rolled down his checks. He fought it because he felt that he had to demonstrate strength, especially now. But he couldn't. Ed took a position behind them. Then he placed one hand on each woman's shoulder. They could not see his face and he was speechless. He couldn't have talked if he had to. Everyone seemed spent from anguish.

Kneeling in prayer, Laleh faced the sky through the small opening they had left, and talked to the clouds.

83

"Eih Khoda, khoda-ye-zibai-ha! Komakam kon; Khoda-ya Sonbol ro zendeh Negah dar! Chetor mitounam vaghti bargardam, margesh ro tonjih konam. Eih khoda, ageh mordeh man rp ham be bar! Bedun-e-ou nemitunam bazardam." *Oh God! God of the Beauties! Help Me! Let Sonbol be alive! How can I explain her death to our family when I return; Oh God, if she is dead, please take my life too! I can't go back without her!*

Claire and Ed also felt compelled to pray to God in their Catholic tradition.

They knelt and crossed themselves. "Holy Mary, mother of God," they began, and quietly supported Laleh's supplications. They prayed for the missing people and asked for God's help in surviving.

The eye of the hurricane passed quickly and the storm's fury was more intense in every way. Eventually, they managed to finish their wall and sat down in semi-darkness. They told stories, recited poetry, tried to recall scriptures and sing songs each knew. Anything seemed to help.

They now noticed that the noise had not returned, even though the wind had returned. There was no explanation.

Laleh, in a stage of shock, forgot all about Jim. All she could think of was Sonbol. "Claire, Ed, I do not know what to do! I am so scared! How can I ever return to Iran? How can I explain to my family what happened? Why did the boat blow up?"

"Laleh, we can't do anything right now. Let's try to be patient and think of what we can do to save ourselves now. God will help us— for it is his will that we are still alive," exclaimed Claire.

Inexplicably, there grew a new resolve to face their fate. Somehow the cave crew, despite the damp cold and their hunger and thirst, managed to huddle together all during the storm's fury and get some sleep.

Finally the storm left, and sunshine was again partially visible. They decided to leave their sanctuary and swim to the shoreline, away from the rugged rock caves to look for any sign of survivors, food or other supplies.

They found nothing there and decided to swim to Privateer Bay, just south of the caves. There they found a small beach with several small foot trails. They climbed to the summit of about 440 feet, to see what they could. They couldn't see any signs of life, even though some tourists must have come often enough in the past to keep the trails open. Below, to the east, they saw the beautiful white-sand beach of Money Bay.

On the way down to the beach, Claire and Ed found some prickly pear cactus. Using primitive survival skills that they had learned in a Utah outdoor recreation class, they started a fire. Ed burned the needles off of the cactus and said, "There's a lot of juice inside this little succulent plant. Chew it well to release the fluid. It will also give us some solid food."

Laleh managed to net a fish with the shirt that she had worn over her swimsuit. The hungry trio fed themselves sparingly. "It's starting to give me energy. The weakness that replaces hunger will start to leave," she announced to her quiet partners. None had been very verbal before eating.

Ed found a machineel tree that had small green apples on it. He started to harvest the fruit for the others, when he realized that the leaves were causing an intense rash on his arms. "Better not eat this crap," announced Ed. He then spotted three Century Plants in full bloom. "You know, similar plants grow in the desert near the Grand Canyon of the Colorado River. This plant only blooms about every five to twenty years even though legend gave the plant its name—Century Plant. These don't really take one hundred years to blossom—the plants are helped by the rain. Too bad we can't eat them."

Old dead stalks from other dead Century plants in the area stood ten or more feet in the air. Ed made a flagpole out of one of the stalks by breaking it off at the base and tying very small strips of cloth

85

each person tore from swimsuits. It looked more like a string, with a tamarind blossom secured on the end.

"At least it helps us feel we're more prepared to get someone's attention if the chance comes," Ed said.

Laleh and Claire stomped the international SOS sign in the sand on the beach. Then they gathered darker earth and leaves to accentuate the lettering.

The Coast Guard had deduced that the flotation ring and rubber raft they had found, with the *MAVERICK* name on them, had been blown to the west by the prevailing winds of the storm. The objects had been found several miles away, toward St. John, but they had correctly estimated where the ship might have been anchored. Several ships had been able to get a distress call out during the storm, but they had not received one from the *Maverick*. The crew of the search plane also may not have spotted the trio, if it had not been for the reflected sun flashing signals off Ed's knife blade. He always wore it when scuba diving or snorkeling.

When the big U.S. Coast Guard Huey helicopter crew first spotted them, they were just finishing their sign-making. Ed waved the flag. The chopper had been searching for numerous vessels reported missing during the hurricane. They immediately changed course and approached the island beach at about twenty feet off of the surface. With shouts of elation, the three ran toward the helicopter. A Coast Guardsman jumped out and welcomed them aboard before smudging their SOS prior to leaving. A Coast Guard officer said that no bodies had been found from the *Maverick*.

Laleh stood at the door of the chopper and looked back, saying in Persian, "Geem, Koja-ee-? Sonbol kojast? Pay dash Kardi? Zendast?" *Jim, where are you? Where is Sonbol? Did you find her? Is she alive?*

The authorities of British Virgin Islands reluctantly accepted the trio's story of the explosion and storm. Laleh was released to fly home to Tehran. She continued to anguish how she would explain to her family what her sister's fate had been. She couldn't be certain of anything but her own guilt. At the same time Ed and Claire were released to return to Utah.

Chapter 6
Palo Alto and Salt Lake City—Day 9

In Palo Alto, the private telephone line was blinking on Mr. Granite's phone as the executive committee for Alpha Omega was discussing a pressing business issue. J. R. knew that it was a priority call because other incoming calls were to be intercepted by his private secretary. It must be an urgent family problem or a privileged friend who was calling, as very few knew this number.

"Excuse me, everyone, I must take this call in my office—I'll be right back." Rock stepped into his adjacent private office. "This is Rock," he answered. "Yes, Alpha Storm. I've been waiting for your call, Colonel. . . . Oh! An accident? With Ben! And he is missing and presumed dead. . . . Hurricane Lili. . . . Oh, what a tragedy. . . . Any survivors?" Rock inquired.

Rock's face would have defeated his overly solicitous verbiage had anyone been in the private office with him. The look of satisfaction changed all too soon, however.

"What, Colonel? You mean all of the passengers did not disappear, three survived? Tell me what happened!" demanded Rock, as his face flushed.

"Laleh Bazargan, Edward Woodsman and Claire Woodsman, found by the U.S. Coast Guard, were the only three existing survivors who speculated that the explosion and fire was from ignited fuel. There was some confusion among the survivors about a mysterious rescue plane that briefly made one fly-by soon after the accident. No confirmation could be made from any air traffic controllers in the Virgin Islands of any such flights at that time. The B.V.I. and U.S. authorities had interrogated the survivors and determined that they had no evidence to hold them very long. The three would be headed home soon or had already left—Dr. Bazargan to Tehran in Iran and the Woodsmans to Salt Lake City, Utah." Colonel Nick Cabal incredulously concluded.

"Loose ends make me very nervous, Nick. What have you planned to insure that there are no other surprises?" inquired Rock. "Hmmmm, I guess you are right, it's best to do nothing sometimes—until you get more data." Rock was obviously disturbed despite the confidence exuded by Colonel Cabal. "You will call me immediately if anything else develops. Call me anytime, Colonel, day or night—you have my home phone number and my cell phone. . . . No, Colonel, only this company phone is a secured phone. . . . Just keep me informed," concluded Mr. Granite.

As he returned the phone to its cradle, he couldn't help but feel that they were very vulnerable. Still, he thought, he'd have to be ready for the events that would follow. Probably Ben's relatives had been notified by the authorities by now and it would be just a question of hours until the company would be officially notified by someone from the government, or an inquiry from the press would reveal the story. He would have to act shocked and devastated. There would be questions and more questions. He would have to formulate contingency plans.

Right now he had to steel his nerves and return to the meeting as if nothing serious had happened. He would tell them that it was his stockbroker with some decisions he had to authorize right then. His biggest concern was what he would tell Dr. Reichstadt. He elected to let that resolve when the company was officially informed of the "accident" and the hurricane. Ben's replacement would have to be selected after the funeral. The memorial service would probably be held in his hometown, somewhere in Jackson, Wyoming. What an inconvenient time, with winter coming early in those mountain towns and air flights near holidays, but Rock would have to attend unless he could convince the family to allow a second memorial service for Ben's many friends in Palo Alto.

In Salt Lake, Edward Woodsman, M.D., was standing in the chairperson's office facing his boss, Kip Kelly, M.D. Ever since Kip had helped get Ed his appointment to the University of Utah Medical Center, he had been more of a peer than a boss. But now it was different.

Ed had asked Kip to act, in his capacity as chairperson, to apportion limited division funds for start-up money. It would be used for an immediate research project involving the new influenza A virus found in Iran. Ed hit a brick wall.

"All of our funds are already dedicated for the balance of the whole academic year! Ed, you could write grant requests to industry and governmental sources—as you know. The first order of business, of course, will be securing the 'seed virus' from Dr. Bazargan." Kip's voice inflection implied the expectation that it would probably never happen because of the strained relations between the U.S. and Iran.

Ed knew also that the possibility of getting any support from Alpha Omega had depended on Ben's advocacy. Ben was dead and so was Ed's vision of creating help to develop a vaccine. Ed was frustrated, angry, and depressed.

"Instead of the state of Utah and the University spending so much money on the Winter Olympics, they should focus more on saving lives!" Ed exclaimed in anger to Kip as he left the office.

"That was a passive-aggressive response," Claire told him later at home. "You knew Kip had a poster about the winter Olympics on the wall in his office and that he is a supporter. You know that you should not have been so hostile. What good's a burned bridge, Honey-chile?" Claire asked in a sarcastic ethnic tone.

"Spike, you are so quick to bounce the blame to me. You are so damned supercilious—what the hell have you done to help the vaccine cause today?" Ed said in uncharacteristic hostility.

"I haven't done anything yet! What did you expect me to do? I do intend to find out what I can about the virus that killed Jaynee. I intend to interview the railroad detective at the Union Pacific as soon as I can. Right now I have several patients who really need to see me. I missed their appointments while we were gone. I need to see them first," Claire retorted.

"And, I suppose, you don't think I have any patients who really missed or needed me!" retorted Ed.

Ed and Claire vented all of their pent-up anger, frustration and hostility of the past weeks. Shouting, screaming, slamming doors and stomping feet were common for them both that evening. Then, just before retiring, each went jogging in opposite directions in the dark. Their habit had always been to go jogging together. When the two came back to their small house in the Avenues, on the north side of Salt Lake City, they were tired and sweaty.

However, the jogging had been therapeutic for each of them. Each realized what had really happened and proceeded to apologize and forgive one another. It had been catharsis for them both, Claire said. Finally, both cried unashamedly as they discovered they each had deferred any genuine grieving until this day. They held each other most of the night. At one point they both awakened with insatiable sexual desire. The soothing caresses, gentle kisses, and movement were climaxed in emotional relief. The two made profoundly simple reaffirmations verbally:

"I love you, Eddie" and "I love you, Spike."

Both were late for work the next morning, delayed by the snowstorm that had come during the night. They also had agreed not to talk about the subject of the Iranian virus for a while, to allow their emotions to heal. They each knew that they were not going to solve anything until someone else, like Laleh, could give them direction. Before the trio had separated they all pledged to keep the others informed by e-mail or telephone. They knew it was very doubtful the Iranian government communication bureaucrats would allow unmonitored communication with Americans.

They would have to look for ways to be resourceful, because the infectious disease data would probably raise concerns about national security with any potential censor. If any authority in Iran felt that Laleh was leaking biological weaponry information to the U.S., she would be in danger. The idea of speaking at international scientific meetings might have been tolerated by the Iranian government, but Laleh's intention of shipping live virus samples to the U.S. would demand intervention.

Chapter 7
Alpha Omega—Days 10–11

In Palo Alto, California, Dr. Martin Reichstadt was the only executive who was available when the federal government agent arrived at the offices of Alpha Omega to deliver the official notification of the presumed death of Dr. Ben Carlson, and to solicit any information that might possibly be relative to their investigation on the subject. Dr. Reichstadt was assured that the federal agent had notified Ben's family of the accident.

Martin Reichstadt was shocked. He mused that the accident was a dichotomy—tragic but convenient. That, coupled with the coinciding hurricane, made him think that it almost had been an act of God. The loss of a close work associate was tragic, and he was relieved to hear that the survivors believed nothing but an accident had occurred.

As all these feelings flashed across Dr. Martin Reichstadt's face, the highly trained federal agent noticed the body language and facial expressions were not consistent with normal expectations. As a trained observer, he knew something else was there to be discovered. Dr. Reichstadt also realized his own behavior and preempted the federal agent's next question by saying:

"I must say I'm relieved that he was not shot by a jealous husband, as terrible as that may sound. He had that one weakness. Some men seem to let their emotional urges, instead of their brain, dictate their actions at times. Having said that, we will be hard-pressed to replace Ben's talent. He was the best Director of Marketing that we've ever had and I will miss him greatly. Is there anything else that we can do for you?"

The agent asked more questions to verify that Ben's reputation as a womanizer was accurate. He also asked the nature of AO's product line and of Ben's business trip. He acted unsatisfied, but said nothing. Dr. Martin Reichstadt felt he needed to reassure the agent. "Mr. J. R. Granite, our CEO, will also be happy to answer any questions when he returns from his business trip tomorrow."

The agent looked pensive and indicated that he would check with Mr. Granite's secretary on his way out.

Dr. Reichstadt worried about what the agent wanted to know, and why he didn't believe that Martin, the presiding executive, could have answered any questions right then. Later a CNN report from Athens, Greece, indicated that relatives of the missing Greek couple had raised the question. "How could there be survivors of the ship explosion that didn't know what happened to our loved ones?" It was noted that a large American pharmaceutical company had paid for the cruise. The representative of the insurance carrier for the sailing ship had said, "We have just begun our investigation. I have no comment."

The next morning when Dr. Reichstadt arrived at the company parking lot, Alpha Omega's security officers were restraining reporters from TV, radio, and the printed media from approaching his limo. The pack swarmed toward the approaching vehicle. Dr. Reichstadt was startled and he instructed his limo driver to divert his normal plans for going into the plant. He told plant security on the car phone, "Prepare for my arrival at the delivery entrance, the press are in a feeding frenzy."

He also called his secretary. "Marsha, would you please alert Mr. Granite's secretary of the circumstances? The press is here in force. I'm trying to divert them for a moment. Prepare the conference room and schedule a press release for later in the day, when Mr. Granite will be back. Then, Marsha, please confirm the plan with Mr. Granite. When that is done, call security and let them inform the press about the delayed press conference plan. Finally, call me back on my car phone when you can confirm that I can enter the plant via the service entrance. I don't want any surprises there."

The press demanded to know why the limo had eluded them and why there was a delayed communication. Then they were informed that the CEO was en route and he would answer all their questions at the press conference. Martin was greatly relieved that he would not have to deal with the press.

Martin thought to himself. "This could be a 'Pandora's Box'— once opened it will be too late to contain what might happen." His limo driver circled the area outside the plant and made an impromptu tour of some of the neighborhood's residential properties. Dr. Reichstadt became aware of one vehicle following them at a discreet distance. He felt it must be some perceptive reporter who was hoping for privileged information. Dr. Reichstadt told his driver, "I believe we have a tail following us." The driver made a quick turn into the service entrance. The Ford Taurus drove on past them, but he noticed two people inside. Martin wondered if he was just getting paranoid. Immediately he retreated to his office where he could relax. "There was something about that tail," Dr. Reichstadt mumbled to himself.

Later that afternoon, Rock Granite made his grand entry into the conference room and appeared very confident. He began by asking for a question. He pointed at a familiar face. "Yes, Dorothy, you can be first." She had read the prepared written press release that was circulating, and asked a nonthreatening clarifying question. He handled all of the questions with disciplined aplomb until the last departing inquiry. It came just as he was leaving. Rock knew that the "door-knob'" questions could be dangerous.

"Mr. Granite, we were told that all of the survivors aboard the *Maverick* had been passengers aboard the *Royal Caribbean* and for some reason they decided to leave that ship to sail on a windjammer. Why did they do that?" inquired the reporter from CNN.

He replied, "The small group had a need to discuss private,

more focused issues unrelated to the main conference and in a secluded atmosphere." J. R. then waxed and waned like a poet describing the beauty of the Caribbean as seen from a small sailing boat.

The CNN reporter continued, "What was the primary reason for your company rationalizing paying additional money for everyone's exclusive windjammer cruise?"

Rock rambled on, "There often is a need for confidential conversations in public relations, government, business, and even religion. This was no different." He then clarified the question with a question. "Haven't you ever been a guest of a public-relations social event, Ron?" He knew full well this reporter had been on many such junkets. Some in the press corps smiled.

One other woman from the newspaper media asked a question later that returned to the theme of possible "quid pro quo" expectations of Alpha Omega.

Rock Granite looked incredulously insulted and said, "Absolutely not, there was none."

"Specifically, did Dr. Ben Carlson imply, at any time on the sailing boat or the cruise ship, that Alpha Omega might assist any health care executives, in any manner, in exchange for their attendance?"

The question seemed loaded and hit a nerve. Rock said, "I must refuse to answer that until I can get a clarification from our legal counsel. I simply don't know for sure. It's too early in our investigation of the circumstances to make any unqualified statements. I hope you will ask me that again, later." With that, Rock terminated the press conference.

Chapter 8
Norman Island—Days 10–11

Paul'le was in a deep sleep. Jim was breathing deeply. His realistic dream began with the image of Laleh coming to him as he lay on the beach—unable in this nightmare to move or respond. She was dressed in a black chador. She looked down on him in puzzlement. It was evident that she was nude under that black chrysalis. He was helpless to stop her from walking away from him toward the beach. Periodically looking back for some sign of life in his motionless body, she paused at the water's edge. Her hands inside the chador came together and reached for the sky. The chador slid off of her body slowly exposing her to her God, for whom she searched the heavens above. Jim's body was aroused in every way. Laleh's image continued to walk into the waves until she turned and faced Jim once more, as if to bid farewell. The water pulsated with her being. With her eyes now closed, she lay back into the water and floated out to sea.

Jim exploded from his nightmare and ran in his semi-sleep toward the waiting waves, peeling off what little clothing he had. He dived into the water before he was really awake. Not until then did Jim feel the pain of his badly bruised ribs and sternum. The shock was almost too much and he gasped. He swallowed saltwater and came up choking for air. He couldn't remember when he was more embarrassed or hurt worse. Paul'le had awakened to the furor of Jim's actions and watched him throw himself into the sea. The more he tried to explain his dream to Paul'le, the more Paul'le grinned. It was the only relief they had experienced in many hours.

Paul'le was still hurting from injuries, and both moved slowly. They ate some dried noodles and cereal out of the small individually wrapped packages they had found floating. The box of foil-wrapped granola bars with raisins finished off their feast. The bottled water washed it down. There were no complaints—they were too grateful. Paul'le was trying to explain some bizarre dream he had in order to show some sympathy to Jim. They resolved that they would get organized after eating. Both would scout the area to determine their location. After climbing a small rise, Paul'le selected the direction he believed they should go.

Jim said, "We need to get back to the other survivors, Paul'le. I don't want to waste any time exploring. Are you sure that is the right direction?"

"Yes, very sure. We go now!"

Both wondered what the cave dwellers had done in their absence. Then they heard it—a helicopter—in the distance, perhaps landing just on the other side of the mountain. The two stood under some broken palms in excited anticipation and searched the sky with hand-shaded eyes. They thought they could hear a plane over the western sea, and finally they heard it soar overhead—just missing them. They belatedly ran from the shadows of the tree line. The plane's occupants were concentrating on possible signs of debris in the ocean. . . . It was too late. . . . The sound went away about as fast as it had come.

All was silent except for the minimal surf and an occasional seagull's call. Their frustration was profound, but Jim and Paul'le struggled in spite of their injuries to reach the summit of the hill and determine their relative position. Having done that, they started trekking to the caves, carrying all they could. But they had arrived too late.

On the beach, south of the upper cave, was a signal— one of the coin buttons that Laleh had found before. It had been left on top of a small cairn of rocks directly below the upper cave. Laleh must have left it to get Jim's attention, a sign of hope. Jim clutched the coin. It wasn't until then that they became aware of the rock arrow on the ground pointing in the direction the three must have gone. They really hadn't given up hope, then, that Paul'le and Jim would return! The two concurred that the trio probably had headed toward the widest area of the beach, some distance away.

Then they saw the smeared SOS scraped in the beach's sand. Someone had done a fair job, however, of obliterating it. No doubt the Coast Guard did not want to activate any more searching there, and had tried to destroy it. But, as most ecologists know, some marks stay in primitive areas for a very long time despite efforts to restore damage.

The two men made preparations for their rescue. They laid a signal fire near the SOS in the sand, to be ignited in case another plane or ship came their way.

As they worked, Jim reflected on the education he'd gained in just a few hours. He had learned a lot about living off the land, thanks to Paul'le who had found some mangoes that the storm didn't destroy. They spotted a two-foot long iguana that did not want to be captured despite the great efforts made to trap him. The two men had found loblolly, poinsettia and oleander. None of those plants were edible, however.

Jim speculated that Paul'le spoke with a French Patois accent. Judging from what Paul'le said, Creole, Dutch, French, Spanish and English were also spoken on the different Virgin Islands.

Paul'le described a local infection unlike anything Jim had ever heard. He surmised it might be bilharziasis, a snail-borne parasite disease. The two men considered themselves fortunate not to have contracted any illnesses. Any fish that they caught, they cooked.

They kept themselves busy with daily living. It would have been quite enjoyable if it hadn't been for the memories of the immediate past. Jim decided he wouldn't tell Paul'le about Dora until after they were rescued.

The sun was low on the horizon when a cruise ship came close enough for one of its crew members to spot them. The ship sent a small boat to pick them up. A Coast Guard cutter in the area met the cruise ship and transferred them. Jim and Paul'le's story matched the record the authorities had from the previously rescued survivors. When Jim finally told Paul'le the story about Dora, he seemed prepared for the news.

When they returned to St. Thomas, Paul'le contacted the owners of the *Latina* and *Maverick* to notify them of the details. He was frank about the disaster. The owners had not been able to afford hurricane insurance, but they did have liability and fire insurance. Paul'le prayed that the insurance adjuster would accept his version of the explosion, afraid that he might be accused of negligence.

The newly bonded pair pledged that they would remain friends and mail each other a letter every year on the anniversary of their rescue. Just before Jim boarded his flight back to Utah, he received official confirmation from the authorities in St. Thomas that Laleh had returned safely to Iran.

He had called Ed and Claire with the cellular phone he had salvaged and recharged from Ben's bag. He then tried a telephone number for Laleh that her government had listed for her. There was no answer. He also tried the number that Laleh had given to Claire and Ed. No answer there either. Jim planned to return the cellular phone to Ben's family or the company. He tried to call Alpha Omega. Unfortunately, Jim could only access Ben's private line, which was set to default to phone mail only. He felt certain that Alpha Omega had been notified of the accident, because the recorded message left by a secretary mentioned that some staff member would get back to the caller as soon as possible. Jim decided he would try again from Salt Lake City.

As he waited at the airport for his return flight, Jim reasoned Laleh was going to need all the help she could get with Alpha Omega, especially with Ben gone. He resolved to talk to the management at AO. He still had Ben's gym bag, which contained his Daytimer notebook and a couple of computer disks, among other personal effects, and thought there might be something in there that might help before he returned it. Why he neglected to tell anyone about the bag, he couldn't say. Perhaps it would be simpler, he thought, if he put his own luggage tag on the bag, to expedite getting it through customs.

Jim pondered his options on the red-eye late night flight to Salt Lake City and didn't even close his eyes. This was quite a departure from his trip to the Caribbean—now he was filled with conflicting emotions of relief and grief and unanswered questions. It was a long flight home.

Chapter 9
St. Thomas—Day 12

In St. Thomas, the insurance adjuster contacted an insurance investigator for V. I. Marine Insurance. Mike Murphy had completed his review of the depositions given to the government investigators and the records from the crewmembers of the Latina concerning the radio transmissions Dora had made just before the "accident." As Mike, a deep-sea diving investigator, reviewed the data, his instincts told him that the wreck might offer some evidence to substantiate his concern. His experience in diving had enabled him to secure employment as an independent investigator for several insurance companies. Mike had received his diving training as a U.S. Navy Seal. He had previously helped solve several outstanding investigations while working for a private investigator who eventually retired, leaving Mike the business and the debt. Mike also "knew the territory." He had lived on St. Thomas for eight years.

The insurance company concurred with Mike that this was an unusual accident; it justified a dive to the wreck. He felt that it was imperative that they mount an immediate investigation with a search team at the site of the accident before nature ruined any more potential evidence. The logistics necessary to conduct a proper search would require coordination with the various governmental agencies that might also want to include their own investigators, if for any reason foul play was suspected. Because the possibility of locating further survivors was improbable, government bureaucracy did not help expedite the departure date. Mike and his three crewmembers were finally en route to Norman Island when they received news over their radio that two more survivors, Jim and Paul'le, had been found and were heading home. Mike got a preliminary government report that Jim and Paul'le's stories supported the basic information obtained from the other three survivors found earlier. Their depositions were also available to Mike.

Mike asked the Coast Guard, to please fax the report and depositions to his ship as soon as possible.they assured him that they would. "I've got to get to a wreck site ASAP," he told them.

After finishing his telephone call, he returned to brief his crew on their upcoming job. "We will photograph the scene on the bottom of the bay first, including any unrecovered remains, where they lay. Scott will use still cameras with telephoto and wide-angle lenses. Dave will have the underwater video camera for use when we get close to the wreckage. We can't predict if there is a section left that will be big enough to explore, or if we will just find scattered small debris. Because of the very clear waters, very concise still photos should be possible. We've all done this type of work many times before and we've got the latest equipment to record our work. But, I want to remind you again that it often is the smallest detail that makes the case. Remember—be careful down there. We don't know what caused the first explosion—there could be another."

Mike was a tough taskmaster and was demanding on himself as well as his crew. He would never ask them to do anything that he wouldn't do. They digitally recorded all of their video work, but Mike was still old-fashioned when it came to the still photographs. He maintained a small color lab for still photography on his eighty-foot powerboat, *Neptune's Snoop*. If the first photos were not good enough, they would reshoot them immediately.

Mike liked the business for insurance companies because the income was certain. He liked the insurance business best, however, because he was his own boss at sea and didn't have strangers to worry about on the site. But when it was slow, he would charter for treasure hunters and various scientific research.

It took a whole day to identify all of the area in question. They tried to avoid touching any of the wreckage or remains until that was completed. Then, piece by grisly piece, the remains were carefully recorded in place before removal.

The single government representative with their crew supervised the removal of the partial remains and their transfer to a morgue in St. Thomas. The explosion ripped and dismembered most of the bodies. Eventually, most of the remains of all of the victims were found. Dora's body was some distance from the others and had deteriorated considerably. There wasn't any incontestable evidence to absolutely confirm foul play on any of the victims, except the fact that for some reason Dora was more traumatized. Stab wounds in such powerful explosions are debatable. Then he recalled Paul'le's deposition, and that explained Dora's condition and location.

This was not unusual in explosions, especially when a hurricane was also involved. All of the remains were placed in body bags and loaded on a Coast Guard launch. The Coast Guard officials on the scene confirmed Mike's team findings with their own diver's report. Marker buoys were established and the area quarantined. The human remains that had been offloaded were taken to the morgue in St. Thomas to be prepared according to the next-of-kin's directions.

Later, on the rock bottom, Mike found a portion of the gas stove imbedded in a part of the galley deck. He noted that the remains of two gas valves had been left in the open position and the pilot light disabled. He knew then that this might not be an accident. Mike signaled the others to photo the valves with both video and the still cameras. As they were finishing that task, Mike swam over to direct them to see a larger piece of hull that had three holes in it. Mike thought they looked like possible bullet holes because they resembled implosion rather than explosion holes. The splinters protruded away from the holes on the side of the wood that had no barnacles. All other hull fragments had splinters sticking out on the exterior surfaces.

When they finished all of their recording that day they were exhausted. Calls were made to various government agencies. The next two days they removed anything that looked important to their investigation. When Mike scrutinized what he felt were possible bullet holes, he noticed that some of the holes in the hull teak wood showed evidence of scorching. Mike didn't need a lab to convince him that incendiary bullets had made these holes and had probably ignited the propane from the intentionally opened gas jets.

"This is a murder scene!" he said to himself.

Mike didn't share his views with anyone yet. He wanted to get the lab confirmation and everyone else's unbiased opinion before writing his own formal report and sharing the evidence. The final results would be included as part of the "team findings'" of the Coast Guard.

He was convinced if the killer or killers knew that their secret was out, they might run or destroy evidence elsewhere. It also wouldn't be the first time a policyholder had wanted to collect on his insurance and had committed murder to do it. On the other hand, it could also just have been a jealous lover or even some political plot against one of the international guests. All in all, he thought, it's best to lull the killers into a false sense of security.

None of the other crewmembers or the government investigator had come to any conclusions yet. They seemed to be assuming they were examining evidence of an accident. Mike listened to the others and did not speculate. He knew he needed to re-interview each of the survivors as soon as possible. He would concentrate on the Americans first and then decide if he needed to get the Iranian's deposition.

Eventually they all left the area and Mike returned to book a flight to Palo Alto via Salt Lake City. He gambled that the Salt Lake residents would be available. He hoped the element of surprise might give him an advantage in seeking the truth.

Chapter 10
Tehran, Iran—Days 12–15

Because of ticketing and customs delays, it had been forty-eight hours since Laleh's rescue. It was almost two in the morning when the plane arrived in the Iranian sky. The captain announced that the plane would land in thirty minutes. Laleh was anxious as she looked down from her window seat. Tehran, the capital, looked so beautiful with the twinkling lights of Iran's largest city. The entire population of nearly twelve million people in Tehran Bozorg seemed to have left a light on. It was an ancient city with a history that stretched back in recorded time 2,500 years, to Cyrus the Great and the Achaemenian Dynasty.

Laleh reminisced sadly about the many events that had happened during her own parent's and grandparent's lives under the Pahlavi Dynasty of 1925–79. Then, November 4, 1979, had changed all of their lives. That was the day the revolutionaries seized the United States Embassy and took sixty-six captives. Then the United States met failure in its attempt to rescue the hostages in April 1980.

The Ayatollah Ruhollah Khomeini took advantage of the people's displeasure with Mohammed Reza Shah's secret police and his failure to guarantee civil and political rights. It was through Khomeini's control of the Islamic Revolutionary Council, that life for any moderately religious people, like Laleh's family, became subject to constant scrutiny by the self-appointed devout Shiites. She hated the religious doctrines for all women that demanded that they wear conservative clothing that masked anything suggesting her gender. She honestly believed that all of the male zealots were misogynists who feared their own sexuality.

Laleh listened to an announcement from the plane's pilot,

preparing them for their approach to the airport. It wouldn't be long now. . .

She continued her reflections about the powerful Americans who had been blamed for the Shah's capitulation to their "immoral influence." Many formerly westernized women in Iran felt pride in returning to the old symbols of a more moral life, and it had become vogue to follow the Shi'ite customs by covering themselves. She was one among them. It didn't make any difference that she had been better educated than most of the women and had experienced things her female peers could not even perceive.

She would be glad to be home amid familiar surroundings, but she was aware of the inherent fear of constant surveillance that she'd not sensed while she was abroad. On the one hand, she would be glad to see her family again, but she dreaded the news that she would eventually need to reveal to them the uncertain reality of Sonbol's survival. She knew that was her main fear. The death of millions of people due to the possible pending influenza pandemic was the other dreaded fear. No wonder she was depressed.

The atmosphere was so clear that Laleh could see Mt. Damavand, a snow-capped 18,550-foot active volcano glistening in the light of the moon, fifty miles northeast of the city. She wondered if some of the villagers living near the base still believe that Dahhak, the legendary chained evil giant was straining to be free when they saw signs of smoke or heard rumbling. She also thought she could see the Caspian Sea seventy miles due north. How could a scene so beautiful allow her to have so many ugly feelings about coming home? How was she going to explain what had happened in the Virgin Islands?

A storm front was approaching, carrying wind and dust as they made their final descent into Tehran's Mehrabad airport. Clouds were gathering and the moonlight was suddenly masked. As the plane taxied to their gate, the security guards became evident. They were obviously ready to insure that everyone first went to the customs area for inspection of luggage. Laleh pulled her scarf forward to show proper covering of her hair. She didn't want to be arrested for not following the Islamic dress code.

Laleh could smell dust in the air mixed with the pollution of airplane fuel exhaust. The abundance of cigarette smoke in the customs area reminded her that old habits die slowly. She stood respectfully in line behind the male passengers of the flight, and eventually submitted her passport to the officer in charge. He looked at her passport and then at her when he said, "Dr. Bazargan, lotfan befarmaid berid daftar-e-etelaat." *Dr. Bazargan, please go to the security and information office.*

Laleh was shocked. Her face turned pale. Two revolutionary guards—pasdar—escorted her to the office.

"Hello, Dr. Bazargan," said Colonel Eshraghi, head of the airport security guard.

"Hello. May I ask why I am here?" Laleh responded.

"Of course! How was your trip in the United States? Did you meet with important Americans? Where is your sister?" Colonel Eshraghi sneered. As Laleh started to answer his questions he interrupted and said, "We need to ask you some questions later. You can go now. Your family is waiting for you. But, you need to report to the Islamic Public Prosecutor's office within forty-eight hours for interrogation. If we do not hear from you then, we will send the revolutionary guards to arrest you. Your luggage has passed inspection by the guards. You may go now."

Laleh left the office speechless. Confused and frightened, she stumbled out of the area. She saw her family outside waving at her—she haltingly waved back. She walked faster and quickly went outside. Her mother and her youngest sister, Narges, reached her at the same time, and both hugged and kissed her. Amir, her brother, stood waiting to give his greeting.

Simultaneously the two women asked Laleh, "Sonbol koush?" *Where is Sonbol?*

"Pasdar-ha negahesh dashtan?" *Have the Revolutionary*

Guards arrested her? Amir nervously asked, the question dripping with fear.

"Berim, Sonbol hanuz Amricast." *Let's go. Sonbol is still in America.*

Amir seemed panicky as he looked at Laleh and asked, "What do you mean Sonbol is still in America? How could that be possible? Tell us what happened!" Laleh's brother was a tall, dangerously handsome man. At the age of twenty-six, he had been interrogated by the Islamic Public Prosecutor's Office on several occasions. Once he was charged for wearing sunglasses and a short-sleeved shirt, and once for looking at and lusting after a woman. All of the siblings had suffered from frustrations imposed on most young Iranians living in Tehran.

Mrs. Bazargan was frantic when she saw Laleh's pale face and diverted eyes. "Swear to your father's soul that nothing has happened to Sonbol. Is she all right?"

"I do not know. The only thing I know is that she is still there. Please, let's go home. I am so tired and frightened. I will explain all about it when we get home," Laleh replied with tears in her eyes.

Narges simply said, "Laleh!" in a demanding tone.

Even though Narges had been rebellious to her mother at times and also defiant to her culture, she was shocked that Laleh refused to respond to her mother immediately. Narges, in her late twenties, was a beautiful woman with long black hair discreetly hidden under a rebelliously risky colorful scarf that could not hide her big brown eyes. A suggestion of perfume also betrayed her facade. Narges, which means narcissus, looked at Laleh with fear in her eyes. Despite their insistence, Laleh refused to discuss the situation any further. The family assumed that she feared something or someone in the air terminal. They reluctantly made uneasy and contrived small talk as they drove home with Amir at the wheel of their Peykon, an Iranian-made vehicle that looks like a four-door Subaru.

During the ride from the airport, Amir urged the passengers to roll each of the windows down a little as Narges insisted on smoking. Laleh was in the front seat and seemed nervous as she talked rapidly and incessantly about a plethora of trivial things she had seen on her trip. She started with a description of the flowers and the Hotel 1829 in Charlotte Amalie. She conducted a travelogue as she glanced out of the car window and viewed the sights. As they drove through a city that seemed to never sleep, the sights of numerous parks were refreshing. There were no derelicts, such as one might see anywhere in the western world.

They approached an intersection where cars, trucks, and vans for all the seventeen daily newspapers published in Iran were arriving at the same time. Farmers' produce trucks were also lining up to deliver their wares. Of the 42,000 miles of paved roads in Iran, the most are in Tehran or from Tabriz in the northwest with its trade center and Azerbaijanian agricultural products.

Amir cursed at one of the truck drivers, "Stupid jackass!"

Trucks with meat, produce and other goods coming and going to other major cities such as Abadan, Mashhad, Shiraz and Esfahan also traveled at night through Tehran. Even though the wide tree-lined streets appeared adequate, the city pulsated with traffic noise.

Laleh asked, "How do the apartment dwellers adjacent to these conduits of clamor ever sleep?"

Amir commented, "I have a friend who was anxious to escape this environment and moved to Abadan to work in an oil refinery on the Persian Gulf. I wonder if he escaped much air pollution by moving there?"

Laleh commented on every facet in a continuing attempt to maintain control of the dialogue. "Oh look, there is the Golestan, the Rose Garden Palace." The Golestan had been the Qajars' royal residence. The main building was architecturally unpretentious, and functioned as a museum. Everywhere Laleh looked modern buildings were going up in a checkered pattern beside nineteenth-century houses.

Eventually they were in the avenues and smaller streets where deep, wide gutters channeled water and looked like small rivers in the spring.

Laleh noticed the baroque and pretentious appearance of the banks built twenty or thirty years ago, and how they contrasted with the proliferation of new houses built with gray utilitarian architecture.

Amir was the only person in the car who was not dozing—even Laleh was silent when they finally arrived home at five in the morning. It was still dark and now no one felt like sleeping. Narges made tea while the rest sat looking at each other in silence—waiting for Laleh to speak.

Amir could stand it no longer. "Laleh jon, dear Laleh, we will not be able to sleep if you don't talk. So many strange things have happened since you and Sonbol left for the United States. Remember I faxed you that you should not come back until I told you to come."

"Yes," replied Laleh.

"Well, on that day they arrested me for no reason. They kept me for two days. At first I didn't know why. Later, they questioned me about you and Sonbol. They wanted to know why you two went to the United States and if I knew where you went after the conference," Amir exclaimed.

Defensively Laleh replied, "The authorities all knew the purpose of the conference. They, themselves, gave us permission to leave the country! I don't understand any of this!"

"Yes, but it seems that another group, an orthodox traditional group was the problem. The Imam's constituents didn't know about the conference," Narges explained.

"I am so confused. I have to find out what is going on! At the airport, a Colonel Eshraghi told me that I have to report to the Islamic Public Prosecutor's Office within forty-eight hours," Laleh said with anguish.

The Mother sternly demanded, "Now, tell us what happened to Sonbol. Just where, exactly, is she?"

Laleh took a sip of her tea, a deep breath, and said, "I must start from the beginning."

She then proceeded to chronicle the past events, day by day. She told them about their trip to the Caribbean and the conference. Eventually she described in detail all that she could recall about the ship exploding and the drama that unfolded like a bad dream. She was shaken by the catharsis—but relieved. Laleh told them that her friend Dr. Jim Schriver, whom she trusted highly, was also missing even though he had not been on the ship when it exploded. Questions continued being asked by the family, until they all were exhausted.

Laleh awakened after the Azan's call to noon prayer, Namaz-e-zhor, that echoed from the neighbors' TVs and radios. Her mother was already facing the Qiblah or the direction of the Ka'bah' at Mecca, in Saudi Arabia. Mrs. Bazargan always prayed five times a day and had once in her life been on a hajj to Mecca. Even though she was devout Muslim, she did not try to force her grown children to follow her example. Laleh dressed and prepared to go to the Islamic Public Prosecutor's Office. Before she left, she decided to call Imam Khomeini Hospital to let her colleagues know that she was back from the United States. Her friend Dr. Tabatabai was in the surgical suite, so she left a message with the scrub nurse.

The austere concrete building of the Islamic Public Prosecutor's Office looked appropriately ominous. The reception clerk, Mr. Talaghani, told her, "You need to go to the Islamic Revolutionary Court of Justice and ask to see Hojat-ul-Islam Panjali. He is in charge of political cases."

Laleh was now not as frightened as she was angry and frustrated. She wondered what political cases they could be thinking about? She had not been involved in anything political. She tried to keep herself calm as she left to drive to the Islamic Revolutionary Court of Justice. It was an equally drab-looking, perfunctory building.

Laleh was stopped at the court's front door. The female Zainab (a revolutionary guard), who looked like an amazon, was doing her job. With a polite but perverted smile she informed Laleh that she would have to submit to a search. Laleh seethed at such an invasion of her dignity. Following her search, Laleh was escorted to Hojat-ul-Islam Panjali's office by the same woman guard, or Zainab.

"Salam-ul aleikum agha, I am Dr. Laleh Bazargan. At Mehrabad airport, Colonel Eshraghi told me to report to the Islamic Public Prosecutor's Office. From there they directed me to you," Laleh announced.

"Oh yes, Dr. Bazargan," said Panjali, peering over a folder. "I have been waiting for you. Please have a seat. There are some important questions about your trip to the United States that need to be discussed. Unfortunately, since I am busy with several cases of monafegh (hypocrites) my schedule is very crowded. As you know, the younger generation these days is not properly aware of true Islam. They believe imperialist propaganda and do strange things. They watch CNN or read anti-Islamic propaganda publications. They all need to learn their lessons by being punished. . . . At any rate, where was I? I do not have time now to question you. So, you will stay in Evin prison for a while until your turn. Va-salam, the sister Zainab, will escort you to Evin," Hojat-ul-Islam Panjali concluded.

"But haj-agha!" Laleh pleaded.

"No, Dr. Bazargan, I don't have time. There are many cases I must take care of first," replied Hojat-ul-Islam Panjali.

"Then please let me call home and inform my mother. I think it is my right to have at least one phone call," Laleh persisted.

"Where were you these last years after our blessed Islamic Revolution? Didn't you hear about the Islamic Judicial System? Is this something that you learned in America, the right to make one phone call? I suppose the next thing you will request is, 'the right to have an attorney'! Are you a dreamer, lady? You should thank God for even having an opportunity to practice as a doctor. Have you forgotten

113

about your mission as a virtuous and good woman? You should be ashamed of yourself! You are not yet either a wife or a mother. Your family will know soon enough where you are. Don't worry, your brother is an experienced visitor here and knows about these matters." Hojat-ul-Islam Panjali replied with barely constrained rage, his dank expression exaggerated by his bushy eyebrows, sunken eyes peering over his beak-like nose and scraggly beard.

Laleh was staggered by his anger. She had heard about political prisoners, but she never believed it was true. She always tried to blame those prisoners for not being patient with the Islamic Revolution. She felt they had tried to exaggerate the situation. What had she done that caused her to deserve such treatment? What was she going to do now?"

Laleh, with terror in her heart, followed the sister Zainab to Evin Prison. As she shuffled behind her captor she remembered Jim telling her that Amnesty International didn't seem to share her perspective of human rights for women in Iran. She also recalled Sonbol responding that when Americans saw the faults of other countries, it is predictable that they wouldn't see clearly in a mirror.

Laleh felt that all of these events were too abstract and strange to comprehend and internalize. All her life she had worked hard to achieve her goal of becoming a physician. She'd tried to follow the good teachings of the Q'uran. She then recalled her father saying, "To be successful in life, never touch politics. Politics are ugly. It is like drugs. When you touch it, you become addicted to it and by the time you realize it—you have risked your life." She'd never been a political person. She assumed it was her research and lecture, Causal Relationship of Parkinson's Disease and influenza type A Induced Meningitis, delivered in the United States Virgin Islands, that had launched her into this mess.

The aroma in the prison reminded Laleh of a sweaty nursing unit mixed with a faint suggestion of urine and feces. It did not smell like a prison used just for political prisoners. Some of the women inside looked like they had led a hard life for a long time. She could not tell if they had been abused recently or if the discolorations were artifacts. Despite her experience with sick and hostile patients in the past, she didn't feel comfortable being with these women, much less relating to the other prisoners. She knew she was neither a political activist nor a criminal. She felt she had nothing in common with the other prisoners.

The sister Zainab unlocked a room labeled "Examination Room." Something that looked like a crude concrete shower stall stood in the corner and a transparent plastic sheet with a black mildewed fringe on the bottom served as a curtain. An ancient surgical table with stirrups was illuminated in the center of the room. The only other furniture in the room was one folding chair.

"Strip and place your clothes on the chair where I can examine them," demanded the sister Zainab. She stood with a sheet over one of her arms and she pointed to the chair with the other. She was a very large woman with features that suggested she could have had excessive androgen levels in her 200-pound frame. Her bulky breasts were her only feminine features. Laleh trembled as she reluctantly removed her outer clothing and then stood shivering in her underwear. She was scared and angry.

"Those also," said Lady Zainab, nodding to her undergarments and then handing her the sheet.

Laleh felt violated as the creature, the sister Zainab, watched her with the same perverted smile she had seen before. Even though the sister Zainab had not touched her yet, she felt her eyes. She took the sheet and did her best to hold it close to her body.

The sister Zainab then removed from her pocket a stainless-steel speculum used by physicians to open or distend a body orifice to permit visual inspection. She squeezed the handles menacingly. At the same time she said, "Get in the stirrups!"

"I AM A VIRGIN! I WILL NOT DO THIS!" Laleh shouted in absolute terror. Memories of a little girl who had been mutilated by rural religious zealots shook her psyche. The little girl had been clitori-cally circumcised and left in her care to be cured of her post-operative infection. Laleh's eyes filled with tears. She knew that she would die defending herself.

The Zainab invaded Laleh's personal aura, and said, smiling, "Very well—you may get dressed."

Laleh dressed and was led, sobbing, to her cell.

Finally, hours later, Laleh was called for her interrogation. She was awash with mixed feelings. She felt dirty and unkempt as she had groomed herself with only a broken comb that she had found. She was relieved, however, that it was finally her turn to have an audience with Hojat-ul-Islam Panjali. She was ushered into his presence. He wore an oversized long black cloak that could not hide the fact that he was short and fat. A white turban on his head only added contrasting emphasis.

He started with, "Besmehi-Taala *In the name of God.* Dr. Bazar-gan, Mr. Kachuee is here as our interrogator. Also, Haj-agha Hossini and myself will listen to your answers. After Mr. Kachuee is done with his interrogation, we will both decide about your sentencing."

"Why? What are you sentencing me for? What did I do?" Laleh yelled, losing her composure completely. She had been secluded from her family and friends. She had seen no radio or TV nor had she read a newspaper. She was beside herself with indignation.

Hojat-ul-Islam Panjali was aware that their mental torture had been effective. In a loud voice he instructed Laleh, "BRING DOWN YOUR VOICE, WOMAN." Then after an appropriate pause he said in a very controlled voice, "Don't you see I respect you as a doctor? It seems your mother didn't teach you about the principles of Islam. Didn't she tell you that it is harum—*religiously prohibited*—for a woman to yell? Don't you know that the men in this room are not halal—*legitimate*—to you? We are not your mahram, with whom marriage is prohibited, brothers, uncles, etc. Keep your voice down and do as we say or otherwise you will be charged and executed as zena-ba maharem—*incestuous!*"

Laleh was shocked and silent, but she boiled as she thought, "What is he talking about?" She realized that she was in a more dangerous situation than she was before her outburst. Her sense of self-preservation demanded a quick response.

"I am sorry. My reaction was totally out of control. I apologize for my behavior." Her teeth ground at what she had forced herself to say.

"Excellent. But, don't dare repeat it again!" Hojat-ul-Islam Panjali replied. "Mr. Kachuee, please start."

Mr. Kachuee, a tall, handsome man in his early forties, came forward.

He tried to avoid direct eye contact with Laleh and politely said, "With your permission, Hojat-ul-Islam Panjali and haj-agha Hosseini." He continued, "Dr. Bazargan, we are aware of your trip to the United States. We know that there you attended a scientific conference."

Suddenly Mr. Kachuee was interrupted. Hojat-ul-Islam Panjali said, "As you know, our Islamic government is very supportive to all kinds of scientific research. But we only approve of the ones which are Islamic and not imperialistic."

Mr. Kachuee submissively accepted the interruption. He continued, "First Dr. Bazargan, I want you to tell us all about your trip and the conference."

Finally Laleh was allowed to speak. "The conference was held at St. Thomas of the Virgin Islands. There I met many international scientists including Dr. Woodsman and Dr. Schriver of the continental United States. There were also experts from China and Greece and many other countries. I presented my paper entitled, 'Causal Relationship of Parkinson's Disease and Influenza Type A–Induced Meningitis.' Almost everyone enjoyed it and congratulated our country."

"What happened next?" Mr. Kachuee inquired.

"Several of my peers and I went to the British Virgin Islands," replied Laleh.

117

"Why?" Mr. Kachuee asked.

"To discuss in depth some of the questions about my research," answered Laleh.

"Why didn't you stay in St. Thomas and discuss the research there?" Mr. Kachuee probed. "Why did you choose the British Virgin Islands?"

"I cannot recall exactly; it just seemed to evolve out of a group discussion," replied Laleh.

"Who paid for this trip? Who contracted with the sailing ship?" Mr. Kachuee demanded.

"I think the contract must have been made by Dr. Ben Carlson, the director of Alpha Omega Pharmaceutical Company," Laleh responded.

"Do you know why or how your ship mysteriously exploded?" Mr. Kachuee asked.

The question jolted Laleh, her eyes widened. "No. But how did you know about that?"

"Woman, we know everything! God is on our side!" Hojat-ul-Islam Panjali answered.

Laleh excitedly inquired, "Is my sister alive? Do you know who was responsible or how it happened?" Her head was spinning.

Mr. Kachuee glared at her, ignoring her questions. "And where were you? Why was your sister alone on the ship?" Mr. Kachuee challenged.

Laleh paused for a few seconds. She needed to answer this question carefully. She did not want to be whipped, lashed or worse for swimming with strange men who were not halal—*legitimate*—to her. "I went with Dr. Woodsman and his wife and a couple of others to visit Norman Island which is also known as Treasure Island."

The interrogation took many hours as they questioned Laleh about everything involving the conference and sailing ship. They wanted to know if she had imbibed alcohol or violated any other religious restrictions. Laleh was very evasive and tried not to lie about anything. Abruptly they concluded and informed her that she was "not providing enough information." They instructed sister Zainab to return her to her cell. Laleh was sullen as the amazon, Zainab, pushed her in the middle of her back to direct her out of the court.

Haj-agha Hosseini turned a thoughtful gaze to Hojat-ul-Islam Panjali. "I think we should let her go, but we need to find out where she has hidden this deadly virus. In the interest of national security this could be a very great psychological weapon. The damage this could inflict would be very useful for ghesas—an-eye-for-an-eye retaliation. People fear the unknown most. We wouldn't need to beg and bargain for atomic weapons anymore. This would be our atomic bomb. Our 'weapon of restraint.' We would use it only when forced to do so."

"I agree! We could name it, DIV—demon. No one would know for sure if it came from the United States originally. America would not admit it, even if it did. But, they just might know how deadly it is and respect the threat it offers. It would be perfect," replied Hojat-ul-Islam Panjali.

Laleh was escorted to the Islamic Public Prosecutor's Office by the same female guard, Zainab. The Islamic Revolutionary Court of Justice then released Laleh a short time later. Her Paykon was still in the parking lot where she had left it. Because of the moist weather, the windows were barely transparent. Her clothing was so dirty that she didn't hesitate to wipe an area on the windshield with the sleeve of her coat. Laleh sat in the driver's seat feeling exhausted and depressed. She finally leaned back for a few seconds and took a deep breath. When the car started reluctantly, it almost caused her to panic. She did not want to go back in for any reason.

She drove cautiously out of the parking lot and then headed toward Argentine Square and her home. As she drove, her mind wandered with strange thoughts. She remembered Sonbol's sudden disappearance and wondered if she, too, would ever return home. Then she thought of Jim and realized how much she had loved him and how much she needed him, especially now. It seemed that her life had changed with the new experiences in the United States and the experiences that she had just been through in her own country. What had happened to her beloved Iran? She was confused and afraid because of the past events.

As she turned on to Vali-e-Asr Street, a taxi driver pulled even with her left side. He rolled his window down and yelled at her, "HEY, woman, go home! Cook your husband a lunch! What kind of driving is this? You woman driver!" The traffic stopped at the light, and the taxi driver continued his harangue, "Our government claims this is an Islamic country. So how come they don't arrest your husband for letting you use the car and drive on the streets, like they do in Saudi Arabia? That's where the real Islam is governing." Laleh, with tears in her eyes, remembered Jim telling her, "Amnesty International does not agree with your country's stand on women's rights." She thought sarcastically, "No wonder this Islamic government is so popular with men."

The taxi driver cut in front of her and waved an obscene gesture.

Laleh slowed down to insure that she did not overtake the taxi again. She remembered late 1978 when demonstrators carried Imam Khomeini's pictures. They also carried placards with Islamic slogans such as, "Independence, freedom, Islamic government" and "God, Quran, Khomeini."

She then mumbled to herself, "As Hojat-ul-Islam Panjali said, it seems our mothers have not taught us Islam correctly, otherwise we would not ask for it. As must keh bar must—that is what we deserve." At that time, she had thought she had obtained a better understanding of the mind set and popularity of the Islamic Republic. It was a historic enigma of her culture.

She drove the rest of the way without incident to Argentine Square and home. She parked the car off the street in their private driveway and took her keys out of the ignition. Before she could locate her house key, Mrs. Bazargan had opened the door and rushed to greet Laleh. Quietly the two engulfed one another, tears glistening on their cheeks. Slowly they turned to face the entrance and walked into the house.

"Where were you? Did they arrest you?" Her mother inquired.

"Yes," Laleh replied.

"Let's go inside and we will talk," said Mrs. Bazargan.

"Yes, but first I need to take a shower and get rid of these clothes," responded Laleh. "I feel just filthy."

While Laleh was in the shower, her mother prepared Chelo Kabob, rice and kabob, with must-o-khiar, yogurt and cucumber. They would drink *dough,* a yogurt drink. Meanwhile Amir and Narges arrived home and Mrs. Bazargan informed them that Laleh was safe and had just returned home. When Laleh entered the dining room, she saw the faces of the whole family around the table, watching her expectantly.

"Thanks be to God. Laleh is free. It is fitting that we celebrate your freedom on Eid Fetr—the last day of Ramadan," Mrs. Bazargan proclaimed.

Chapter 11
Hayden Lake and Palo Alto—Day 14

It was a sunny day in Hayden Lake, Idaho, when Nick Cabal heard the CNN report that two additional survivors, Jim and Paul'le, had been found on Norman Island. The Colonel went ballistic. The channels of communication to his associates in the Virgin Islands were risky to contact on an impromptu basis, but Nick took the chance. His associates confirmed the news.

Upon hearing that Laleh had returned home, the Colonel shouted over the phone "Bad news! The Iranian is already in Iran! What a mess! There are five survivors! Five!" It was in Nick's nature to believe that the survivors knew more than they were revealing to the press. Sure, it sounded as though they all believed the ship blew up by accident coincidental to the hurricane, but who knew for sure? "The five survivors are now probably all back safely in their homes. Such gutless, jelly-brained incompetents! Those stupid idiots in the Caribbean have the balls to call themselves professionals! Unbelievable! Now I don't know who I can trust to accomplish such delicate missions." The aide at Nick's elbow simply shook his head in disgusted sympathy.

Nick quickly formulated a damage-control plan and assembled new "patriot" assassins for the delicate missions he envisioned. "I want a daily report. Put surveillance on all of the Americans and determine if there is some way we can discredit the Iranian. Check the deck hand, Paul'le, to determine if he's a risk. I want an up-to-date dossier on all of them ASAP."

Colonel Nick Cabal felt compelled to call J. R. Granite at Alpha Omega with an "Alpha Storm" update. Rock answered the phone and could not believe his ears, which were turning bright red with increased circulation. His heart started to pound. His whole right side went numb as he continued to listen. He couldn't talk. He became nauseated and dizzy. He collapsed and dropped the phone. He vomited and started choking on the vomit as he stared helplessly at the ceiling. . . .

Nick Cabal could only hang the receiver back onto the phone. He had a downed comrade. Quickly he looked up the Alpha Omega's regular telephone number and called Rock's secretary, Edith. "Hello, this is Bill Jones and I have reason to believe that Mr. Granite may have been stricken by some health problem while he was talking to me just now. He suddenly sounded sick and I couldn't get him to respond on his other open line. You'd better check on him!" Nick admonished.

"Please hang on—I'll put you on hold and get right back to you." Edith called for help in the immediate offices to assist her as she rushed to Rock's side. Pathetic sounds emanated from the stricken CEO. Shocked, she paged the emergency service available in the plant, and the EMTs came almost immediately. Rock was taken by ambulance to the nearest hospital for treatment of a possible stroke. He was in critical condition, because no one knew exactly how long he had been without oxygen before he was resuscitated. Events seemed to be compounding by the minute.

Edith found no Bill Jones or anyone on the line when she returned. She hung up.

Nick said out loud to his staff, " We need to get control of the situation promptly before it gets totally out of our control." He couldn't know how prophetic that statement was going to be.

In Washington, DC, the foreign ambassadors of the victims' various countries were demanding more information about the "accident" from the U.S. State Department. Rumors had begun about the suspicious nature of the impromptu windjammer sailing trip. A confidential foreign drug-dealing informant indicated that she had heard of a clandestine seaplane being prepared in the accident's area at the time of the accident. She was believed to have some connection with the CIA. One group in the Watts area of California implied that the CIA had used certain shadow organizations in the British Virgin Islands to accomplish their money laundering during the Iran-Contra affair. They also said that a high-ranking government official often was on board such missions in the past.

The other doctors and nurses who had attended the lecture during the seminar on the *Royal Caribbean* but had not been invited to sail on the *Maverick,* were suddenly experts on what might have happened. Nothing could be confirmed by any agency. The director of the CIA denied to everyone, including the president, that any clandestine activity had been authorized. He insisted that they had never even heard of such a mysterious virus from the National Institutes of Health or the World Health Organization, and the CIA certainly had nothing to do with the fateful accident.

One sensationalist newspaper in San Francisco interviewed a "source" that said, "We have information that several important people in the world, such as Attorney General Janet Reno, evangelist Billy Graham and the president of China, Deng Xioping, all may have contracted their Parkinson's disease from the mysterious biological virus weapon. It is an Islamic religious conspiracy." On the same front page they had an interview from a space alien. Most considered the stories bogus.

Nick Cabal addressed his damage-control committee. "We had only two reliable patriots operating at Alpha Omega and one of them, Rock Granite, is now out of commission! Bill Balencamp is now our only source for our virus supply. He has informed me that under the circumstances, he can't produce or ship any more virus until the current situation is settled." Nick paused, hoping that he might hear some enlightened suggestions. Silence. "Well, we must take some calculated risks and terminate the five threats to our national security. I want each of you to develop a plan to eliminate these vermin before it's too late. We can't risk action that has the appearance of anything except unfortunate accidents. Let's meet again in three hours with a battle plan. Understood?" Everyone answered in unison, "Yes, sir!" Nick handed out individual assignments.

The colonel motioned to one of the departing staff members to remain. "Lavar, I want to talk to you briefly."

"Yes, sir," Lavar responded crisply.

Nick referred briefly to a note he had scribbled earlier. "Lavar, you grew up in Salt Lake City and I think you may have met one of the operatives who facilitated the arms merchant's money-laundering Iran-Contra operation in Iran. Remember, Admiral Poindexter and William Casey, the CIA director at that time, had dealings with Adnan Khashoggi. I can't remember the other name in the agency who was Adnan Khashoggi's American facilitator source who may still live in Salt Lake. What was his name?"

"Do you mean Manuel Florentine? He grew up in Iran," Lavar clarified.

"Is that the contact known as '*Manny*'?"

"I believe that's the guy."

"Why don't you ask him how and who we might reach in Iran to do what needs to be done. Accidents happen to the famous all over the world. We need something creative. Remember when William Colby was reported missing on one Sunday in April 1996 and then buried in May of that year after a presumed accidental drowning? Remember Princess Di's car accident? Construct something creative but untraceable. You are our point man, and we need your best effort on this Iranian problem."

"You can count on me, sir. I'll find a way."

"Good man, Lavar, I knew I could count on you." Nick saluted his "point man" before he left.

Chapter 12
Salt Lake City and Alta, Utah—Days 12–13

Jim had a brief emotional telephone conversation with Ed and Claire while he was in St. Thomas waiting to board his plane. The next morning, Jim, Ed and Claire hugged and chatted at the air terminal in Salt Lake City. They told Jim about the news media's feeding frenzy and how lucky they were that they had not been spotted.

They dropped him off at his apartment because he said he needed to be alone for a while, but he had flashbacks to Jaynee's life in their apartment and was greeted by the dark shadows of thoughts temporarily forgotten. Pictures were everywhere, on the mantle, on the walls, on the refrigerator and in his mind. The answering machine was maxed with messages. Jim knew he could not stay there that night. The pain of his losses was unbearable.

Jim wondered out loud, "Why does God allow everything bad to happen to good people? What have I done, what has anyone I've known done to deserve this? If there is really a God, a he or she or it, you owe me an explanation!" There was no reply.

Jim packed every bag and box he could find with essentials and loaded them into his red Toyota 4-Runner. He didn't really know where he was going—just away from that crypt full of bad memories. He gathered his mail to be dealt with later. He left all of his pictures of Jaynee . . . again. . . .

Jim drove by instinct, south from the apartment, toward Wasatch Boulevard. He had always escaped his worries by heading to the hills. The boulevard, set against the eastern mountains, periodically allowed five arteries to exit from it and rise to the various ski resorts and scenic vistas in the Wasatch Mountains. He thought to himself, "I've got to sort stuff out." After the breeze had blown away the smog, the valley below looked clean and fresh in its pristine new snow cover. He squinted with the bright sun, even though he had his sunglasses on his nose. Jim knew that the weather in the mountains would be different because of a storm front blowing in from Canada. He knew well that the mountains could make their own weather.

He decided to stop for gas and call ahead to get a room reservation at The Alta Lodge, up Little Cottonwood Canyon. He knew his chances at the peak of the ski season were slim, but he called anyway. He was surprised when a recent cancellation allowed him to book a room.

His steel-studded snow tires made a scratching hum as he drifted south on the semi-dry pavement. Soon the noise was lost on the snowpacked road leading to some of the best skiing in the world. He reached out to play the tape in the deck, but stopped when he realized it had been one of Jaynee's favorites. Even though Jim had his skis on his roof rack, he was only looking for a sanctuary far away from death, fear, and memories.

Jim thought to himself, "I need to escape to the tranquility of quiet snow and the warmth of a fireplace." Snow dervishes whirled with increasing vigor as the four-wheel drive vehicle churned through six inches of new snow on the Little Cottonwood Canyon road, still untouched by the fleet of snow plows. Small black flags were waving frantically atop ten-foot poles that punctured the banks of snow on the edges of the road to guide the plows on their course. These flags were essential guides for Jim as he drove up into the Wasatch National Forest.

The higher he went up the canyon, the higher the snow banks on the mountain side became, up to six feet deep in places. But the canyon side remained void of any snow or concrete security barrier. Jim could not see the bottom of the canyon, but he knew it was at least five hundred feet down to the icy creek. His knuckles turned white from his tight grip as he "crabbed" the steering wheel to maintain a proper traction with the front wheels. He used the slight oscillating maneuver he had learned on the ranch as a kid, driving the old Jeep. He had prided himself on his four-wheeling talent, but tension was inherent with the precarious road and conditions. If he dared stop, he would be stalled until the snowplow came.

Finally, the covered walkway from the parking lot down the wooden stairs to Alta Lodge became visible ahead. It took Jim a few seconds to relax his hands and release the steering wheel. Not until then did Jim recall that he had not seen a single vehicle coming up the canyon or going down, a very rare event.

When he reached the small check-in desk of the lodge, the clerk asked, "How did you miss the avalanche?"

"Avalanche? It must have occurred just behind me. I wondered why I hadn't seen any canyon patrol vehicles. I guess I am very lucky."

Jim carried everything into his room. Judging from the amount he had packed, it looked like he was planning to live there permanently. After getting comfortable in front of his fire, he watched the snow fall and billow outside. He listened to his John Denver CD. The Lazy Boy chair served him well, and soon deep, deep dreamless sleep overcame him while the flames from the fireplace warmed his relaxing muscles.

Not until he heard the muffled booms of cannon shooting down the snow cornices high above the ski slopes to release planned avalanches, did he awaken. The beeping of large "groomers" backing up, smoothing the new snow drifts and bumps, announced to Jim where he was. It was morning and it was still snowing and blowing. The wind chill factor made it −10 degrees Fahrenheit outside. Jim elected to stay in his room and enjoy a muffin and coffee while he meditated.

He looked at the pile of luggage and discovered he had brought Ben's bag as well as all of the others with him. One of the canvas bags included the urn that contained Jaynee's ashes. "I don't remember packing that. I must have done it subconsciously." Jaynee and Jim had talked about his uncle's request to spread his ashes in the hills if the cancer got him.

He remembered Jaynee and he had signed up to be organ donors. They had also vowed to have their ashes spread in the mountains. The two of them had spent so many good times together here.

Jim dug out his backcountry gear and prepared his metal-edged touring skis by fastening the sticky "skins" on the bottoms to allow him to climb. He knew that if he asked for permission to deposit Jaynee's ashes in the mountains, he would be told "no," by the authorities. He looked again out the window. In the backcountry no one would ever know, and it will do no harm. "If I am caught, I can ask for mercy."

He knew the area like the back of his hand, but in blowing snow it would be easy to get lost. He did wear his transceiver radio-locating device that everyone called a "Pieps." The Pieps transmitted an almost inaudible sound to help locate victims of avalanches. He elected to climb up through the spruce trees to avoid as much risk as possible from an avalanche.

It was slow going to reach the perfect spot they had found before. Jim was warm from the exercise and felt introspective. There was certainly no danger of seeing any other human being in this weather. Jim tried to imagine what his Uncle Andy would have said, as he was casting Jaynee's ashes.

"Dear God, you know I haven't been true to all of my promises I made to you, but I hope you can forgive me. Jaynee was my only love and I commend her ashes to your mountain and her spirit to you. Help me to feel your presence in my life and guide me from now on. I don't have Jaynee to keep me on the straight and narrow anymore. I'll leave her in your care now—I hope you can let her know somehow that I will always love her. Also, I feel that you and she know I've met another woman. Somehow, I hope you can make me feel that it is okay."

When Jim finished casting the ashes in the wind, he struggled to find his way back down to the lodge. It took him almost as long to get down as it did to go up—but he made it. The tears that he had shed remained frozen on his face.

But something happened to him that he hadn't expected. A serene and tranquil feeling had replaced the chaos of emotions that had previously bothered him. "I know what I must do from this point forward," he thought.

He recalled the frustration in Ed and Claire's voices as they discussed the future of the vaccine because of Ben's death and Laleh's situation. Jim decided to fly out to Palo Alto to deliver Ben's bag and lobby the powers that are there to consider making a vaccine. It was the last wish of Ben before he was killed, and maybe that would make them consider the idea. He felt he must also find a way to communicate with Laleh.

At noon he decided to catch up on the news by watching the local TV. He watched while eating lunch in his room. The local leading news story was about the mayor and her conference concerning some of her campaign financing during her recent reelection. Then the scene switched to a residence fire in the avenues of Salt Lake.

"Oh my Gosh! That's my fourplex apartment house! Those are my neighbors!" His neighbors were standing with blankets around them, watching the fire department struggle with an inferno during the middle of the night. Flames roared out of every opening, exploding from every window and door.

Jim dropped his beer as he reached for the phone. He called Claire and Ed but they did not pick up as they both were at work. He decided not to leave a message, and instead paged Ed at the hospital.

Ed was greatly relieved to hear from Jim and filled him in on the story as he had heard it from the battalion chief fire fighter. "It started very quickly, possibly in your apartment. The arson investigators will be finishing their investigation today to confirm if it was arson—I guess to see if an accelerant was used. I was told that the explosion made it difficult." Ed and Jim agreed that it was a very strange set of circumstances.

Jim asked Ed, "Will you please reassure the fire department that I'm okay and that I will be back from my 'religious retreat' as soon as I can safely get back to town from the canyon?

"For the time being, just tell them where I am and that I'll be back in town later today to relate with the authorities." Jim added, "I intend to stop by the apartment first; maybe I'll see an official while I'm there."

"I'll notify them right away, Jim," Ed said.

Chapter 13
Salt Lake City—Days 13–15

Jim packed his gear, paid his bill and left. He arrived in the early afternoon and went by his apartment. The explosion and intense heat had collapsed the second story onto the first floor apartments where Jim's unit had been. After a brief look at the ashes, it occurred to him that it was going to look quite suspicious for him to drive up to the front of the fire station with all of his prized possessions conveniently packed safely in his vehicle. He parked almost a block away, on a side street, away from the fire station.

Jim asked the fire marshal, "Can you give me permission to look beyond the yellow tape at the fire? I'd like to see if there is anything . . ."

"I'm sorry, but you'll have to wait a few more hours."

Jim then, with candor, answered all of the questions the fire marshal asked. The firefighter asked Jim if he needed the Red Cross help in finding emergency housing assistance.

"I have renter's insurance. I think it will allow me to stay in a hotel. I'll be at the University Park Hotel."

The fire marshal replied, "That's fine, but please don't leave town. Also, keep in touch for the next few days until we complete our investigation." Jim knew they had no court order to retain him, or they would have used it.

In his hotel room looking out on Research Park. Still, he was unable to contact Laleh. Nothing seemed to work: telephone, mail or fax. Snow continued to fall lightly in the cold, crisp dry air as two cross-country enthusiasts trekked on the foot-deep base covering the lawns of the large corporations adjacent to the hotel. The pine and spruce trees contrasted with the Gambel Oak that wove between the large new buildings.

At the same time, a group dressed in the University of Utah Athletic Department's sweats jogged up the plowed street, each with unique headgear to distinguish the individuals. It reminded Jim of a United Nations team. One large black man with a Muslim, fez-like hat, another man with a yarmulke, a fellow with what might have been an ear-flapped hat woven in the Andes, one with a billed cap turned backward.

The wide, almost empty streets were convenient for students needing a cheap, quick and easy outlet for exercise in Research Park where the hotel was located near the campus.

Jim called his insurance company concerning the fire. He then called the College of Pharmacy, and retrieved numerous phone messages that had been left on his voice mail and his e-mail at the campus.

Finally, the next morning, Jim tried calling Alpha Omega, hoping that eventually he would be able to reach Laleh and obtain a seed virus. Dr. Martin Reichstadt finally responded to his phone call, after Marsha told him Jim's relationship to Ben. He was very pleased to host Jim at Alpha Omega—almost to excess. "We would be very pleased to talk to you. We have several questions to ask you. We will change our agenda to accommodate you this week." Jim made immediate reservations to fly to Palo Alto the next day.

Jim had still been denied access to the burned remains of his apartment, as had the other members of his fourplex apartment because of the arson investigation. Strangely, Jim was relieved to be restrained. It was one unpleasant thing he could avoid right then. He had not shared the passion nor joined in the sorrow of his fellow apartment dwellers. He was content to have been an escapee.

Jim called the fire marshal to inform him of his need to go to California. He was informed that they would like to meet with him that day before he left. Jim knew it was serious when he saw a court reporter in the office to take dictation. A police detective, an ATF—

Alcohol, Tobacco and Firearms—agent, the fire marshal, and an insurance investigator, Mike Murphy, were also present. The court reporter and Jim were settling in for hours of questions.

It wasn't until the middle of the deposition that everyone came to understand who Mike Murphy really was. Jim initially had no idea who he was or why he was there. He assumed that he was investigating for the apartment owner's insurance company. After a great deal of discussion, Mike revealed how and why he was there before he became included on the panel.

Two reporters from the news media were present outside when Jim left the meeting. They tried to ask him about his relations with the "Iranian germ warfare agent," referring to Dr. Bazargan, how he could have survived the original "accident" and now, how he had been able to dodge another close call. Jim felt angry but kept repeating, "No comment."

Jim now wished that he had hired an attorney for the hearing, even though he knew that he'd done nothing dishonest. They made him feel guilty, somehow. He felt like a prime suspect.

Ed and Claire both got on the phone when Jim called them concerning the insurance investigator from St. Thomas. Had he really just dropped in to Salt Lake to do a little research? None of them believed that. Jim advised them they would probably be visited by the same investigator. They agreed and Claire and Ed decided that they would call their attorney to get his opinion on the need for counsel.

Chapter 14
NW Salt Lake County—Day 15

Kendra Yazzie, the Navaho teacher's aide at The School With No Name, had witnessed Jaynee's accident. She had suggested that Claire interview the railroad detective. Claire finally obtained an appointment that morning with the U.P.R.R. special agent who was identified as the investigator of the flatcar/trailer burglary. He was in a single-story rectangular building with light-colored brick that sat next to the old Union Pacific Station. Its tall tower still proudly displayed the red, white and blue crest, but it was no longer used for passengers. The main business of this era was freight. Much of the work of the special agent is related to theft of material on rail cars, an occasional accident, employee theft and general security of all areas.

"Hello, I'm Jack Winehart—I was the special agent in charge of the tractor-trailer burglary aboard the flatcar you were inquiring about."

Something about this case still haunted Jack, but he never could put his finger on it. That was probably why he had scheduled this interview instead of referring her to the sheriff's office or other local police agencies–the people who usually inherit anything they don't feel the railroad has a vested interest in. Claire expected Jack to be a redneck and a white bigot. He wasn't.

That morning, when she told Ed about her negative expectations, he had warned her: "Spike, don't go in with a chip on your shoulder. The railroad has had to deal with racial and ethnic differences for a long time and I'm sure that lack of prejudice has been a goal for hiring special agents for quite some time."

She reminded him how naive he was. "Remember Texaco's recent legal problems with bigotry?"

Ed still admonished her to keep an open mind.

Now she stared at an old eight-by-ten picture on Jack's bookshelf behind his desk and it lessened her concern. A younger Jack had his arms on the shoulders of two black friends all posing in their high school football uniforms.

"How can I help you?" inquired Jack.

Claire told agent Winehart everything she knew about the case, and then asked him if there was anything he could add to what Jim had told her.

Jack said, "Perhaps you didn't know that this vial had fallen out of a special shipping container. I found the remnants of packaging designed to protect a shipment of vaccine or live virus—not computer parts. The carton evidently had been left resting or was tossed onto the track in front of a train moving through the yard and was mashed and shredded. When I checked with our records for shipping, I discovered that for some unknown reason, the carton was not on a manifest as a biological agent or anything else. Plus, it was fraudulently labeled. In fact, none of the names or addresses could be located and we didn't have a manifest to affiliate it with our burglary or any other shipment.

"I initially assumed that the package was just another one of the computer chip boxes that had been thrown off the slow-moving freight. I had an informant tip us off previously that a group of five men were conspiring to steal the shipment. The sheriff arrested a local merchant the next morning. He had conspired to steal the computer parts for his place of business. We recovered all of the items mentioned in the manifest, only five cartons. Four of the waiting accomplices were arrested while hiding adjacent to the track where we recovered the five boxes of computer parts that night. The broken box was not found until the next morning.

"When I found the ruptured box, steaming dry-ice fragments and a smashed vial, I had to believe the broken box was a biological-substance box. However, we had no paper trail for it, so I notified the FDA. They came and hauled it away to be held for future evidence.

The coincidence of such a similar-looking package being in the yard at the same time and not being part of the same burglary was too hard for me to accept. But, no 'missing shipment' forms have ever been filed claiming the mysterious extra box.

"The company shipping the computer parts, Fairchild, plus the insurance company were content with five boxes. My boss, the deputy chief, was happy—I had recovered the loss. We, and the sheriff, apprehended all five of the perpetrators I had identified. The county attorney got convictions on all of them. However, we never identified who had been on the flatcar pitching boxes. It evolved from testimony of the other defendants that the merchant must have been the one in the trailer on the flatcar. But no one testified that they were certain it was he. His attorney did not object to the assumptions. The county got immediate confessions of complicity and plea-bargained minimum sentences for all of the defendants. I was instructed by the chief to forget the informant's count of perpetrators. And as far as the mystery box was concerned—delegate it to the feds and forget it."

"Could you tell me anything else about the mystery box, how you knew it was a biological container?" Claire inquired.

"I did a little research and learned that federal regulations for shipping viruses differ depending on the degree of danger assigned to it. They call it the Dangerous Goods Guidelines. The vials that hold the specimens are usually six centimeters long. Plastic bubble wrap is then wound around the vial or vials to accommodate placing it all in the larger snap-cap plastic container about ten centimeters in diameter and eighteen centimeters high. A cloth packet of 'dry mop' encloses each vial. It is similar to the little packets included with new cameras or electronics. This container is then put in a much bigger cardboard box with a styrofoam insert, which is pre-formed to fit the plastic container and includes a slab of dry ice, which, incidentally, was still smoking or steaming in individual pieces when I found it.

"The resultant package is about the size of a small-sized picnic chest. The required six warning and identification labels were not on it, only the fictitious shipping label. All of the computer parts 'boxes' were wrapped with red sealing tape—as was the mystery box. . . .

"Now, tell me again, why are you so sure that particular vial had the unique virus in it that killed your friend?"

"The Parkinson's Disease Syndrome that was associated with Jaynee's case of influenza A is almost unknown. The odds of this very unique virus occurring naturally and then infecting only one person in this state at that time defies statistical law. Especially when that type of virus and constellation of symptoms hadn't been seen any-where in the world—except possibly in Iran—before," stated Claire. "I can understand your skepticism, Mr. Winehart. Why don't you call right now and talk to my husband who is an infectious disease expert at the University of Utah. He's in his lab at this hour," admonished Claire. She retrieved Ed's business card from her purse and handed it to Jack.

"I hope you are not offended, but we have to document every-thing these days, " replied Agent Winehart.

Claire pointed out the number and settled back in her chair to collect her thoughts while she listened to Jack Winehart ask numerous questions of Ed. But Ed corrected one of Claire's perceptions. "We haven't yet been able to positively identify the virus as being the exact same virus as the type in Iran. But we're anticipating a comparative virus to be sent soon by Doctor Laleh Bazargan in Iran."

After Jack finished talking he sat back in his swivel chair, folding his fingers so that just the tips touched. He pursed his lips in a puzzled way and studied the ceiling. After a very long pause, Jack leaned forward on the edge of his chair and rested his hands on his desk. Claire said nothing.

"Mrs. Woodsman, I think I would like to take a second look at all of this. This is clearly out of my jurisdiction, but perhaps I can help you by gathering some information. Then you may wish to take it elsewhere. I can't officially be involved anymore; I hope you under-stand," said Agent Winehart.

"I really appreciate your willingness to help. When can we get together again?" Claire asked.

"Well, let me look at my calendar. We have people gone for vacations. . . . I have two critical meetings tomorrow. . . . How would 2:00 p.m. tomorrow work for you?" offered Agent Winehart.

"Whatever fits your needs is fine with me," said Claire.

"Then let's say at two tomorrow." Agent Winehart marked his schedule.

Claire confirmed the time and then left his office convinced that something or somebody was behind a real conspiracy. She was sure she would not have to convince Eddie now.

Jack Winehart stretched his authority to the limit in gathering information about a closed file the U.P.R.R. had mothballed months ago. He took the rest of the day off and did most of his research on his own time. His close work associates knew that there was "fire in his belly," as one secretary had confided. Jack was a big lovable bear who was usually slow-speaking and slow-moving—unless, like a grizzly bear, he was provoked. His pace quickened and his motions were forceful now.

Jack could not dismiss the fact that there was no record for the mystery box, so that is where he decided to start. He knew that the originating freight forwarding firm was called EXPED Inc. When he had asked people in the railroad's business office—who knew of the firm's reputation—he found some provocative facts which he wrote down.

1. EXPED was believed to have federal contracts with import/export licenses for a multitude of products for dual use (domestic and military).

2. Tooele Army Depot of Tooele, Utah, was alleged to have sent to foreign destinations all kinds of weapons and heavy equipment through them.

3. Dugway Proving Grounds at Dugway, Utah, was believed to

have shipped biologicals through them.

4. Computer components from different Utah firms, who supplied special-orders for the federal government, often went through EXPED.

5. The property on which EXPED was located had belonged to a corporation believed to have been associated with one of the Iran-Contra agents for many years.

Jack could not help but wonder if the company wasn't part of one of those quasi-government organizations that received undocumented support from the CIA, FBI or the National Security Council. He went to the Salt Lake County Recorder's Office to see who might be listed as owners of the EXPED property, and found the appropriate document in the recorder's files in less than an hour.

When Jack brought up the historic microfiche, he saw an interesting history. The record went clear back to the creation of the entire Salt Lake International Center near the international airport. Jack then recalled an old newspaper acquaintance's story about Howard Hughes and Adnan Khashoggi having been partners to make the original purchase of the property. The newspaperman had told him about flying as a guest with Adnan Kashoggi in his private jet. They flew to a remote island to meet some sheik and negotiate a multimillion-dollar deal while he and another Utahn watched in awe.

Jack also recalled news media accounts of the Iran-Contra hearings in which Adnan Khashoggi from Saudi Arabia was implicated, along with Manucher Ghorbanifar from Iran. It was that decade that the Salt Lake Triad Center construction and the addition of an educational wing to LDS Hospital were started with the promises from Mr. Khashoggi of a million dollars. It was never clear to Jack why Mr. Khasoggi felt compelled to select Salt Lake City for his generosity above any other location in the world. Early in 1996 Jack vaguely recalled a Wall Street Journal article describing Adnan Khashoggi as a Saudi international arms merchant who was alleged to have sold airplane parts in the Middle East.

There was nothing concrete that he would dare suggest without further confirmation. There was no document with the name of EXPED Inc. on it to confirm any association, and he had no way of knowing which firm of record was leasing to them now.

Jack made some quantum leaps in logic. "Suppose EXPED Inc. is the result of some front group, created to shield politically sensitive international business transactions? Couldn't some misguided zealots also mask a shipment of virus by mixing it with a shipment of computer parts? If the plot had been discovered by the secret agency requesting the virus shipment, it would be mired in confusion and misinformation. The public also would never need to know—if the agency did not file a complaint. Motive, opportunity and means had all been postulated concerning the burglary. Four hobos were hired to catch five boxes of computer parts thrown from a slow moving train. One dishonest local merchant, who unwittingly allowed an informant to overhear him talking to the hobos on the phone duping them about their involvement, was identified. Also, at the trial, the merchant could not remember from whom he had obtained the initial information about the potential shipment. Nothing was on any court record about a box of virus or anyone who claimed it.

Recent rumor indicated that Winehart's informant had also disappeared. Unfortunately, he had contracted TB during one of his month-long bouts of drinking. He had refused to take the free treatment offered by the public health department. Then, after the trial, he left the state by hopping a freight train. But, it was all too pat—it smelled like a setup. The only clue was a single broken vial that the feds had taken away along with the remains of the biological shipping container. It would take official action to retrieve such evidence—if they still had the evidence available—because the case had been cleared.

Winehart was frustrated because he had no railroad authority to warrant further investigation. He knew he only had a hunch, and a definite risk of losing his job because of his violation of company policy guidelines.

"I have only a few years left until I can retire. I really should not expose myself to such risk. I can't tell my wife—I don't need her anxiety added to my own. So why, I ask, am I doing this?" He had no logical explanation. Perhaps it had something to do with his religious convictions. He had been a member of the United Church of Christ all of his married life, about thirty-five years. Maybe Christ was guiding him. Defend the wronged and help the suffering. He finally felt that he had to do this investigation, regardless of his personal risk!

He called the EXPED office to inquire if they could handle a bogus railroad client's need to package a live virus shipment. They assured him that they were well-prepared and experienced to do just that. They could even expedite international banking and shipments to most countries. They could also coordinate with various means of transportation worldwide. Jack indicated that the client would get back to them if they selected EXPED's service.

Jack next visited the Salt Lake International Center, an industrial center in the northwest corner of Salt Lake County. The Great Salt Lake bordered the northern extreme of the vast center. EXPED was located in the northern area of the International Center adjacent to a railroad track spur. Two old open-passenger touring cars and three ancient boxcars were awaiting their grave on another track three hundred meters away. Tumbleweeds rolled in the dusty wind. EXPED had more than fifty truck stalls for loading on the north side of the building and only two doors to accommodate rail cars on the south side. It was obvious that most of their traffic went by truck, either eighteen-wheelers or other large trucks. A lot of trucks simply shuttled their loads to the nearby international air terminal. Only a relatively small number went by rail. Jack noted EXPED's equally large neighbors did not have the security that EXPED seemed to need.

Jack knew what it had cost to institute what they had built. Chain-link fence with an angled summit of razor wire and inconspicuous video cameras were standard. Protected floodlights could illuminate everything at night.

Jack thought, "If a rail car were isolated inside the perimeter, it would be very unlikely common thieves could get near it. The accomplice must have had access to the interior of EXPED."

Jack knew that some of the "special shipments" had sensors built into the trailer seals, narrow tapes designating a destination point. If one of them was broken before its destination, it would emit a weak signal to the electronic scanners that read the bar codes as the train moved down the track.

"The burgled trailer on the flatcar in question wasn't sealed with one of those seals," Jack recalled. "And, it wasn't loaded in the U.P.'s north yard where most tractor-trailers are done. This must have been an inside job!"

Jack parked near the manned guard station at the curb and casually walked up to chat with the guard. It was cold and windy and Jack went inside the pedestrian entrance. The guard reminded Jack of his pals in the old days in the M.P.s. The black pants were carefully bloused before being tucked into highly polished military-style boots. His matching black Ike jacket was neatly pressed and his leather gun holster, mace holder and cell-phone belt retainer were spit-polished. It made Jack feel a little slovenly in his wrinkled tweed coat. Jack expected to see captain's bars on his lapels, but only a badge designating a security guard was evident. The burr haircut was the final touch. Jack struck up a conversation by showing his credentials to the guard and indicating that he was curious what kind of an outfit EXPED was to work for.

Jack told him, "I had to make a trip out here to check on a complaint and passed by your firm. I got to thinking—in a few years I might want to take early retirement if I could find a part-time job. Does your company consider part-time work? I wouldn't want to work full-time. It looks like a good place to work compared to some places I have seen." Jack could almost predict what the response might be in this man's situation.

"I've never heard of part-time guards being hired with EXPED and they are one of the biggest in the world," commented the guard.

"I wonder why they don't?" pondered Jack, yet knowing the answer.

A big semi pulled up to the gate at that moment, requiring the guard to leave Jack alone at the counter, which was visible from three glassed-in sides. But Jack was a consummate observer. He noticed that the guard office had TV monitors showing all of the angles outside the main building. The large building was a rectangle two stories high and as big as four football fields. The only entrance for people, vehicles or trains came through this monitored portal. The rails and truck entrance were on one side of the security building, a covered pedestrian walkway passed through the security building, and a passenger car entrance was located on the other side of the parking lot. Executive and visitor parking had been located close to the main pedestrian entrance. A traffic-barrier bar was controlled by the guards on duty inside. The employees had designated parking on the rest of the area. The executive parking with small signs showed specific names for each stall, but they were too far away for Jack to read. He did notice the usual status symbols of expensive vehicles—all different.

One vehicle, however, looked somewhat out of place. It was a new black Humvee. The distinctive broad, low profile of the vehicle made it conspicuous with its four wide wheels. It looked poised to leap like some science fiction transformer. Jack was surprised to see that it had a Stars-and-Bars emblem in the window. The state of Utah made no provision for such emblems on the usual license plate brackets. Jack thought he saw two rifle racks through one dark window.

On the guard's desk was a recent copy of the *Phineas Priesthood Reporter.*

Jack had read in an article the November issue of *Intelligence Report,* a project of the Southern Poverty Law Center, that "the Phineas Priesthood movement was rooted in the racist theology of

Christian identity. A doctrine that considers whites the only true children of God, Jews the spawn of Satan and all other people subhuman."

Such literature, in the absence of any other printed material being visible, was conspicuous. "The guard must feel secure that leaving it out is not a cause for concern." Jack thought to himself.

Jack could not help wondering how many other people working here shared that philosophy. Whatever executive owned that vehicle probably was committed to one of those so-called patriot groups. Anyone who would spend that kind of money for one of those vehicles and flaunt the Confederate flag was definitely trying to make a statement.

The guard finally returned to answer Jack's question, "Our clients wouldn't permit casual guards like other firms can hire. They wouldn't even consider it."

"You must get a lot of military and government agency contracts as well as regular industry business here," Jack speculated.

"I can't comment on that, " responded the guard, embarrassed by his own stupid initial remark.

Jack saved any further awkwardness by telling the guard, "Oh well, I obviously have more work to do on my plan for retirement. Thanks for your time. I had better get on down the track to check on that complaint sent to the railroad."

Jack reviewed what facts he had gathered. The flatcar burglary had to have had inside conspirators at EXPED. Someone in there had just added a hitchhiking parcel to the bonafide shipment of computer parts—someone who was confident that any of the other perpetrators would not dare implicate him.

The others would do their time and never expose their accomplice inside EXPED. Even the dishonest merchant failed to recall the EXPED conspirator. This indicated far-reaching power. It even suggested a potential for retaliation inside prison. Jack was a practical man. He knew that alone he wasn't going to be able to spend the energy, much less the time, determining exactly who the EXPED conspirator was. He assumed that the conspirators must be part of some bigger group or gang. The type of heist, the devious way it was staged, suggested that the whole burglary was set up to mask the real goal. The focus of transferring some virus to an illegal recipient was diverted to the "straw dog"—computer parts. Someone inside EXPED must have boarded the train car and had remained inside the boxcar with the shipment, to act as the pitchman. It also would have to mean that EXPED security records would show that someone checked in and did not check out on the date in question. A time card or electric records would have been forged. This had to be the work of some sophisticated radicals or crooks. They also had access to some high-level privileged data to know the how, when and where the potential shipments would be made. It was probable that at least one company executive was a co-conspirator, maybe even the Humvee owner. Jack reasoned that it was possible that the guard he met was part of the conspiracy.

But the conspirators had made an error. The package got pitched at the worst possible time. It got pitched just when another train was going nearby. Someone made an error in timing, or something caused him to make a hurried decision. He had rushed to retrieve the contents of the box—but he lost one vial of perhaps ten or twelve that were recovered and sent on to some clandestine group.

Jack kept coming back to the one fact. No individual, business or government had yet reported any missing biological package.

He came to a conclusion. Whatever entity was responsible for allowing it to get lost, must have wanted it to stay lost.

Jack wondered if someone in the government had used their influence on the biological people out at Dugway. Something of this magnitude should have been detected. The virus could have originated in a manufacturer's plant or a government research lab, anywhere in the world. But the package—what was left of it—sure hadn't helped identify the source.

He postulated that maybe someone in EXPED pasted new bogus labels over bona fide labels to mask the source and divert it. He doubted he would have the opportunity to examine the package, but he decided to call the Feds anyway and ask them if they could check. He would call his good friend at the FDA, Wil Ruth, and ask him to check the labels for a possible "paste-over" and inquire if there was anything new that might suggest a source for the shipment.

Jack had spent most of his day on his private quest and arrived back at his office at the U.P. just in time to telephone his buddy Wil at his FDA office before closing time.

"Wil, this is Jack. How have you been? Won any marathons recently?"

"Good to hear from you Jack. Thanks for asking—I won my age group at that race in New Mexico last week. It was supposed to be warm down there, but I about froze my buns. What's happening in your life?" inquired Wil.

"Well, as you know, we closed that case about the mysterious biological box and broken vial that you received from us, but my damned curiosity has been haunting me. Wil, do you think that there could have been a 'paste-over label,' and that the bona fide original might still be under it?" inquired Jack.

"Do you always get these ghosts haunting you when I'm trying to get away a little early?" countered Wil. "Hang on, buddy, I'll just go into the old evidence room across the hall and check that out. You know it's not unusual for some packing containers to be recycled. But, this class of biological container cannot be reused according to strict regulations. It should be destroyed when its original mission is terminated. Hang on, I'll be right back."

Jack thumbed through his mail while waiting for the results of Wil's search. Jack knew that anyone else would have insisted that he call the next day. He was grateful.

"Jack, you're in some luck, even though I ruined part of the label when I pulled one off. But, I can tell you that it originated from

Alpha Omega Pharmaceutical in Palo Alto," responded Wil. . . . However, no lot number, date or legible recipient."

"Bingo," shouted Jack. "Wil, that helps a heap, I owe you one!"

"Maybe you can help me by being my bridge partner next Saturday. My regular, Dave, is going to be out of town," said Wil, exploiting Jack's offer.

"Sounds like a deal. Call and remind me Friday and tell me the particulars," said Jack. The two had played duplicate bridge together for a few years whenever their schedules would allow.

"I'll call you Friday morning," said Wil.

Chapter 15
Salt Lake County and Alta—Day 16

Claire met Jack at 2:00 P.M. as planned, and he gave her all the information that he had gathered. Claire recorded their conversation on her little pocket recorder.

Jack said, "I don't want to have any record of anyone you are talking to, when or where you are. This is just for your own 'off-the-record' use to share with your husband and Jim." Jack kept asking himself why he felt compelled to do all that he had done. Then he finally told Claire, "It would appear the mystery package originated from Alpha Omega Pharmaceutical!"

"How could that be?" Claire had Jack repeat all of his suppositions again, just to be sure. "Not from Iran or some other foreign country? It came from a U.S. company—Alpha Omega!" Claire reaffirmed. "That doesn't make sense."

"I know how you feel, but with my limited time and resources, that's my best guess. I really can't afford to get more involved—I hope you understand," said Jack. "You may want to take this to the FDA or the FBI and let them advise you, at least." She thanked Jack for all of his help and promised that she would let him know if she could make better sense of the mystery.

Claire left the agent's office confused. She knew Eddie would be skeptical when she saw him that night, but she had him listen to the tape anyway.

"Spike, why in the world would Alpha Omega have spent all the money, and gone to all of the trouble that they did in the Caribbean, if they already had all the answers?" Ed inquired. "Or, at least the virus."

"I don't know—I don't know," Claire said, raising her voice a half an octave.

"Why don't we drive out by this EXPED firm? Something is missing. Agent Winehart must have missed something or made some mistake. I can't buy all of this Alpha Omega stuff."

"We may have assumed the wrong thing at the wrong time, or he may have. If we don't have other social obligations tonight, we could go right now," Ed said.

"Let's go now while we still have a little sunlight left," said Claire.

Most of the traffic on I-80 was eastbound at 4:30 P.M. and it was getting near dusk. Their lane west was moving quite well. Ed was driving their Jeep Cherokee at a little above the speed limit of sixty-five miles per hour, while Claire used the cosmetic mirror on the sunshade to check her lipstick.

She said to Ed, "I believe we have a 'tail,' I really do!"

"Claire, for a psychologist, I can't believe you are becoming paranoid," said Ed.

"Just look in your mirror at the dark-colored Ford Taurus, two cars behind us." Ed looked. "See what they do if you change lanes. It looks like an out-of-town car license," Claire suggested.

Ed decided. "I'll play their silly game and mollycoddle your suspicion, Claire." He made a couple of maneuvers. "They didn't instantly change, but they did follow to the right lane and passing lane. They *are* following us!" Ed admitted.

When they signaled right to turn off into the Salt Lake International trade center, however, the Ford drove right on by.

"See Claire, it was just a coincidence. The Ford drove on down I-80. Please try to keep your fertile imagination from causing panic," cautioned Ed.

They drove down Wright Brothers Drive and turned west on Harold Getty Drive. After a while, they came to EXPED Inc. They just stopped across the street from the big trucking dock entrances and watched.

"What do you see, Eddie?" inquired Claire. She had that tone in her voice like a school teacher testing him. Ed hated this game.

"I see about twenty eighteen-wheel semi-trucks backed up to docks, but the building doors are all shut. I also see about three big garage doors that are open, and a cadre of about twenty or so drivers milling about inside. What am I supposed to be seeing?" Ed inquired impatiently.

"The truck drivers don't look right," Claire observed through their binoculars. "None of them are overweight. Their clothing all looks tidy and they aren't wearing cowboy boots. Their shoes are oxfords and hiking boots. None of the trucks had women's garters or other trivia hanging from the inside mirrors. The logos on the trucks are all different, but they are all about the same size. It's almost 5 P.M. and most of the drivers have not left for home even though their trucks seem to have completed their assigned tasks. They are waiting for the exact quitting time. I believe that they are all employees of EXPED. They might just as well be wearing a military uniform—they are so regimented. Nothing at all looks conspicuous—which is suspicious," Claire responded.

Ed conceded that her postulations were worth thinking about. They waited until 5:00 P.M., when they noticed most drivers left on cue and went to their private cars to go home and other replacement drivers drove in and took their places.

At that moment, they both saw a dark Ford Taurus driving toward them. It made a quick right behind some large buildings ahead of them and innocently parked in a parking lot and turned off its lights. No one got out.

Ed then said, "My pager just went off—I wonder what that is all about—I'm not on call tonight. I guess my cellular is out of range—I'm going to drive to that Quality Inn we saw on the way in and call on their pay phone before we return home."

Ed called the number he recognized as his answering service.

"This is Dr. Woodsman—what's up?"

The operator responded, "Hello, Dr. Woodsman, we had a call from a person who said he was Dr. James Schriver calling long distance. He requested that you obtain a computer disk from the Alta Lodge that he evidently left there. It is urgently needed. Their lost and found person will give it only to you—after you present proper identification. Dr. Schriver indicated that you know where he is and he would like you to send it to him there, ASAP."

"Why didn't he ask them to mail it to him?" Ed inquired.

"We just take the messages, Doctor," the operator replied.

"Yes, I understand," responded Ed. "Thanks for your effort."

"Jim's dependence on us for everything is beginning to annoy me." Ed growled. "I could understand when he was grieving so much. But now? Really!" He repeated the peculiar message to Claire when he returned to the Jeep.

"Do you suppose it's one of those disks that Ben had in his bag that Jim talked about? Perhaps he forgot and left one in the Alta Lodge's vault or something?" inquired Claire.

"Damned if I know. Honestly—he can act so irresponsibly sometimes," complained Ed. "I guess we might as well head on up Little Cottonwood Canyon while the weather is stable. They're predicting another 'dump' of snow for tomorrow. It will only take about fifty minutes now to get up there."

After they pulled out the Ford Taurus followed.

"I don't think we have much choice," said Claire. "I'm going to finish recording the data we have collected up to now, if you will shut off the radio."

Claire did a monologue into the little pocket recorder as they transferred from I-80 to I-15 and proceeded toward I-215. The canyons glowed from the incidental city lights. By the time they reached the beginning of Little Cottonwood Canyon road, Claire had finished her addendum on the recorder and placed it in her purse.

The Ford Taurus followed in the shadows without Ed and Claire's awareness.

Chapter 16
Little Cottonwood Canyon—Day 16

Claire and Ed approached the three-lane entrance to Little Cottonwood Canyon and read the large, illuminated road condition sign that was updated routinely. The sign was cautioning "Black Ice— Four-Wheel Drive or Chains Only," a common warning to those who frequented the ski areas of Alta and Snowbird. It was about 5:30 P.M. Because of the winter darkness, headlights were needed, even though the incidental light from Salt Lake City helped illuminate the clear, moonless night. The city light was periodically shadowed, however, by the tall mountainsides and evergreens of the canyon. As the road snaked its way up the mountain, traffic from behind cast headlight beams brightly into the rear view mirrors. This was usually noticeable only on the straight segments between curves in the road. It was impossible to see what type of vehicle was traveling behind them unless it passed.

Claire and Ed continued to be bewildered by Jim's request. "It was so strange that he hadn't called us earlier—but then perhaps he had tried and not been able to reach us on my cellular," Ed postulated. Neither of them could explain why cellular phones work so well in some places and not in other locations.

"I know the mountains block signals from cells, but why won't they work on the flat area around the International Center when the battery is fully charged? This is frustrating. I think we should consider changing equipment and service provider," Claire suggested.

"Wow! Look at the speed of that vehicle coming up from behind us, probably a teenager with hot pants," commented Ed while scanning his mirrors while on a brief straight segment of road that quickly evolved into a sharp curve to the left. "What a place to try and pass!" The road at this point was only two lanes wide, with snow on the hillside and no guardrail on the Woodsmans' side.

The drop-off was close to six hundred feet. "He's over the double yellow lines! He doesn't need to drive that fast. . . ."

"Just don't get cute with him now," cautioned Claire.

"YOU ARE TOO CLOSE—YOU IDIOT!" Ed screamed.

The Ford Taurus was just about three-fourths of a car length ahead of them when it suddenly veered in front of them. The Ford's right rear side struck the left front fender of the Jeep. The black ice was invisible and neither the guard rail nor the snow inhibited their flight.

"YOU CRAZY DRIVER!" Yelled Ed.

"WE ARE GOING. . . . OVER!" Claire screamed.

Ed struggled to control the Jeep before it became airborne. It was so sudden! So surrealistic, it was like slow motion. Quiet, cold wind passed by the windows and hinted that fate was going to deal their cards to the angel of death. Then the inertia ran out and the Jeep plummeted nose down toward a steep rock outcropping of the canyon wall. They were in a vertical fall when suddenly the air bags deployed with the noise of a cannon. Immediately Claire and Ed felt the horrible impact of the Jeep's engine breaking loose, as the whole front of the vehicle was crushed like a flattened aluminum can. Doctors Claire and Edward Woodsman lost consciousness. The Jeep flipped end over end, dislodging cascades of snow behind them. Then it rolled over and over pulverizing all of the glass into tiny pieces. The roof was hammered with each contact, compressing it down to the vehicle's headrests. The gas tank ruptured, the ski racks, outside mirrors and every other appendage were ripped away down the remaining hundreds of feet of rock and snow. The pathetic Jeep remnant stopped against some huge boulders bordering Little Cottonwood Creek. The torrents of dislodged snow buried most of the wreck.

Only one second behind them and about fifty yards up the canyon—the assassins met their maker. Their initial impact had caused them to lose control on the black ice and they too had spun off of the road. Their wreckage landed upside down in four feet of freezing water beneath the broken ice. There was no glass remaining in the Ford, either. The shock was the coup de grace to the broken bodies of the pair of men without seat belts on. Miraculously, there was no fire, but there was deathly quiet everywhere.

Ironically, the traffic traveling minutes later up and down the canyon road was not aware that an accident had occurred. There were no skid marks or debris from either wreck on the road. It would have been almost impossible to see evidence in the daylight, much less the dark. The wreckage could be seen only if one knew to look for the black piece of the underside of the Ford resting in the creek.

Ed did not know how long he had been unconscious when he awoke. "Spike! Claire! Are you okay?" he screamed. No answer. . . .

He struggled to assess his own condition. Despite the fact that both he and Claire had their heavy winter coats and wool sweaters on, he was shivering. He thought that he might be able to see, but it was pitch dark. He became aware that he was suspended in his seat belt. The Jeep must be on its side. Claire must be below him. He reached out for her even though still tightly secured by the belt. His chest hurt when he tried to reach her. Suddenly, he realized that the car was full of loose grainy snow.

"She's under the snow!" cried Ed.

He had to free himself, whatever it would take. He tasted the warm, salty taste of blood in his mouth. His head pounded. He groped for the seat belt release button. It wouldn't release. He wiggled in the darkness to get a purchase on something so that he could relieve enough pressure on the belt to escape its grasp. It worked.

He straddled her still form. Everything hurt, but his legs still supported him. Ed remembered that the penlight he used to diagnose patients' ailments was in his coat pocket. He searched his clothing with trembling hands.

He found it, and quickly he directed the light beneath him to where Claire should be. He held the light in his mouth while he dug through the granular snow like a dog.

It seemed futile as the snow kept sliding back as he dug. He was praying out loud that Claire was alive. Tears ran down his checks as he tried to call out Claire's name with the light in his teeth. He took off his outer shell jacket and proceeded to fill it with snow. The only solution was to stand on the steering wheel and lift the snow out of the tight remaining window space. The driver's side was barely protruding above the snow.

He could see the road high above him. Car lights were appearing and disappearing because of the curves and trees, occupants unaware of the tragedy below them. He worked frantically until he located Claire's beautiful dark skinned face turned almost ashen by the cold. He could feel a pulse in her neck!

Hope gave him renewed energy. He couldn't feel her breath on his almost frozen hands. He bent over in the cramped space to give her mouth-to-mouth respiration. She soon started gasping and finally was breathing on her own. But she was still unconscious. Ed had to get help, and fast.

Ed recalled his Boy Scout Morse code training—Use S.O.S. to signal for help. But it was pathetic. Ed with his tiny pen light flashed at the road with dot, dot, dot—dash, dash, dash—dot, dot, dot—over and over. Finally, he thought he saw a car stop on the road.

He yelled at the top of his lungs, "HELP—HELP—HELP!" All the while he was signaling with his tiny light, he knew his voice wasn't carrying that far, yet he kept yelling.

Miraculously, a Sheriff's Canyon Patrol deputy saw the light signals in the moonless dark. He responded by turning his spotlight in the direction of the wreck. Ed then knew that someone was aware. He returned the signal with his S.O.S. The deputy turned on his emergency colored lights in addition to his spotlight.

The deputy signaled something in Morse code, but Ed didn't

know any more than S.O.S, which he just continued to signal.

Cars with curious passengers began to slow on the dangerous stretch of road to see what they could despite signs that said "No Stopping" because of the avalanche danger. The deputy got his binoculars out and finally spotted Ed. His bloody face told the officer that this was not some childish prank. He reported on his radio the status of what he could see, then he moved the spotlight about to determine anything else that might explain what had happened. This unnerved Ed as he felt that perhaps the deputy was really not sure they were there. He was greatly relieved when the beam returned to their location.

Ed returned to Claire. It was less frigid inside the wreck. He found a car blanket that had been ejected from the Jeep, and he thanked God out loud. Ed straddled Claire's seat-belted body and became aware of the myriad glass particles in her hair and ears. He restrained himself from moving her as she obviously had a head injury with perhaps neck and back fractures. He doubled the blanket as best as he could and tucked it about her.

He kissed her gently repeatedly and called loudly, "Hang on, Honey, hang on. Help is coming." He thought he heard her respond with a groan.

His cell phone—his cell phone! Maybe it would work. He pawed through his pockets and found it. He dialed 911. It went right through. He thanked God again. Ed was eventually patched through phone and radio to the deputy.

"This is Officer Carl Pickett," he said. "I will stay in contact with you as more help is coming. Tell me what you know about your situation and if you know anything about the other car in the river."

"I didn't know there was another car down here! It must be the one that collided with us. The crazy man ran us off the road!" Ed said.

He proceeded to concentrate on Claire's situation and make suggestions to the deputy for a medical evacuation.

Officer Pickett had Ed patched through to University Hospital and Ed was able to give some basic information before his phone quit working. He stuck it back in his pocket even though he really wanted to throw it in the snow. He returned to Claire and put his face next to hers in an attempt to share his body heat with her.

He recited every bit of biblical scripture he could recall—even if it wasn't accurate. Somehow he knew that the Holy Mother of God would understand. As a scientist he was terrified with the potential injuries that Claire might have.

His patience evaporated. "Where are they?" he yelled through the glassless door. He was unaware of the challenges that the rescuers faced. The outside wind-chill temperature was below zero. A gentle breeze was preceding a storm front that was due to blow in before noon the next day. It could come early. The sides of the canyon were extremely steep, and there was no safe place to land a helicopter. The area was also the frequent resting place for avalanches spawned thousands of feet above.

The only off-road parking that could be snowplowed was about two miles up the canyon at the White Pine trailhead. Access to the wreck could not be made with snow machines. People on cross-country skis would be needed, pulling litter sleds. Paramedics with "Jaws of Life" might be needed to cut Claire out. Ed was getting frostbite on his fingers and nose. He was getting very stiff, and multiple pains were surpassing his pain tolerance limits. Ed could not allow himself to lie on top of Claire, and yet he wanted to share body heat. His body was going to collapse if he didn't get up and away from her for a while. When he straightened up, the muscles in his back spasmed, and Ed couldn't lift himself out of the wreck. Even though Ed knew what had happened, he still cried out in pain.

"OH . . . oh!" Time seemed frozen. "What is keeping them?" thought Ed.

At last a voice from the darkness yelled out, "They're over here. Bring the sleds!" A rescue dog was soon rubbing his nose on Ed's outstretched hand that extended in pain above the opening in the snow-covered wreckage. The German shepherd barked as it looked behind and uphill at the first member of the rescue team skiing through a tight grove of aspen trees.

Ed was barely conscious when he was lifted away from Claire. He was still muttering his concern to the rescue team. "Get Claire. She's below. . . . Broken neck and back! Careful! Careful. . . ."

Hours later Ed and Claire were admitted to The University of Utah Hospital.

Chapter 17
Salt Lake City and Palo Alto—Day 17

It was almost 3:00 P.M. the next day before Ed awakened in his hospital bed. A student nurse was startled when he yelled. "Where is she? Where is she?" Sharp pain stabbed him in his back and head before the frightened student nurse responded. The bandages on his face and hands reminded her of some old horror movie about a mummy.

"She's—she's in the next bed, Dr. Woodsman. She's right here," stammered the young woman.

The hospital administration had put them both in the same room. It was a judgment call that Ed instantly knew was made after consideration of several factors. Ed assumed that his injuries must not be too severe, despite his pain, or they would have had them each assigned to different care areas. Ed asked to speak to the physician who was assigned to their care.

The chief orthopedic resident, Susan Cartwright, was a large-boned woman about six feet tall. Her strong features did not belie the fact that she was a caring and tender person. The chief resident addressed Ed's main concern, Claire's prognosis. "Claire has been given full body X-rays, a CAT scan and an MRI of her head, neck and back," she said. "She has a fracture of C-7 of the neck vertebra near her shoulders. Her skull was not fractured, but a subdural hematoma requires a neurosurgical intervention. As you can guess, a hole needs to be drilled into her skull to relieve the pressure on her brain from the blood pooling there."

Ed replied, "I'm with it—I know what you are saying."

"Good. She's still comatose, but all of her other vital signs are miraculously as well as could be expected. She has multiple contusions and a bunch of small lacerations, only a couple of required stitches.

"Most of the small lacerations on her face did not bleed much because of the cold. We are going to keep her in a halo neck brace until further evaluation. Her reflexes seem to indicate that she still has adequate spinal cord function. She is breathing on her own—no respirator. If she doesn't regain consciousness within the hour, we should operate to relieve pressure on her brain. At this point it is a relatively good prognosis. Considering what she has been through, she is one very lucky lady."

Dr. Cartwright then informed Ed, "You might have a ruptured disk at L3 and 4, but it's not as bad as many I've seen. Actually, it may even have been an artifact of a previous injury. I feel that most of your discomfort is probably muscle trauma. You, too, are badly bruised, to be certain, but no broken bones could be seen on X-rays. The frost-bite on the tips of your nose, ears and fingers may turn uncomfortable soon. You have been unconscious, so you need to avoid too much exertion. You are free to get up and about, but bed rest will be neces-sary until I'm convinced that you are truly out-of-the-woods and free to resume limited activity. Do you feel like talking to a sheriff's office detective?"

Ed replied, "After I check my phone mail first—okay?"

A message from Jim was the first call of his phone mail. "Ed, I tried to call you two before I left on my flight to Alpha Omega, but missed you. I'll be interested how that talk with the insurance agent, Mike Murphy, turned out. I'll try and call you again from Palo Alto as soon as I have anything to report."

Conspicuously, there was no record of any later call about the forgotten computer disk from Jim. The rest of the phone mail mes-sages were just routine. Ed suddenly was filled with anger. "If it hadn't been for Jim's stupid and selfish request that we drive up to Alta Lodge to get Ben's computer disk that he left, we wouldn't be in the shape we are now," he thought to himself.

It took Ed a bit of doing to get the phone number of Alpha Omega's executive area where Jim Schriver was in conference, but at last the phone was ringing.

"I'd like to speak to Dr. Schriver, please," demanded Ed.

"This is Jim Schriver," the mystified voice replied.

"Jim, this is Ed. Have you any idea what has happened to Claire and me?" Before Jim could answer, Ed continued. "Because of your request that we retrieve that damned computer disk you left at Alta Lodge, we're barely alive today!"

"WHOA—Ed, I don't know what you are talking about?"

"That God-damned disk you asked us to get almost caused us to get killed. I am right now calling from a hospital bed and Claire is unconscious! What are you trying to tell me? You don't even remember leaving that request with the hospital operator?"

"My God, Ed, she's unconscious and you are injured? What happened?" questioned Jim incredulously.

Ed spoke so emotionally that his old West Virginia accent broke through his usually controlled dialogue. "What the hell are you all doing there that you don't recollect from one damned day to the next what you ask a body to do? Did you call me or didn't you?" demanded Ed.

"I have been touring the facilities nonstop since I arrived and I haven't called anybody in Utah, Ed!" replied Jim. He wanted to speak out of earshot of the other people there in Alpha Omega to continue the discussion. Jim excused himself from the others and was shown into Ben's old office, which was next door to the conference room. "I've got all of the computer disks I need, both Ben's and mine, even though I haven't used them yet. There must be some mistake."

Ed tried to recall all that had happened since they last talked. He explained Claire's and his injuries. He also tried to recall exactly what the detective had said and then repeated it to Jim. He dumped the entire story on Jim like a computer downloading. Jim could barely keep up with the dialog. It was obvious that Ed had been severely traumatized.

"What are you telling me, Ed? We have all been victims of some sort of elaborate conspiracy? I could understand if it was Claire telling me this theory—but you believe all this?" Jim inquired. "Tell me again why the railroad detective believes that Jaynee's virus came from Alpha Omega—there was a label with their return address on it underneath a fake shipping label? Is that right? And it clearly said Alpha Omega? Are you sure?"

"That's the gist of it," said Ed.

"None of this makes any sense," responded Jim.

"I know!" answered Ed. "But with our *real* wounds and close calls, I can no longer just dismiss it all as coincidence. We must consider the possibilities, man."

"You've convinced me, Ed, but what, then, am I doing here at Alpha Omega? If they already have the influenza A virus, they could and should have made a vaccine before now. This is preposterous," said Jim.

"I know it doesn't add up, but I believe there really is a conspiracy to silence us all. We're all in danger, Jim. You had best watch your back while you are at Alpha Omega," cautioned Ed.

"Ed, you two need special protection, even in the hospital. You're both really vulnerable in there," Jim responded.

"The railroad detective already suggested that we get the FDA or the FBI involved," said Ed.

"He did? WOW! He must be quite confident of his theory. I have not tried to use Ben's two computer disks—maybe I can get access to a terminal to see what I can find out that was so important on them that Ben took both with him on the cruise. As a matter of fact, I am in his office right now—they put me in here for a little privacy. I'll call you as soon as I know anything. I'm staying at the Stanford Arms Hotel, if you need to reach me. I'll be careful—you can bank on that."

"Jim, I'm sorry I exploded on you—I've just been out of my head," said Ed.

163

"It's understandable, try to rest and regain your strength. I should be back soon. Bye—I love you two." Jim said.

With tears in both eyes, Jim thought, "I haven't told any man that I loved him since I told Dad that years ago as a child. Cowboys just don't do that, much."

Chapter 18
Alpha Omega—Day 17

Jim did not hang up the receiver, but simply depressed the switch on the phone cradle while he regained his composure. He had excused himself from the walking tour of AO's facility to answer the telephone call from Ed. As he was about to hang up, he reached into his tweed sport coat pocket to feel the computer disks he had concealed. Temptation was too great. He looked at the ornate solid wooden door and wondered how many security agents would crash in to accost him for breaching their computer files if he could figure out Ben's password.

He still held the phone receiver to his ear—it was telling him to hang up and redial. Jim recalled some of Ben's old habits in college. He wondered if Ben still followed his old protocols for selecting PIN codes and passwords. Jim remembered that Ben would use a favorite ten-letter word and assign the corresponding digit to the letter in the word or words. He remembered Ben's system for his little black book of women in his life. He used SINGLE LADY (1-S, 2-i, 3-n, 4-g, 5-l, 6-e, 7-L, 8-a, 9-d, 0-y) so that he could put down Mary Jones' phone number: NYL ENL LGLD, which was (307) 637-7479.

Jim continued to hold the phone between his cheek and shoulder, freeing both hands for his search. Just in case someone came looking for him, he could quickly return to a normal posture. He frantically searched Ben's desk for some hint. He opened all unlocked desk drawers. He had turned on the computer but refrained from trying bogus passwords because many systems would lock up after three wrong tries.

He heard someone coming. Both hands became visible even though the monitor was still cued to requesting a password. It was Dr.

Martin Reichstadt, the man he came to California to see.

"Yeah, there you are. I'm Dr. Reichstadt."

Jim assumed the posture of just hanging up the telephone as he simultaneously and surreptitiously turned the monitor off with the other hand. The computer was still on.

"I'm glad to finally get to meet you, Dr. Reichstadt," said Jim. He quickly came from behind the desk and shook Dr. Reichstadt's hand in a firm cowboy grip.

Reichstadt said, "I apologize for the delay, but some critical management problems came up. I know that you will want to complete the tour of our manufacturing facilities. It is a coincidence that we had this special tour set up for other visiting VIPs anyway, so . . ."

"I understand completely, Dr. Reichstadt—no apology needed. I enjoyed what I got to see very much and did get to see firsthand how your state-of-the-art vaccine production really works."

"Good—good," responded Dr. Reichstadt. Before he could continue, Jim reached in his pocket and retrieved the remaining disk he had in his pocket and withdrew it and held it up in a position to demonstrate what he had and also be ready to install it in the drive of the computer.

"Dr. Reichstadt, in addition to his company cellular phone, Ben had a computer disk that I thought may be related to company business. I took the privilege of removing it, along with the phone, from the things that I intend to send to Ben's parents in Wyoming." Jim didn't mention the other disk that was already in the disk drive. "I was wondering, while I was here, could we determine if this is his personal business or company business?" Jim gambled that the temptation to safeguard possible company privileged information would preempt any reservations Dr. Reichstadt might have.

Dr. Reichstadt replied, "Dr. Schriver, we can look into that before you leave. It sounds like a good idea, but right now I have some of our research staff and executives assembled and waiting to discuss your ideas about this Tehran virus."

"Certainly—I didn't realize you were ready for me," Jim responded condescendingly. Jim returned the one disk to his pocket, but was stymied in his ploy to retrieve the other disk. He left the room with the computer on.

Dr. Reichstadt led Jim down the hall toward the president's boardroom. He queried Jim about his accommodations and his air flight coming to Palo Alto. When they entered the boardroom, all eyes turned to them and casual talk ceased.

"Ladies and gentlemen, I would like to introduce Dr. Schriver," announced Dr. Reichstadt. He then proceeded to introduce the research staff and executives: Dr. Mary Matheson, Vice President of Planning and Development, who was in charge of alpha interferon focus group; Dr. Rosa Martinez was director of the antigen-antibody research project; Dr. Bill Balencamp, Vice President of Production, was in charge of vaccine production; Eric Mittles was the Chief General Counsel of the legal department; and Dr. Lu Chan was head of the Molecular Biology Engineering area.

Jim felt that this was a curious gathering of interest groups and wondered about the criteria for their selection. Because of the quiet, pensive expectation of the group, Jim sensed that this was his opportunity to present what they really needed to know. But first he wanted to find out what they might already know. Jim used Laleh's syllabus that he had obtained from the Continuing Education Director of the Caribbean conference as a source of his opening remarks. He felt that they were waiting for something else and assumed that the lack of questions meant that they were more than ready for him to indicate how soon they would be able to evaluate Laleh's live virus for themselves. He indicated that, though he had not been able to contact her, he expected her to send the frozen virus in the very near future. He invited them to comment or ask questions.

Dr. Matheson began by explaining in very technical terms why she thought the virus might have been a natural virus instead of an engineered one, "To facilitate the postencephalitic parkinsonism associated with any influenza A virus infection, as was seen in the 1918-24 period, it would seem that a heretofore unknown cause, maybe a recognition protein, had to have been present. In this Tehran virus, it would seem that an unknown natural enabler or unnatural molecular-engineered enabler would have been necessary. A special protein encoded into the virus could make it a super antigen and cause viremia in the brain that the virus invaded. The inflammatory process is believed to be the cause of tissue destruction—of course in this case primarily the midbrain, including the substantia nigra.

"Possibly it may have been designed to produce alpha interferon at a predictable time, if it were engineered by man. But premeditated malice of this degree would require a whole team of intelligent sociopaths to engineer and produce such a virus. In summary, it would seem to me that this virus could have evolved as a result of an error, even if it were engineered. Or, even more logical, it was a unique naturally evolved pathogen with retroactive effects."

Jim noticed that Dr. Reichstadt seemed very tense and strangely quiet. Dr. Matheson's postulating seemed to make Dr. Reichstadt squirm and avoid eye contact.

Dr. Martinez spoke up next. "If Dr. Bazargan can get us an uncontaminated live virus with such characteristics, we have the technology to test it against most known influenza A viruses. But, to my knowledge, there are no cultures of the original 1918 virus available anywhere in the world. That was just too long ago. The Von Economo encephalitis rarely appears nowadays and I don't think anyone has frozen virus stored anywhere. We can't compare the Tehran strain with the 1918 strain."

Dr. Reichstadt felt compelled to speak. "There have been no documented reports, outside of a few cases in Iran, that would suggest a pending worldwide epidemic of a natural or unnatural virus, and no further reports coming from Iran. It is a documented fact that the U.S. Defense Department had gone on record indicating that BW—bacterial warfare—agents do not have a dependable profile in battle. Conditions must be just right. Slightly moist ambient air and very little wind are necessary conditions for effective results. A BW bomb must spray droplets less than three microns in size over a wide area to be effective. Then the virus must be quite virulent, fast, and demonstrate no cross-immunity from other past virus infections or vaccines."

Dr. Lu Chan seemed eager to offer his perspective, even though only half of these scientists would fully comprehend his technical jargon. "If a biological bomb were to be used today, much more effective solutions could be developed. For instance, Cone Shell venom can cause death in twenty-four hours by the production of neuro-transmitters and individual proteins of 156 peaks, HBLC. There are select areas of the brain for all of these different proteins that are released by the Cone Shell. Some proteins cause sleep or the subject becomes narcotized. In theory, one could select specific neurotrans-mitters with individual proteins for specific uses. Like a key in a lock, they could cause non-fatal or fatal consequences. It would be theoretically possible to genetically alter a virus after splicing in the desired specific Cone Shell protein for a given effect and then proceed to propagate the new virus on cloned human brain tissue."

Dr. Balencamp weakly supported Dr. Chan by saying, "I suppose, if we had to replicate the Tehran natural or engineered virus— we could do it now if we needed to do so." Jim noticed controlled hostility in Bill's face. He wondered why.

"People, people! We seem to have lost our focus. Do we need to consider making a vaccine to prevent a threat to mankind? Is there a clear and present danger from this Tehran influenza A virus worldwide? Isn't that the first question?"

"The next question is, can we safely make a vaccine that comes from either an artificially altered or naturally occurring virus that is associated with a cause of Parkinson's disease?" Dr. Reichstadt challenged.

The attorney, Eric Mittles, knew his cue. "From a malpractice perspective, we would face the risk of hundreds of frivolous suits from patients who will naturally develop Parkinson's disease even though the vaccine would not be the actual cause of their malady. We would be sitting ducks for bankruptcy. We are self-insured, as you all know, but our deep pocket is still limited. We would end up paying for the care of any Parkinson's disease patients who received our vaccine anytime in their lifetime. What are the odds of a court ever ruling in our favor? You know the answer before I give it to you—nada, zip, zilch, zero!"

All eyes were now on Jim. He stood slowly and directed his response to Dr. Lu Chan. "It is my perception that it is possible to design a protein that could function as a marker or identification tag, if you will, with molecular engineering. It would function like a DNA test. Isn't that possible?" asked Jim.

"Yes, that is possible, but of course it would take time and an FDA approval. We would have no way of predicting, with certainty, how such a tag would adversely influence a patient response without a great deal of documented study," replied Dr. Chan.

Dr. Reichstadt again responded, "If only Ben could be here. I remember Ben telling me it takes an average of five hundred million dollars to bring a new chemical entity or vaccine to market. That's before we make a dime on the product. I have to ask you all, who might buy such a product right now? Where is the market and what or who will pay for it?"

Jim, who had been standing with his arms folded, unfolded them. "I'm glad you mentioned Ben, Dr. Reichstadt, because I know exactly what he would say. He actually told us in the Caribbean that this company has taken humanitarian risks in the past to co-develop certain vaccines with other foreign governments to protect their citizens from diseases that are indigenous to their country. It is also my understanding that foreign costs are much lower, especially when the U.S. domestic market risk would not need to be included. Ben also told us that your management could also utilize the foreign experience for possible future marketing of the same product later in the U.S. market and it might be easier to rationalize."

Jim took small liberties with the truth, but he felt Ben's intent was correctly expressed. Everyone seemed to feel hesitant to comment now as they knew politically they were going to be on thin ice from that moment. The silence was deafening.

Dr. Reichstadt understood what had happened. Jim had managed to gain high moral ground despite all of the negative opinions concerning the need to make a vaccine. It would not be wise to expose the company to worldwide public criticism. He could see the press reports describing the crass materialism and cavalier attitude of their management who didn't even investigate the possibilities of making a vaccine to protect the public. He knew that Jim did not need to limit his offer to work with Alpha Omega. He could go to any number of their competitors and cause public relations damage if they took the risk and Alpha Omega did not. Besides, he knew what no one else but Rock Granite knew. They might possibly have a head start with the ancient frozen viruses Martin had brought with him from academia, years ago.

"Why don't we do a cursory feasibility study to at least explore the possibilities?" he asked. "Let's assume that world events force us to make a vaccine on an emergency basis. Consider this as a contingency plan study for an epidemic, if and when one would develop. I would like to ask all of you here to look at all of the possibilities and meet again at 4:00 P.M."

"Can you continue functioning as a visiting facilitator, Dr. Schriver?" Jim's head moved affirmatively as he checked his plane ticket. "What about the rest of you?" Dr. Reichstadt inquired.

Everyone knew that this was more of a command than an inquiry; they would be there.

Before leaving, Jim reminded Dr. Reichstadt of his desire to use Ben's computer to determine the origin of the computer disk in Ben's effects.

Surprisingly, Dr. Reichstadt said, "I'll ask Ben's secretary to assist you in gaining entry to check on that. I'm sorry I can't do it for you as I must attend to some phone calls that my secretary has been hounding me about. Will you be headed back to Salt Lake City tonight then?"

"Unfortunately, I am homeless because of an explosion and fire in my apartment. And I must help some close friends who are in the hospital in Salt Lake," Jim replied.

"My, I had no idea. You have had so much bad luck this year. What about this fire and explosion? What caused that?" inquired Dr. Reichstadt.

"They don't know yet." Jim studied Dr. Reichsdadt's face to detect any clue of guilt. He could see none. Jim's tension was evident.

"These past couple of weeks have been terrible for you," Martin Reichstadt commented, while looking genuinely concerned and a bit puzzled.

"Thank you for your concern. I guess I should go see Ben's secretary now," Jim said.

"Her name is Mary Whiting and her desk is just outside Ben's office in the 'common area' of the executive suites. She's really the best person to help you anyway, she's been here longer than most of us," Martin indicated.

Jim thanked Dr. Reichstadt again and assured him he would be at the four o'clock meeting. He found his way back to the common area and Mary Whiting's desk. She was not there.

He saw an older woman on a telephone in a room fifty feet away. It housed the copy machine, FAX, paper shredder and another terminal and computer. He guessed this was Mary, copying data while talking. Jim sat down near her desk. She had only one guest chair and it was at an angle next to her chair. She obviously was trained well as a communicator. No barrier desk between herself and her visitor. She had fresh flowers in a homey arrangement on the opposite side of her desk, and rows of pictures that Jim assumed were her grandchildren. A hand-carved wood name sign confirmed that it was her desk. Her chair had a special cushion that suggested Mary might have back problems.

Jim noticed that other, younger women seemed to be waiting for Mary's advice as they queued for their turn while she finished her phone call. Jim was reminded of the senior emergency department nurses in his hospital. They were the glue that kept everyone and everything running smoothly. Without such devoted and intelligent people he suspected all institutions would simply collapse.

It was obvious that she was going to be delayed longer and Jim allowed his eyes to survey the typed memo cards she had written to herself—notes tucked under the edge of her large desk blotter. One caught his eye; it simply said Ben Carlsom at the top and then a list of words and letters:

BEN CARLSON
Personal-MMB
Budget-MME
Day Planner-MMN
Old Pharmaceuticals-BMM
New Pharmaceuticals- EMM
Influenza Vaccines-MMC
Type A: MMCB
Type B: MMCE
Type C: MMCN

Jim knew immediately what those meant. This was a guide for Mary to enter secured codes for Ben's files. The misspelled name of Ben Carlson—the m—on the Carlsom was the flag. It was the ten-digit system associated with the letters of Ben's name. B=1, E=2, N=3, etc., and M=0.

At that moment he looked up to see Mary headed his way with a kind smile. She was a motherly looking woman with salt-and-pepper well-groomed hair and a conservative suit. Her jewelry was understated.

"Hello, you must be Dr. Jim Schriver," she announced as she approached with her hand extended.

Jim guessed she might be five foot five inches and, as they used to say on the ranch, "of sturdy stock." Jim greeted her. "And you must be Mary Whiting."

"You are correct. Dr. Reichstadt indicated that you would be coming and I was to allow you access to Ben's personal file on his computer terminal."

At that moment the phone rang again, this time on her desk. Also another secretary seemed to be discreetly hovering to await her chance to communicate with Mary. "You know Ben's office, don't you Dr. Schriver?" Jim nodded yes. "Why don't I just give you this code to enter and you can see if Ben's floppies belong here or with his family?" Mary wrote on a little post-up note:

Type Ben Carlson first, then when asked for a password,
enter: Personal MMB

Jim tried not to bolt over to Ben's office. The office was just as he'd left it earlier. Jim went in and put a chair close to the door without quite blocking it. He wanted to cause an unannounced visitor to slow down and assess what was happening. This would give him time to recover his composure if he heard a noise.

He turned on the monitor, then clicked the mouse to activate the A drive. Nothing happened. Jim felt his heart skip a beat. Then he realized that in his haste he had not turned the computer on. But, had he not left the computer on when he had to leave so quickly?

Perspiration beaded on Jim's upper lip. Was this a setup—a trap of some sort? He pushed the disk ejection and out popped the disk. "Thank God," exclaimed Jim. He started the computer and rein-serted the disk. At the password prompt he typed Personal-001. A menu instantly sprang up for Ben's personal life, his address and tele-phone list of friends, sub-lists of service people he used, birthdays of relatives and friends and sub-files of athletic statistics and on and on.

Jim decided to take a risk and see what would happen if he

typed: Influenza Vaccines-004 and then Type A-0041. It worked perfectly. A whole directory of data on influenza A viruses scrolled across the screen.

Jim began to wonder why Ben's secretary would allow him to check out the disk without explaining the code. Supposedly, he wouldn't be able to access anything, including the personal data, unless he could break the simple code. Quickly Jim exited to a menu that would allow him to copy the disk to an unlabeled blank disk he found in a box on top of the desk. He did the same thing with the disk in his pocket. Jim knew time was critical. Mary Whiting was waiting for him to return to her and tell her that he couldn't access the data with the password that she had given him.

Sure enough—Mary Whiting had a fixed gaze on the door when Jim brought out the single disk with a dejected and quizzical look on his face. The other disks were secure in his pockets. Jim sauntered at almost a slow pace. When he was in speaking range he started talking to her.

"I guess you can take the cowboy out of the country, but you can't take the country out of the cowboy. I either don't know how to use your system or this is proprietary information that belongs to Alpha Omega exclusively," Jim complained. "Let me go back with you to Ben's office, my computer is busy at this moment." Mary led Jim back into the office and activated the system.

She then apologized to Jim, "I'm sorry, but I must use a privileged password."

Jim said, "I understand," and he moved to the other side of the desk.

He had no sooner moved than Mary invited him to see only briefly the menu of subjects that were obviously confidential, with cost data and control information.

"I'm afraid that these are company floppies, Dr. Schriver."

"I guess you are right. Well, I'm glad that we were able to clear it up," he remarked. "Too bad we couldn't have salvaged his laptop computer also."

"I'm sorry we can't help Ben's family with his private affairs. But, if we do find any private or personal data, I will personally send it to his family. We have his parents' address in Jackson, Wyoming," Mary Whiting tactfully replied. "Thank you for this information because this may be the only record of Ben's last work. It will save us a lot of time and money."

"I guess I will gather up my stuff and 'slap leather,' as my ancestors used to say. I checked the weather back in Salt Lake and there's a nice window of opportunity between storms for flying. I'll be leaving after our meeting this afternoon. Thank you for all your help."

As he walked down the hall toward the security controlled production area, he noticed Dr. Bill Balencamp's office door was open.

"Hi, Dr. Balencamp, I saw your door was open," said Jim.

"Yeah—come in," Dr. Balencamp said in a somewhat hostile tone.

"I failed to ask, during the meeting today, if you folks ever did special contract production for other firms. Either our government or other countries?" inquired Jim.

"Yes, we have had several customers with special needs that we have accommodated," responded Balencamp crisply.

"Have you ever done a special vaccine run for a relatively small amount?"

"Sure, we have made special vaccines for other countries who hold the licenses and patents. That is, if our State Department will issue a permit—a license. We then act as their agent and they assume liability for the use. For instance, we have made vaccines for unique tropical diseases indigenous to a local area. Often this international business is complicated legally, because technically it is a joint venture. But one of the big problems is the cost. That is why the U.S. Orphan Drug Law was put into effect. Federal support is often required to fund unprofitable but essential drugs. Each case is different," Dr. Balencamp answered while glaring at Jim.

"So, technically, it might be possible to produce a virus or vaccine if all of the financial and legal challenges could be satisfied?" inquired Jim.

"Sure, if some country like Israel could get the U.S. Government to allow a joint venture, I guess that Alpha Omega would do it. If the price was right, and the risk was controlled," answered Balencamp in an impatient manner.

"Out of curiosity, how is Rock Granite to work for?" inquired Jim. "I understand that he's recovering from a stroke right now."

Balencamp stiffened his back and reacted. "If he were at the helm now, he would have made a decision today. He wouldn't be procrastinating—he is a true leader. They won't keep that old lion out of action very long. He's a real captain of industry, both on and off campus. Our country needs more like him. We don't need all of these foreigners corrupting our industry and way of life. First it was the automobile industry and the clothing industry—and now it will be pharmaceuticals. We have got to stop them. Mark my word, the last days are at hand," pontificated Dr. Balencamp. His face reddened.

Jim was somewhat amused by Dr. Balencamp's "salute the flag" answer. Dr. Balencamp's beard and mustache looked like steel wool. His aviator-styled glasses seemed to accent the rest of his face. His khaki starched shirt and pants did not go with his wrinkled flowered tie and gray suspenders. His six-foot-nine-inch, thin and gangly frame did not seem synchronized with his calculating intent. Every time he stooped over, the white plastic pen and pencil pocket protector tended to empty its contents. Bill's hand would fly up automatically to catch what he could.

"He looks like an angry Ichabod Crane," Jim thought.

Jim couldn't help but notice Bill's desk cluttered with stacks of papers, journal articles and a yellowing potted plant that looked like it hadn't been watered for weeks.

The bulletin board above his desk had a collage of pictures dominated by mountaintops with family groups, smiling faces and wild flowers.

In contrast there were also pictures of camouflaged men with weapons. All were standing about with camouflage makeup on their faces. Tacked around the border of the bulletin board were notes of upcoming events. One poster had a confederate flag emblem with an invitation to STRIKE Patriot Seminars to be held in Hayden Lake, Idaho. It showed a training conference–to be held sometime in the spring.

Bill Balencamp noticed the focus of Jim's eyes. "I think I'll take that conference in; of course, you folks in Utah don't live like we do here in California with hordes of illegal immigrants. We must be prepared!"

Jim considered carefully his response. "I guess we don't."

Sensing an ambivalent response, Dr. Balencamp inquired, "You don't have a problem working with Iranian foreigners either, I guess? I remember 1979 when they overran our embassy and held our citizens captive."

"Dr. Bazargan may be an exception, but I believe Iran is changing. A lot has happened since 1979. Besides, this is a worldwide humanitarian concern now and not a political matter," Jim responded.

"I sure wish we could've had Mr. Granite here today." Balencamp responded, ignoring Jim's logic.

Then he thought silently, "I can't believe this Reichstadt crap. Mr. Granite should have gotten rid of that old fart a long time ago. And this Schriver is a wide-eyed dangerous fool!" He wished he could ignore the chain of command and contact Col. Cabal directly, but he figured he would see him at the conference in Idaho. It was just a matter of days. Colonel Nick Cabal would be there among the brethren. Possibly J.R. Granite would be there by then. He knew he could make sure no vaccine is produced until after then.

"I guess you will be returning to Salt Lake?" Balencamp said in a manner to terminate their discussion.

"Ah, yes, I'll be on my way to pick up my stuff at the gate and head out for Salt Lake tonight, right after our next meeting," answered Jim. "I'll see you then, I presume."

"Okay—see you at four o'clock," Balencamp concluded tersely.

Jim arrived early to the meeting room. He noticed that folks who had special assignments were also there early. They were engaged in some informal debate.

The others quit talking when Jim entered the room. Dr. Reichstadt was almost on Jim's heels.

"Well, everyone, let's get right to it. If we decide that we need to make the vaccine in a hurry, can we do it?" Dr. Reichstadt began. "Assuming that Dr. Bazargan can supply us with the seed virus. Let's begin on the left and go clockwise. Dr. Balencamp, you start."

Balencamp gave the only negative report. He described some phony technical production problems that he needed to solve first. The rest of the team did a remarkable job in such a short period of time. It became clear to all that they could mount a formidable campaign when and if the feared epidemic started. All they needed was the seed virus.

Dr. Reichstadt acknowledged consensus. "We are all confident that Dr. Balencamp can conquer his production problems, given a little more time." Even though Jim could not bring himself to completely trust everyone there, especially Dr.Balencamp, Dr. Reichstadt and Jim seemed to be on the same wavelength.

But he still felt uneasy about Dr. Reichstadt. "It is what he doesn't say that bothers me." Jim recalled what Ed had said about, "watching your back."

Jim got his suitcase at the security office on the way out. Alpha Omega had a company limousine standing by to take him to the airport. Jim was surprised to see another passenger waiting with the driver. Jim elected to go by cab instead, much to the consternation of the public-relations woman in charge. "My university has certain reservations about such things," Jim lamely explained.

Jim put the three disks under a lot of data sheets in his briefcase before being checked by the airport security. "I am very obviously paranoid," he thought to himself. He began to feel there must be only a few bad apples in the Alpha Omega barrel. Almost everyone he'd met so far seemed okay, except perhaps Bill Balencamp. He couldn't trust someone who was such a bigot and a radical—even if he was so bright. And he was still curious about their CEO.

Maybe their CEO would be healthier by the time Laleh and he could communicate. There was also still something about Dr. Reichstadt that he couldn't put his finger on. . . .

Though exhausted, Jim couldn't sleep on the plane; he just daydreamed. He had no photographs of Laleh, only his mental image of her standing at the bow of the boat with her yellow silk swimsuit and a filmy scarf moving with the ocean breezes. He fantasized holding her in his arms and feeling her body next to his, her long black hair gently moving in the wind and her dark eyes staring into his. He saw only his dream as he stared out the window of the plane at the cotton-like clouds, his mind thousands of miles away.

"When will Laleh ever get through to me or me to her?" Jim pondered to himself. "It's been so long, so much has happened. I hope she's okay. . . . Oh Lord, I hope she's all right." He wondered if she even knew he was alive! She probably thought he was dead along with her sister, Sonbol. Still, CNN news went worldwide, so hopefully she knew the correct facts. That is, if she had access to TV at the right time. Nothing would have any meaning, not the vaccine, not anything—if something had happened to Laleh.

The sudden intrusion of the aroma of an oppressive perfume made him aware that the seat next to him was occupied by an obese woman with a beehive hairstyle popular with some of the older matrons of Utah. She had on a dress with large flowers that accentuated her excess. The Mormon religious garment subtly suggested itself beneath her blouse. He knew this meant that the woman had been married in the LDS temple. How could he not have noticed her

when he sat down? She seemed to be quietly working on some genealogy forms. Her half-glasses were about to slip off her nose. She, too,
was in her own world.

The flight attendant handed Jim gin and tonic water with a
lime that he had requested. The flowered lady had orange juice and
ignored Jim as he had her.

"I hate bigotry, racial or religious, but now I am guilty of
stereotyping her and making deprecating judgments before I have
even spoken to her." He decided he needed to do something. He
always thought of himself as a gregarious and loving person, but the
recent events of the past had changed him. He hadn't told a joke to
anyone in a long time. And now, this seemingly wholesome woman
next to him was full of repressed hostility. "Why?" Jim pondered.
"What would Uncle Andy ask me about my feelings, as if I were a kid
back on the ranch?" Jim mused.

Jim turned to the flowered lady and asked, "I couldn't help but
notice that you were working on genealogy. Does that take as much
work as people say it does?"

The flowered lady smiled broadly and said, "Yes, I suppose it
does. It's kind of like making a patchwork quilt. You gather little
scraps of material from all of your relatives and weave them into a
fabric that makes you feel all warm inside. It's worth it."

Jim and the lady talked the rest of the way to Salt Lake City,
sharing some of their families' histories with one another. Jim philos-
ophized that if he could always concentrate on the positive qualities
of other people instead of their differences, he would be a happier
person, and so would they. If only people could set aside their polar-
ized religious, ethnic, political or other prejudiced mindsets and see
the inner human being of their fellows, the world would be much
better. It would be like physical exercise—once it became routine, it
would grow on people.

The lights of Salt Lake Valley could be seen below, adding their luster to the clear night. Various hues blended to beautify the area, Jim thought. It was symbolic of what tolerance could mean to people everywhere. If only humans could just stop killing one another long enough to try to see each other's light.

Chapter 19
Tehran—Days 15–17

To Laleh, the hours in prison had seemed like a lifetime. Now it was Eid Fir, a holiday on the last day of Ramadan, the Muslim month of fasting.

Mrs. Bazargan insisted that Laleh eat her lunch as she brandished a cleaning rag like a foil near her. "Were you fasting in prison?" Laleh's mother inquired impatiently.

Laleh, puzzled, looked at her mother pensively. Her mother knew that Laleh had never fasted in her adult life. Laleh knew her mother wanted to know if she had been forced to fast or just pretended to fast.

"I didn't want to be whipped one hundred lashes, so I went on a diet," Laleh responded with her beautiful smile, betrayed only by the sadness in her eyes. As she looked at her surroundings, her deceased father's picture caught her gaze.

"Laleh, I understand, we both miss your father even more at times like these," her mother consoled in a gentle voice. Mrs. Bazargan remembered Laleh's innocent look when she was only a little two-year-old girl. She and Laleh's father, Mohandes Bazargan, Engineer Bazargan, had to answer their daughter's question candidly about where they had met.

She had replied, "I met your father when we were locked together in a bakery shop during the 1963 religious upheaval led by the Ayatollah Khomeini. Father and I had to seek refuge quickly. We hid in the bakery. The Ayatollah Khomeini led the opposition to the Shah's agrarian reforms and the law giving women the right to vote. A year later, he was sent into exile in Iraq."

When Laleh was twelve years old, the Shah had commanded that a celebration be made of the 2,500th anniversary of the Iranian Kings. Mr. Bazargan had said, "The *New York Times* reported that the Shah spent one hundred million dollars for the event while citizens went hungry!"

Then she recalled when Laleh was twenty years old—eight years later—there had been a celebration for the "Restoration of Iran to Imperial Greatness." It was soon converted into the Celebration of The Islamic Revolution. It was February 1979, when the Ayatollah Khomeini led the revolution from exile. The images of hostility raged in her memory.

Those memories were too painful, so she allowed more pleasant visions to come into her mind. The decade of the Iranian oil boom, 1963 to 1973, under the Shah, were great years for the Bazargan family. They had been able to purchase their own house. They had been able to send their children to private schools. Both Laleh and Sonbol had completed their university education in Iran. Sonbol obtained a degree in art and Laleh had been fortunate to get her medical degree in Oxford, England. Sonbol had been active in student demonstrations against the Shah's policies and had made her a target of his assassins, but she was a heroine on campus.

Then her mood darkened again as she remembered that Laleh's brother, Amir, and her sister, Narges, hadn't been able to participate in the higher education system. Laleh's brother and sister couldn't pass the Islamic test for being admitted to the Islamic university. They could not demonstrate that the family had any Shahid (martyr) history. Laleh was softly crying. Her mother groomed Laleh's hair with her fingers and patted her softly as she continued to remember the past.

During the trying times, the other qualifying students enjoyed the Worldly Shawhadat Benefits. They included free housing, education and health benefits for the Shohadas. The Shohadas, Shadid families who had lost a family member to the Iran-Iraq war, had all the advantages.

184

Laleh's father was so very certain that his children with university degrees would automatically become government employees or have other good jobs. The degrees would always guarantee them a secure future. But it only proved to be a beautiful dream that was gone with the wind of change in Iran. Their son, Amir, after finishing his two years of mandatory military service, was still unemployed.

Her thoughts shifted again as she thought of Laleh's future and her own past. Laleh's mother still repressed the hostile memories of Mohandes forcing her to have unprotected sex, which led to a fourth pregnancy. The ancient traditions demanded at least one son be born. That was the most important and prestigious element that could be met by a religious family, She hated it! Where was the love?

Mrs. Bazargan's recollections were interrupted when she heard Amir say, "Laleh, your colleague, Dr. Tabatabai, called you from the Imam Khomeini Hospital while you were gone."

"What did he say? Did he leave any messages?" Laleh inquired.

"No, he was returning your call. He was happy to hear that you were back from the United States and asked when you would be back to work," replied Amir.

"You didn't tell him that I had been arrested, did you?" Laleh inquired anxiously.

"No. I honestly could not tell him anything, as I was not sure what you were doing. I wasn't sure that you were under arrest and he did not ask."

"Well, I need to contact him as soon as possible. There are a lot of important things that I need to discuss with him. I have the feeling that the government soon will be interfering with my practice. If they start asking questions and raising suspicions at the hospital, I may lose my job as Infectious Disease Specialist," Laleh anguished.

"What do you mean?" Narges asked.

"I think they are going to make trouble for me. The type of questions they asked me and the way they asked them convinced me that I am vulnerable. I have done nothing wrong, but it seems that the influenza A virus has become a serious political matter. It is no longer just a scientific challenge to do proper research and save lives.

"It is so unfortunate how beneficial health science can become corrupted. It can be transformed into something destructive and dangerous. Remember the betrayal of Einstein's research and the consequent advent of the atomic bomb? This reminds me of discussions with Dr. Schriver about the nidus, or nest of creation. Both bad and good things can originate from the same source. It depends on the motives of human beings.

"I believe that we must find a way as soon as possible to make a vaccine, before it is too late. We must do as the Romans said in Latin, Carpe Diem, or *seize the day*. The whole international community needs this vaccine, not just Iran."

Laleh realized that she had been preaching. She rose to her feet again to make a phone call. She dialed 930040. The number was busy so she tried 930041. She finally got through after almost giving up in her impatience.

"Allo, Bimarestan Imam Khomeini, Dr. Tabatabai lotfan." Hello, Imam Khomeini Hospital, may I talk to Dr. Tabatabai, please?

"Allo?" Dr. Tabatabai answered.

"Allo, Yusef, Salam, Laleh-am." Hello, Yusef, this is Laleh.

"Salam, Laleh jon, Kojai Khanum? Chetori?" Hello, Dear Laleh, where have you been? How are you? Dr. Tabatabai inquired with concern.

"I am fine now. Yusef, how is your schedule tomorrow? I'd like to stop by and see you. Maybe we can have lunch together," Laleh suggested.

"Well, I am not so busy tomorrow that I can't change my schedule for you. I would like to see you very much. Why did it take so long for you to call me back? I have been concerned; are you okay?" Yusef inquired.

"I'm all right. I am anxious to see you tomorrow," responded Laleh.

"I can make time to see you at eleven. Please meet me at my office and we will go to lunch from there. Oh, by the way, tomorrow is the twenty-second of Bahman. The Anniversary of the Islamic Revolution Celebration is one of the hospital's holidays now. I will work for only a few hours in the morning. Ask Amir to give you a ride to the hospital and I will take you home. Oh yes, please give my regards to your mother," said Dr. Tabatabai.

"Thank you, I will see you then. Good-bye," Laleh replied.

The next day Amir dutifully agreed to drive Laleh to the Imam Khomeini Hospital. As they drove from Argentine square to Vali Asr street, the tulips were beginning to bloom along the roadway. It was a beautiful day, with the spring waters converging in streams down the gutters.

When they turned on Dr. Hossein Fatemi Street and past Laleh Park, she remembered that as a teenager she liked to drive down Fatemi Street for that reason—she would tell anyone who would listen that it was her park. Today, the park was very crowded. Many people had gathered there to celebrate the anniversary of the Islamic revolution.

Laleh inquired, "Amir, have you noticed how many parks we have seen built since the revolution?"

"Yes, thanks to Tehran's mayor, Mr. Karbaschi. You know, Laleh, I am impressed with him. This mayor has done so many positive things for this city, just as he did for Esfahan where he was also mayor. His effort to make Tehran colorful with flowers and green with vegetation in the parks has been as noticeable as the high-rise buildings and roads he has developed. Just his facilitation of the transportation system is amazing. However, many people do not like him or appreciate his efforts. I heard a joke that you should never stoop over around him, or he'll plant another flower," said Ami, chuckling.

"I wish people would learn that the public places are like their own houses and together we all make the whole village. Everything is part of them and they are part of everything," Laleh commented. "Why can't they see that the whole universe is a circle of life? If you love yourself, you are able to love everything around you. You respect everything around you and appreciate it. It's that simple!"

Laleh paused. Amir gave her a look out of the corner of his eye. "I know what you are thinking, 'Laleh's on her soap box again,'" Laleh laughed. "But, sometimes I get angrier at ourselves than I do at the government. If we have someone like Mr. Karbaschi, who cares about beauty and the cleanliness of the city, people should congratulate him. Unfortunately, they don't see the parks as their own. They refer to them as his parks. That explains why you see so much trash—sunflower seed husks, orange peels, cigarette butts, and food wrappers, even though there are trash containers everywhere," Laleh observed.

Amir chose to add his thoughts. "Also, people get angry at Mr. Karbaschi because he levies fines, which forces the people to protect the public facilities and respect the laws and regulations. Remember several years ago when a group burned some buses to protest his actions? His reaction was unique. He simply said that if they burned their own buses he would just tax and fine them to purchase new buses. He told them that they would be the ones paying for their mistakes."

"However, I believe that cultural poverty evolves out of economic poverty and contributes to the people's actions," exclaimed Laleh.

While Amir and Laleh were discussing Tehran's cultural poverty, a pedestrian jumped in front of their car, attempting to cross the street. Amir had to take evasive action by maneuvering the car to the right side, locking the brakes and stalling the engine. Laleh pitched forward, her head hitting the windshield. "Did you hit him?" Laleh inquired as she rubbed her forehead.

"No, I missed him, but it was close. That stupid fool did not even see us coming. I wonder if he is one of those people who try to make drivers believe that they have been hit and injured so that they can get some money?" Amir responded. "I am still shaking; how is your head?"

"If we had been going faster I would have had a severe injury. It's nothing now but a small swelling. I will be all right," Laleh answered. "It's a shame that in Iran seat belts are not used or are missing."

Amir turned the car into Yusefi Street. The double-decker buses passed them with billowing diesel exhaust that invaded everyone's eyes and nose. "No wonder Tehran is one of the most polluted cities in the world," commented Amir.

Laleh remembered, "I rode the buses with mother when we went to the bazaar shopping. I loved to sit on the top deck in the front row seat before the revolution. It made me feel like I was riding on a vehicle with no driver. The sense of freedom and abandon made me imagine what it might be like to ride a motorcycle—which, of course, father would never allow me to do."

She wished out loud. "Our whole lives could have such freedom—no constantly enraged pious drivers who hate women who can drive. I would like to see buses that have no bars dividing the front from the rear—no rules that women must ride in the back of the buses, enforced by the revolutionary guards."

She paused and looked at Amir. "It reminds me of the Afro-American segregation that used to exist in the United States. Anti-female prejudice is rampant in this Muslim country. It is a major insult, yet I hope that our country will change, as did the United States. There is so much change that is needed everywhere for women. I would change even the Islamic Law that insists that women must be seated behind a curtain in Allah's house—the Mosque."

Laleh then wondered, "Will Faezeh Hashemi, the Majlis Deputy and daughter of President Rafsanjani, have to sit in the back of a bus or sit in the back seats of the Islamic Parliament?" She quoted Ms. Hashemi, "Men always have been the main scholars of Islam, interpreting Islamic laws and implementing these interpretations. Only men have manipulated Islamic laws during history, corrupting them to secure their own interests."

Laleh wondered what Islamic rationale would be offered as an explanation for other obvious violations of female rights.

Amir, amused by Laleh's gender questions, turned into the parking area of the Imam Khomeini's Hospital. "Do you want me to go in with you?" he asked.

"No, thanks. I will see you at home. I am sure that Dr. Tabatabai will take me home," responded Laleh.

Laleh went directly to Dr. Tabatabai's office. The bright, modern hospital was busier than usual because of an influx of patients with special problems caused by a recent earthquake in western Iran. This hospital was the most prestigious and best staffed and equipped in the country.

Dr. Tabatabai's corner office looked out upon beautiful, well-kept grounds. As she walked the long halls, Laleh became introspective. Why did she trust him so much? What made him such a close friend? Perhaps it was his prematurely gray hair. Dr. Tabatabai was a surgeon of about forty years old, nice looking and financially secure. He had been instrumental in advocating Laleh's inclusion on the hospital staff. Because of his politically powerful position, she was accepted without opposition. Laleh thought maybe she saw him as a surrogate father—one to replace her real father who had been so protective of her before he died, or maybe like an older, mature brother. Laleh pondered and realized that she could not sort out how or why she trusted him so much.

When Laleh opened his door, Dr. Tabatabai jumped up from his desk. "Hello, Dear Laleh. How are you?" Dr. Tabatabai said with unusual emotion. An observer might have guessed that he was in love with Laleh, yet cautious. His restraint to express his love for her was driven by the fear that he might lose her friendship if he was too direct.

"Hi Yusef, I am fine. How are you? How is everything?" Laleh inquired as she hugged him. The touching was certainly not the usual habit of Islamic men and women associated professionally, but Laleh felt he was like a family member. Yusef struggled with his feelings.

"There has not been much news since you were gone," Yusef said. "We are still understaffed and our shortage of beds is acute. There is more work than we have time to do, and not enough money to meet our goals.

"I don't want to give you a headache your first day back. Let's go somewhere, perhaps to a nice restaurant and then perhaps a walk in the park. I want to know all about your trip to the United States. I want to hear about your conference, how your talk was received, the places you visited and the sights you saw. Everything," said Dr. Tabatabai.

Laleh sat back in her chair, not moving. Tears reflected like small, shiny pearls down her cheeks. "I do not want to be arrested again. I don't want to get you in trouble either. We are neither related nor married to each other. It would be too risky now to go to a public park to talk—no matter how innocent it might be. My brother Amir was arrested several times in the park just because he was walking with his female friend. Once we even had to pretend that the girl was his fiancee," Laleh explained.

"What do you mean arrested again? What has happened to you? Is that why you did not return my calls sooner? Amir did not tell me you were arrested. Why were you arrested?" Yusef stammered. His concern was genuine and it showed in his face.

Laleh took a long, deep breath and wiped her tears. "Let's go to my house. We can talk safely there. I can't go to your home. Gossip might get back to some revolutionary guard. Being single is hell in this country! We will be safe there; my mother is at home. We can have lunch in peace there. Actually, she suggested that we might consider that. Now I realize that I am happy that she did," said Laleh.

"I'd love that, Laleh."

As Dr. Tabatabai drove, Laleh told him about the conference and how her paper was received. She told him about the extra trip to the British Virgin Islands and her conversation with Ben Carlson, the marketing director of Alpha Omega Pharmaceutical Company. She stressed the verbal agreement with Ben to work toward an international contract to produce a vaccine for the unique influenza A virus. She reminded Yusef that Alpha Omega had dealt successfully with other deadly viruses to make good vaccines.

"This all sounds like good news, wonderful information. What I don't understand is, why were you arrested?" Dr. Tabatabai inquired.

Laleh explained. "When we took the cruise to the British Virgin Islands, for a short while we had a great time. Much was accomplished, especially an agreement of all the doctors attending that we should work together to lobby for the vaccine against the dangerous virus. When we reached Norman Island, some of us decided to go snorkeling into the ocean caves there. It was beautiful—clean, crystal clear water. I had never in my life seen such colorful fish before—and in such abundance."

Dr. Tabatabai interrupted Laleh. "Weren't you afraid then that someone would report you to the revolutionary guard because you were in a swimsuit and snorkeling with men who were not relatives?"

His facetious and somewhat sarcastic remark did not go unnoticed by Laleh. "Please, Yusef, this is serious. Somehow I believe that someone did report me. Maybe they have spies there, too."

"I am sorry, please forgive me for the interruption. Then what happened?" replied Yusef.

"Claire, Edward, Jim, Paul'le and I went back to the caves a second time and the others stayed on the sailing ship. It was then, while we were away, that suddenly out of nowhere, the ship exploded. They have not been able to locate any of those who were on the ship when it exploded. I don't know if Sonbol survived or not."

"Oh Laleh, I did hear that news. My nurse told me that she

heard it on CNN. I thought I heard that several people did survive. However, I did not watch it myself. I did not know that it was your ship! I can't tell you the names of any of the survivors. I must believe, though, that I would have remembered Sonbol's name. I will ask my nurse tomorrow if she can recall any of the names."

"The story does not end here," continued Laleh. "When I arrived at Mehrabad airport they told me that I would have to report to the Islamic Revolutionary Court of Justice. I went there the next day. They kept me in Evin prison for several hours and interrogated me about my trip and my research with the virus. Finally, on Eid Fetr, they released me."

"That means yesterday, when you called me," replied Yusef.

"That is correct," Laleh confirmed.

"Here we are at your home. How much do your mother and your family know about all of this?" Dr. Tabatabai inquired.

"They know everything," replied Laleh.

Yusef parked his Mercedes Benz and they walked toward the front door. Laleh's mother liked Dr. Tabatabai very much. She had always wished and prayed that these two angels would marry each other. Every time she approached the subject, Laleh would refuse to talk about it. Mrs. Bazargan believed that Dr. Tabatabai could make Laleh happy. He was well-educated and financially secure. Sometimes Laleh's mother felt that the old way of parents arranging a marriage was best after all.

To Laleh, Yusef was just a good family friend.

As they approached the front door, Mrs. Bazargan opened the door to greet them. "Hello, Doctor, how are you?"

"Hello, Mrs. Bazargan, I am fine, thank you. How are you?" responded Yusef.

"Fine. Please come in. Have a seat." Mrs. Bazargan gestured to a chair that had been her husband's favorite. "Would you like some Maulshair—Islamic beer?"

"Yes, please. Thanks for your hospitality." Yusef replied.

Mrs. Bazargan left the room and Dr. Tabatabai addressed Laleh. "What is next? What are your plans? I hope you know that you can always count on me. I will help in any way I can." Yusef felt the moment. He perceived that he could now rationalize trying to become emotionally close to Laleh. She was desperate and he was there for her, he thought.

"Well, I do appreciate your concern, Yusef. But at this moment I feel brainless. I need some time to set my priorities and become more focused. I must first concentrate on Sonbol. I must call Dr. Jim Schriver in the United States. He promised me he would do all he could to find Sonbol. Second, I need to determine if Alpha Omega Pharmaceutical executives will honor the proposal Dr. Ben Carlson made before his untimely death. When we were on board the *Maverick* he agreed with my proposal that we should involve the World Health Organization, and obtain their confirmation of a need to make a vaccine from the virus that I have isolated. The next step that we agreed to was that the WHO would be allowed equal access to the virus to produce vaccine concomitantly with Alpha Omega. I believe Alpha Omega has a competitive edge because of the magnitude of both facilities and staff."

Laleh began to pace. "I have heard unsubstantiated rumors from patients who were in Afghanistan on business. An influenza epidemic might be developing in Afghanistan, if what they have told me is true. Some of the CNS (central nervous system) symptomatology reported makes me wonder if they might have a virus infection similar to the influenza A that I have been working with. I feel morally obligated to abide in principle with the concept that this should be an international effort. But, we have an imminent responsibility to protect the citizens of our own country first and I feel we should start developing a vaccine, by ourselves, right now. We can work with the international community later.

"I have not been able to communicate with Alpha Omega or my friend Jim Schriver, and time is running out. Perhaps we will be able to expedite Alpha Omega's efforts with our experience. By the time the bureaucracies of the various countries move to production authorization, it will be too late for us. Yusef, I need your help to do that. Will you support me with this project?" Laleh requested with confidence.

"Laleh, I will do whatever I can to assist you. You have my commitment. I will contact a friend of mine at the Tehran University of Medical Science. His name is Dr. Azar. He represents Iran in the World Health Organization. In fact, maybe it would be helpful if you went with me to see him," suggested Dr. Tabatabai.

"Thank you, that is a good idea. I would like to do that after I produce a small pilot plant vaccine that could actually be tested for potency. There is so much happening right now that concerns me. I feel a great sense of urgency to at least start a pilot project prior to talking to him. You have heard it expressed, a bird in hand is worth two in the bush," said Laleh.

Yusef nodded in agreement.

"We could produce adequate quantities of attenuated live virus to test potency. We could do the pilot project using the Soviet method. The soviets used an attenuated live virus vaccine, which would be more effective and quicker for our situation. We could use fertile duck eggs, and I know a good supplier of duck eggs locally who will work with me. Fertile chicken eggs are also available, but have had some problems with contamination with certain avian viruses and low yield. We could make a nasal spray vaccine. It would be easy to instill nasal spray into test animals such as birds, horses, ferrets or swine. Of course, swine are not very available in this country.

"We can use some of the sterile empty containers that we used for an older combined A and B Russian Federation vaccine. They were surplus from a cooperative study we did with them a couple of years ago. We could then take the plasma specimens from the test animals and inoculate rhesus monkey kidney, cynomolgus monkey kidney or Madin-Darby canine kidney cell cultures. We would detect virus by the cytopathic effect or hemadsorption. In the second week after infection, subjects experiencing primary infection with influenza virus, develop antibody. The antibody could be detected with neutralizing, hemagglutination-inhibiting (HAI), complement-fixing (CF), enzyme-linked immunosorbent assay (ELISA), and/or immunofluorescent antibodies in serum.

"We will also need a supply of amantadine or rimantadine to use in emergency treatment of personnel who become accidentally exposed. These drugs have been 70 to 90 percent effective in preventing illnesses of some known strains of type A influenza viruses. We would assume that one or the other might have some effect in an emergency."

Dr. Tabatabai said, "Perhaps Dr. Azar could be of some assistance in selecting which of these tests would be most cost-effective or efficacious. This is clearly out of my field of expertise, Laleh. I can only give you morale and political help with some of the hospital committees. But I marvel at your ambition."

"I would be so very grateful if you could help me with the political assistance in the hospital committees. It would greatly boost my morale if I did not have to worry about such things and could just concentrate on my job," said Laleh. "I can use the funding left over from some other projects to do this pilot project. In that way I won't need to go before any committee to beg for funding. I would rather plead for forgiveness than for permission."

"That is very risky, Laleh," Dr. Tabatabai cautioned.

"It's worth the risk. I truly believe that people on a peer review committee, presented with a successful vaccine, would understand. Once they saw the good that could be done, they would authorize reimbursing me for the funds that I borrowed from other accounts," Laleh postulated.

"Laleh, that is very risky and complicated. What would you have me do?" Yusef queried.

"Initially I would just appreciate some privacy in my lab. The fewer people who know what I am doing, the better. If you could just intercept intruders, that would be all I could ask. If I could dodge some of the hospital meetings so that I did not have to compromise my work by answering prying questions, I know that I could succeed in producing a test vaccine. Would that be too much to ask of you, Yusef?" Laleh requested.

Dr. Tabatabai instinctively knew that he was way out on a limb. He knew he wouldn't even consider such legal exposure if anyone else had dared to ask such a favor. But, this seemed to be a test of his true affection for Laleh. He would have to take the risk. "Laleh, my heart will not let me do anything except help you. I am sure intellectually neither of us would normally consider such circumvention of protocol. But to take such risks with you seems so right and exciting. My common sense has surrendered to your desires."

Laleh took his hand in both of hers and said, "You won't regret this decision, Dear Yusef." Yusef expected a more amorous response. Instead, it was a warm response that any woman might gratefully give to a brother.

Laleh sensed his partial feeling of rejection and compensated with a final gesture of brushing her hand slowly on his face while saying, "Thank you so much, Yusef."

Fortunately, at that moment Laleh's mother bustled into the room with a tray of cups of Iranian beer. There followed a plethora of small talk. Eventually it became evident that the intimate discussion was over and that it was time for Yusef to depart. "I should return to my office, Laleh. I will stay in contact with you and if you need anything, anything at all, I am at your service," Dr. Tabatabai concluded.

Laleh and her mother walked Yusef to the door to bid him farewell. Mrs. Bazargan bubbled with misconceptions of Laleh and Yusef's relationship. She did not listen to anything Laleh had to say about the matter. She could tell what Yusef felt. "Mothers have special intuition about such matters," Mrs. Bazargan often said as

197

Laleh insisted on trying to correct her.

The next day was the first day of Hajj. The ritual pilgrimage, or Hajj, to Mecca in Saudi Arabia, is a duty for every Muslim once in his lifetime.

Dr. Tabatabai was anxiously walking up and down in his office while holding a cordless phone to his ear. He had attempted to reach Dr. Azar at the virology section in the infectious disease department of the Tehran University of Medical Sciences. He rechecked the FAX number, +98(21)6462267.

Dr. Tabatabai had sent two messages, both the same. "Urgent, please contact me concerning my request to have a meeting with you. Yours, Tabatabai." There was still no answer on the telephone either.

Yusef began to fear that Laleh and he may have waited too long to communicate. Dr. Azar might have gone to Mecca this year to perform his Hajj. Dr. Tabatabai sat down at his desk feeling frustrated. The phone rang once before Yusef answered.

"Hello, Yusef. I am sorry I couldn't get back to you sooner, we had some very urgent concerns. Are you all right—anything wrong?" Dr. Azar inquired.

"Thank you for returning my call. I am all right, but one of my associates, Dr. Bazargan, needs to see you as soon as possible," replied Dr. Tabatabai.

"Let me look at my schedule a moment. I have 10 A.M. available. Would that work?" Dr. Azar asked.

"That would be great. We will plan on seeing you at your office then. Good-bye," concluded Dr. Tabatabai.

Laleh and Dr. Tabatabai drove down Shahreza Avenue. Street vendors were hawking their fresh walnuts and plums. Laleh always loved these first-fruits—nobar. She hoped that they might buy some on the way home after their meeting. After they parked in front of the School of Public Health and the Institute of Public Health Research, they walked toward Dr. Azar's office. Laleh felt tense, but excited. They entered the office a few minutes early.

"Hello, Dr. Azar, this is my associate and friend, Dr. Bazargan," Dr. Tabatabai announced.

"Hello, Yusef. I am pleased to meet you, Dr. Bazargan. I feel like I already know you because of your research publications."

"Thank you, I am pleased to meet you also," said Laleh.

Dr. Azar was thirty-eight years old, nice looking and a successful physician. But, somehow Laleh had a peculiar feeling about him. There was something about him that did not feel comfortable.

Dr. Azar invited Laleh to describe her research.

"I have a copy of my paper that is soon to be published. I would like you, Dr. Azar, to lobby the World Health Organization to accept my data concerning the new strain of influenza A virus. It is more dangerous than the strains in the current recommended combination vaccines. I have many fears about the preliminary news coming out of Iran's eastern neighbor, Afghanistan. I am afraid that it is just a question of time until we see it all over the Mideast and finally the rest of the world!"

Dr. Azar spoke condescendingly to Laleh in an all-too-common male chauvinistic manner. "Dr. Bazargan, I know you have an emotional need to respond to such a health threat as if it were already pandemic. My wife also tends to feel as though every case of the sniffles that our children get is a portent of doom. Right now, this doesn't seem to be that urgent. Certainly not of magnitude to alert the whole world to institute a crash program. That Afghanistan virus has not been classified officially as an influenza A, much less typed to exactly which strain it is."

Dr. Azar looked at her in a patronizing manner. "This may be why only men, who are not so emotional, are entrusted with a decision of this magnitude. However, maybe you will have more information later that you will share with me that might change my opinion. Is there any other data that you may have neglected to include?" Dr. Azar baited Laleh.

Laleh struggled to keep her composure; she knew that this man was critical to securing the authority to manufacture the vaccine in her country. Tactfully she responded, "I can understand your reticence to make the same mistake that the Americans made in 1976 with the swine influenza vaccine. But, I ask if it is prudent to wait until we can conclusively prove that the Afghanistan virus is the virus that I identified? Wouldn't it be better to at least start preparing a vaccine? No large-scale production would need to take place until the conclusive evidence was in," Laleh argued.

Laleh resisted the temptation to tell Dr. Azar that she already had proved to herself that the vaccine would be safe in select animals. Yet, human evaluation was another story. She wouldn't reveal that she had worked on a vaccine before the conference. Dr.Yusef Tabatabai sat biting his tongue and waiting for Laleh to reveal the information she had said originally would be the key to Azar's support. Laleh sat waiting for Azar's rebuttal.

Azar looked at Yusef sensing that he was swallowing words without a sound. The awkward silence seemed to speak to Laleh. Yusef had obviously communicated with Dr. Azar without her knowledge, and this was the clandestine result! This had been one of those "man-to-man" privileged conversations. She was furious with her conclusion. She looked from one man to the other. It was obvious to her that they didn't know what to say.

Finally Azar spoke. "Dr. Bazargan, I may have been premature. Perhaps if we could test your virus here in this lab, I might get a greater appreciation of its virulence. Also, we could do some immunology comparisons with one or two Afghani patients who have recovered from the current epidemic. I feel that this approach would be the most prudent for us to take at this time. Why don't I send over a courier with a proper virus-safe container to collect a specimen of your alleged Parkinson's disease-causing influenza A virus? Say— next Monday at 9 A.M.?"

Laleh immediately stood. Yusef was startled and attempted to join her in an upright posture, not knowing what she might do or say.

"I will consider your proposition and call you tomorrow," said Laleh.

She said nothing else—much to Yusef's dismay. He knew her well enough to realize that she might pick up Dr. Azar's fish bowl that both of her hands were resting on and pitch it at either one of them. She glared at Yusef's guilty face. He quickly made excuses for Laleh as he followed a few steps behind her. She marched out of Azar's office and immediately went to a public telephone.

"Who are you calling?" Yusef blurted.

"I am requesting one of the three hundred taxis-for-women-only here in Tehran. It seems only fitting, that as a woman, I should 'enjoin the lawful and prohibit from the unlawful, as the Revolutionary Guard describes it," Laleh said angrily.

"Laleh, you do not understand the politics of these matters," said Yusef in obvious admission of his conspiracy. "You asked me to assist you in political matters and this was a choice that I had to make for you," he continued defensively. "You should be grateful to have such a broadminded man for your friend. What other man do you know would have taken the chances that I have for you, a woman?"

"I can't believe what I am hearing," Laleh screamed. "Now, I am but a mere woman!" She turned her back on him. "I expected better from you, Yusef, you have been a close friend. I felt like a sister or daughter to you."

It was a severe cut to Yusef's ego and a shock of reality that he didn't expect. "That's what you thought of me? That's what you think of me? It is just as well that you take the taxi!"

He turned on his heel and headed for the parking lot and his car. Laleh stood rubbing her temples. She feared that she had lost a good and powerful friend.

The taxi would not arrive for forty-five minutes.

Chapter 20
University Medical Center-Day 18

Ed waited impatiently for Jim Schriver to answer his page. Ed had been researching data for his presentation on epidemiology for the week's infectious disease conference that was being held for all the board-certified infectious disease physicians who practiced in the State of Utah. That meant that most of the specialists would be coming to the University of Utah for a luncheon meeting. Infection Control Nurses and Infectious Disease Pharmacists would also attend this special academic session. Ed had discovered information he knew Jim wanted to be aware of prior to that meeting.

"Hello, this is Jim Schriver."

"Jim, this is Ed. I just picked up some data from the World Health Organization. They are reporting an epidemic of influenza A in Afghanistan that seems to be other than A(H1N1) or A(H3N2). As you know, that means that the current vaccine might not be effective against it. It seems to be a new virulent strain with a lot of morbidity and mortality. I have been in touch with the CDC in Atlanta and they also say there have been reports of unusual CNS activity reported. The central nervous system symptoms include Parkinsonism syndrome. They haven't typed its H or N designation yet, however."

"Really!" said Jim. "Afghanistan is the eastern neighbor of Iran. I wonder if there is any connection?"

"The data is very thin," said Ed. "Also, do you remember anything about the Iranians experimenting with a nasal spray immunization perfected by the Russians just a while back?"

"All that I remember is that it was to be an attenuated live-virus vaccine. They forced the virus to grow in other animals so that it would change to adapt to critters other than humans and not be as virulent when it was reintroduced to humans. The final form was a nasal spray. The idea was to have a more effective vaccine than one that used killed virus," responded Jim.

"Precisely! All of the vaccine in the U.S. is made from killed virus, because of the concern that there could potentially be more problems with side effects," said Ed.

"It seems that someone in Iran might be using the Russian technique to develop a nasal influenza vaccine against the new A-influenza virus. The single WHO Iranian physician representative denies that any new virus has been typed in their country to produce either virus or vaccine. Other sources have rumored that an Iranian physician secured a contract for fertilized duck eggs. No mention of fertilized chicken's eggs like the U.S.A. Doesn't that sound familiar? There's no way to determine if Laleh's Tehran virus might have been the one included in the live virus vaccine. I got a friend at the CDC to talk off the record that he also believes that the Afghanistan virus is the same as the Iranian virus! Have you heard anything from Laleh yet?"

"I haven't heard a thing yet, and I am getting very concerned," said Jim. "I don't know what to think. None of the phone numbers seem to work and she hasn't responded to any of my letters. I wish I had an e-mail address or Internet location that would work in Tehran to check on her. I'm going to talk to one of my Iranian students here and ask him to try and get a message through to Laleh. I will let you know ASAP," said Jim.

Jim decided to change the subject. "What do you plan to include in your lecture?"

"I'll probably give a brief review for the usual audience plus a few medical students, nurses and pharmacists that the chairman invited. I'll explain that the subtypes of A viruses are designated by H for hemagglutinin and N neuraminidase, the two different viral proteins. That will help everyone to understand the system for labeling."

"I'll remind everyone that influenza type A viruses undergo two kinds of changes. One is a series of mutations that occur over time and cause a gradual evolution of the virus. This is called antigenic drift. The other kind of change is an abrupt change in the hemagglutinin and/or the neuraminidase proteins. This is called antigenic shift. In this case, a new subtype of the virus suddenly emerges. Type A viruses undergo both kinds of changes; influenza type B viruses change only by the more gradual process of antigenic drift. That will explain what the vaccine labels A(H1N1) and A(H3N2) mean that were included in the U.S. marketed vaccine in 1996–97. The formula is actually: A/Wuhan/359/95(H3N2) plus A/Singapore/6/86(H1N1) and B/Beijing/184/93. I'll remind them that there are about eighty countries that participate in WHO to collaborate in selecting a formula each year."

"Sounds like a good start for a broad audience," said Jim.

"I'm also going to include a brief epidemiological history of human influenza. I'll read you what I've got so far: Influenza A and B viruses continually undergo antigenic drift. This process accounts for most of the changes that occur from one influenza season to another. Antigenic shift occurs only occasionally. When it does occur, large numbers of people have no antibody protection against the virus. This results in a worldwide epidemic, called a pandemic. During this century, pandemics occurred in 1918, 1957, and 1968, each of which resulted in a large number of deaths:

"1918–19: "Spanish flu" A(H1N1)—Caused the highest known influenza-related mortality.

"1957–58: "Asian flu" A(H2N2)—70,000 deaths in the United States.

"1968–69: "Hong-Kong flu" A(H3N2)—34,000 deaths in the United States.

"Influenza viruses continually change over time, usually by mutation. This constant changing enables the virus to evade the immune system of its host, so that people are susceptible to influenza virus infection throughout life. This process works as follows: a person infected with influenza virus develops antibody against that virus; as the virus changes, the 'older' antibody no longer recognizes the 'newer' virus, and reinfection can occur. The older antibody can, however, provide partial protection against reinfection for some people.

"Soon we will be entering the next century; what do you think are civilization's odds on encountering another pandemic influenza virus?" Ed took a breath and waited for Jim's response.

"Ed, I think you are right on course with this review. I thought of only one subject that you didn't cover. . . . You might emphasize that all this drift and shift is natural evolution of the influenza viruses without any artificial genetic manipulation. Some of the students may miss the point," added Jim. "It sounds like the start of an interesting lecture. If you need any of my slides, you are welcome . . ."

"Thanks Jim, I'll probably borrow some—especially if you can get anything new from Laleh."

Ed concluded their conversation by discussing Claire's recovery. "She's doing fine now. No problem with short-term memory and ibuprofen is all she needs for the discomfort. She's still got some psychological problems, relative to driving, and she gets an occasional panic attack in the middle of the night. Trying to sleep with an Aspen neck brace on is not the best for sound sleep. Physically she's doing okay. I'll tell her you asked."

"Hey! Jim, I almost forgot something. You may not remember Claire's little waterproof camera. Well guess what . . . I finally took her film to be processed and you won't believe what she had a picture of," Ed said with excitement.

"I'm all ears," Jim replied.

"When we were in that little port at Tortola, Claire took some pictures. One picture was of our group all gathered on the ship for a group picture. In the background a seaplane is banking for a turn to land on the water."

"Don't tell me—it looked like the same one that buzzed us that night," Jim responded.

"Right on! You've got to see it and tell me what you think," said Ed.

"Can you see any markings or numbers with a magnifying glass?" inquired Jim.

"That's why I want you to look at it. I don't want to jump to the wrong conclusion."

"Okay—I'll meet you at lunch in the hospital cafeteria by the windows. I'm excited," said Jim.

The sun was reflecting off the snow-capped Oquirrh Mountains west of Salt Lake City and the lower campus buildings were outlined by beautiful evergreens. Being located high on the hillside gave the hospital a prominent position over the rest of the campus. The hospital cafeteria's view would be hard to beat anywhere. Mexican fiesta music was playing over the P.A. system to accompany the food entrees offered that day. The aroma of fried onions and peppers stimulated everyone's appetite. Considering the usual quality of hospital chow, this was quite a feast.

Jim had arrived a little early to obtain a window table, and he had brought a magnifying glass to inspect the colored prints Ed was bringing. Jim looked toward the interior of the cafeteria and saw Claire's wheelchair being wheeled in carefully with her tray filled with food. Her posture was stiff and deliberate. The rigid, padded Aspen collar reminded her of her vulnerability. Her nurse's aide relinquished the navigation of the chair to Jim.

Jim stood up and scurried to assist Claire. "Claire, I'm so glad you feel good enough to join us for lunch." Jim gave her a gentle hug, took her tray and guided her to a seat. "Are you supposed to be carrying this stuff?" Jim inquired.

"Jim, you have no idea how happy I am to be able to walk and do this. Just think of Christopher Reeve's accident. I may not be Super Woman, but I know how lucky I am. Today is a special day for me, to carry my own tray for lunch. I have a weight limit, but what little I eat is not a problem for me to carry, especially if I indulge myself by riding a wheelchair. Have you found a place to live yet?"

"I'm still a resident of the hotel. I guess I'm still in shock from all that has happened and can't face anything else yet. But thanks for your concern."

"No news from Laleh yet?" Claire inquired.

"Afraid not," Jim responded dejectedly.

Ed came through the crowd with his tray full of fajitas and side dishes. "What a beautiful day, my two favorite people and a fiesta meal. The one thing we are each missing is a frozen margarita. Did you show him the pictures yet, Claire?"

"I just got here," said Claire. She fished the photos from her jacket pocket and handed them to Jim. Claire and Ed seemed pensive as they waited for Jim's response.

"Boy, I don't know. Even with this magnifying glass I can only make out a letter N and perhaps a number 5. They weren't banking enough to read the wing very well and the sun is reflecting off the rest of the aircraft. But, that's something. We should be able to get somebody who's a pilot or someone who knows such things to tell us what kind of plane it is. I think it looks similar to the one we saw that night."

Ed asked Jim, "What are your thoughts now, about a possible conspiracy?"

"I'm convinced those thugs that ran you two off the road were no coincidence. The fire at my apartment was the work of an arsonist, even if nobody can prove it yet. That insurance investigator knew more than he was telling us about the ship accident. The relabeled shipping carton that contained the mysterious vial that may have killed Jaynee seems to have originated from Alpha Omega."

"But, having said all of that, how do we tie it all together? The magnitude of such a conspiracy is beyond me."

"Who had the most opportunity and motive?" Ed asked.

"We have discussed all of this and are as frustrated as you are. Ed and I wonder if we are not just paranoid because of some extraordinary coincidences," Clair answered.

"Oh, my pager just went off. I'll have to get back to critical care. Sorry, but I have to run," Ed said, looking expectantly to Claire.

"I can find my way back to my office. Pick me up any time you are done here tonight, I have a lot of work to catch up on. I have a couch in my office and I will take a rest this afternoon. . . . Remember, the doctor said it won't be long and I will be driving again."

"Spike—don't overdo it," Eddie said to Claire. He gave her a kiss and waved good-bye to Jim.

Jim finished lunch with Claire and the two rehashed conspiracy theories to no avail. He concluded, "I don't think we can seriously believe it could be our own government, just because the FBI has failed to I.D. any suspects yet. Alpha Omega may have had a motive. They may have felt Iran was a threat to them somehow. All I know is that I don't trust them. They have enough resources to do more than a small country might have the power to do."

"Jim, I see what you mean. Maybe the FBI will get something on Alpha Omega."

"Claire, I really don't know what to think about the FBI. But, I do know you need to get to your office and I to mine. Let me push you, it's on my way."

Their conversation switched to another topic when different well-wishers encountered them.

Jim returned to his office after his lunch with Claire and Ed. It was a good day to get a lot done because there were few interruptions. The first hour was very productive. Jim cleared his desk of items marked "Urgent" and was starting on "Round-to-its" when he heard cautious steps in the hall. Jim often kept his office door open and sound traveled a long way in the uncarpeted hall. Someone was alternately moving briskly and then stopping, moving briskly and stopping, but definitely getting closer.

Jim got up quietly from his seat and moved toward the open door. He thought to himself. "What do I think I'm doing?" If it was someone meaning harm he was defenseless. He had taken classes on martial arts, but this could be the real thing!

Jim elected not to close the door. He speculated that the element of surprise could work for him as well as a potential assailant. He assumed a defensive posture out of sight and adjacent to the open door. The steps came closer, using the same measured pace TV cops used when ducking in doorways with guns drawn, looking for a suspect. Suddenly a figure ducked into his doorway. Jim was ready to kick when he saw the hand, preceded by a paper flyer announcing an upcoming social event.

"Oh! Dr. Schriver! I—I didn't know you were working today," said the startled student.

"I was—ah—catching-up today." Jim said, embarrassed.

"Yeah. Well. Have a nice day." The startled student felt confused and left hurriedly.

"I am certifiably paranoid. All of our earlier discussions of the day have caused me to flip," Jim thought to himself.

Jim then remembered the picture of the seaplane. He decided to call an old retired pharmacist he knew who had been a pilot in the Air Force during WW II. Dick Davis had served in the Pacific theater and Jim thought he might help him identify their mystery plane.

"Hi Dick, this is Jim Schriver at the U. How are you?"

"Well, Boots, I haven't talked to you for years. Not since you did that clerkship in our pharmacy. To what do I owe the pleasure?"

"It's such a long story. I'll try to be brief."

Jim explained the mystery plane as best as he could. Dick quizzed him at length before he made his best guess.

"I think that there is a high probability the plane is a J.4F Widgeon, which was known as a flying-duck. It is a five-seat seaplane with two engines. Each engine was a two hundred horsepower Ranger L-440C-5. I bet that it probably was purchased from an air transport company." Dick paused to think. "It wouldn't surprise me if the plane now belongs to one of those quasi-CIA front organizations, either that or some drug runners. At any rate, I'd be willing to bet that it's not registered to some legitimate company. Any pilot that would fly with all of his lights out was definitely trying to keep a low profile."

"You don't think it was just a small commercial outfit whose pilot just forgot to turn his lights on?"

"Possibly, but not probable. Think about it. No cabin lights. No red or green wing lights. No landing lights. No indicator lights. No light of any kind," Dick challenged.

"Very interesting. I really appreciate your opinion, Dick."

"Glad someone still thinks my opinion is worth something. I hope I get to see you at our next Pharmacy CE program up there," said Dick.

"I'll look forward to that. Thanks again, Dick."

Jim was jolted by the idea that the plane might have belonged to some sinister group and not a potential Good Samaritan.

"If that is true, why were they in the same area, at the same time, as our *Maverick* disaster?" Jim asked himself.

Jim then called the Salt Lake Fire Marshal's office and talked to the secretary who had taken notes regarding the apartment fire. Jim got a telephone number for Mike Murphy from his business card that she had in her Rolodex card file.

Then Jim phoned Mike Murphy to try to confirm his suspicions about the aircraft.

"Off the record," Mike told Jim, "it might be a good guess. Some of my more reliable snitches have confirmed that possibility." Mike Murphy confirmed, "I have authorized payment of the claim to the owners of the *Maverick,* as the investigation showed no culpability on the part of the policyholders. But I haven't ruled out foul play on the part of some other unknown parties whose motives seemed obscure."

That was enough for Jim. He concluded that some sinister

organization did own the Flying Duck airplane. It might be possible the plane now belonged to one of the CIA's front organizations, drug dealers, or even a pharmaceutical company like Alpha Omega. Nothing could be proved either way—yet. But, the more probable choice that had known motive and opportunity was—Alpha Omega!

Jim started to postulate. His apartment fire might be another piece of the puzzle. Especially if it was some Alpha Omega assassination hit man that missed getting me in the Caribbean. And not just him, but the others also! Oh my God! It didn't make sense, but more and more pieces of the puzzle pointed in AO's direction.

"Oh, No! What about Laleh? Maybe that is why I haven't heard from her. Maybe they got her already! Oh, crap!"

Jim got up, and after looking down the hall, closed the door. He suddenly felt vulnerable. He walked to his window and looked all around. It was getting late and the pink alpine glow on the Wasatch was contrasting with the dark purple mountains covered in white snow. The clouds looked impaled by the mystic peaks. Normally, Jim thought, he would be tranquilized with this view. But this day it seemed ominous.

He called Ed to find out the name of the FBI agent that they had talked to in the hospital.

"His name is Albert Lind," said Ed as he gave Jim the phone number. Ed went on to explain that, normally, the FBI would not be involved, but because of the interstate circumstances involving two men with no ID in an Idaho rented car, they got into the case. A friend who had worked in the FBI lab and was now working for the hospital said, "Unless $25,000 or more is involved, your case won't get much attention. Especially now that it was almost a closed case for all of the other law enforcement agencies. It would remain closed until someone could raise new evidence to reopen the case."

"I guess I should let him know that we think we have some new info with your picture of the mysterious plane," Jim said.

"I doubt if that picture and Dick's guess will do it, Jim."

"Who knows?" asked Jim, ending the call with a question.

But first Jim called the FAA to see if any flight plans had been filed by seaplanes of the "flying duck" type, a Widgeon. "If any did file a plan in that area of the Caribbean near the time of the mysterious flight, it might answer some questions," Jim thought.

"There is no record of any such flight plans," the FAA clerk indicated.

"Well, thanks for your trouble," said Jim.

"However," the FAA clerk added, "flights were altered often to avoid the tropical storm and hurricane."

Still, Jim became more suspicious of any plane that would be flying in risky weather and didn't file a flight plan. It might have meant that some clandestine flight could have been in the air without a flight plan at that time. Maybe the FAA was too busy tracking storm-generated concerns, but he was cynical.

"Thanks for the info," Jim concluded.

Jim cautiously left his office. He felt ridiculous and paranoid.

Later, he called the Coast Guard to see if they had any other data that others might have overlooked. He inquired about any records of Widgeons being involved in any activity proximal to the time of the hurricane in the American or British Virgin Islands. He was rewarded with the news.

"We show only one entry logged that requested information about such a seaplane. At the time of the storm a plane of that description was flying too low without running lights and was spotted by some fishermen. No other reports were made, and no follow-up was done because no other incident reports were filed. I hope that this information is helpful," said the melodious female voice at the Coast Guard.

Jim's pulse rate had increased with the news about the plane. So had his paranoia. "Thank you very much! That is indeed the information I hoped you could supply." He paced the floor as he evaluated his new information.

The phone rang. It was Ed. "Jim, I just finished talking to the coroner. You will be interested in this: The two men killed in that car that rolled into Little Cottonwood Creek were both tattooed with similar swastika designs that included the same word, STRIKE, plus a snake picture on their left chests. Neither had any valid ID or a police record. No fingerprints were on record! However, they were both in great physical condition. It is just my hunch these two healthy specimens might have been in the armed services at one time. However, you would think that the FBI would have a slam dunk if that were true. A Utah Highway Patrol clerk told the coroner that the car was rented in Boise, Idaho, but the trail just ends there with false ID. It all seems too tidy to me. Considering what that railroad detective told Claire, it smells like a conspiracy of some type that went bad," Ed said.

"Ed, why don't you have the coroner fax you a picture of the tattoos? Then try to see what you can find on the Internet concerning those tattoo symbols," Jim suggested.

In minutes Jim's phone rang again; it was Ed. "I've got the answers to the swastika, snake and STRIKE search. It belongs to a 'false' patriot group. Certainly the authorities would have found the same data. I can't believe the investigators couldn't identity the two men killed in the wreck. It didn't take much time to do just what I had done."

"Did you say STRIKE? STRIKE? Now I recall where I have seen that name! Bill Ballencamp of Alpha Omega belongs to that organization and he said their CEO, Rock Granite, would be at their next meeting. Ed, those people working for Alpha Omega are trying to kill us! Can you believe that? Alpha Omega! Why? It's hard to believe that the CEO and head of vaccine production of one of America's largest corporations could be involved in such activity," Jim responded.

"We may never know why, but you can bet we should protect ourselves. Jim, I'll call the FBI and fill them in about the plane and the STRIKE connection. In fact, if those individuals in Alpha Omega could reach out to the Caribbean and Utah through STRIKE, Iran is probably not a safe haven for Laleh!"

"Ed, I'm going to my office to phone and e-mail her again. Talk to you later."

Chapter 21
College of Pharmacy-Day 19

Jim walked to the nearby College of Pharmacy. He worried how he was going to reach Laleh and warn her of the documented newfound danger and how he was going to catch up with the backlog of work he had missed. He prayed that somehow Laleh would get a message to him.

As Jim opened the front door of the Pharmacy Building, he heard a bird chirp as he stomped the melting snow off his feet before entering. Two robins were perched high on a limb right outside his second story office window. He assumed that they were scouting for a new nest site. "Where's Laleh? Every idle minute that I allow myself, I see her image fading," he thought to himself.

Jim found it difficult to concentrate. He filled his coffee cup, sharpened his pencils, emptied his garbage, opened and sorted his mail, checked his e-mail—and still there was nothing from Laleh. He tried to send another e-mail message to the only address he had for her and it was not deliverable—again. He finally forced himself to concentrate on his overdue work.

It was dusk when he realized that most people had left the building. He still had his lab coat on. He had not taken time to find an apartment, with all that had happened, and the idea of going back to the hotel wasn't inviting. He decided he'd been in a survival mode for too long. He would have to find a way to resume a more normal lifestyle and vowed to locate something to rent before the week was out. He knew he had some sort of problem facing reality. It really bothered him to think of living alone now. Sure, the hotel had lots of people around, but he still felt the loneliness as much as if he rented a house. He didn't know what to do. . . .

He went back to the hospital and ate dinner in the cafeteria before returning to his office to work. It was past midnight before he walked to the hotel and collapsed into the bed.

Jim awoke at 6:00 A.M., grabbed a pint of coffee from the hotel cafe for his mini-vacuum stainless steel bottle and rode his bike up the hill from the hotel. He quickly took a shortcut through old Fort Douglas to the College of Pharmacy. He wanted to see if the e-mail service had been restored. He had been informed it had been down because of some backhoe cable-cutting accident. He knew he would have a lot of messages whenever it was restored.

Jim jogged to the college and raced up to his office. When he finally got on line to check his e-mail, he saw a list of messages that had exceeded two pages, and he was overwhelmed. The mail went back over a week. Then one name jumped at him. Dr. Laleh Bazargan, Tehran, Iran had been listed! Jim quickly clicked on her name with his mouse. It had a message from the 'webmaster' that, "This message could not be left because of technical difficulties." Jim was relieved to at least know that she had tried to communicate with him, but he was dismayed that he had such rotten luck not to get her message. He copied her new e-mail listing address on his Rolodex.

Two students knocked on the door casing as they walked through his open door. Both were convinced that his last test was simply not fair. Jim spoiled most of them by his patience, but today had to be an exception. He was polite, resolute and brief.

After they departed, he quickly typed her a very restrained message:

Dr. Laleh Bazargan,

I was very pleased to realize that you had tried to communicate with me concerning the joint effort to develop the influenza A vaccine. Unfortunately our e-mail service has had technical problems and has also been out of service for quite a while due to an accident. I must apologize for this. I received notification that you had attempted to communicate today.

216

I did NOT receive the text of your message. Please repeat your message. I very much want to respond. How is your family? How did your family receive the news about your sister? I need to talk to you about several things. Some of the data that I might send you is proprietary in nature and we should decide how a secured message might be sent and received.

Sincerely, Jim

Jim sent the message and pondered what other mode of communication he might have overlooked.

Then as he gazed out his window at the robins, Jim noticed one of his former students, a doctoral candidate from Iran, Cyrus Kamali, walking through the courtyard toward the front door. Jim bolted from his office and dashed down the stairs to intercept Cyrus.

"Cyrus! Cyrus! . . ." Jim called in a restrained tone as he trotted on his tiptoes to minimize the echo on the marble tile. Cyrus stopped.

"Hello, Dr. Schriver!" Cyrus responded, somewhat surprised by Jim's animated approach.

"Cyrus, do you have a minute?" Jim inquired.

"Sure, I just came in to check some data on an experiment I started yesterday."

"I could really use your advice on how I might contact someone in Iran who has been hard to contact. How do you communicate with your family back home in Tehran?" Jim wondered.

"I just call them on the telephone, when I can afford it," Cyrus said.

"If I offered to pay your phone bill, would you be willing to call your family for a chat and then ask them to look in the telephone directory there and see if there is a listing for Dr. Laleh Bazargan? I'm not sure my listing for her is accurate," Jim said.

"Boy, I won't pass up a chance to have my phone call paid for. I will be happy to call. Can I do anything else?" Cyrus responded.

"If they or you think of any other way that I might contact her, please let me know," Jim said.

"What project are you working on with her?" Cyrus inquired, taking advantage of this new relationship.

"We hope to collaborate on a new influenza vaccine," said Jim. He then gave Cyrus a brief history of their professional experiences and told him of their hope to jointly develop a vaccine.

"Sounds cool! I'll call tonight, if that's all right." Cyrus had obviously adapted some of the American expressions.

"That's fine," said Jim. He was now optimistic for the first time in quite a while. He might really get to talk to Laleh. The cryptic, and certainly formal, e-mail he sent did not express any affection. He hated curbing his language to placate government censors or paranoid religious zealots. Hope sprang in Jim's heart to a new level.

The phone rang; it was Cyrus. "I have been thinking about what you asked me to do and I feel that I should talk to you now. Do you have any more free time right now to talk about this?"

"Certainly, come on up to my office now, if you want." Jim replied.

Cyrus came up immediately. Jim poured them both a cup of coffee and thanked Cyrus for his concern and asked him what the problem might be.

"You must forgive me for being so presumptuous, but I felt that I needed to warn you about one of my culture's idiosyncrasies. In general most Americans are very direct. When they want to know something, they simply ask a direct question and then expect a direct answer. Our history and mores evolved differently than America's. Persians usually are not so direct. If we want to know something, we usually are more furtive. For instance you might inquire, 'Are there any government immunization programs that include new influenza strains that the international community should be aware of?' You would not ask, "What is the Iranian government's plan to handle potential outbreaks of influenza?' I know that I may sound excessively fastidious, but my way will probably get you a more accurate answer."

"Thank you, that's very insightful. I will try to be more tactful. By the way, have you heard that there's an influenza A epidemic in Afghanistan and an Iranian influenza live virus nasal vaccine is being used to fight it?" Jim asked.

"Yes, I saw some mention of it on the net yesterday," answered Cyrus.

"Well, that's even more reason for me to contact Laleh."

"Laleh? Not Dr. Bazargan?" Cyrus inquired with a slight smile, his dark eyebrows arching. "I didn't realize."

It took a second before Jim understood that. He had just revealed publicly what he would never do in Iran. He had a personal need to talk to her besides his professional one, and in his direct American way, instantly revealed that fact. He had done so just after he had been warned about being so direct. "Will I ever learn?" Jim thought.

"It was just a Freudian slip," said Jim, unwilling to discuss that subject anymore.

"I will call with my credit card from the lab, and let you know what I can find out. It is already late in Iran," Cyrus tactfully concluded as he turned and walked away.

Jim expressed his thanks to Cyrus for his understanding and willingness to help. Still, he was embarrassed and confused for many reasons. He couldn't help but wonder if this was going to be an impossible relationship.

Then something occurred to him. Had Laleh and her government decided to proceed without the technical expertise and large-production capabilities of America's Alpha Omega? After all, they had no written contracts. Had Laleh just used him to delay any American activity toward production of her own intramuscular vaccine? Had he been a typical romantic, naive chump? But then, maybe he was just being presumptuous. Maybe the epidemic was just a coincidence and the press was jumping to conclusions. Maybe it was the result of a lab accident. Jim struggled to contain his building anger. Why had she been so elusive up to now? Jim repressed the questions and started to gather all the information he could on intranasal vaccines. A host of questions plagued the concept when compared to the traditional intramuscular injection.

Suddenly, Jim felt a wave of hostility come over him. "SHE USED ME!" he yelled. He threw his favorite coffee mug at the phone, knocking it off of the desk, splattering coffee everywhere and exploding the cup like a fragment grenade. Jim cursed at Laleh's memories. Hate seemed to emanate from every cell in his body. How could he have been such a fool? He shouted. Echoes of profanity resonated through his door as he continued to kick the garbage can around his office.

The knock was timid but persistent. Dr. Tia Milanno, Jim's office neighbor, stood compassionately staring into Jim's eyes, saying nothing but obviously expecting an answer as he opened the door.

Jim blurted with moist eyes, "I'm sorry—I just lost it. I just couldn't help myself."

"Let me help you," said Tia. She gently put one hand on Jim's arm and with the other moved his chair out of the mess. "Why don't you sit here for a minute." It was more of a command than a question. She put both hands on his shoulders and guided him into his seat.

Jim had always thought of her as a pretty woman with a great intellect and a spitfire tongue when provoked. But he had not seen her compassion and understanding before. His embarrassment was complete. She cleaned up his mess without saying anything. She seemed to know what to do.

As she started to leave, she simply put her hand on his and said, "I've-been-there-and-done-that too." She closed the door behind her.

Jim rubbed his temples and rotated his chair to look at the alpine glow of the mountains in the sunset outside his window. He found himself praying for guidance. He resolved he would soon find out the truth by telephone or e-mail and until that time he would force himself to concentrate on some data that he had read in *Infectious Diseases and Their Etiologic Agents,* by Mandell et al.:

> Influenza virus type A has been shown to be relatively stable in small-particle aerosols at a variety of relative humidities and temperatures, but survival appears to be favored by low relative humidity and low environmental temperature. In experimental influenza in volunteers, inoculation with small-particle aerosols produces an illness that more closely mimics natural disease than does inoculation with large drops into the nose. Finally, in such experimental infections, doses of 137–300 times the median tissue culture infective dose (TCID 50) are required to infect by nasal drops, whereas 0.6–3.0 TCID 50 is infectious by the aerosol route.

Jim knew that information would be critical to anyone attempting to make a live virus vaccine. He went on reading:

> Influenza A viruses commonly infect other species, most notably horses, swine, and avian (bird) species, but not primates. Equine (horse) influenza is a milder disease without complications. The disease in swine is very similar to that in humans in that it produces a respiratory and systemic illness with low mortality and with occasional pulmonary bacterial superinfection. The disease in waterfowl varies from an inapparent infection to a lethal infection involving primarily the gastrointestinal and central nervous systems and also the sinuses and the trachea. There are many antigenic relationships among avian influenza viruses and those isolated from humans.

Jim knew also that the influenza A virus would change and adapt in order to survive, especially when it is forced to change from one animal species to another. He went on to read about what actually killed patients with uncomplicated influenza and no other secondary infections or preexisting physical problems:

> The lungs in fatal influenza viral pneumonia, in addition to sloughing of epithelium in the tracheobronchial tree, show extensive hemorrhage, hyaline membrane formation, and a paucity of polymorphonuclear cell infiltration.

> The onset of illness from the time of exposure varies from eighteen to seventy-two hours depending in part on the inoculum or size of dose.

Jim knew that in China, pigs, ducks and humans lived in close proximity with one another. Influenza A could change and adapt quickly and easily. That explained why many of the new strains of flu often came from there. If some Far East or Middle and Near East countries, with similar environments, chose to use an intranasal live virus, couldn't it mutate quickly and become more virulent? Especially if the nasal spray was not used by properly trained technicians. What would happen if some farm child had the opportunity to play with a spray in the farmyard? Near the end of the text he read another worrisome statement:

"Other types of genetically engineered live influenza vaccines are currently under development."

Jim went to the medical library and pored over the reference articles mentioned in the text. By the time he left the library it was dark. The walk from the library to the college was brisk and breezy.

Cyrus was leaving the College of Pharmacy as he met Jim coming back from the library. "Dr. Schriver, I've got it all set up for tomorrow night. My folks have it arranged for us to talk to Dr. Bazargan at 8 A.M. Tehran time—8 p.m. Salt Lake time."

"Fantastic, Cyrus." Should we meet in my hotel to place the call, so it will go on my bill automatically?" Jim asked.

"That sounds fine; I'll meet you there then tomorrow at 8 P.M."

Jim had to ride his bike back to the hotel and it did not have a light. He tried to be careful on the back road because it was not very well lit. He was tired and hungry but didn't want a big meal. Maybe he would just have some Happy Hour hors d'oeuvres in the hotel lounge. After the day he'd had, he was ready for a few beers.

When he sat down he didn't see a soul that he knew. None of the waitresses looked familiar—all new crew. He felt as lonely as a sheepherder in a blizzard.

Two hours and eight beers later Jim satisfied his thirst generated by the spicy tidbits. A Utah Jazz basketball game was on TV.

The rest became a blur until a familiar voice called his name. "Jim! Jim!"

He looked up to see Tia. Twice in one day she had seen him at his worst. "Oh, hi," he said with a fishtailed tongue. It was plain to see he was almost drunk.

"I just got out of a dinner meeting here, down in the ballroom. I saw you alone over here, and thought I would just check on you," she said with sympathy. Her beautiful eyes were fixed on his.

Jim wished the long-predicted Wasatch Earthquake would come right then and swallow him up. He knew he couldn't walk right if he got up—he remembered that awful conspicuous feeling he learned as a freshman. "Tia, I donnn knoww what say."

"Don't say anything. Come with me," Tia said. "You still are living here, aren't you?"

"Yass," Jim managed, despite what seemed like marbles in his mouth.

"What's your room number?" Tia asked.

"Isss 814, but . . . but . . ."

"I know you haven't had a better offer tonight, Jim. Or is that your trouble, you got turned down?" Tia said facetiously. She locked her arm under his and laced her fingers through his while tucking his arm close to her side, just as she had done so many times before with patients in the hospital. She was small-framed but strong because of all of her mountain biking and other exercise.

"Thhan you—again," he managed to say.

Tia got him to his bed with great effort and dropped him on it. "Boy, some date you have been tonight," she said joking, then left him clothed and nearly unconscious.

"Thhan you."

When he awoke the next morning he remembered how he had vomited until he saw bile the night before. He was furious with himself and totally embarrassed when he recalled Tia tucking him in as if he were an idiot teenager.

In a way he was lucky—he lost most of it early. He couldn't imagine how he could feel any worse than he did right then. He was depressed, nauseous, dizzy, and his head throbbed with every beat of his heart. Everything hurt. Grasping the sink with both hands he looked in the mirror with contempt.

He suddenly remembered who he was mad at. "Laleh Bazargan—is the woman who betrayed me. You're the cause of all of my misery. It was all your fault." He wondered why he had been such a schmuck to believe her? He tried and tried to communicate with her only to be rejected. He had thought that it was her government restricting her—but it was really just her way of dealing him out of the project. Her country wouldn't have to co-license and pay anyone else. Jim almost wished that the epidemic would teach her and her country a lesson.

He wondered if he could safely encourage Alpha Omega to develop an independent vaccine by getting a seed virus from one of the Afghani patients. He would call Alpha Omega tomorrow if he didn't hear from her. "To hell with Laleh Bazargan!" He would find a way without her if she didn't get back to him.

Then he said out loud, "Damn you, Jaynee!" He didn't need a psychologist like Claire to explain why he vented his anger that way. He recognized his hostility was augmented by the memory of his wife Jaynee and her death. She had left him alone.

The transference of anger from Jaynee to Laleh had blind-sided Jim. He sank to his knees in boxer shorts and tee shirt amidst his squalid fetid clothing and towels, left where he dropped them the night before.

"Lord, help me. I've screwed up, again. . . ." He was paranoid, depressed, anxious, lonely and angry.

There didn't seem to be any clear direction to anything he had been doing since Jaynee died, he knew. He wondered why humans had to suffer so much? Why do people pray to someone they can't see? Why does everything about an omnipotent God have to be so mysterious and unprovable? Why can't we scientists find proof of God's existence to show everyone? Why are we left with faith that somehow God is with us listening to our diatribes. "I guess what I want is a small miracle, some sign from you, God." Jim concluded.

Jim struggled to his feet with his head pounding. Dizziness threatened to steal any vestige of control that remained to him. He was in 'survival mode' as he propped himself in the shower. His fumbling of the water controls produced a blast of very cold water. Jim slapped at the faucets to correct the temperature of the water. He frantically swore at himself for his error.

He finally got the water temperature right and started to calm down.

Chapter 22
Tehran and Mashad, Iran—Days 19–21

Soon it would be Norooz, the Persian New Year and the first day of spring. Norooz has been celebrated for more than three thousand years in Iran. Unlike other ancient Persian celebrations, Norooz had not withered away after the invasion. Throughout history Iran tenaciously preserved her unique identity. This perseverance made Iran different from other Middle Eastern countries. The Arab invasion, the triumph of Islamic philosophy during the seventh century A.D., nor the Mongol invasion or any other invasions of Iran had been able to destroy this ancient celebration. From the time of Zorastrianism, the first ancient Iranian religion, to the time of the Safavid dynasty, and even now when Shi'ite Islam was recognized as the official state religion—this Norooz celebration had been valued, shared and handed down for generations.

As Norooz approached, Laleh became depressed. Every moment of preparing for Norooz brought memories back. She remembered how excited Sonbol was when talking about Norooz to the American scientists.

She hadn't received even a post card from Jim. Her e-mail wasn't working. "I don't know how to feel any more," Laleh ruminated. She had to hold herself back due to her status in her family ever since their father died. Being the first child in the family had always put a lot of pressure on her. She always had to play the virtuous daughter for both mother and father. She had to be the role model for two sisters. She had to prepare herself to be the future good wife and mother—as the country's mores demanded. At times, she even had to take on the surrogate role of deceased father for her younger brother. Everyone in the family turned to her to make important decisions.

With all of these responsibilities and experience, she was just plain confused concerning Jim. Even dreaming of freely loving a man like Jim, an American, was almost impossible. She wasn't sure if he really cared anymore.

To Laleh, love was not based on just needs and responsibility, but full of passion and burning. She had felt a real chemistry, a real burning with Jim, and she didn't want to lose that feeling. No matter what, she wanted to keep that! It had given her spiritual energy with which she was able to confront all of the problems that she'd had to face.

Laleh received a "strange" phone call. It came about 7 P.M.

"Alo." *Hello.*

"Salam" *Hi.*

"May I speak to Dr. Laleh Bazaragan?" requested the female voice at the other end.

"Khodam hastam, shoma?" *This is she; you?* Laleh responded.

"You don't know me. My name is Forough Kamali. My son, Cyrus, is a university graduate student at the University of Utah in Salt Lake City, Utah."

Laleh's heart stopped. That was where Jim lived!

"He has requested us to call you and arrange a time for you to come to our house," announced Mrs. Kamali. "Of course it would be after the specific transition time to the new year." Saat-e-tahvil-e-sal-e-no.

"Why? I don't know your son Cyrus," replied Laleh.

"I know. My son and his professor, Dr. Schriver, would like to congratulate you on Norooz and wish you a Happy New Year," Mrs. Kamali answered.

Laleh's heart stood still. She felt tense and excited. "Finally— there is a miracle for me. He hasn't forgotten me!" she thought to herself.

Laleh tried to contain her emotions. "Mrs. Kamali, when do you want me to visit your house?" she inquired eagerly.

"Well, Tuesday, the first day of Norooz, at 7 A.M. would be best to see you. Our address is 1953 Jam-e-Jam street." Mrs. Kamali said.

"I'll be there. Happy New Year," Sal-e-no mobarak. "Good bye," she replied.

Laleh was very excited. She counted every minute until Tuesday morning. She couldn't wait to hear Jim's voice again! She wanted to tell him so many things about the vaccine that she'd made, her imprisonment and the oppression brought on by the power of the mullahs. There was so much!

Before her trip she had always been so proud of her country but now, it was being ruled by people like Hojat-ul-Islam Panjali. There were so many feelings that she couldn't even whisper about because of the network of informers. "I wish I could tell him how much I love him." She almost said.

Laleh suddenly knew what was in her heart. "I must leave my country. I pray that Jim truly still feels for me what I feel for him." She felt herself perspiring. "I also know that my vaccine will never get worldwide use unless I can escape with it." The word, *escape*, seemed so alien to use when thinking about her country. She needed to make a plan. She must tell Jim of her needs without the ubiquitous telephone monitors learning anything. She was going to need to be devious but articulate when she talked to Jim. She had to plan every word.

The phone rang loudly at that moment and startled Laleh. She flinched and jumped for the phone. It was Dr. Tabatabai.

"Hello, Laleh, I have been trying to contact you since our misunderstanding. Your phone has been busy. I have to show you something," Dr. Tabatabai said.

"Hi, Yusef. I also regret that meeting. I would like to talk to you. What is it that you want to show me?" responded Laleh.

"Well, your office secretary brought me a copy of an e-mail message from Utah that she downloaded for you. It is from a JR Schriver and she felt it might be urgent. Would you like to come see it now?" Dr. Tabatabai knew without asking that she wouldn't want him to read it to her over the phone.

"Yes, yes!" Laleh responded joyfully.

"I'll be there in about two hours," Dr. Tabatabai concluded.

Laleh was shocked. In only about half an hour, she had gotten two messages from Jim.

"What a beautiful Norooz gift I have received this year," thought Laleh. Then guilt seeped into her mind with thoughts of Sonbol's absence and probable death.

With Tehran's heavy traffic, Dr. Tabatabai arrived at Laleh's house in about an hour and a half after their telephone conversation. As he handed Laleh the e-mail copy, he could feel Laleh's anxiety. Although he was curious to ask her about Jim, he could not bring himself to ask. He managed to hide his curiosity and continued, "What did you want to tell me?"

Laleh was relieved. She read the message and mumbled, "That is why he never got my e-mail." She didn't think there were any technical difficulties. She was being audited, monitored and restricted by the SAVAMA, the National Information and Security Organization of the Islamic Republic of Iran.

Looking into Yusef's eyes with determination, Laleh announced, "I have decided to leave Iran. I will take some of the vaccine with me. From abroad, I will let the world know about this deadly disease virus and our vaccine. I no longer trust this government. I am afraid that they will use this virus as a weapon. This is very dangerous for the whole world. It is more dangerous than the atomic bomb. I need your help to get out of the country," Laleh said.

Yusef's mouth fell open in disbelief. Shock preceded a sense of betrayal. He struggled with different emotions as he tried to formulate a response that wouldn't destroy what love for him she still might have.

"How long are you going to stay away?" asked Dr. Tabatabai.

"I don't know. As long as it takes," responded Laleh.

"Have you thought about where you'll go?" He asked.

"Ashkhabad, Turkmenistan," Laleh said.

"Why there?" He inquired.

"Well, that is one place close to Mashhad. The Iranian government has had close relations with Turkmenistan and I don't need a visa as an Iranian citizen. With so little time, that route is the best way for me."

"But why in such a hurry?" asked Dr. Tabatabai.

"I am scared. I have to watch my back all the time. I don't even feel comfortable working at the hospital anymore. Besides, what kind of a life do you think I can have now in Iran?" Laleh inquired.

Dr. Tabatabai suddenly felt dizzy. He dropped into the nearest chair and tried to think of a way out of the mess. He struggled with his love for Laleh. He didn't want to lose her. When Laleh was in the Virgin Islands, he decided to propose marriage to her as soon as she arrived in Iran. This plan was disrupted when the government arrested Laleh. Now this! He knew Laleh well and knew that she had made up her mind—it was too late for him. His heart was broken. He couldn't utter a word. His mouth was dry as if the desert wind had been blowing through it.

He tried very hard to lie to himself. There was no danger that he couldn't protect her from—all she needed to do was marry him! Then reality prevailed as he realized it was too much to ask. He knew that in reality, her life was in danger and he couldn't stop the government. He then imagined how it would be if Laleh left the country, and he followed her! He was also tired of working in a place where human life had little value. He loved her. . . . As soon as she was settled abroad, he would join her and marry her there.

Yusef leaned back in his chair and said, "I will help you by any means I can. I also would rather work somewhere else! So I think the best way is to arrange a family trip to Mashhad. I know your mother would love to go on a pilgrimage to Mashhad to visit Imam Reza's shrine." Imam Reza was the eighth Imam in the Shi'ites' twelve

Imami believers. "We could arrange to arrive in Mashhad on Eid Gurban when Muslims sacrifice a sheep. Eid Gurban is one of the most important feasts of Islam. It is the same ceremonial ritual followed at Mina during the Hadjj in Mecca."

Laleh pondered what Yusef had just said, considering the consequences.

"You could leave for Ashkhabad on Eid Ghadir, the Shi'ite Twelver's holiday," he continued. According to Shi'ite tradition, the Prophet Mohammad had chosen Ali, his son-in-law, to be his successor after his death. On that day, he became the right Caliph or head of the community and state.

Laleh told Yusef, "That is a great plan!" She would tell Jim about it when she talked to him at the Kamali's house on Friday, the first day of Norooz, though as she thought about it, she realized she was a little worried about the real intentions of Yusef. "Yusef, that's a great idea. You are such a good friend."

Yusef felt Laleh could read his mind and his unspoken intentions. He was happy, but he was also naive and mistaken.

When the day came, Laleh asked her sister Narges to accompany her to the Kamali house. They drove from Vali-e-asr, and passed Vanak Square. The two women struggled through gridlock traffic as they approached Jam-e-Jam Street.

The two talked about the funny moments the three sisters had during their teenage years. Narges was three years younger than Sonbol and ten years younger than Laleh.

Narges reminded Laleh, "I always covered for you two and your secret dating with boys. I must admit that I was jealous of the close relationship that Sonbol had with you. I always felt that somehow I had lost your affection after father died and you had to assume a different role. Your family responsibilities seemed to double. I guess that feeling might have been one of the reasons why I was so rebellious. And after the revolution I was even more frustrated. I haven't been able to achieve the dreams I had envisioned nor the status I felt I deserved having worked so hard as a student. I hadn't been as pro-revolutionary as Sonbol."

A moment of silence ensued. Laleh waited.

Narges then said, "I never blamed the United States. I was too young and don't remember anything about the late Shah Pahlavi dynasty. I only heard that there had been more individual freedom during that time. The word *freedom* is very confusing to me."

Laleh just nodded and allowed her sister to vent her pent-up feelings. It could be a long time before they had this opportunity again.

Narges continued. "When I was in high school, I had class-mates who believed that Khomeini's Islam was the only path to free-dom. It was such a dichotomy. Veiling women was a path to freedom, as opposed to the Reza shah's unveiling women. Becoming a martyr was a path to freedom. Everyone should tolerate their misfortunes and wait for the return of the Twelfth Imam . . . the last Imam, the hidden Imam, Mahdi.

"All of these old men and their religious politics robbed me of my childhood. Why couldn't I and my friends just be like other kids in the world and concentrate on living and loving one another?" she inquired, looking to Laleh for an answer.

Laleh shrugged to signal that she didn't know.

"Why were we made to feel guilty and inadequate if we were not political?" asked Narges.

Trying to relate to her sister's serious concerns and still manage to drive safely, Laleh recalled to herself what she had learned in the Caribbean. Real freedom was in America and she must suffer with the secret that she was going to America and dared not tell Narges, at least not at this moment. If things went wrong, it would be best that the other family members continue to live the same way as they are accustomed. Perhaps, if her plan went the way she wanted, she could show them all what real freedom is. She would sponsor their coming to the U.S.

They both became nervous and argued about Laleh's fast driving. The fact that they were going to be late getting to the Kamalis made her foot heavy.

The phone call was due at any moment when they stopped in front of the Kamali home.

Mrs. Kamali was waiting at the door and quickly invited them into her living room to meet her family. After she insisted that they accept her offer, the two sisters sat and received tea. As Laleh was asking Mr. and Mrs. Kamali about their son Cyrus in Salt Lake City, the phone rang.

Not until evening had Jim felt like checking his messages at the hotel desk or his phone messages and e-mail at the college. Cyrus Kamali, the Iranian doctoral researcher, had called to tell him that he had made an appointment through his family in Iran for Laleh to communicate by phone with him at his house in thirty minutes. Jim drove with abandon to get to Cyrus' house on time. It was near Olympus Hills Shopping Center on the east bench of the mountains in Salt Lake County. The stage had been set for Cyrus to phone his family in Iran and be prepared to talk to his parents, his real brother and sisters, and the last voice would be that of Laleh pretending to be another of his sisters.

Jim entered Cyrus' cigarette smoke-filled house. There evidently was more risk involved for his family than Jim had realized. They all were going out on a limb for him and were nervous about the consequences for family members in Tehran. It wasn't a question of whether or not their conversations would be monitored, but what the Revolutionary Guards' interpreter would deduct from the dialog. He would have to be very careful. Cyrus placed the call. . . .

The phone rang and Ali Kamali, Cyrus' father, answered the phone on the first ring, near 8:00 A.M. in Tehran, as it was on the opposite side of the earth, Jim reasoned. The family seemed stilted in the conversation with one another, and Jim prayed that the monitor listening in Iran would not be able to sense that.

233

It was finally time for Laleh to speak. She limited her salutations to her pseudo-family and then Jim was handed the phone.

"Hello, Jim?" Laleh inquired.

"I'm here, Laleh—for you," Jim answered.

There was a brief awkward silence as Laleh was taken back momentarily. Jim would not be able to explain why he answered her that way.

Narges' curiosity was killing her, but she realized that she should relate with Mrs. Kamali when the conversation shifted to Laleh and Jim.

"Your English is getting very good Jim," Laleh quickly recovered. "You must continue your studies of English in that country to be better able to serve Allah in our tradition. My time is limited today, so I will be brief. You wondered about the earthquake in Tabriz, Iran, and if it had been felt in Ashkhabad, Turkmenistan. You had a friend who was going there, you said. As far as I can determine, if he stays in the Hotel Ashkhabad he should be able to meet his party there. He should feel safe. You also mentioned that he could be going to that location soon. If he could leave tomorrow he'd have no problems arriving there Friday.

"From what you told me, his friend could come from the south to meet him then. His friend will have a lot to tell you also about his hajj. I am sorry I must go now, but I am looking forward to seeing you all someday soon. Perhaps we could meet somewhere closer to here in the future, as my time is limited now and somewhat frantic. It is so hard to get away from my work. I'm scheduled to be so busy that I doubt if I'll be able to call again. So, I shall close, with hope from Allah that we will see each other again soon," Laleh concluded.

"It would be my pleasure, Darling. Sister." answered Jim in a tone that Laleh worried might be too affectionate. "I shall also say good-bye for the rest of the family now. There is only one God, Allah, and Mohammad is his messenger."

Jim now knew what he needed to do. He had to go to the Hotel

Ashkhabad in Turkmenistan and wait for her arrival next Friday. He assumed he should buy their tickets from Ashkhabad to the U.S., departing on the following Monday.

"I wish to thank all of you for helping us," Jim addressed Cyrus for the whole Kamali family. "I know how stressful and difficult this has been for you. I pray that nothing detrimental comes of this to your family in Tehran. We will always be in your debt."

Jim concluded his social obligations and again thanked Cyrus and gave him a hug as he departed to go back his University Park Hotel.

After Laleh hung the telephone receiver slowly, almost reluctantly, she asked for permission to leave. Mrs. Kamali insisted that they both remain a little longer. Mrs. Kamali had an almost immediate bonding to Narges and she to her. Their brief chat together, while Laleh was on the phone, had been like two computers downloading their lives to one another. Narges' rebellious eyes had caught Mrs. Kamali's attention and Narges' courageous spirit impressed her. She needed to get to know Narges better. Narges talked with Mrs. Kamali for quite a while after the telephone call had been concluded.

"She would be an ideal woman to take care of my son," Mrs. Kamali thought to herself. "Cyrus should consider Narges a very good candidate for marriage."

Laleh finished her trivial conversation with Mr. Kamali and then both sisters repeated their thanks and said their farewells. Mrs. Kamali said, "Narges, I have the feeling that you will be meeting Cyrus this summer." Laleh and Narges left, and Laleh began to prepare to leave the next day.

Laleh, her mother and Dr. Tabatabai flew to Mashhad on the Eid Gurban holiday as planned. The Iran Air flight was full of pilgrims. At the airport were many children who were starting their holiday travel. They were playing, jumping up and down, spilling their drinks, soiling their clothes, and the sound level was nerve-

235

wracking. Some of the little boys, below the age of five, were still treated as extensions of their mothers. Still clinging to their mothers' skirts and accompanying them into the women's restrooms and other segregated areas, the little boys seemed to know what the future had in store for them. All too soon they would be thrust into the harsh Islamic world of men. No mollycoddling then, just harsh discipline by proud fathers.

Even though Mashhad is only 966 kilometers, approximately six hundred miles from Tehran, it would be the trip of a lifetime for many of the travelers. For some, it could be the only trip away from home.

The flight was relatively short, the flying time only a little over an hour. However, with the great influx into Mashhad during the holiday, it took twice as long to get anywhere on the ground. It took a long time before they caught a taxi to the Hotel Ferdosi.

Mrs. Bazargan was very happy. She hoped this would be a great chance for Dr. Tabatabai and Laleh to get to know each other as more than just work associates. Plus, she could pray at the shrine of the Imam for the eventual union of Laleh and Yusef. Dr. Tabatabai prayed at the Imam Reza's shrine for Laleh's love. Laleh prayed for Jim and her safety when they attempted to join in the coming days.

Mrs. Bazargan, Laleh and Yusef stayed in Mashhad until it was time for Laleh to leave for Ashkhabad. During their stay they visited the Bazaar where Mrs. Bazargan bought lots of saffron. Mashhad saffron was known for its excellent color and taste. Laleh wanted to buy Jim a souvenir of the famous Mashhad turquoise.

"Don't you think it's premature to buy that for Yusef now?" her mother asked.

Laleh realized that her mother had assumed that the gift was for Yusef. "Perhaps it would be best that I save it for another time."

They all went to visit Ferdowsi's tomb. Laleh, for the first time, recognized her cultural duality. A traditional pilgrim would visit Imam Reza's shrine first. Shi'ite pilgrims consider the Imam Reza as the eighth Imam. Then they would visit Ferdowsi's tomb second in Tus.

Laleh read from a tour book, "The poet Ferdowsi is famous for his work, Shahnameh. The Shahnameh is a poetry book in a heroic-epic style about ancient myths and the history of Iran before Islam. The artistic book has given Iranians a kind of self-identity as Ajam, non-Arab, which separates Iranian culture from Arab culture. Just as the Iranian Indo-European language, Farsi, or Persian, is not derived from Aramaic Semitic language."

Yusef, not to be outdone by Laleh, read from his own brochure. "At the time of the Archenemies in the great Persian empire which was founded by Cyrus the Great, the national faith of Persia was Zoroastrianism. The dualistic teaching, characteristic of this religion, was evident in the story of the cosmic battle between good and evil that has affected Iranian life. Zoroaster believed that all human beings should choose for themselves between the forces of good and evil. Thus his teaching was based on free will, a characteristic seen in Shi'ism as opposed to orthodox Sunni belief, which is based on pre-destination. Ferdowsi's sources were based on his collection of infor-mation from Zoroastrian priests, Mobeds, and other old classes of nobles taken from Middle Persian–Pahlavi–literature."

Mrs. Bazargan felt compelled to respond. "Maybe you young people don't think we elders learned anything from history. Ferdowsi and his characters in the Shahnameh are the symbolization of Iranian nationalism and heroism for all Iranians. Some of today's secular Iranians replace the Qu'ran with the Shahnameh, in their Haft Sin, the seven items with the starting letter 'S' sound, is used on their New Year's table setting. That is done in order to show their real connec-tion with ancient Iranian celebration."

Although the trio enjoyed their time in Mashhad, Laleh's mind was focused on her trip to Turkmenistan. It was the day of the Eid Gurban's holiday for the Shi'ites, the most important day in the Shi'ite year.

Yusef was casually explaining Shi'ism and Sunnism to a group of high school boys in Mashhad on holiday, which had been debating loudly. "The day of separation of Shi'ism and Sunnism is over a dispute about who should be the Caliph, Prophet Mohammad's successor and the head of the state and community—the day that Sunni believed Abu-Bakr, the eldest and closest friend of the prophet, was selected the right successor. Shi'ites point to this historical day as Allegiance Day, rooz-e-byat, of World Shi'ites. They believe that the Prophet Mohammad had chosen Ali, his son-in-law and closest friend, as his successor. In reality it was not a question of nomination of candidacy, but a legal and doctrinal, plus an emotional and psychological, difference between Shi'ites and Sunnis."

Laleh and the others heard again all of the old arguments and discussions about Mohammad's actions. It was like visiting museum after museum, eventually getting tired despite the worthiness of the information. Laleh was ready to leave.

Laleh had decided that this would be the day to reveal her plans to her mother and say good-bye. Her mother's hopes that Laleh would consider the fine prospects of marriage to Yusef vanished. A river of tears ensued.

Yusef then took Laleh's hand and placed his cellular telephone into it. "Laleh, I want you to have this in case of an emergency. When I come to the United States I can retrieve it from you."

Yusef could hardly speak when Laleh gently touched her hand to his cheek.

"Thank you for your concern Yusef, it will be a good luck token. I'll call you, if I can, from Turkmenistan. . . . Good-bye . . . Yusef."

Laleh gathered her carry-on baggage that included a stainless steel vacuum bottle containing two vials that she had labeled Insulin 1 and 2. She also carried a blood sugar testing kit and some disposable insulin syringes to reinforce the ruse.

The frozen virus in 1 and the vaccine in 2 were packed on top of dry ice. Regular ice had carefully been placed on top of the vials.

Laleh knew that it was still risky because a knowledgeable inspector would question the steaming or smoking from the bottle if she were requested to open it.

Her mouth was dry as she lined up to board the bus to Turkmenistan. She tried to control her trembling hands and quivering legs. She consoled herself by thinking that any government spy would not expect her to travel by bus, especially alone. The government would not know that she had left until she did not return home with her mother and Yusef. It was thrilling but terrifying. Laleh had not lived on the edge much as a physician.

Since she felt it was essential for world health, it was worth the risk. Yet, it was so difficult to leave everyone in her family behind. There was also the guilt she felt about Yusef.

At the Imam Reza's shrine, she promised to donate a chandelier to the temple if all went well with her trip. She vowed that she would go to a Christian church and thank Jesus by lighting twelve candles.

The bored bus driver took her ticket and examined her travel paper from the public security department of the ostendari in Mashhad giving her permission to visit Sarakhs. He motioned her to the rear of the bus. Sarakhs was the closest tiny border town of Turkmenistan, only 178 kilometers east-northeast. It had been a camel caravan center for centuries. The tour bus pulled away without any problems. At last she was on her way to Turkmenistan and Jim.

Laleh sat near the middle of the tour bus, just behind the men's front section. She sat beside a woman whose husband was just in front of her talking to another man about mining. "Would you like to share some of my lunch?—I have way more than I can eat," Laleh told the lady.

"We have been fasting since we went on our pilgrimage to Mashhad, but we forgot to buy something for our trip home." She looked in her husband's direction. "I don't think I should."

"I insist," said Laleh, thrusting an orange, a wrapped candy bar and a bag of nuts into the woman's lap.

"Are you sure you have enough?" The woman and her husband were obviously not in the same socioeconomic class as Laleh.

"Oh, yes. I've stuffed myself already with this pocket bread. It is delicious. It's made with cucumber, tomato, onion, goat cheese, sweet basil and tarragon."

"Thank you so much," said the hungry woman. "My name is Mary. I was born in Turkmenistan in the city of the same name, Mary."

"I'm pleased to meet you, Mary."

"We live now in a mining village west of Bajgiran, Iran. It is high on a mountain that is still snow-covered. Where is your home?"

"I was born in Tehran and I still live there." Laleh was tempted to tell her that she was soon to live in the U.S.A.

"We do not have any children—yet. And you?" Mary asked.

"I am unmarried—still," Laleh replied without any other explanation.

The ochre and tan desert terrain moved past them with dull monotony. The sun was not as hot as during the summer inferno, but the bus driver had not turned on the air conditioner, or it was broken. Most people were dozing, as were Laleh and Mary. They all were fortunate that the bus was a newer, quieter vehicle.

Out the windows, images of the past were a contrasting sight for the modern travelers. People riding camels, wrapped in traditional clothing of the northern nomads, were seen out of the dusty bus window. The vistas seemed infinite in all directions at that moment. Laleh tried to catch up on her rest.

She slept for almost three hours before she awakened feeling very sick at her stomach. She also felt that she might be coming down with diarrhea. She probably shouldn't have bought her lunch from an independent migrating vendor. The pocket sandwiches had looked and smelled great. But, she had been eager to escape Iran.

When they reached Savakhs, the bus driver let everyone off, but first he admonished them. "Everyone must return to this bus within two hours for the return trip to Mashhad. You are not allowed to stay overnight here."

Everyone with the tour leader was herded to Shaikh Loghaman Baba's mausoleum. He was a teller of fables during the tenth century. The domed structure was impressive amid the oasis of several beautiful palms. There were paved roads in the city, but it was obvious that camels were still a popular mode of transportation.

Unfortunately, Laleh's hopes dimmed that she could drift away from the tourists and get transportation to Ashkhabad. The environment and security were harsh. Besides, Laleh was becoming very ill. She returned in despair to the bus.

Mary noticed Laleh's distress and asked her husband, "Zayd, would you ask the bus driver to direct us to a restroom. My friend Laleh is quite ill."

Zayd raised his large frame and nimbly traversed the aisle to the front. The driver directed them to a close primitive restroom.

"I'm very ill," mumbled Laleh as Mary assisted her to a secluded area reserved for women. Laleh vomited repeatedly and then suffered from explosive diarrhea. She lost so much fluid that she passed out upon the windblown dirt.

Mary again summoned Zayd to help her carry Laleh back to the bus. All the women on the bus were quite eager to adjust their seating positions to allow Laleh's barely conscious frame to be laid on the seat at the very back of the bus. The aroma from her sickness also demanded distance.

Mary finally convinced Laleh that she should rest at their home in Bajgiran. The town was many kilometers in the opposite direction, but still near the Turkmenistan border, with easy access to Ashkhabad. They changed buses in Mashhad to go on to Bajgiran. The bus finally stopped at Bajgiran and discharged Zayd, Mary and Laleh. Laleh was barely aware that she had been off-loaded into a truck bed and bundled with blankets for the trip to the copper mine. Zayd and Mary's small mobile home had two sleeping areas and Laleh was placed semiconscious on a bed. The next day, Laleh awakened with a consuming thirst.

Mary was greatly relieved when Laleh had regained full consciousness. "Can I help you in any way?"

"I am very thirsty and disoriented. Where am I?"

Mary said, "You are in our home near Bajgiran. "We got your luggage. It's here." Mary pointed to the cases. "We took the liberty of reading your identification papers when you were unconscious. We discovered that you are a doctor, so we delayed going to the nearest hospital, which would have been another two hours away. I was beginning to think that we did the wrong thing."

"Thank you very much, you both are very kind. I believe that I had bacterial food poisoning; it was very severe, but short-lived. I'm sure that I shall feel better as the hours pass. I simply need to replace the fluids that I lost. I should be out of your way soon. Oh, what day is it? How long have I been out?"

"You got sick after lunch today, it's still Friday," Mary responded.

"My head is pounding. I must think. Oh, yes, do you have a refrigerator?"

"Yes we do!" Mary responded proudly.

"Would it be all right if I put my vacuum bottle in your freezing compartment? It's small."

"You are most welcome. Just don't forget to take it with you when you go."

"There won't be any danger of doing that. Ah . . . I have my personal medicine in there. Thank you." Laleh stood up to put the bottle in the freezing compartment. Her head spun and she instantly dropped to her knees and put her head down. "I was supposed to meet someone tonight in Ashkhabad."

"You couldn't have done that anyway," Mary interrupted.

"Why is that?" Laleh inquired with disbelief. Her head was pulsing like a large metronome.

"When the border guards stopped vehicles on the highway, a freight train on the track that was crossing the highway hit a stalled truck." Mary gestured with her hands. "Some toxic substances were released and they have stopped all traffic until they can correct the danger. It may take a week because of the location at the most steep and narrow section of the canyon. There is no way around it."

"I don't understand, why did the border guards stop everybody?" Laleh asked.

"The rumor going around was that the border guards had been ordered by SAVAMA to search for an enemy of the state. Someone who had stolen some state secrets was believed en route to Turkmenistan."

"Are there no other roads to get to Ashkhabad from Bajgiran?" Laleh inquired.

"No; why are you in such a hurry? There are no other ways for a woman to get there from here except by bus and train."

"Maybe I can trust you? You are a woman—you may understand," Laleh confided cautiously.

"I envy you, a woman of means, that can travel like you—without a man to lead you like some pet," Mary commented wistfully.

"My close friend awaits me in Ashkhabad! I think he wants to marry me, but I do not have permission from my family. I am desperate; I must at least call him!" Laleh said.

"There is only the mining office phone for emergency use here at this camp."

Laleh then remembered the cellular phone that Yusef loaned her. "I just remembered, a friend loaned me a cellular phone."

"I have never seen one. Only on TV have I seen one. You must have a very rich and powerful friend," Mary said with wide eyes.

"He is a very good friend of our family," said Laleh shading the truth. "I must try and call him now." Laleh had stuck a piece of tape with the hotel phone number on the phone before boarding the bus. She knew that remembering the number would be risky, or she might misplace a piece of paper with the number. She dialed as Mary watched and prepared to eavesdrop. The cellular unit read, "Out of Range."

Laleh continued to drink water as she explained to Mary the workings of a cellular phone. Laleh needed to get high enough on the mountain and in an unobstructed visual line toward Ashkhabad, almost forty kilometers away, to get the best possible reception.

"That might be only a poor gamble, but I need to take it—now!" Laleh emphasized.

"We may need to ski there," announced Mary. "Fortunately, we have some skis. They are very old and very simple. They just have a leather strap to hold your foot on to the ski. Zayd made them. He made poles also. But you are too ill . . ."

"I'm getting stronger every minute," said Laleh, not exactly lying. "Let's go if you have the time." She noticed an ancient army backpack and frame hanging on the wall. Laleh pointed to the pack and inquired, "Can we use that also?"

"Certainly, but we must hurry. I have only a little time before Zayd will be home and he expects to be fed immediately."

Because the shallow, windblown snow was difficult to negotiate, the two elected to hike from Mary's front door in an easterly direction, gaining elevation as they traveled. After a while they turned north and eventually crested a ridge on a shoulder of the mountain that allowed a great vista of the vast desert north of Ashkhabad. The scale gave some dimension to the city in the distance. Mary hadn't thought it would have taken so long to get where they were. But, they hadn't skied, and hiking had been slower.

She took a deep breath and activated the phone. Then she dialed the hotel number. No one answered for six rings. Laleh was just getting despondent, when a voice answered.

"Hotel Ashkhabad." The first automatic answering message was spoken in English with an instruction to press one if the caller understood. The message was then repeated in German, Russian and

The NIDUS: CRADLE OF TERROR

Turkmen with different reference numbers.

Laleh pressed one.

"How can I help you," inquired an English-speaking desk clerk. Laleh's pulse quickened. "I'd like to speak to a guest, Dr. James Schriver, please."

Chapter 23
USA and Turkmenistan—Days 21–24

Jim had so much to think about and so much to do after the phone call at Cyrus Kamali's. Through a coded FAX from the Kamalis, Laleh told Jim that she would be carrying the virus and the vaccine vials frozen inside a vacuum bottle packed with dry ice. It would need replenishing in Ashkhabad.

The Turkmenistan Ministry of Foreign Affairs said that his visa would be confirmed upon his arrival in Ashkhabad. Evidence of hotel accommodations would be necessary to complete the authorization. Jim was assured that such requirements were not unusual. He had simply filled out the form he had obtained off the Internet. A visa good for thirty days had been promised to Jim for twenty dollars, U.S. currency. The new currency of Turkmenistan, the manat, replaced the old USSR ruble in 1993. The coins were tenges. However, U.S. dollars would be accepted most places.

He had his round-trip ticket and Laleh's one-way ticket to the United States.

He reserved two adjoining rooms in the Hotel Ashkhabad. Jim knew that the social mores of the Islamic culture demanded that Laleh have her own accommodations. As he waited, he imagined their meeting in the lobby when she arrived. He prayed that they could get the vials safely into the U.S. despite violating regulations of many countries.

Jim even fantasized about a possible wedding. It would be something outdoors, perhaps by a waterfall or stream in Utah. He wondered if Laleh would feel the same way.

Then Jim felt his pulse quicken and his mind race with thoughts of Laleh in bed with him as his wife. He forced himself to concentrate on less stimulating thoughts. He wondered if Laleh might want to select a unique restaurant to celebrate their reunion. Jim decided not to pay for a Turkmenintour, the all-inclusive package that included meals.

His enthusiasm couldn't be contained. "This is going be the most awesome, most marvelous meeting! I can see her now!" His emotions started to race again and his practical side intervened saying, "Patience, patience, patience. . . ."

The reservations were confirmed. He would fly out of Salt Lake on Delta Airlines and then transfer to Lufthansa Airlines in Berlin for the final leg into Ashkhabad, Turkmenistan. They would fly back to the U.S. together.

"Together!" Jim was again bubbling with thoughts of the two of them together—close.

Everything was working out perfectly. Fortunately, Jim was able to take advantage of spring break at the College of Pharmacy, and thus not lose his job. He was so infatuated with Laleh that he was willing to sacrifice everything, if necessary. He considered that the trauma of losing Jaynee had made him realize just how precious his relationship with Laleh was. She had decided that Ashkhabad, the literal translation being "The Place of Love," was the right place. "I hope she is right."

To cool his ardor, Jim decided to do some research about health concerns in Turkmenistan. He opened the tour guidebook he had taken from the library.

"Most of the water mains had to be replaced after the 1948 earthquake, which measured 10.5 on the Richter scale. The city had been razed after more than the officially reported 30 percent of the population had been killed. It's taken a long time to rebuild their infrastructure." Considering that many water sources were still not trusted in the country, Jim felt it would be better to be safe rather than sorry. He'd never experienced the waterborne ills so many people have when they travel abroad because he'd always taken precautions. This would be no exception. He decided to take his small "Pur" brand bacterial water filter that he used in the backcountry. The hand pump was quick and small enough to fit inside one of his empty hiking boots. The big challenge might be to find some water without any dangerous elements like arsenic, or any water at all.

Because cholera and diphtheria are present in that part of the world, Jim went to the Salt Lake County Public Health Service and obtained immunizations. Some other health tips he read about: He shouldn't accept ice in drinks and should eat only properly cooked meat and vegetables. Fruit should be peeled before eating. Many countries have unpredictable sources of toilet paper supply.

Jim also decided to include a small medical kit, a first-aid kit and his pocket GPS, a Garmin Global Positioning System. He remembered that he needed a reliable map that could be used with the GPS and he eventually got one off the Internet.

His friends were often amused at his compulsive attention to proper planning when Jim traveled with them. He didn't mind their joking. He'd backpacked for weeks at a time in the wilderness and knew what it meant when you forget a critical item. There were no stores.

"Damn, I love that woman. I can't think about anyone or anything else. I wonder what she is doing over there right now?" He sat in his office watching the robins work on their nest. The birds seemed to make their bond of parenthood a total commitment.

"If only human beings could meet their covenants with as much dedication. When Laleh and I marry we will be dependable parents. We will be there for our children."

Jim recalled how Jaynee and he hadn't wanted to have children right away. They had their careers and fun-in-the-sun priorities. He wondered how Laleh felt about a family. He was ready now!

"Back to work," Jim said out loud. The selection of clothes was not easy because spring had just arrived on the calendar. He decided he should pack for a warmer climate. Ashkhabad was on the edge of the Kara-Kum Desert. However, it was at the foot of the Kopet-Dag Mountain Range and might have fluke storms. He wondered if they might have sandstorms like some other deserts.

He decided to pack layers of clothing—fleece and wool—and he would wear his old cowboy boots. They were like a security blanket. Jim piled the potential contents for his two carry-on bags in the middle of his bed. He tossed a round two-pin continental AC conversion plug onto the bed. It would allow him to use his electric razor. He studied the mess and wondered what he could have forgotten.

Jim was buoyed by his anticipation of seeing Laleh as he parked his vehicle in the long-term parking area at the airport and jogged with his luggage to the shuttle through melting slush. He was oblivious to the weather. The Delta flight left on time to Atlanta. The transoceanic leg was uneventful as they prepared to land in Berlin. Jim had never been to Europe and he regretted that he couldn't take the time to tour this famous city.

"Who knows if any one of these people have the new flu?" Jim glanced briefly at a TV in the airport lounge area. A Reuters News Service story was being aired on the CNN news. The announcer was speaking in German, but Jim could tell that some epidemic in Afghanistan was being featured. He looked around him and saw several people coughing and red-eyed in the airport. He hurried on to his next flight connection.

The plane departed in a rainstorm. Dark, ominous clouds cloaked the city from view. His fellow passengers' dialects and clothing suggested what might be ahead in Ashkhabad.

Jim couldn't help thinking about the dangerous virus and the potentially lifesaving vaccine he and Laleh were attempting. "I can't do anything for those poor souls right now." But his love soon interceded and he grew oblivious to anyone else on the plane. His only thoughts were of her.

A passenger several rows behind Jim kept an eye on him throughout the flight. He was very unobtrusive. His olive skin, black

249

goatee and the half-eyeglasses pinched on his nose did nothing to distinguish him from most of the other travelers. The fact that he never talked to anyone near him nor closed his eyes, went unnoticed. He held a copy of an old American novel in his hands but never turned a page.

The large plane circled over the Firyusa Gorge in the Kopet Dag Mountains south of Ashkhabad while waiting for some technical difficulties to clear up at the airport. A woman associated with the Sister Cities Organization from Albuquerque delighted in explaining everything to Jim that could be seen in the clear moonlit night. She was leading a small international group on a tour of Turkmenistan. She was a tall, trim woman Jim judged to be in her fifties. She was also a retired professor of geography.

"See the gorge below? It is a summer retreat for many people of the city of almost a half a million people." She announced, "Now you can see the Hippodrome, where horse races are held. It is only ten kilometers south of Ashkhabad. I'll never go there again because there were no restrooms at all when I went there last. It isn't far from the Turkmenbashi Stud Farm."

That interested Jim, as he had grown up on a ranch in Colorado.

She continued. "Famous horses, the Akhal-Teke or Akilteken, are bred there. It is believed by scientists that they could be the root-stock from which the world's great thoroughbreds originated. Their speed is legendary. The horses, long-necked with concave cheeks, are about fifteen hands high. They hold their heads up to look over the desert. Their golden color matches the golden steppes of the Kara Kum. I have read that their lean, small frames allowed them to go for hundreds of kilometers and as long as three days without water. They were the early Turkmen's secret weapon."

At last they approached Ashkhabad and another traveler pointed to an old ruin. "That's Geok-Tepe, an old fort forty kilometers west of the city where as many as twenty thousand Tekke Turkmen were killed by the Russian General Skobileff in 1881."

"You must have been here before," said Jim in an inquiring tone.

"Yes, many times. My work brings me here often from Germany," the man said.

Jim asked, "What are those tiny little isolated dark sites in the desert sand? I see them all over down there."

"Oh, those!" The German acknowledged knowingly. "Those are some of the listening posts that the KGB installed in the desert bordering Iran during the Cold War. The Red Army built the control towers surrounded by barbed wire. I don't think any of them are manned any more, especially those far away, next to the mountains. There isn't enough reason to justify the expense these days."

The bright moon actually made some objects easier to see at night than during the day because of contrasts. The German traveler, a talkative history buff, began relating the stories about Mongols intent on obliterating the Muslim civilizations in the eighth century. "Genghis Khan came here in the 1200s, then Marco Polo and the Great Silk Road. The Turkomans, caravan merchants, came in the thirteenth century."

"Alexander The Great was influenced here by great horse-women. This is the Land of the Amazons, bordering Chorasmia. The women rode tall, swift horses, shot arrows, and threw javelins at their enemies with such speed that it spawned legends. You probably have heard about the queen of the Amazons who tried to seduce Alexander, but he had declined with a promise to return later."

"Actually, this is the first time I have heard of it." Jim responded.

"Well then, you probably haven't heard that Alexander owned a horse, Bucephalus, that was an Akhal-Teke. Cyrus the Great of Persia had a close companion who was alleged to have received a gift of such a horse also!"

Jim and the German then shared brief personal histories and Jim learned his name was Hans Pasternak.

The woman from Albuquerque introduced herself to them both. "My name is Shawn Johnson. I could not restrain myself from listening to your fascinating conversation. I was curious, Mr. Pasternak, have you visited Kou-Ata?" Without waiting for an answer, she insisted on telling the two men about an underground mineral lake in Turkmenistan. It is fed by hot springs in the Kou-Ata, which means father of caves. It is located about ninety kilometers southwest from Ashkhabad. Even though there are no accommodations there, many people visit," the Johnson woman indicated.

"The hike down inside the cave is quite long as it goes down for hundreds of feet with crude lighting all along the way. The sulfur-smelling water is full of calcium oxide, which requires that visitors carry their own bottled drinking water with them. You should wear hiking boots, because there's a long climb up afterward. The upper part of the cave has mud swallows nesting in the ceiling and the lower portion has bats. Also, I almost forgot, if a person can swim about three kilometers in the subterranean lake, they can end up under Iran. But I'm not that good of a swimmer."

Then Hans said, "You probably will find it difficult to go there as a foreigner. The whole Kopet Dag mountain range is considered a state security zone. It borders Iran and I think it would be considered off-limits to Americans. I saw a Turkmen Red Star newspaper that had published a picture of the city with the mountains in the background a few years ago. They received 'inquiries' about a possible breach of trust by some political authority."

Shawn Johnson then pointed and said, "That's the Kara-Kum Canal, which was completed in 1962 and alleviated the chronic water shortage."

Jim inquired about the railroad yard starkly lit below them.

"It's the Trans-Caspian Railway. Another state security zone, of course," Hans responded.

A voice came over the intercom apologizing for the delay caused by stalled ground equipment, saying they would be landing directly.

Jim was ready to deplane even though it could be several hours before Laleh would arrive. It took a long time to exit the plane and proceed through customs.

Jim's baggage had been chosen by the inspector to be inspected closely. He watched in horror as the inspector opened his Thermos with dry ice. It steamed carbon dioxide. But the inspector simply replaced the cap and said nothing. Jim feared he was visibly shaking and could hardly believe he was cleared. He forced himself to walk slowly out of the area.

The man with the goatee and half-glasses was delayed in his deplaning but did not have his baggage checked. He had only one attaché case. He tried to appear nonchalant, yet he was always in sight of Jim. His stocky frame and tight jacket exposed the bulge of a weapon on his hip. The security people at the gate seemed to act as if the man was invisible—he just melted into the swirling crowd. Jim wondered who this gun-toter knew or who he had bribed. The Goatee seemed to know where everything was without reading signs or asking questions. He was on his own turf.

Jim went to an information booth to inquire about taxis. He noticed that people could send a telegram or Telex via dual Cyrillic and Latin keyboards. Long distance calls were being made through an international operator who could speak English. There didn't seem to be a way to make international direct calls. A fax machine was available for a fee. He hoped they wouldn't have to contact anyone.

An English-speaking bureaucrat advised that all of the taxi drivers were independent and might not be licensed. A verbal contract would be necessary with each ride before he started anywhere.

Jim gathered his luggage and started to approach a taxi. He sensed that he was being ignored in preference to others. Then he noticed that the man with the goatee—some distance behind him with only a briefcase—got a taxi driver to scurry to his side immediately. Jim was ready to do battle.

However, the goateed man was polite and insisted with a motion of his hand that the taxi operator should attend to Jim first.

Jim waved a thank you to the man and entered the taxi. As Jim slid into his seat, the taxi driver noted the fact that Jim had loaded his own bags in the seat beside him.

The driver spoke to Jim in German or Russian but he did not understand what the driver said. But he knew the international tone was derogatory.

Jim informed the taxi driver, "I'm sorry, but I speak only English."

"Hmmm—Da! Amerikan." The cab driver affirmed his worst suspicions with his look. He may as well have said out loud, "This traveler is one of those disgusting Americans who knows no customs of the East and is too egotistical to learn any other language."

Jim tried to communicate with hand signals and corrupted high-school German. In this way Jim negotiated the cost to get to the two-star Ashkhabad Hotel. But he was at the cab driver's mercy and finally agreed on the terms of their verbal contract.

"Okay, four dollars American," Jim concluded.

The taxi driver had determined he would be paid in advance. Then the driver motioned for the goateed man to come and another contract was negotiated in a fraction of the time that it took Jim. The man did not pay in U.S. dollars; Jim could tell that different-colored paper money was used. The bearded man smiled broadly and sat down in the back seat with Jim. He uttered what might have been a Turkmen greeting. The taxi driver then told a joke. The other passenger and driver laughed heartily. Jim felt it was probably at his expense.

The cabby refused to get out of his cab or make a gesture of helping Jim unload his bags when they arrived just short of the entrance. The cabby was very solicitous, however, with the goateed man, and they bid each other a Turkmen farewell. Jim tried to appear oblivious of the slight and departed the man's company with a smile and a wave, juggling his bags.

Jim felt the stored heat generated from the black sand desert as the evening began to cool. A contrasting breeze from the south off the snowcapped Kopet Dag Mountains began to blow.

Two armed guards at the entrance of the hotel observed Jim leaving the cab, and smiled at each other in a knowing way. When Jim entered the lobby it seemed he was the only English-speaking client there. A long line of people was waiting to check in, and they all seemed to be talking at once. It was noisy.

He hoped his room would be quieter. "If they still have one for me," Jim said to himself. He watched a native of Turkmenistan pay in advance for a night's lodging with ten American one-dollar bills.

When it was Jim's turn, he asked how much he needed to pay in advance." He showed his credentials.

The desk receptionist did not hesitate. "The $120 is accurate as stated in your confirmation."

Jim guessed that he would have similar accommodations to the native Turkmen that only had to pay ten dollars. Jim's $120.00 was 288,000 manats, an average annual income for most Turkmen.

"I need to pay for the room of Dr. L. Bazargan. She will be checking in later."

"Konyechno! Yes, certainly! She has not yet checked in, but her moneys have been received."

The desk clerk then indicated, "Her identification, she needs to present—to get key."

Jim asked for his room key and whether there were any bell-hops. He was given a contemptuous look. He guessed that he must have said something that sounded obscene.

He surveyed the lobby, hoping to see someone who looked like a bellhop. "That person over there would look like a comic in the U.S.A.," he thought. He wore a black leather jacket and colored eye-glasses. But the way he lurked about the check-in area suggested he might be a hotel security person.

The German engineer Hans Pasternak, who had just checked

in, nodded in the direction of the man in black leather and sunglasses. "Former KGB." Jim almost laughed. The man did look like someone typecast as a baddie in a 1960s movie.

The elevator had a sign with an international symbol that meant that it was out of order, so Jim had to lug his baggage up two flights of stairs. He guessed that the building had five floors. Even though it was cool, he was sweating profusely by the time he reached his high-ceiling room. After Jim examined his quarters, he was glad he had brought his own toilet paper, soap and light bulb. He needed all of it.

Jim looked out the window over the city. Few old landmarks were visible in the moonlight. The people of Askhkabad hoped to get money and an enlightened bureaucracy to finish rebuilding most of the structures that had been leveled by the devastating earthquake of 1948. The Soviets had rebuilt most of the buildings with very utilitarian gray concrete rectangles.

There was a knock on the door and Jim jerked from the window. He bounded across the room to unlock the door, expecting to find Laleh. It was instead the leather-coated man with the sunglasses. Jim took a step back. Without saying a word, the black coat handed Jim a note from the "Desk Registration Clerk." Jim stood baffled and unfolded the note.

It said, "Dr. Schriver, you have a telephone call from a Dr. Laleh Bazargan in Iran. Please come to the Public Room as soon as possible, your call is being held."

The formal note reflected that his room phone either did not exist or was not working. The old KGB messenger was serving as a bellman, whether anyone wanted to admit it or not.

Jim bounded down the flights of stairs and almost flew to "The Public Room."

The old bellman tried to keep up, but bravely kept Jim in sight. His arthritic knees restrained him.

Jim snatched the phone receiver up. "Hello—Laleh?"

"Jim. Jim . . ." She started crying and struggled with her emotions.

She was still weak from the food poisoning and stood shaking in the mild breeze on the mountaintop. The peculiar skis strapped to her borrowed hiking boots, and the long wool dress protruding from under a stylish coat and a borrowed fur hat perched on her head, made her look warm but rumpled. Her teeth tended to chatter as she continued. "Darling, I don't know where to start. I came down with food poisoning and my new friends, Mary and Zayd Ashari, rescued me off the bus after I fainted from losing too much fluid." Laleh paused.

"I'm staying at their home on a mountain near Bejgiran. I won't be there with you tonight and I don't know what to do. . . ."

"Laleh, I can tell by your voice, you're not telling me something. What else is wrong?"

"Oh, Jim." She convulsed with more tears.

"Laleh, tell me!" Jim demanded.

"I heard that the authorities are looking for someone with state secrets who is trying to escape. The Border Patrol between Iran and Turkmenistan set up a road block on the highway and the train hit a stopped truck on the tracks. Some sort of toxic waste was spilled as a result. Mary just heard that it might be a week before the roads are opened again . . ."

"So you are stuck there—maybe for a week?"

"Yes! But I do have this borrowed cell phone."

"Laleh, what does Zayd do there in Bejgiran?" Jim inquired.

Laleh counseled with Mary. "He works at the Prophet's Copper Mine here. It's west of Bejgiran about ten kilometers. I would guess we're at about 3,500 meters in altitude on the south side of the Kopet Dag mountain range. You are on the north side and about forty kilometers from the border. This side of the mountain is only about forty-five degrees in slope, but the north side is quite vertical, sheer cliff. I can't just walk off this mountain, I'm told . . ."

"Let me think," requested Jim. "I think there may be a way," He mumbled to himself as he considered different options. "I am going to come and get you, Laleh! Stay there at your friend's home and I will be there sometime tomorrow. What is your cellular telephone number?"

Laleh gave him the number and said, "I'm sorry I've made a mess of things."

"You didn't do this. It was done to you. It's not your fault, Laleh." He could tell that her lack of response said volumes. "We'll find a way," Jim replied, in an exaggerated western drawl.

"Jim, how can you be so flippant? This is not one of your western movies where the good guys always win!"

"Seriously, don't worry any more. I have a plan."

"Jim, you are an American in a strange, hostile country. You don't know the language. What are you going to do? Call for the cavalry?"

"I can't tell you over this phone, but trust me. I have met some people who I know will help me find you tomorrow and bring us both out."

"Jim, it is so very dangerous—especially now. You don't know all that has happened to me. . . ."

He did not understand what she was trying to tell him. "Rest, save your strength, drink lots of fluid and prepare to leave tomorrow. Locate a backpack. . . . We best get off this line. It's hard to say how many eavesdroppers there may be. I love you."

Jim knew he had to contact his new friend, Hans Pasternak. He finally located him by telephone at Hans' girlfriend's shop in the large bazaar, not too far from the hotel.

"Hello, Hans Pasternak?" Jim tried to confirm.

"Ya, this is Hans."

"Hans, I hope this is a good time to request a big favor from a new friend."

"What is za problem? I'm here to serve."

Jim could tell Hans must have been drinking a bit.

"This will be a very big favor, with lots of complications. Are you still willing to serve, Hans?" He didn't wait for a response. "Let me tell you more about what I need before you commit yourself. Could you possibly meet me tonight—say in an hour here in the hotel bar?"

"I'll be there with the love of my life—right, sweet thing?" Hans put music to his reply while evidently looking to his intimate partner for her consent.

"Hmmmmm," a female voice responded. A pause ensued, while sounds of passion preempted Jim's sense of urgency.

Finally, Hans responded. "We'll be there in an hour." The phone went dead.

Jim's mind went into high gear brainstorming the possibilities. He figured he would need a good map, his Garmin global positioning device, horses to go across the desert to the base of the Kopet Dag mountain, rock climbing gear for two on the mountain, two ice axes, water, a little food, winter clothing for the snow on top, and advice and counsel from someone who knows the area. He started writing a list of needs, including key questions for his new friends.

There was a restaurant and a hotel bar accessible by a separate outside door. It reminded Jim of Utah, where visitors often didn't expect to obtain alcoholic beverages and were surprised when their favorite spirits were waiting for them. Jim's eyes were sweeping everywhere in search of a table.

He noticed the employee cafeteria and a souvenir and news shop. A candy kiosk featured boxed candy, candied fruit of different types and rock candy of different colors. A large man in a blue blazer approached Jim with a mouth full of gold teeth that reminded him of some character out of an old James Bond movie. His hand was extended as he neared.

"Velcome Dr. Schriver, Ashkhabad is honored."

"Hello," Jim responded with a rigid smile. "Who are you?"

"I am Djura Niyazov, representative of the Turkmen Friendship Society. Ve have Pepsi in the bar. Can I buy you one while you wait?"

Jim wondered if this offer was made to impress him that he could purchase expensive drinks—not just vodka. Or, it might have also been a tacit way to let him know that Djura was aware of the predominant Mormon culture of Utah and their aversion to alcoholic drinks.

"I'm sorry, but I am waiting for professional associates, perhaps another time," replied Jim while looking around Djura for some sign of his guests.

"On the stools, we could sit at the bar end while you waited for Dr. Bazargan," suggested Djura.

Jim wasn't surprised that Djura was so knowledgeable and intrusive. He needed to find out how much he knew. "The Pepsi sounds fine—I'll wait there with you."

"It is good that you do this. Good relations between our countries start with small steps, " responded Djura with his teeth flashing from the overhead lights.

"Is it your job to greet all foreign visitors with such attention?" Jim inquired.

"We need tourists to help our economy. Can your business here help us?" Djura inquired with a big sly smile, all the while trying to read Jim's body language and facial expression.

"As you probably already know, I am in the medical field and anything that can help people stay well, save a country and its citizens from illness and death is good business. Is there anything else that you feel you would like to know about my business?" Jim inquired.

Djura was caught off guard with this American's directness. Such candor was unique. He just stood staring as he considered his next reply.

"I have great respect for your national security capabilities," Jim blurted before Djura could think of a diplomatic answer.

"You must have mistook, I am the Turkmen Friendship Society Representative. We help your needs wherever and quickly," the smiling teeth replied.

"Good," said Jim, "help me locate four good riding horses and saddles to rent for a day."

"The doctor will need them when?" Djura was obviously disturbed that his "friendship efforts" might get complicated. But he risked asking, "Where vill you horseback ride?"

"Where would you suggest? We just wanted to ride in the desert tomorrow."

"Come back to you, I will. Arrangements with horses and saddles for four, I will get. One hundred U.S. dollars, it will cost in advance." Djura challenged the American's sincerity.

"We'll pay on receipt of the animals," Jim said with authority.

"It would be correct to have a guide also. I am a very good guide. Know all places."

Jim thought, "I won't risk discussing anything other than horses with this guy, no matter what he wants to call himself. I wouldn't even do this if we had time to do otherwise." Jim sipped the warm Pepsi, wishing he had requested vodka. He thought to himself as he became mad and impatient. He said, "I'll consider the guide offer."

Djura waited for Jim to say something of gratitude. The Pepsi was very expensive and hard to obtain.

Jim lifted his Pepsi in salute and said, "Thanks, this was refreshing. I see my friends looking for me now. Wait right here, I want them to meet you."

Both Jim and Djura heard the voices of the two loud guests come into the bar. Hans and a pretty woman, arm in arm, smooching with every other step. "Dr. Livingstone—I mean Schriver, I presume," greeted Hans. Obviously neither was feeling any pain. I would like you to meet Lillia Sopiev. Lillia . . . Jim Schriver."

Hans formally introduced Lillia Sopiev. She was a widowed shopkeeper in the city's main bazaar. After a few moments of chatter the three agreed that they had a lot of work to do to meet all of Jim's needs. They would have to work all night.

Lillia spoke fluent English and Jim wondered where she learned to speak so well. She told him that her father had been with the Russian Embassy. She had been schooled in England when he was posted in London as an attaché. She had married her husband, as her father had arranged, when she was fourteen years old. Since then she had lived in Ashkhabad and had been running the shop in the bazaar for five years since her husband's stroke and death. She had not been able to have children. Hans had met her about a year ago when he was shopping while in town for business. They had fallen in love.

Jim was relieved by the presence of his friend in the doorway of the Public Room. The two newcomers scanned Djura for recognition and awaited introductions. Jim whispered, "He claims he can get some horses for us."

Hans whispered back, "KGB, be careful."

Jim said in a loud voice, "I'd like you to meet Djura Niyazov before he leaves. He is about to go and locate our riding horses for tomorrow." The other two thanked him for his efforts to locate the animals. Jim mentioned that Hans would serve as their guide and tour leader.

Djura excused himself and started to leave. He turned and said, "We meet here in the hotel lobby at 6 A.M.—is okay?"

"The earlier, the better," said Jim. Djura nodded and quickly left.

Jim was motioned by Hans to follow him. Without a word, the trio walked briskly toward the large front doors and steps. Two men standing outside the building watched first as Djura and then the trio exited the bar. They hustled across the street in the moonlight, and ran into the shadow of the building. A different man with a goatee bolted from a parked car to jog after them. There was no attempt to hide the fact that they were under government surveillance. At least, that's what the trio assumed.

The goateed man slowed to the trio's pace about five meters behind them, almost in earshot. The three walked briskly block after block, turning arbitrarily onto different streets in a circuitous route until they could hear the panting of the overweight, aged tail. Jim recognized their shadow as the goateed person he had shared the cab with from the airport. Jim noticed Hans was steering them toward a parked car. About fifty kilometers away, they started to sprint to the car. Quickly they scrambled into the vehicle.

Hans could see the dark figure behind them struggling to catch up. Hans immediately lurched into motion. He swerved back and forth while departing, thus making a license identification more difficult. It worked. When they were three hundred kilometers away the confused agent gave up trying to get a fix. They quickly turned again and were lost from view.

The trio stood ready with the mountain climbing gear, clothing and all of the other essentials by six o'clock. It was all packed in duffel bags and secreted in the trunk of Lillia's car, parked out of sight near the ranch where they would start their ride. Lillia was shuttled by another friend to the hotel in time to meet up with Hans, Jim and Djura.

When they met Djura Niyazov at the hotel the next morning, he asked if they still needed four horses, as there were only three of them. Jim explained, "The fourth rider was detained but will meet us later."

Djura escorted them to the horse barn south of the city, driving them in his own Fiat. Cash payment was made and a bond given for four people's use of the valuable horses. Djura handled all of the money and arrangements. He was very happy to wave at them as he left with his cut.

They got organized and were briefed on the proper use of the animals by the wrangler. Jim was in awe of the fine quality of the Akhal-Teke horses. They were everything he had heard about. They rode the horses to Lillia's car and retrieved their duffel bags.

They had an eighteen-mile ride to get to the foothills of the Kopet Dag. They knew that the horses could make the ride, but none of the people had ridden for years. They got under way quickly.

Lillia left her little car out of sight, off the main road and behind a barn. Jim checked his GPS to confirm where they were on the map. It worked perfectly, the horse ranch was where it was supposed to be. As a precaution, they took extra water bags because of Jim's past bad experiences on other desert trips in Utah. The riderless horse carried water and feed for the animals.

The ominous southern ochre cliffs could be seen clearly, glistening in the sunrise. They rode west until they were out of sight of the ranch and main road, then turned south, ignoring the advice of the horse wranglers that "You can ride in any direction except south. The government prohibits that."

They passed an old guard tower that looked abandoned. The electric power lines had been disconnected. The sensing devices located here and there on the desert looked weathered and non-functional. They decided that the old Soviet security system was only a legend now because of the new Turkmenistan government's inability to pay for the manpower to monitor Iran's border. The two countries had just finished building a joint railroad, and a gas pipeline was in progress.

Jim commented, "Look at that beautiful contrast of shadows. Notice the bright sun shining on the melting snow near the top. It gives me an adrenaline rush."

"My friend, I hope you know what you are doing," said Hans.

"Oh, you're going to climb up THAT!" Lillia exclaimed, in an unbelieving tone.

"Yes, and hopefully back down safely with Laleh, who has never done rock climbing. I know what you think. . . . Talk about fools rushing in where angels fear to tread," Jim answered.

"Oh, my. It just looks too intimidating. It always has, even from the air," Lillia said, looking at Jim as if he were demented. Then she looked again at the feat before them. "I'm glad Hans and I are only expected to wait at the bottom for you two."

They reached the base of the cliff in time for lunch.

They secured the horses in the shade of the only trees that could be seen for three hundred meters and were well out of sight of the main road, ten kilometers away. Jim was pleased with the climbing route he felt would be the easiest.

"It looks like I will only have to do one pitch at the top. The rest will be scrambling on stone ledges," Jim announced as he peered through his small binoculars. "We won't need crampons for ice at the top—if we can start down while the snow is soft. I will take both ice axes. . . . Might have to watch for an avalanche, however. . . . We have plenty of rope." There was a granite veneer on some of the mostly unstable rock monolith. Perhaps it wouldn't be as unstable and crumbly as he had feared.

"We must stay out of sight of any airplanes that might come over. Use the flashlights only in an emergency. Do you have any other concerns?" Hans asked.

"Nothing more than the usual. Watch where you step. I was warned that there are a few poisonous snakes about. You should feed the horses and give them each a little water. Sleep as much as you can because we will want to start riding back in the dark." They wished each other good luck and Jim started up the cliff.

Jim marveled how fortunate he was to have found such accommodating new friends. There seemed to be an unspoken bond between them for some unknown reason. Jim felt that maybe being ardent lovers themselves, they empathized with Laleh and his situation. Jim thought to himself, "Love will always find a way."

Chapter 24
Turkmenistan and Iran—Days 24–26

Jim always hated hiking in sand. It reminded him of childhood nightmares in which a monster could move by leaps and bounds while Jim's feet were always stuck in mud or sand.

He thought about a climbing friend he used to climb with up Little Cottonwood Canyon. Jerry would always pay homage to the mountain by making a deep bow just before starting a climb. Then, mystically, he would take one step forward and scan the mountain while mumbling some mantra. Now, Jim was heavily laden with his yellow helmet, climbing clothes, shoes, harness, rope, hardware, rosin bag, water, food, ice ax, plus a duplication of everything for Laleh.

The jingling noise of the carabiners, rappelling devices, chocks, bongs, cams and snow screws, sounded something like a wind chime. Hiking and scrambling with the weight he was hauling made him quite warm. Even though it was early spring and snow still clung to the apex of the mountain, Jim was soon perspiring.

He wouldn't need the technical gear until almost at the very top. But, he was glad Hans had friends who loaned it. It would be necessary for the final assent.

He stretched his muscles by reaching little ledges and shelves as he sought out his route. He found himself traversing long ridges first to the right and then back to the left, zigzagging as the mountain dictated.

Jim mumbled as he faced a wall and slid sideways. From the ranch and trail, the cliff looked a lot more vertical. The "surface cracks" were really ledges over a half to a full meter wide. With the open exposure, he was glad he didn't have acrophobia and he sure hoped Laleh didn't have it either.

Lillia was looking up while shielding her eyes with one hand from the sun. "Look at him now! He looks like a human fly walking sideways on a glass windowpane. I can't watch, Hans. What if he falls? What could we do?"

"I think he's done this type of thing before. He should be all right. If I weren't so terrified of heights, I'd be up there with him."

"If you had—I wouldn't be here to watch, I assure you!" Lillia retorted.

Periodically Jim stopped to clear the route of loose stone slabs which would fall one hundred meters or more before striking and exploding on the hard rock below.

The first rock explosion sounded like a gunshot to Lillia. "Oh, no! Who's shooting at us? I knew we shouldn't have come."

Hans couldn't help but be amused. "As a wild child, I used to drop chunks off of bridges over deep canyons, just to hear that noise."

Lillia felt silly. "I am not amused!"

"Lillia, it's not the loud booms that unsettle my nerves. It is the dull thuds," commented Hans.

"That is a terrible thought, Hans!"

During the next hour Jim made quick but noisy progress. At times he would set off cascades of debris that both Lillia and Hans worried could be heard ten kilometers away. Sometimes Jim would pile up three flat rocks on top of one another to make trail marking cairns. However, as an environmentalist, he was careful never to scratch the wall to permanently deface an area. He planned to destroy the rock-cairns on the way down, being careful that nobody was below when he did. He would leave nothing but footprints—which the wind could blow away.

As Jim neared the top, the shadow of the cliff moved further north, shading and chilling him when he rested. The melting snow, drizzling from protruding rock overhangs, made the climbing surface very slippery. Sometimes it would drizzle on his helmet and splash behind his sunglasses. Then the wind, which was causing a sandstorm below, carried fine dust the consistency of sifted flour onto his wet glasses—producing mud. Cursing, Jim stopped to clear his lenses.

"I sure hope Hans and Lillia are doing okay. I wonder if they can see that old halftrack truck that I see way out there in the desert. I wonder what they are doing. Could they be searching for us? If so, I pray the sandstorm will delay their ardor," Jim said to himself.

The climbing became more than a scramble. Jim had to use hand jams and some upper body strength to gain purchase on some areas. He reminded himself to tell Laleh to always use a three-point descent on this. Keep two hands and a foot, or two feet and one hand on the mountain at all times.

Finally Jim reached the snow. Soft, it lay on about a sixty-degree slope. It was novel to use the ancient old wood-handled ice ax. It had a heavy leather strap with a loop on the end that was securely encompassing his wrist. He faced the steep slope, placing one foot pointing right and the other left. He would squat slightly, retrieve his ice ax and briskly rise to plant its point firmly above him.

Watching from below, Hans said to Lillia, "Come look at him now. He's the dark smudge on that snow chute. Tell me, what does he look like to you?"

"He is doing a plie." As a child I took ballet. Now he's doing first position." Lillia said as she continued to peer through the binoculars.

"Exactly! That's what I thought. Fascinating. Ballet on a mountain."

"Now I think he is screwing in one of those fifty-centimeter snow screws into what must be hard snow in the shadows. Now he's fastening a carabiner through its loop. . . . Threading the rope. . . . Fastening it to his climbing harness. I don't know how he does it all so fast," Lillia marveled.

"He's doing it all by himself, too. He should have a partner," Hans reflected. "Now he's off snow and onto rock."

Jim continued to creep up, little by little, securing carabiners into the loops of cams and bongs that had been wedged in cracks of hard rock.

The mountain was made of such variable stuff, sandstone, basalt and shale one minute that would break loose on a whim. Next it was solid granite, conglomerate and hard clay. It was no place for a novice.

At last Jim could see the end of the technical climb, when he realized there wasn't going to be quite enough rope! He was going to be short by about ten feet. "Bad luck! Oh well, I'll have to improvise." He still had enough hardware to use nylon webbing and make a sort of etriers, rope or nylon web ladders made of loops.

Jim finished constructing his etriers and prayed that he would not need anything else. He wouldn't have bothered if it had just been him alone to get down. He could have easily free-climbed much of the slope. But, he and Laleh would need to hurry down this at dusk and he was getting tired already. He'd had no sleep the previous night, then a long horse ride. He figured it would be worth it though, to have Laleh in his arms within the hour!

The crest of the final little climb gave him a vantage point into the southern valley. "Wow, I can see for a hundred kilometers at least!" The lengthening shadows across the desert were beautiful. The Atrak River ran in the valley due south and west. Bajgiran was to the southeast. Some of the incidental light was visible in the shadows. His GPS showed where he was on the map. The tiny mining town must be between him and Bajgiran in a straight line. "Piece of cake."

Jim called with Lillia's cellular phone to Laleh's cell number.

She answered, "Hello."

"I'm on top of your mountain looking down at you. Did you find a pack to load your essentials into? You must leave your suitcases."

"Yes, I've got it loaded. I'm all ready and excited!" She responded.

"I've found a route to get us out. Be discreet, but look for me. I should be there within the hour. Can you do it?"

"I'll find a way," Laleh said.

"Say no more. Monitors—you know." Jim hung up.

The windblown snow on the south side of the mountain was already firm again, due to the receding warmth of the sun. It would be only about a three-kilometer jog over the shoulder of the mountain to the Prophet's Copper Mine and little village below.

Jim knew better than to spend too much energy running. They were going to have to come uphill and then climb back down the other side, some of it in the dark.

He had to stay focused on pacing himself, but he was so energized he was almost euphoric. He had to avoid falling and dropping into some bottomless shadow.

The snow was softer, and only a few centimeters deep. Jim crested the foothill and looked down upon the mobile home village. His eyes were sweeping the area for some sign of Laleh.

Most of these people ate early, so they were having their supper. Jim wouldn't attract the attention of the rest of the village. Someone there was bound to dislike strange westerners who dropped in. With the steep, shale slope someone could glissade down to the village, but Jim restrained himself. He missed seeing a dark figure leave the perimeter of the town and creep up toward him from his far left. The figure moved quietly with the stealth of someone on a mission.

"Jim? Jim?" The figure cried out in the dusk of the cool evening.

"Laleh?" Jim said in startled unbelief.

Neither restrained themselves any longer. They raced toward each other with abandon, Laleh, who was barely able to move under the large, antique pack she had bought from her new friends, threw it off. Jim ran, jingling all the way. He dropped his ice ax just prior to their explosive embrace. The action startled a vulture which flew out of harm's way. They fell and rolled in the snow together as they kissed and embraced.

Their situation prevented them from dallying long, though. Already someone in the village was shouting something their way. It was impossible to see who it was, but they knew that the whole village would soon be craning their necks to see what was going on. Laleh took Jim's hand and they retreated up Jim's tracks in the diminishing light.

Jim looked to the east and said to Laleh, "The full moon will be a blessing, but also a problem. Others might be able to see us."

After jogging on the wind-hardened snowdrifts, they were warmed up and eager to get to freedom. But then, when they reached the edge of the cliff, Laleh glanced down the steep drop into Turkmenistan. Jim lowered her pack with a small cord to the base of the first small descent.

"I can't do that," she said with the tone of a frightened child. She kicked a small rock that sailed through space for a few seconds before it exploded several meters below them.

"Ohhhhh!" She cried out as she backpedaled as far away from the edge as she could. She sat down abruptly, her feet still pushing away from the precipice.

Jim dropped everything and rushed to her aid. He held her for several minutes, using all of his persuasive skills to calm her fears. He realized that she generated new fears in him. What were they going to do if she couldn't even try?

He took out a roll of string-like five-millimeter cord and said, "I'm going to tie this to your harness. I won't let you fall." Jim hated himself for lying to her. He knew a cord that small could not break her fall. But, psychologically, it would help. The rope ladder was secure.

"It's only going to be used for these first few meters. Then, I'll belay you with a genuine climbing rope," Jim said to her.

"You're sure, Jim?" Her lower lip was quivering and tears were running down her cheeks.

"Face the mountain and bow like me, Laleh." She turned her back to the vista below and did as he instructed. "We must honor the mountain before we descend." Jim and Laleh did a deep bow very slowly. "Now take a very deep breath and let it out very slowly. " He demonstrated. She followed. They repeated it. "Now, I am behind you. Walk backward looking down only at your feet." They slowly backed up to the edge. Jim squatted down and grabbed hold of the first loop with both hands and then he placed one foot in a loop below his hands. The next foot went lower.

Laleh followed his instructions as she watched him make loop knots in the cord dangling from her harness and then clip them into a carabiner. The first steps were Laleh's most terrifying. "Jim, if I didn't love you more than life itself—I wouldn't do this." She complained, "My mouth feels like a dry cotton ball, I'm so scared."

The progress was slow and Jim kept reminding Laleh about the three-point stance. "Remember, only one of your limbs should be free at any one time, the other three on the mountain. Don't look at anything except where your hand or foot is going."

At last the first few meters were done. Jim had Laleh rest and drink some water while he went back up to retrieve the hardware.

He then yanked the thin cord that had been her "lifeline" and secured her to the real climbing rope. She was too trusting to question him at that moment. His instructions were simple. "Every time you hook onto or off the rope you must yell, 'ON BELAY' or 'OFF BELAY.' Now, Laleh, you must again face the mountain and try to follow my old footprints as I belay you until the next comfortable spot where we can rest, down there. After you are there, I will rappel down to you." He used his most authoritarian tone. He couldn't be a lover— not now.

"On belay," she said as she started down.

Jim the climbing mentor and Laleh the student. Jim kept coaxing Laleh and demanding her response, focusing her vision on the route down. Jim was glad there wasn't much melting in the evening. But now there was clear ice hiding in shadows that demanded their attention.

It was almost midnight before the pair left the snow and ice, and came to the narrow ledges and shelves. Jim stopped there to rest on a mini plateau. While they were resting, an irritating aroma stimulated their noses.

"Is that sulfur, Jim?" Laleh asked.

"It is! There is a large underground cave, Kou-Ata, in Turkmenistan. People often visit to swim in the sulfur-smelling water. It is in this Kopet Dag mountain range, in the Firyusa gorge, not too many kilometers from here. Some say that one can swim under the mountain into Iran. Maybe we should have done that instead of climbing over this mountain," Jim said, half-joking.

"Not me—claustrophobia. If you think that I'm afraid of heights, it's nothing like my fear of tight places. Even the idea upsets me."

"I wonder where that smell is coming from?" Jim pondered. He stood up and let his nose lead him around the limited area. "I think it's coming from these cracks over here."

"Jim, I want to go down now! I remember an earthquake as a child that smelled like that. It makes me very uneasy. Can I take my harness off now?"

"Best not. It's like a seat belt in a car. I'd prefer you keep it on until we are back to the others and ready to get on our way." He caught himself before saying "horses." He hadn't mentioned that mode of transportation yet.

Beautiful moonlight illuminated their route, but thoughts of romance were preempted by fear. They carefully descended.

Tethered together, Jim led them down the switchbacks and scrambles on the cliff face, putting in protection hardware even when he didn't think it was necessary, just to pacify Laleh's fears.

An hour later the moon started to hide behind the mountain. They would soon be in complete darkness. "We've been moving too slowly," Jim thought to himself. He had a headband flashlight, but was afraid everyone for fifty kilometers around would see it.

They came to a very narrow ledge only seventy centimeters wide, or about two feet. It was almost pitch dark. Reflected moonlight was all that was illuminating their path.

"AH EEEeeee!" Laleh screamed as she suddenly fell from the cliff.

Jim instinctively braced for the inevitable impact. The rope tightened and stretched with the quickness of an airbag response, but the weight of her fall gained force to test all of Jim's safety protocol. He had her belayed for the moment, but he couldn't be sure if it would hold. He had been putting in safety anchors in holes and cracks he couldn't adequately see. Sickening sounds of grating metal suggested that something was slipping somewhere. Jim dare not move. He yelled.

"Laleh! Laleh!"

No response. Explosions of the rock that she had dislodged echoed back to Jim. "Laleh! Laleh!"

From way down below Hans and Lillia responded in the darkness. "Jim, what's wrong? What happened? Can we help?"

"Laleh fell! I've got her on belay! But I can't see what happened. She's not answering me."

"Oh, God—no!" Lillia said to Hans.

A faint groaning echoed off the solid rock.

"LALEH!" Jim screamed.

"Jim?" Replied a wee voice in the darkness. "I think I'm all right. I must have fainted. . . . I don't know where I am—but my toes seem to be dragging on a ledge." Jim cursed himself for not bringing a flashlight for her. He had screwed up. With great effort, he struggled to find another anchor location. He forced in a cam and tied off her rope. The grinding metal sound stopped. He donned his headband light and pointed in Laleh's direction. He could only see the rear of her backpack when she would slowly swing out. Hans and Lillia had retrieved their lights and beamed them toward her on the cliff.

"Jim—do you think I hurt the vaccine and virus in the bottles?" Laleh yelled up to Jim.

"Darling, right now I only care about you. Are you hurt anywhere?

"I don't think so. I may have wet my pants, though. . . . I'm all wet."

"The least of our problems, Laleh. You can change at the bottom. Can you see where your feet are?" Jim asked.

Hans yelled an answer. "She's touching a shelf with her toes. I think if you give her a little slack, she can swing into it."

"I think Hans is right, Jim," Laleh confirmed. "Jim, I also see a little cairn at the end of this shelf."

"GREAT!" Wait there until I get down to you. That's got to be part of our route down. Does it have three stones—one on top of the other?"

"Yes"! I think so; it's hard to tell in this poor light."

"I'm going to let you down slowly and you let me know when you have enough rope to get to the back of the shelf and unhook your carabiner. Then I'll retrieve the rope. Then just stay there until I climb down to you," Jim directed.

Hans yelled at the two. "Laleh, isn't it a crazy way Jim has chosen for us to meet?"

His light humor was helpful to Laleh. She released her rope and remembered to say, "Off belay!"

After the accident, they had decided to risk the lights in spite of the danger of being seen. It was after midnight and the odds were in their favor. It was another half hour before the two got down to Hans and Lillia. Introductions were amusing and brief. Laleh seemed to be on an adrenaline high. She had conquered one of her worst fears, falling off a cliff.

Jim was exhausted. "Why don't we all sleep a few hours? And then we'll mount the horses and head back at daybreak."

"Horses? What horses?" Laleh inquired.

"Some gorgeous Akhal-Tekis over there," Jim pointed into the darkness.

"I'm allergic to horses," Laleh said. "My nose runs and my eyes swell. And they get so red and water so bad that I can't see."

"I've got some allergy medicine back in town," said Jim.

"How far must we ride these animals before I get treatment?"

"We'll get started early in the morning and we'll get back before it's too hot. Let's hit the hay. I'm exhausted!"

After kissing Laleh goodnight, Jim fell immediately asleep. Laleh lay beside him looking at the stars, enjoying her salvation.

She thought. "All my adventures will be worth it if we can get the vaccine produced before too many others die."

Lillia and Hans cuddled like pets. They had rested all day waiting for the other two. Now they were ready to play. They found a secluded sandstone alcove not too far away, but out of sight. Eventually everyone fell into deep sleep, exhausted.

It was almost dawn when Hans and Lillia awakened to sounds echoing off of the stone wall. It was the noise of a vehicle stuck in the sand and several men laboring to free it. One loud voice seemed to be shouting commands to the others. It sounded like only a kilometer or less away.

Quickly they tiptoed toward Jim and Laleh motioning to one another to be quiet. They both knelt beside their friends and synchronized their efforts to cover Jim and Laleh's mouths to assure quiet awakenings.

"Mmmmmm" Laleh struggled to scream before she realized what was happening. Lillia whispered in her ear.

Jim refused to be awakened at first. Hans quietly told him what was going on.

The four travelers quickly darted about using their hands to mask their flashlights and locate their gear. Stealth was difficult in the dark. The horses sensed the tension and started moving about anxiously and whinnying. At last the four were ready to ride.

Jim used sign language to signal the others in the limited predawn light. He motioned for them to follow him east. He had to do it twice to confirm what he felt they should do. He followed the foot of the mountain toward the hard rock. He started to gallop his horse off in that direction with the others close behind him.

Hans thought to himself, "He'd better have a more practical plan than what it looks like." The two women simply followed—terrified. There was the risk that a horse would fall while galloping in the dark. And the noise of their passage was amplified for the military people behind them. The echo of hooves on rock was heard everywhere.

They could hear the vehicle accelerating to join in the chase. It seemed to be gaining on them, when suddenly it stopped. Curses exploded and echoed down the base of the rock mountain. Sounds of doors opening, people scrambling, and frantic confused voices met the small group's ears. Jim had remembered the little mini-canyon he had seen from his perch while climbing down to get Laleh. It had been between where they slept and the east, just big enough to trap a vehicle, if they went the way Jim led them. It had worked. To continue the chase the pursuers had to resort to chasing them on foot while the four continued to ride the famous racing horses of the desert.

Jim soon raised his arm and directed them to the right. They followed Jim's lead north across deep sand in a low channel of sand dunes and occasional hard clay. Jim slowed his horse to a walk and allowed the others to catch up to him.

"Let's follow this north. It heads in the right direction and is out of line of sight if our pursuers stay on foot."

Jim knew horses. "Everyone dismount and lead your horse while you jog. Then we will mount again." They all trusted the man known to his old friends as "Boots." They continued the procedure for almost an hour. When the sun came up, Jim realized that the path was leading them too far west.

"Rest the horses and yourselves while I sneak a peak. I think I got a glimpse of one of those old guard tower roofs." Jim handed his reins to Laleh and climbed up a small sand dune bordering their ravine. There it was, another old guard tower. Hoping it was still abandoned, he dashed to its stairs and climbed two steps at a time. He looked back the way they had come and could see nothing except the beauty of another cloudless day. The early morning cold was giving way to heat. A few brave plants had started to bloom already in the harsh desert. From far away he thought he could hear the sound of a half-track, but he was not sure.

The sounds of a ranch were coming from the opposite direction and Jim clearly saw their destination.

"We will have the horses back to the ranch before noon." Jim had hurried back to the others to tell them the good news. But, he cautioned, "They might have a radio. Someone still could intercept us. The leader probably knows that the horses came from the ranch. If he does, I think the best thing we can do now is simply make a run for it back to the car and get lost in the city as fast as we can. What do you all think?" They agreed with him.

Before returning the horses, the foursome stopped at Lillia's car to deposit the climbing equipment. They left a big tip with the grateful wranglers. No other visitors from the government were there—yet.

It was dusk and they were all starved as Hans drove down Makhtymkuli Avenue past the Hall of the Accomplishments of the Turkmen People. Finally they found a restaurant called Shishkas—Pine Cones.

Lillia explained that the name had more than one meaning in her culture. It could refer to cone-bearing trees that are very rare in a desert, or to people who fancy themselves as "big shots" or elite people. A Turkmen band, Akysh, was playing Central Asian rock with amplifiers that one could hear outside on the street. The balalaika, drums, bass guitar and electric keyboard gave the place a lively feel.

They pushed through a traditional, blue-bead stringed veil that functioned as a door and were met with the aroma of pirozhki—small pies stuffed with chopped potatoes, cabbage, lamb and seasonings that included garlic and onion. The room was full of men enjoying the food and entertainment. The conspicuous foursome were treated as celebrities, as the manager stumbled to their table to assist them.

"Salaam Aleikham," he greeted them.

"Aleikham Salaam," they responded.

The manager fixed his eyes on the men, even though Lillia was the only one ordering. She wondered if he even would know what she looked like. Jim and Hans simply smiled at him. The manager then thanked the men for the order.

The owner served them radishes, green onions and other zakkushkis (hors d'oeuvres) and vodka with his compliments. He stayed to toast his honored guests, though his Russian/Turkmen dialect was not understood well by any of the foursome. Only Lillia could get the gist of what he said. Whatever he said caused those at other tables nearby to raise their glasses and salute, drinking down the whole contents of their glasses. The women gasped for air and a drink of water, while the men's glasses were all firmly planted back on the tables.

Lillia had not expected such attention and only felt she caught a few isolated words. "I heard movie-maker and wealthy—little else."

She was glad that they had requested bottled water first. Lillia said, "I have never drunk with strange men before in public. I'm afraid that they will think of us as prostitutes."

Laleh said, "I'm afraid you're correct."

Jim and Laleh needed desperately to have some privacy. Because of the loud music, Laleh found she could speak furtively to Jim, knowing that no one else could hear them. Before they talked long, Jim felt he had to confirm Laleh's worst fears. "Sonbol is dead." Jim held her while she wept. Jim told Laleh everything he could remember that had happened since they had been apart. Laleh revealed everything she could remember about her life since they had been separated. They talked quietly about the virus and vaccine being left in the pack out in the car, unguarded. Neither Hans nor Lillia knew of their real mission. Jim suggested that he carry the seed virus and she the vaccine.

Laleh and Jim moved close to Lillia. "Laleh and I need to return to the hotel and get me checked out before our friends catch up with us. And, we need a place to stay tonight before we board our flight tomorrow."

Lillia insisted, "You two must stay with me. I assure you, I can accommodate you at my home above the shop. Hans and I can sleep below in the shop tonight."

Jim and Laleh had only told Hans and Lillia that they were seeking to escape their unknown pursuers. They had not told them about their need to replenish dry ice on a deadly virus and vaccine. Laleh seemed quite uneasy about involving Hans and Lillia any further.

"My shop is in the bazaar and you won't have to talk to any hotel security people there," Lillia insisted.

Laleh mumbled, "But what if . . ."

Lillia said, "We will stop at the hotel out of sight, and you two can run up and get Jim's baggage. We will whisk you away. At this late hour we can do it without a concern."

Jim and Laleh replaced the virus and vaccine's dry ice that Jim had brought.

A new hotel clerk was on duty. Jim paid his bill with cash and checked out. Apparently, the old former KGB agent had left for dinner and a little vodka, though the usual police guards stood outside the hotel in the shadows.

Once they arrived at the bazaar where Lillia's shop and loft apartment were, everyone collapsed with exhaustion. Laleh and Jim slept upstairs. Hans and Lillia disappeared below in the shop.

The roar of old trucks and rattling of handcarts with metal rims became part of the cacophony of a market coming to life. The foursome slept until almost noon.

Afternoon Islamic prayer time had ended. The sounds of turkeys, chickens, birds, lambs, camels and people of a hundred tongues awakened them.

The smell of Turkmen coffee further awakened Jim and Laleh. Even though most of the people drank green tea, Lillia knew how to make good coffee for her guests. Jim and Hans enjoyed their coffee as Lillia and Laleh sipped the green tea. The threesome tried to be of help to Lillia with her shop.

Unfortunately, foreign guests were unique and many voyeurs came past just to see Lillia's guests. Jim and Laleh decided it would be best if they left their gracious host to go shop other parts of the bazaar. First they carefully checked on the virus and vaccine. They elected to carry the vacuum bottles with them in a big cloth market bag along with their other purchases. Jim found himself clenching the straps until his hand hurt. It was near eighty degrees Fahrenheit even in the shade, which felt especially hot after their recent snow experience.

Jim and Laleh watched the men of the bazaar move in the heat without removing their telpeks—tall brown sheepskin fur hats. Jim wondered if they considered the hats essential to their identity.

They saw one man purchasing a white fur hat as they elbowed their way through the shopping areas. They were told it was probably for his wedding. He also had purchased a red and yellow striped silk robe or khalat, instead of the common long dark robe. There seemed to be three colors of men's pants—gray, brown and dark blue in both light and heavy fabric. They were the typical Turkenbalak or pantaloons.

Laleh said, "The women wear one of five tribes' characteristic yokes of bright patterns. Don't you think we should dress less like native tourists, Jim?"

"Probably a good idea," Jim answered.

Laleh purchased one of the bright-colored shawls and a long blue dress. She also bought a yoke she felt would look good with the combination. Back in Lillia's loft, she put the outfit on. Jim was not to be outdone. He donned an outfit complete with gray pantaloons, tall black "snake" boots, a billowing shirt and a white fur hat. He carried his new colorful robe on his arm.

Laleh said, "It's all too hot, but we actually will be less obvious."

Jim observed, "With my dark tan and your natural coloring we almost look native." Laleh and Jim sipped tea at a table and watched shoppers pass them by without pausing to gawk. Their guise seemed to work.

Jim commented to Laleh, "I can't get over the variety that is available to those with money. Look at all you can purchase. Silk, carpet, licorice root, green and red tomatoes, wood, carrots, apples, potatoes, raisins, grapes, melons, cherek—that round bread baked in clay—ovens, audio tapes, and any of the animals."

Laleh added, "Of course they are purchased live and people are expected to take them home to slaughter."

Jim was so happy that he started to whistle some tune, but stopped when he became aware that he was disturbing many of the native Turkmen. Later Lillia told them, "It is considered bad luck to whistle indoors. It is a superstition that to do so invites the evil spirits."

Soon after, a Western-looking man came walking down the aisles of the bazaar, looking people over carefully. "It's pretty obvious that he isn't shopping," Laleh told Jim. The man passed quickly without staring, and escaped from view.

"Laleh, Hans has to be careful, because he must bribe the old political bosses to get anything done. The old apparatchiki are still in high places. It's risky business, plus the secret police must keep track of all foreigners. That puts Lillia at risk and we just compound the risk." Jim remarked, then continued, "We have good disguises—not just souvenirs. We can explore the whole city in our new clothes without raising too many suspicions. We can get to the airport just before it's time to depart tonight. It will be less risk for Hans and Lillia."

Laleh suggested, "Let's check on what Lillia thinks of this."

Lillia stood looking at them. Then she said, "I feel that it is possible—if you are very careful. However, you must allow me to drive you to the airport." Lillia cautioned them both and agreed to meet them only an hour and a half before flight time.

Jim said, "It's just too bad I hate wearing this hat."

The two tried to copy the natives' gestures, walk and demeanor. They knew they wouldn't fool anybody unless they got their act together. It was an exciting challenge for them and they got braver as the day went on.

At one point Jim said, "Laleh, here we are walking around the city like no other foreign tourists dare do." He had to direct his comments over his shoulder, as Laleh was dutifully following behind him a few steps, as properly married people of that country did.

They found themselves on Shevchenko Street at an open market that served lemonade, ice cream and candies.

"What more could one want for lunch?" Laleh asked rhetorically.

"How about some vodka?" Jim asked facetiously.

A bookstore and a tailor shop were also nearby. A tall water fountain burbled in the center. It was a red metal structure with seven jets of water shooting out. It commemorated the 1948 earthquake. The pair sat on the edge of the fountain splashing water like children.

"Jim, so much has happened. This is the first time that we have had a chance to really be alone, just you and I. We have paid a lot of money for expensive hotel rooms and haven't even slept there. Fate continues to keep us apart. . . . Do you know what I'm trying to say?"

"Only too well; it will be different in the U.S.," Jim promised. "Laleh, I know that if we had gone back to the hotel, we would have been in trouble and possibly deported. Now, we're simply going to leave when we want to, when our airline tickets say we can. Plus, we have maintained control of the virus and vaccine!" Jim consoled.

Laleh reminded Jim, "You have not experienced what I have. You haven't been jailed like I was in Iran. How do we know the U.S. won't send me back to Iran!" She broke into tears.

Jim held her, trying to console her while she wept. She seemed so fragile that he did not know what to say or do.

Finally, when she seemed to grow quiet, he commented, "I can't guarantee that you won't be sent back. We must assume that your ticket to Germany and the U.S., as well as mine, will be honored. The Turkmenistan government might notify the Iranian government and have your visa canceled. Our passports could be confiscated while we wait for the two governments' bureaucracies to decide what to do. But, I do know that we should enjoy ourselves until the final moment and avoid ruminating over considerations that only fate will decide."

"I guess you're right," Laleh answered halfheartedly.

"Laleh, I can hear the railroad steam locomotives not far from here. Let's visit them. I haven't seen old trains operating since I was a kid," Jim suggested.

"I will go with you," Laleh condescended. She wiped her eyes and nose and pulled the scarf around her head more tightly to hide her red face.

The train was about to pull out en route to the village known as Mary. Jim and Laleh started walking along the passenger cars toward the front of the train. The windows of the compartments, hanging with little white curtains printed with small, light-blue camels, caught Laleh's attention. Jim was most interested in the alternating sound of steam being released by the pistons of the massive engine.

Laleh pointed toward the station. "That's a rare sight—a saxaul tree. The leaves of the saxaul tree are thin and resistant to drought, a very practical plant for the desert. But, from a distance, it looks like the wind has blown all of its foliage off. There certainly seems to be an ample supply of botflies searching for nourishment." Laleh brushed herself. "They invade any shade of a person's garments."

"A few larks are lunching on the flies," said Jim. "And, I just saw a pink-winged grosbeak and some sparrows."

Laleh sought shade while Jim studied the train. As she did, she became aware of a man with a goatee watching her. He used his thumb and index finger to inhale a cigarette through a silver holder. He had no luggage. She turned her gaze away and wished she could dissolve into the shadows. She tried to whisper to get Jim's attention. He was too engrossed with the machines.

An armored lizard chose that moment to scurry in front of her. "Eeeek!" Laleh screamed.

Jim wheeled to her aid with the simple response, "Laleh?"

The man heard Jim call her name and, extinguishing his cigarette, started heading in their direction about one hundred meters away. Jim was at first concerned about the lizard but then saw her head signal toward the goateed man. He recognized him as the taxi companion at his arrival.

Jim caught Laleh by the arm and headed toward a yellow, old-fashioned trolley. The trolley car was already moving when they swung on board. Though he was obviously after them, the man did not move quickly enough, or he wasn't motivated enough, to catch them.

"Perhaps his job was simply to make sure we didn't leave the city," Jim observed.

As Jim and Laleh sat on the trolley going to some unknown destination, they discussed a plan. "Laleh, let's just stay here until we must get off, then transfer, if such a thing is possible," Jim suggested.

Large buildings with metal facades were common in the area they were approaching. Massive works reflected the old Soviet mind-set. Parks went by with new young trees, not five years old, bordered by concrete sidewalks.

Jim commented, "This reminds me of some new comprehensive developments in the desert cities of Nevada, Utah, Arizona or New Mexico."

Laleh observed, "At least the apartment houses are painted pleasing colors of pink, green and pastel blue. But still, there's no grass."

The avenues were designed to expedite traffic and contain sand. Only around the Kara Kum canal, did the parks display pretty, wild, red poppies and yellow chamomile flowers. Even a few saxaul trees grew near the canal.

Jim found a newspaper on the seat. Though neither could read, two pictures caught their eyes. The first was of a person with a wound on his leg. The other picture was of three different snakes.

"The cobra, gyurza and efe are three poisonous snakes that live in the desert," said Jim, recognizing the serpents from what he had learned before coming.

Jim told Laleh of his travels with Jaynee in the Southwest of America. Laleh realized that Jim felt at ease talking about his deceased wife. They continued to ride different routes all over the city.

"Jim, I feel like a tourist in the Virgin Islands," Laleh said. "We're flying like birds on wing through this city." Laleh relaxed and talked with a young mother who was feeding her small child.

"What do you feed the baby?" Laleh tried to ask.

"Kissloe," the mother responded. "Kissloe is a substance made from curdled sheep's milk and looks like yogurt and cottage cheese.

As they rode through a business section in peace, Jim knew he should ask formally about their marriage. Then he decided it might be best to wait until they were safely on the airplane out of Turkmenistan.

Laleh and Jim managed to tour by trolley and on foot until dark. They were exhausted when they reached the bazaar and their gracious host, Lillia. They talked with Hans and Lillia as long as possible, knowing that they might never see them again.

They devised a plan to get Jim and Laleh to the airport. It was going to be risky at best.

Before dark, the desert wind started blowing. Jim and Laleh began to worry that their plane might not be allowed to land, even if they were given permission to board it for Germany. The sandstorms of the desert are legendary the world over. In developed cities like Ashkhabad, the wind and relatively small amount of sand were not a problem. But out at the new airport at the outskirts it could present difficulty. Many of the abandoned ancient desert cities around Ashkhabad had been all but consumed, with ten to fifty feet of sand deposited over them through the centuries.

Jim told Laleh, "Jaynee and I spent a lifetime, in one twenty-four-hour period. We were inside a small backpacking tent a few years ago in southern Utah. I remember minute grain particles sifting through the fabric of a double-walled tent and invading every orifice of our bodies. We had dry nostrils and irritated eyes from grit under our contacts. Our ears felt like sandpaper, and our hair was like a couple of dirty mops."

Jim stood up. "We might as well head for the airport. This storm might be a blessing in disguise. The police may not be overzealous during the dark annoyance of a sandstorm. If all goes well, we will simply hang out in the boarding lines in our costumes until time to leave and pray no one will try to stop us until we're aboard and out of Ashkhabad's air space." The other three concurred.

Hans had been concerned that Lillia's car might be harmed driving through the storm, but she insisted that she would take the risk. Lillia dropped the pair off within walking distance of the airport entry area. Family or visitors were not allowed to stay with passengers. The winds had forced the door guards to retreat inside to protect their weapons from being jammed with sand. They were preoccupied with their tea. Sunset wasn't due for another hour, but the sand had already shut out the sun at this remote desert location.

Few vehicles were on the highway. At the airport only a handful of babushkas, women in scarves, armed with brooms, were waging war with the blowing sand. Everyone else acted as if they were in hibernation. One guard kept a big plastic bag over his machine gun, which was slung over his shoulder. The years in the desert taught him well. He was smoking a cigarette and reading a small paper as he slouched against the wall.

Of the multiple windows for service, only one was in use. Laleh and Jim queued up with their passports, visa and tickets in hand behind six other people. The clerk was lethargic as she perfunctorily glanced at the papers of the travelers. Eventually, it was Laleh's turn to have her papers processed. Her heart raced as she stood in her costume. The clerk never looked up and proceeded to stamp and sort all of the paperwork. Still with her head down, the clerk said something in Turkmen and pointed toward a gate. Laleh gathered her carry-on baggage and kept to the slow pace of everyone about her. Jim followed shortly after.

Laleh was still worried about the new rapport that Turkmenistan had recently developed with Iran through their partnership, building a gas pipeline from Turkmenistan to Turkey. "I can't believe our luck," she said.

Suddenly, the peace was broken. Two policemen burst into the terminal lobby at the other end of the building. With loud voices they demanded something of the guard with the plastic bag over his weapon. A heated discussion continued as the trio drifted in Laleh and Jim's direction. A woman airport employee was persuaded to join the group. All four marched past Jim and Laleh as if they were invisible. The terrified pair expected a strong hand to grasp their shoulders at any moment.

They listened while the restrooms were invaded and the occupants roused. Then the soldiers promptly left and ran out of the building into the sandstorm. The armed guards nervously looked outside for intruders.

After the storm had abated, several police and military guards still swarmed in the building as Jim and Laleh's plane departed

Ashkhabad air space. Their precious vacuum bottles were safe, unopened. They were on their way to Germany and the U.S. Both fell asleep almost as soon as they knew they were safely out of Turkmenistan. It was not much later that Jim was awakened.

"Jim. Jim. . . . JIM!" Laleh whispered as loud as she could, as she poked him with increasing vigor.

"Hmmmm. Yeah little darlin'—What is it?" Jim whispered in response.

"The man with the goatee—the man with the goatee!" Laleh whispered in Jim's ear.

"What!" Jim said out loud, craning his neck to see who Laleh was talking about. "Oh no!" Jim whispered back. "It's him!"

"Oh Jim, what can we do?"

"He's just sitting four seats behind us back there. He's acting like everything is normal, reading that pocket book. Why do you suppose he didn't arrest us before we took off, while we were still in Turkmenistan jurisdiction?" Jim questioned.

At that moment the goateed man glanced up and looked directly toward the two and smiled. Jim and Laleh spun back down into their seats looking shocked at each other.

"What the hell is going on?" Jim asked rhetorically.

"Do you think the plane is really going to Germany? Or could they somehow have tricked us and we are going to Iran?" Laleh theorized.

"That pompous dog! He's just sitting there with that self-confident smile on his face. I'm going back there right now and confront him!" Jim announced as he unbuckled his seat belt and prepared to stand.

"No, JIM! Wait! Talk to me. Tell me what you are going to do," Laleh said as she grabbed his shirt. Jim lunged upward with his face reddening. Laleh hung on, and with her other hand patted Jim's discarded seat belt. "Sit. Tell me."

"I think I'll just punch him in the nose and talk later." Jim whispered loudly.

"Jim, I think he would have moved on us before now if he could. For some reason he hasn't. This is like a chess game. Maybe he is setting us up for something that he can use against us later."

The goateed man continued to look nonchalant. He had redirected his gaze at his novel. The smile was gone. He was the perfect example of a confident man.

The aisle seat next to Jim and Laleh was vacant for the moment because the assigned occupant was in the rest room. The overhead sign was illuminated and the flight attendant had just announced, "You are free to move about the cabin now." At that moment, the goateed man made his move. He came forward and stood next to Jim's seat.

"Hello, I'd like to introduce myself," said the goateed man.

Jim and Laleh would have bumped their heads on the ceiling if they hadn't been fastened into their seat belts. "Whaaa!" Jim managed to utter.

"I mean no harm. Please be calm. I don't have much time to talk," the goateed man said.

"What the hell is going on?" Jim demanded.

"I work indirectly for your government, Dr. Schriver. We are on your side and also want to help protect you, Dr. Bazargan," The goateed man said, turning to face first one and then the other. "I can only advise you to ditch these clothes before you get off the plane and be careful. Get back to U.S. territory A.S.A.P. My company can only do so much in foreign countries. . . . We didn't have this conversation. . . ." The mysterious man quickly left to resume his assigned seat.

"He's got to be CIA," said Jim, as he watched the mystery man return to his proper place.

"What should we do, Jim?" Laleh asked.

"I am certain that Alpha Omega was instrumental, somehow, in all of our problems. Now this guy! I don't know who to trust, Laleh."

"Could he be working for your State Department to foster U.S. business in Turkmenistan?" Laleh postulated.

"Who knows for sure, Laleh? I think he acts like a 'spook.'"

"A spook?"

"A CIA operative or other secret agent."

"This is all so confusing, Jim. Where can we take the vaccine now? Our time window for stopping a pandemic is very limited," Laleh whispered.

"We've been so busy surviving that we really haven't decided who should make the vaccine. The time crunch is frightening. We still have connections with Alpha Omega—if we dare trust anyone there. I don't think we could get any other vaccine company management on board in time. . . . Damn it, Laleh, I think we're locked into gambling on Alpha Omega—no matter what the personal risk might be. What do you think?"

"Jim, using an organization that may have somehow been responsible for Sonbol and others' deaths seems insane! But, I have to admit—we have no other choice! Everyone in that big company couldn't be evil. Most of their scientists must be humanitarians or they wouldn't have their favorable image worldwide. We just won't know who the bad guys are. I don't think it's going to be much different than working in Iran."

She continued, "If we let the company believe that we have notified authorities and others of our intent to do business with Alpha Omega, it would be insurance that they would not harm us. At least, until they hear our proposal."

Jim said, "It's a heck of a risk, Laleh. But I agree, we must take it."

They agreed to a plan. Using the plane's phone, Jim telephoned Dr. Reichstadt's secretary, Mary Whiting. "Dr. Bazargan and I are on our way to Alpha Omega. We would like to confer with Dr. Reichstadt as soon as possible, if you can find us some time. . . . Yes, Dr. Bazargan is seated right beside me—on the plane. . . . Yes, that will be great. We will both see you then," Jim concluded.

Jim turned to Laleh and said, "Darling, it is all set. I think we can indulge ourselves now with a little cautious optimism. What do you think?"

Jim demonstrated a high five. Laleh seemed amused and somewhat relieved.

They changed clothes in the restrooms before deplaning and boarded the plane from Germany to the U.S. Their "souvenirs" had served them well. The goateed man had disappeared as mysteriously as he had appeared. Now they were flying from Germany over the Atlantic Ocean. They were speechless, looking into each other's eyes, not as fellow survivors or scientists, but as lovers.

"We're on our way to the good ol' USA," Jim announced jovially.

"Laleh, I want you to consider what I am going to ask you as a carefully thought-out proposal, and it wasn't born out of a rebound to stress. For months I have not been able to think about much else in spite of the virus problem. I now know what is critical in my life. Nothing else in my life is of greater priority. . . . I can't live without you. . . . I need you desperately. I love you and want you to be my wife."

"Jim, this is too soon. So much has happened. I do love you, but it is so sudden. If I listened to my heart, I would say yes right now. But I need time to think—to consider. I hope you can understand. I am, how do you say? 'I'm on overload.'" Laleh's dark eyes were searching his for understanding.

"I feel the passion like breath blowing on a glowing ember. Yet, I don't think I can allow myself to be consumed by the flame until a little later. Please, please be patient with me. I do love you. . . ."

"Laleh, I am so afraid I will lose you. Every fiber in my body says that this is right. I can understand what you are saying. But, it doesn't mean that I want to accept a delay. I hope I can assume that the answer is probably yes and it's just a question of when?" Jim asked hopefully.

Laleh answered with a kiss.

Chapter 25
Idaho—Days 24–26

"We need to bring this executive planning session to order. All officers please take your seats," commanded Colonel Nick Cabal. "As you all know, this year's STRIKE Patriots training program is being conducted on the property of Captain Rock Granite's ranch near Sun Valley. What you all may not know is that he has been incapacitated with a stroke. Unfortunately he has not progressed well with his therapy and still can't communicate. However, his wife insisted that we should go forward with our plans just as though he were with us. He is now in a comprehensive care facility and it would appear as if he will be there for some time. It is a sad story that I won't go into at length. It is enough to say that he was felled while trying to serve his country through STRIKE's outreach. If any of you would like to send his wife a card, I am sure she will read it to him. We believe that it might be therapeutic for him to know that his patriotism will live on in our activities.

"We have some other disturbing news. Our two comrades who were killed in an unfortunate accident in Utah are being accused of intentionally causing the accident. You should all be aware, the federal government will try to associate STRIKE with that tragedy. Those two comrades had responded to a concern that the source of our tactical virus was about to be compromised. You all are admonished to decline discussing anything about that. Our information officer, Sergeant Black, will address all inquiries," the colonel announced.

"Now some good news. The Taliban Muslim army in Afghanistan is now being fought by a coalition led by Rashid Dostum and Ahmed Shah Masood. Our bacteriological agent, our influenza A

293

virus, has started to do some good for the coalition—the new influenza A virus that we obtained from Rock Granite via Utah a while back. Our government can't be associated with such foreign operations.

"If it wasn't for our STRIKE efforts, those Muslim idiots could continue to disrupt the balance of western influence in that critical Mid-East country. Our intelligence reports that the influenza A epidemic has reduced their fighting effectiveness 40 percent. By the time summer comes, Masood's men should have control of Herat, a key city in the northwest corner of Afghanistan. After that perhaps Kabul will fall. Just imagine what will happen when a million Afghan refugees try to escape in panic through Iran's east border. They are both primarily Muslim countries, but their animosity toward each other is historic. The Iranians will be forced, however, to deal with the logistics caused by such an influx of humanity. America won't have to spend a dime to keep Iran tied up in their underwear for at least a year. Something to be proud of, gentlemen," summarized Colonel Cabal.

"Because of our involvement with BW, bacteriological warfare agents, I think it would be good for us to discuss incorporating protection from such agents in our training program this year in Sun Valley," suggested the colonel.

Debate ensued about leaks to the press, hinting of their concern with BW. Some reporter might stumble on to their association with the past use in Afghanistan. They concluded that training with the equipment used for tear gas would have to be an effective but practical compromise, under the circumstances.

The fact emerged that they had only five vials left of the original Utah shipment of the deadly influenza A virus, and this brought up questions about future availability. Cabal assured them all that their other contact in Alpha Omega, Captain Bill Balencamp, would be able to supply them in the future.

He went on to tell them, "Our unique funding will again be

underwritten with a 20 percent increase during the next congressional budget session." He mused at the creativity of certain members of Congress, but also reminded the staff that other funding sources had to be explored if they were to meet their goals. He then told the true story of Willie Sutton, an infamous bank robber in the U.S. "When the press asked Willie after his capture, 'Mr. Sutton, why did you just rob banks?' He replied, 'That's where the money is.' . . . But just remember, he was being interviewed in prison," cautioned Nick.

The rest of the executive meeting reviewed reports of their "brother" patriot organizations in the South and elsewhere. They applauded their brothers' success torching un-American ethnic churches and synagogues. The trial in Denver of the alleged Oklahoma City Federal Building Bomber was discussed. They resolved that their group would not make stupid blunders that had caused their associates' downfall. Careful planning and focus was critical. The mistakes of the past, the Caribbean fiasco, and the subsequent apartment explosion and car wreck failures, would not be tolerated in the future.

"The whole operation has been sloppy, and I accept complete responsibility," said Nick Cabal. "I've decided to terminate the use of volunteers. Instead we will use only previously documented professionals."

He then indicated that a few corrective actions were still needed in Boise, Idaho. They gave him carte blanche authority.

"You should all have in your hands the agenda for the training camp and your respective job assignments. It will be a logistical challenge to accommodate almost a thousand STRIKE trainees this year. Our quartermaster corps should be receiving some free beef from our Montana member, Zeek King, and the other supplies are being delivered from local supporters in Boise. Isn't that accurate?" Nick inquired of his aide. He then went on to solicit an action report from all of the other committee members.

The parking areas for the motor homes and trailers had been

prepared, and a picture posted on the map on the wall. First Aid, fuel and water stations were discussed as well as rented Porta-Johns. A garbage and a trailer dump station was available. Security would be a big problem because of the size of the operation, which had doubled since last year. Ever since the Ruby Ridge and Waco incidents, federal agencies and the media were like vultures. They had prepared their public-relations story very well in advance to preempt speculations. Infiltrators could be expected, as within any new group open to "believers" who simply wanted to become trained members of a potential force of American patriots. They knew others would see them as men playing army in the woods, dangerous in their ignorance and highly malleable to questionable charismatic leadership. Each of the trainees had paid five hundred dollars for the privilege of attending. It was not a bad fee for a few days work, plus gaining an expanding pool of activists.

"When the revolution comes, these patriots will be ready to defend their country!" Colonel Nick Cabal had said often. "Many new recruits come to STRIKE from areas with large populations of recent immigrants. We all know that those wetbacks and those boat people will join up with all those unemployed blacks and take our jobs away—then take over our government."

The sale of weapons was going to be a moneymaker for STRIKE, as they would have a booth for attendees to shop. STRIKE would also get fees from survivalists' business booths. All kinds of prepackaged freeze dried food, water storage containers, radio and cellular communications, book and videotape sales and camping gear would be on display outside the compound, in the vendor's area. This training was just about money. The real work of STRIKE would be hidden from the public and casual trainee.

Only a small cadre of highly trained patriots could be trusted to do what really needed to be done in Idaho. Everyone would start arriving that night, about twenty miles south of Sun Valley at Granite's ranch. They would be ready the next day to begin registration.

The phone rang in the conference room, despite the orders of Colonel Cabal to the contrary. He knew it had better be important as he reached for the phone.

"Colonel Cabal here," Nick announced in an impatient voice. The voice on the other end could be heard by those seated close to him. It sounded excited and punctuated.

"What do you mean, a vial of the influenza A virus just exploded in the lab? We'll be right down there!" The lab had been financed with funds from surreptitious accounts of the U.S. Treasury. The front, being a legitimate import/export business in an industrial area of Boise, had served their purposes well. The whole discussion group followed Cabal along in curiosity until they reached the perimeter of the lab. A red line drawn on the floor designated, "Safe Suits and Masks ONLY Beyond This Point."

Just as they reached the line, the windowless hall turned pitch black—a power failure. The colonel had just reached for the door to the air lock separating the lab from the dressing room, when the lights went out. He fumbled in the dark to try and see a safe suit in the dressing room as the emergency auxiliary power unit started and the lights resumed. Confusion seemed to reign inside the lab as Nick rushed to pull on the balloon-like suit over his other clothing. Normally one of the other workers would insure that a person was properly dressed and then they would tape the connections to insure an air lock in each other's suit. Nick was hasty. Once in the lab he hooked up his airline and quickly moved to join three workers cleaning up broken glass and using disinfectant.

"How did this happen?" inquired Nick.

The workers pointed to a broken air hose. Evidently a pressurized air hose broke and commenced to whip, flipping the vial off the table, shattering it. Unknown to everybody in the lab, the hose continued to whip, spreading the virus all over the lab. At that very moment, the third person had started to come out of the air lock. He was waved back by another person who was entering from inside the lab amidst blinking lights and alarms. In that brief moment, a large amount of the aerosolized virus wafted into the air lock and drifted into the dressing room where the Colonel had just donned his gear. He did not realize yet what had happened. He did not know that he had inhaled the lethal inoculum, a quantity adequate to make hundreds of people sick. The departing worker in the lock entered the dressing room with a false sense of security. When he left the dressing room after changing, a cloud of concentrated virus hung about him and followed him past the staff waiting at the red line for Nick.

It was determined that someone had tripped a wrong switch in confusion and caused the temporary blackout. Ambient airflow out of the dressing room deposited virus on the surface of the executive staff's eyeballs and nasal mucus membranes. None felt anything, however. Nick Cabal cursed himself as paranoid when he felt that he might be coming down with something.

"Such hypochondria is for shirkers and neurotics, not real men like myself. It is simply going to be mind over matter!" Nick Cabal told himself. A short time later he left the Boise area in his Humvee. The others would follow with the larger trucks full of gear. Nick had instructed them to use CB channel seven or thirteen and absolutely not channel nineteen, which truckers used as a party line. The verbal abuse by a few truckers traveling I-84 the previous year had been counter productive.

They would travel a short distance on I-84, then turn on US 20 and then north on a private road, above the Shoshone Ice Caves before state road 75. The ranch setting was beautiful, with the Sawtooth National Forest in back of it. By nightfall they all would be encamped and secure; the advance people had everything well prepared. Nick always enjoyed the subtle show of their convoy. The camouflaged vehicles were spaced like a legitimate army unit going down the highway. His command car was at the lead with the stars-and-bars flag on the radio antenna. They did not need Klan hoods, as most of the local people knew who they were and what they could do.

"It is too bad that we don't have some armor," thought Nick. He winced from a sudden pain behind his eyes, and thought, "It's probably just the bright light. I'll take a Tylenol at camp." His driver extended his arm out the window, pumping his closed fist up and down, signaling to the driver behind him to speed up. Nick could have just called him on the CB, but there was some satisfaction in signaling that way. "When you observe radio silence, you must use hand and arm signals," the colonel had been known to say. Most of the other drivers on I-84, especially the commercial semi-trailer truck drivers, were amused with this display. They drove at fifty-five miles per hour the whole way, even though the maximum was seventy-five mph on the interstate. Nick was oblivious to the other drivers' hand signals, including the "bird." His head continued to pound.

It was almost dark when they deployed to their assigned parking areas and unloaded at the Rock Granite Ranch compound. They were directed by their own M.P.s to the lodge and headquarters area. The smell of baked bread and roasting meat hung in the air. However, Nick wasn't hungry and his headache was worse. He went over to the first aid tent to get something stronger than Tylenol for his headache. He was surprised to see two other of his staff officers there for the same reason.

It concerned him, but he didn't bring up the strange coincidence and neither did they. The virus incident was never mentioned to the group physician on duty. The three knew that such information was confidential, top secret.

The physician examined each of the men separately behind a screen and noticed that each of them had bloodshot eyes, swollen lymph glands, inflamed nasal passages, rales and other abnormal respiratory sounds—indicating some pathological condition. He got a history from each of the men. None of them mentioned the virus accident. Subconsciously, however, each of the men started to harbor repressed fear. During supper the three men did not sit together, but felt it politically prudent to mingle with the troops. All three started guarding coughs and violent sneezes. Their eyes watered and their noses ran. They ached in every joint. Each made an excuse about retiring early to be ready for the very busy morning they had planned. The nasal discharge became worse when they were lying down. Their coughing jags denied them sleep even though they were exhausted.

The physician knew the next morning that the three men were too ill to participate in the morning maneuvers. Normally he would have hospitalized them. But the camp was to be simulating battlefield conditions, and the leaders had to accept responsibility in a big operation. Besides, the three seemed to be having just a bad case of the flu, and he and his staff already had their hands full of cooking-fire injuries, knife and hatchet lacerations as well as overweight and underconditioned older men complaining of possible heart and blood pressure problems. They had underestimated the average age and basic health condition of this group of men who desperately wanted to serve their country. A number even lied about their basic health when they sent in their forms with their advanced registration. How could they have predicted this?

The opening address was made by one of the local politicians who had unsuccessfully run for a state office. Many people in STRIKE revered him for his support of the patriot movement. Several jobs had to be reassigned due to illnesses. It seemed the whole cadre of leadership from Boise had been put under the weather by the flu bug. The troops were dismissed to reassemble with their individual patrols and companies. They would attend classes on weapons, self- and home-defense, civil disobedience, tear-gas protection, obstacle courses, close-order drill, waterfront activities, "over the counter" explosive manufacture; lectures on such subjects as "The Siege of FREEMEN in Justus Township, Montana;" "Formation of a More Effective Gun Lobby in America" and "Prepare for Armageddon." Eventually, all expected to participate in joint maneuvers by the end of the training period.

At the end of that day, a privileged few were informed of the three men who had died in their tents. The physician on call was almost catatonic about his discovery and unable to respond normally. Three new attendees, who were also physicians, were attending field training and had been unavailable for consultation until dinnertime that evening.

It became clear to the other physicians that this was a serious public health issue that could not be contained within the compound. The distasteful job of involving governmental agencies was necessary.

The staff physician was then assisted by the other doctors to establish an emergency protocol. The military zealots were suspicious of a conspiracy when the state police arrived to preside. The news media started to descend. The Idaho State Public Health Director ordered the whole area quarantined. The Communicable Disease Center was notified through other federal agencies and immediately sent a team to central Idaho. The Idaho National Guard was ordered by the governor—who knew the political risk—to assist the quarantine.

Captain Bill Balencamp, employed by Alpha Omega, had left Boise just after the lab accident and had headed home to Palo Alto. He had been summoned home because one of his children had incurred a head injury. Bill drove non-stop to Palo Alto, hesitating only at self-service stations for gas and snack foods. He would see no one else until he reached home. He became concerned when he started to get a headache and fever, but tried to convince himself that it was just a common cold. He had to stop twice to take short naps on the way.

In Palo Alto, Bill was met with the latest good news about their hospitalized son—he would be able to come home the next day. He had improved rapidly. Bill was greatly relieved about his son's condition and yet regretted that he couldn't go to see him that very minute. His fever was 102 degrees Fahrenheit and he had a splitting headache. He might give his son something contagious in his compromised condition.

At that very moment, the phone rang and someone from Alpha Omega indicated that they urgently needed to talk to Bill.

"This is Bill Balencamp, you'll have to forgive me but I have a splitting headache. And I am officially on vacation! Yeah? What lousy timing. . . . They can't wait? What? I just came in the door. I came home to see my son who was hospitalized from an accident. . . . Yes! Sure—enough, I will leave after I check on my boy's condition with his doctor. But I must warn you I'm coming down with something. It may be contagious. . . . Good-bye."

Bill then telephoned his son's physician and obtained an update on the boy's condition. He was assured that the son would be discharged the next day. The doctor advised Bill to avoid exposing his son to anything right then and perhaps it would be best if only his wife pick up his son. Bill talked to his son over the phone. Then he begrudgingly left his home after taking some cold medicine, and headed for the plant to meet with the long-awaited Drs. Bazargan and Schriver.

Chapter 26
Palo Alto–Day 27–28

Laleh and Jim were exhausted by the time they arrived in San Francisco. They had to wait for customs to spot check passengers' luggage and carry-ons, which in their case included their vacuum bottles. But, the inspectors didn't detect anything unusual.

Jim confided in Laleh, "I'm glad those vials are mislabeled insulin."

They rented a car and drove to Palo Alto, California. The eucalyptus perfume in the warm moist air acted like a mild aphrodisiac on the two weary travelers. Jim pulled Laleh close to him as they drove past Stanford University.

Laleh felt truly emancipated sitting so close to a man in public. "America is wonderful," she said. "I am so glad that Dr. Reichstadt at Alpha Omega will see us on such short notice. That airplane telephone was very helpful to us."

Jim gave Laleh a kiss at each red light along El Camino Real. He knew that the pheromone level in the air would have been extreme if they had not rented a convertible. He wondered if she knew.

It was dark when they checked into the Hyatt on El Camino Real. Jim felt like a chaste Catholic priest when Laleh insisted that they get separate rooms. She struggled with her own chemistry as her cultural mores could not be shed; Laleh was actually shaking when they parted with a passionate kiss outside her room.

Jim stood at her closed door in disbelief. He fantasized knocking on her locked door. He turned and kicked his suitcase instead, bruising his big toe. The swelling in it seemed to relieve swelling elsewhere on his body. He cursed under his breath and limped sullenly to his room several doors away. He was mad at all of

Islam's religious leaders. Though her family and religious leaders were thousands of miles away, they had succeeded in ruining this beautiful night.

Jim picked up the phone in his room and dialed Laleh. Jim whispered erotic suggestions and Laleh cried as she tore at her new nightgown. Late-night revelers could be heard next to each of their rooms enjoying the passions that they denied themselves. The night would last a millennium before they would be together again. Jim stood in the cold shower until he was satisfied that he could refocus on his sleep. He was no more successful than Laleh.

The next morning the lethargic pair met to drown in coffee. They both realized that a prolonged engagement was not going to be possible for them. They felt that they might be able to wait until they finished with their business in California—but immediately thereafter they would get married in Utah. It would be Laleh's first marriage, and she had certain priorities that had to be met to satisfy her emotional expectations.

"Laleh, tell me what your fondest dreams are concerning a marriage ceremony," Jim asked, looking deep into her eyes.

"If I could wish for perfection, I would have all of my family and close friends come from Tehran. But, because I can't do that, I would like our marriage to be a special celebration, a model that others might consider for a bicultural wedding ceremony. It should be very different. After all, it is a large turning point in my life. I will be separating from one family life and creating a whole new family in a strange country. All my life I have modeled my life after my parents, friends, teachers and Iranian leaders. Now I feel that I can be an example to the next generation," Laleh began.

"I never did believe in certain old customs that exist even today in Iranian society.

"It was always people's performance of such customs that made me honor them. I have always been a . . . ah . . . maverick. I want my wedding to be a special memory, not only for myself but also for others who will attend the ceremony. I want a ceremony that can be celebrated by peoples of various faith traditions and international customs. The principles of a wedding are shared universally, even though the ceremony is performed differently," Laleh continued. "I would like to see the differences between Persian and American cultures combined in a beautiful way. The combination should demonstrate unity in one—purity in love.

"I would like to invite guests from many different religious beliefs that worship only one God. They may call the creator Yahweh, Allah, Supreme Being, the Great Spirit or God. I don't care. I would like to convey a respect to all who come so that they can feel the ecumenical essence." She hesitated, looking for Jim's reaction.

"Laleh, that sounds like a tall order. I wouldn't know where to start. I guess I'm such an old cowboy at heart that I would probably just opt for some peaceful ceremony by a waterfall in the mountains," he responded.

"I'd like that, too, very much, Jim. I believe in harmony with nature and that setting would be perfect. Where would you do it?" Laleh inquired.

"There are several places relatively close to Salt Lake City. We could select one together," said Jim. "I'm curious; what else would you want to include?"

"I have talked before about the Haft sin of Norooz, the seven "S" sounding items placed on a table celebrating the Persian New Year. I would like to have items on the 'Unite in Matrimony Table,' the Sofreh Aghd. I would like a mirror and candlesticks, which are customarily given to the bride by the groom symbolizing his love and purity," Laleh said, smiling coyly.

Jim smiled and nodded approvingly.

"The groom should first see his bride and the candlelight being reflected together in the mirror. The candle and candlelight, and the meaning of light have three thousand years of tradition among nations. We Persians celebrated the birth of Mitra, the Goddess of

Light, on the longest night of the year, and still do in the name of Yalda," Laleh noted.

She continued, "Jews celebrate Hanukkah with the same meaning, and of course Christians celebrate the birth of Christ. I would like to use a menorah, a seven-candle Jewish candelabra, for the Shamdon-e-Safrehe aghd, candlestick of the matrimony table. I would place a white candle in the middle symbolizing peace and three yellow candles on each side of the white one. The yellow color has been used in my culture to symbolize hate, sickness and a pale face. It is my desire to challenge this negative superstition and change it to a positive symbol of love. I believe that all the colors of the rainbow are very beautiful.

"It also reminds me of the hostage crisis in 1979 when the eighty Americans were held captive. Loved ones at home used yellow ribbons to remind them of their missing loved ones. Our menorah would stand for peace and love for us. What do you think?" Laleh inquired of Jim.

"It's a beautiful idea and I think that my Jewish friends will understand when it is explained to them," Jim responded. "You are steeped in tradition, my dear."

"I am considering including a basket of colored eggs symbolizing fertility." Laleh paused, looking at Jim with an expectant smile.

"Excellent idea!" Jim said with great enthusiasm, moving his eyes in a provocative manner.

"Jim, I'm serious," she said.

"So am I," he said, reaching for Laleh.

"Do you want me to go on?" Laleh inquired indignantly.

"By all means," Jim replied with a restrained smile.

"I would like to color the eggs all silver except for one, and it would be gold. It would mean several things. The gold one would stand for one God. It would also mean to me, one man and only one child." Laleh noticed a puzzled look on Jim's face.

"Only one child, Laleh?" Jim interrupted. "Why only one?"

"I believe that we, as civilized people, must be concerned about overpopulation. Each of us, if we desire, should experience having a child, nourishing that child and watching it grow. We should learn from it and teach it at the same time. That is the symbolism of the golden egg," Laleh preached.

"I still don't understand the silver eggs," said Jim.

"They could be symbolic of the adoption of children. There are thousands of children that need loving parents in the United States, to say nothing of the rest of the world," Laleh explained.

"I guess I always thought of a boy for me and a girl for you to continue the gene pool of our family lines." Jim said.

"Do you think that principle could be compromised by accepting the possibility that God might want us to care for and love his other creations?" Laleh inquired.

"I guess I am not inclined to think of a partnership with God when I think of us creating a baby. But, I have to admit intellectually, you are probably right. It will take me a while to accept this emotionally," Jim admitted.

"Jim, it is so important to me that you really do accept this in your heart. I don't want you to have doubts or second thoughts after we are married. Why don't we sleep on this thought before you commit to this?" Laleh implored.

"I think we should sleep on this together," he said with a seductive tone.

"JIM!" she scolded.

"Okay, Laleh. I will search my heart about this. I know I should. Why don't you tell me your other ideas now?"

"I would also like to have fresh flowers and sweets for people to enjoy," she added. "Also, instead of the custom that an older woman should participate, I want to have a beautiful teenager rub cones of sugar together, pouring sweet joy and happiness down upon the bride while other teenagers hold a square of lace or silk over her head. Usually, unmarried young people are not allowed in the room.

The Iranian Islamic superstition that such virgins would compromise chances of getting married anytime soon, are archaic. As a bride, I want always to remember a youthful spirit, because we all have a child inside us. In Iran, we would be criticized for violating the custom of selecting an older, wiser, married woman.

"I also will not include the custom of carrying a needle with seven strands of different colored threads to sew up the mother-in-law's mouth if needed. I have enough courage to defend myself and do not need to rely on superstitions," Laleh pronounced proudly.

"Jim, I suddenly realize that you have never talked about your mother. Or, for that matter, anyone else in your family except your uncle Andy!" The statement was an implied question to Jim.

"Laleh, it isn't your fault that you don't know much about my family. I have always changed the subject or simply avoided talking about my dysfunctional family."

She waited silently for him to continue. Her eyes searched his until he avoided her stare.

Finally Jim spoke with his voice cracking. "When I was twelve years old, my mother was driving too fast north of Walden, Colorado, up in the mountains of Wyoming, when she lost control on a curve and crashed. My older sister Donna and my brother Dick were both killed. Dick was my Dad's favorite and heir apparent. He had been raised to do all of the 'important' chores around the ranch. My sister was my mother's best friend. My father became a workaholic. My mother became a depressed alcoholic. She ended up taking too many sleeping pills and killed herself."

"Oh, Jim!" Laleh said empathetically.

He continued, "Now there is my Dad, and he and I don't have much of a rapport." Jim had never revealed such intimate facts to anyone else that he could remember. He hadn't even told Jaynee everything. He didn't know why he hadn't. He just hadn't.

"Jim, I had no idea." Laleh managed to say with tears in her eyes.

"I guess that I was always groomed by my Uncle Andy to be the family medicine man. He encouraged me to medicate all of the farm animals and consequently I gained experience as an untrained veterinarian. I felt that my Dad always hated medicines. He said it was the fault of the medicines that my mother killed herself. In fact, when I announced that I wanted to go to college to be a pharmacist and eventually to get my Pharm. D degree, he all but disowned me. If it weren't for my scholarship and some clandestine help from my uncle Andy, I wouldn't have made it," Jim shared.

The two were holding each other. The American cowboy and the Iranian rebel seemed made for each other, despite their cultural backgrounds.

Jim sensed that he had exceeded his sense of propriety. Cowboys don't talk like he had. He still had not heard all of Laleh's thoughts on the wedding ceremony. "Laleh, tell me the rest of your ideas about the wedding ceremony."

"I guess I don't believe in the Mahr and Jahaz custom either. The Mahr custom is supposed to be a sum of money or property that the groom agrees to give the bride for her financial security. The Jahaz is the bride's dowry. In Iran, both the Jahaz and Mahr would be recorded in the marriage contract, the ghabale aghd," Laleh said.

"How do you conclude the ceremony normally?" Jim inquired.

"There is the Shirin Polo, the wedding feast," Laleh said. Then she looked sad with misty eyes again.

"Why the wistful look?" Jim inquired.

"I just remembered Sonbol talking about Shirin Polo to everyone when we were all in St. Thomas. I have included enough, Jim. What do you want to include from your culture?"

"Laleh, I guess I have been a Christian all of my life and that is about all I know. I have had many friends from various Christian denominations, some Jewish friends and one Buddhist friend whose wedding I attended. But I think most accept the advice of their priests, rabbis, pastors or ministers when making arrangements. This is really new. . . ." Jim seemed to be pondering.

Laleh searched his face for specifics.

"I guess most include some sort of entrance ceremony including the procession of the bride's maidens and finally the bride's entrance accompanied by the traditional music of the wedding march, 'Here Comes the Bride.' She stands next to the groom, but not touching until the proper moment. Then there is the minister's greeting, prayer, reading of scripture and sermon to the couple and the congregation."

"They don't say anything, they just listen to the minister?" inquired Laleh.

"Oh yes! Usually it is followed by the wedding vows, a covenant between the couple and God. The last part includes holding hands and the giving of rings to the bride and groom." Jim symbolically stroked her ring finger. "Finally there is the kiss of the bride and groom after the minister proclaims them man and wife, and the dismissal by the minister. The guests follow the bride and groom to a reception. Some Christian faiths like the Mormons have a private wedding ceremony in their temple followed later by a public reception. Legal documents are signed in private by the bride and groom as well as the witnesses and a legal authorized official."

Jim then added, "I can only remember the name of one hymn that is sung in our church—'Oh Perfect Love.' However, I would think we might also include some music that means something special to just the two of us.

"I would like to include the Christian ritual of Holy Communion." Jim looked to Laleh for a response.

"I think we can blend everything—we will be able to marry our cultures."

"Oh, Laleh, look at the time. We had better get going or we will be late." Jim hugged Laleh and gave her a kiss.

Jim and Laleh's appointment with Dr. Reichstadt at Alpha Omega had to be delayed until 10:00 A.M. It had turned very warm and humid because the morning mist had burned off early. The clothing that Jim and Laleh had brought with them was more suitable for a cooler climate. Laleh dressed in her only smart suit, which was made for the cooler weather of Iran. Jim also had dressed for early spring in the cool windy weather of another climate.

"Jim, I'm very nervous," Laleh confided.

The opulent curved roadway entering AO was beautifully landscaped, but there was no mistaking the security associated with the visitors' entrance.

"There's no denying that I'm anxious to know who our enemies are here, and who will be our friends," Jim confided to Laleh.

When they picked up their visitors' clip-on tags they looked somewhat out of place with their warm attire. The gate guard was thorough with his evaluation of their identification. He even called the administration building to confirm their appointment before he assigned them their passes.

Laleh had brought the computer disks and her essential published papers with her in her briefcase. Jim clutched the vacuum bottles with the frozen virus and vaccine vials inside. In his pocket he had the one remaining computer disk that had belonged to Ben. The other luggage was left in the hotel rooms.

Dr. Reichstadt was waiting for the two doctors in the Board Conference Room, Alpha Omega's most prestigious facility. His chief legal counsel and a certified court recorder were seated and ready when the two were ushered into the opulent surroundings. Formal introductions and greetings were made.

"We wish to officially welcome you both, Dr. Laleh Bazargan and Dr. James Schriver, to this meeting on April 29th, 1997. It is 10:10 A.M." Dr. Reichstadt officially opened the meeting, nodding to the court recorder, who was poised at her stylus recorder. Laleh looked absolutely radiant despite the fear that she felt. Jim had a tired, serious look. He still didn't trust Dr. Reichstadt.

"We are very pleased to hear your proposal of a joint effort to produce a vaccine from the influenza A virus that you discovered, Dr. Bazargan," Dr. Reichstadt formally announced.

"It is my intent that whatever mutually acceptable vaccine is produced, we will make it available to any country in the world that needs it, including Iran," Laleh began. The chief counsel looked at Dr. Reichstadt with raised eyebrows, but politely refrained from interrupting. "I would like to go on record indicating that I was able to produce a live attenuated virus nasal vaccine from the virus. We have in our possession a vial of that vaccine as well as a vial of the original seed virus with us today. They are in the vacuum bottles that Dr. Schriver is holding," Laleh announced.

"Mein Gott! You have brought these dangerous substances into this boardroom in nonapproved containers? What are you two thinking of?" Dr. Reichstadt exclaimed.

Bill Balencamp had entered the room quietly from the back. He had arrived late. His long drive from Idaho had tired him, and now he was exhausted from the infection.

Dr. Reichstadt noticed Bill at that moment. "Dr. Balencamp, would you please accompany Dr. Bazargan with her two vacuum bottles of vaccine and seed virus to your production facilities and lock them in the safe freezers? She can advise you there how to properly utilize their containers. I hope that is not too presumptuous of me, Dr. Bazargan, but in this country we have a host of federal and state guidelines relating to safety. Can we presume that Dr. Schriver can speak for you while you are gone?"

"Certainly he can," Laleh answered.

Jim whispered in Laleh's ear. "Be careful! Remember, he's probably not the only STRIKE member working here. Watch your back!"

Dr. Balencamp and Laleh hurriedly left for his production area with the containers.

"Before we start recording, I would like to speak off the

record." Jim waited for Dr. Reichstadt to nod to the reporter, signaling her to stop.

"First, I need to say all data will need to be reviewed by our own legal counsel before we consider any verbal agreements as binding," Jim pensively began.

"Now, just for your information, Dr. Bazargan has gone to great personal risk to bring these items to this country and this corporation. She and I knew that the conventional legal protocol should have been deployed but it could not be facilitated. In short, she and I did the best we could, under the circumstances, to get through several countries' customs inspections to deliver this today. At any moment we could have been arrested or killed, but we felt that this calculated risk was essential in the interest of saving lives. We were incredibly lucky there, but I still worry about her safety here. I believe you should all know now that you could be defacto accomplices from this moment forward if you vote favorably to accept our proposal. Perhaps you all would like to consider this thought while I step out into the hall." Jim stepped out of the room to allow them to consider what he had just said. Stunned faces watched him leave. Jim looked anxiously down the hall where Laleh was being led by Balencamp. He waited for ten minutes before a secretary came out to inform him that they would be a while longer. Jim was sweating because of the tension and the dress coat that he wore. Finally, he was invited back into the boardroom.

"Dr. Schriver, I would like to apologize for my curt response to Dr. Bazargan in my concern for undue biological risk. Now we would like to go on record. Please give us the specifics of your proposal. We will need to involve many other people in the final decisions," Dr. Reichstadt said.

Jim proceeded with an outline of expectations, including certain rights-of-veto. He brought up financial rewards for the two of them upon completion of the signed agreements. All liability would transfer to the Alpha Omega Company upon completion of the con-

313

tracts. A letter of clarification concerning any publication of scientific papers relative to the virus or vaccine was to be developed giving Dr. Bazargan and Dr. Schriver control of selection. The legal documents had to be prepared and completed before they left this week. All of the attendees at the table objected that the time line was unreasonable.

Jim responded. "We've got to race to beat this pandemic."

There were several who questioned the validity of an epidemic that could affect the whole world in such a short time.

"We must consider it a threat to every country in the world, including us. These days, with air travel and other mass transportation, we could be too late if we start production tomorrow," Dr. Reichstadt said to the surprise of most. His comment had the force of finality. The company would find a way.

Laleh followed Bill Balencamp to the biological production area where he ushered her to the secured biohazard air locks. They dressed in the traditional bunny suits with the airlines attached. She could not help feeling guilty about the risks they had taken while in transit with the vulnerable vacuum bottles.

The two scientists labeled and locked the vials in two separate storage containers and placed them in the freezers reserved for such things. Then they exited the area and rejoined after each had gone through the required decontamination procedure. Laleh noticed that Bill was perspiring profusely and seemed unsteady on his feet. "Are you all right?" she inquired. Bill looked angrily at Laleh. He had been barely civil to her since she left the conference room.

"It's none of your business—how I feel," Bill Balencamp said, squinting at her through red eyes, wiping his nose with a tissue. He turned and weaved as if he was going to leave her standing alone in the outer office. Then he just crumpled in his tracks and lay motionless in front of Laleh on his back with his eyes open. Laleh dropped to her knees and did a brief examination. His eyes were both somewhat dilated and his breathing was undetectable. She palpated his neck for some sign of pulse and could only detect a faint one. She picked up a telephone and asked for assistance from the operator who said she would alert the necessary people. Laleh hurriedly looked for some emergency intubation devices that are used to safely give mouth-to-mouth resuscitation. Being unacquainted with the area all she could see was one first aid kit on the wall. An intubation device was not included. She looked at the clock on the wall. A whole precious minute had almost passed!

In desperation Laleh rushed to the door and screamed, "HELP! I HAVE A MEDICAL EMERGENCY IN HERE!"

Two production workers rushed to her, but no one could find what she needed. She had no choice. She began unprotected mouth-to-mouth resuscitation.

She worked at her task with one of the other workers listening to the chest of Bill Balencamp. His heart was beating very rapidly, but weakly. The man had not yet regained consciousness. He did not seem to be able to breathe on his own.

Laleh was ready by now to trade duties with the other worker, estimating that she had been at it for almost five minutes. Just when she was about to trade, the plant EMTs arrived with the proper equipment to relieve her.

Laleh then announced, "I need to talk to your chief of security. I don't think anyone here should leave until I talk to him."

The workers noticed that she was wearing only a visitors' tag on her suit. Their expressions implied that she would not be able to make any demands unless she convinced the security chief.

A worker announced, "He is on his way now. It is the usual protocol in such emergency situations."

Laleh picked up the phone and told the operator, "Get a message to Drs. Reichstadt and Schriver as soon as possible. Don't wait until they finish the meeting! Give it to them now! It is urgent that they contact the production area's main office as soon as possible! We have a medical emergency."

The phone rang almost immediately. "Dr. Balencamp has collapsed in the office from some unknown cause, possibly an infection. You may need to quarantine all of us here for the time being. I have the chief of security standing here waiting for your order, Dr. Reichstadt," Laleh announced. Jim listened on another phone.

While Laleh was queried at length by both of the men, Dr. Reichstadt asked to speak to the chief of security.

"Keep everyone there until we can get the company's head physician down to communicate with you," the chief said. "Locate a safe bunny suit for him to wear before entering. He can use a phone to speak to you while he stands outside the offices. It has a glass-fronted door. Dr. Schriver and I will head over there immediately."

The security chief, Chuck Morris, initiated the accident procedure for which all the employees had been trained. The State Office of Emergency Management had to be notified of an unconfirmed yet possible contagious disease problem. He had been left holding the bag two years ago on a previous minor accident involving a spill of a potential toxic substance that had not been promptly reported to the state, and Chuck was not going to go through that again. The state person indicated that they appreciated the alert, but would not require any other action be taken unless Chuck Morris called them again with a greater level of concern.

Chuck said he would let them know the diagnosis when it was made.

Drs. Reichstadt and Schriver stood outside the door with a cordless phone. Jim finally got to talk to Laleh.

"Darling, what happened?" inquired Jim. Laleh gave him what limited information she had concerning Bill Balencamp.

"Jim, I am concerned. We could not find an intubation device and I had to give him mouth-to-mouth without any protection," announced Laleh.

"Oh, no!" Jim exclaimed, aware that any communicable respiratory disease would almost certainly be passed on to Laleh. "An exposure of such a large quantity of virus or bacteria will most probably overwhelm your resistance. You're going to get whatever damned disease he has!" Jim said as he paced in a circle with the phone to his ear. "I can't believe you would do that!"

"Jim, I had no choice. He would have died—or his brain—if I didn't act fast."

"I know, darling—I know," Jim replied, repentant of his hasty judgment and lack of concern.

"The company physician has taken blood samples and cultures from Dr. Balencamp. We won't know anything else for at least forty-eight hours," explained Laleh.

"The chief of security, Chuck Morris, called Bill's home to see if he could determine more about his recent health. He hoped to get a lead. Chuck hoped it was just some childhood bug one of the kids brought home," Jim consoled Laleh.

"I don't know, Jim; you might call it intuition, but I fear it might be something other than a common cold," Laleh responded. "He should be conscious. His pulse is weak, but I have treated other patients with weak hearts and they would be conscious by now."

Suddenly, Dr. Ballencamp began hemorrhaging from his nose and mouth.

"OH—OH! He's convulsing!" Laleh exclaimed as she rushed to him.

Jim felt helpless. An old crushing feeling came over him—the same feeling he used to get when his father would ignore his presence and ask for his older brother to help in some crisis on the ranch. Everyone else in the plant, except him, seemed to know what their role was in this emergency.

"I've got to focus on something, do something of value. I can't tolerate being a voyeur," he told the person next to him. He decided to call Ed.

Ed put a patient on hold, then told Jim that he would call him right back. Claire was busy in the hospital with patients and couldn't

317

be reached. Finally the phone rang. It was Ed.

"Hi, Jim! I'm glad you're back from the old Soviet Union, how are you doing? Did you get Laleh out of Iran?" Ed inquired.

"Actually we are both in Palo Alto and everything went okay—until now," Jim responded. He told Ed all that had happened. It all poured out so fast that Ed couldn't get a word in edgewise. Finally Jim realized he had talked Ed's ear off.

"Well, that's about all we know. How is everyone there?" Jim asked.

"Claire and I have been very busy—but our health is okay. What about Laleh? When will you know what she has been exposed to? Did you pop the question yet?" inquired Ed.

"It will be forty-eight hours at least. Meanwhile we just have to wait. We'll let you know as soon as we know something. And I didn't know you were aware that I was going to ask her to marry me. Anyway, she said yes!" Jim responded.

"Keep me posted on both of you, Jim. Claire and I are going to give you two a big party when you set a wedding date. How long will it take to make the vaccine?" Ed asked.

"We have quite a lot to do, and her health will dictate how quickly we can do it. I'm stuck here in limbo, sitting outside of the action and unable to do anything. I can only worry," said Jim.

Distracted, Jim watched through the glass door as Laleh and the others attended the tall, thin Dr. Balencamp, his wiry beard and mustache glistening from sweat. "Hang on a minute, Ed."

Dr. Balencamp was having a seizure. The medical team became frantic.

"I'm sorry, Ed, but something seems to have gone wrong with their patient, Dr. Balencamp. It looks like he's seizing," Jim told Ed on the phone.

"Jim, call us from your hotel or the plant when you know more. Where are you staying?" Ed asked hurriedly.

"We're at the El Camino Real in Palo Alto. I'm sorry, I hope you understand," Jim said.

"No problem, Jim. Hang in there, buddy. I hope everything works out okay," Ed said. "Stay in touch."

"We will," Jim promised.

He continued watching. Unable to help Laleh and too distracted to talk to anyone, he watched the team struggling to save Bill Balencamp, only to see them defeated. Dr. Balencamp suddenly became still and unresponsive to their efforts. He was dead.

Various health agencies, plant security, the county coroner, and the sheriff's office and company management all became interested with the mysterious death.

When Bill's devastated wife rushed to the plant, though many people tried to comfort her, they also questioned her concerning his recent health to find possible explanations for the suspected infection.

All that she could bitterly tell them was, "He just went to some camp in Idaho for STRIKE militia training. Our son got a head injury falling off his bike and Bill came home prematurely from the training. He had not even unpacked when the company called and insisted that he come to some crazy meeting. He was exhausted and suffering from the flu when he came home and they made him go to work."

Jim went back to their hotel to fetch Laleh's clothes and cosmetic case. Everyone who had close contact with Dr. Balencamp was ordered to stay in the production area. Jim had been encouraged by Laleh to try not to worry. She had suggested that he return to the hotel and get some exercise in the hotel pool or do some running.

She said, "It's going to be a difficult forty-eight hours, but this will soon pass and we can resume our efforts with the vaccine plans."

They agreed to see each other again through the side window of the production facility and talk over the phone that night at ten. The need to communicate with loved ones was going to require some disciplined use of the limited phone lines.

Jim thought, "Only twelve hours have passed since we arrived at Alpha Omega. So much has happened. I wonder what else can possibly go wrong. I hope that Murphy's Law is not in effect." He dressed for his run. He needed to think.

Chapter 27
Israel—Days 27–29

The dank, ancient stone room on the outskirts of Tel Aviv could have served a similar band of malcontents hundreds of years ago. The smell of ancient dust merged with perspiration and cigarette smoke. Intent men swore their commitment to the Jihad and joined in prayer. They knelt on their mats to face Mecca at the appointed mid-afternoon prayer time. Their cleric, Shaikh Muhammad Homani, stood upon a rectangle stone to address the group of Majd, the armed security and intelligence members of the Hamas organization of Palestinians.

"We must collaborate with Amal. Soon we will have the new deadly virus we have been waiting for. We will hit the Jewish infidels' parliament, the Knesset, with a message from Allah. . . . The Ayatollah Khouni has spoken for the International Party of God, Hezbollah, and it's official! He has condoned the strike by the Hamas against the Knesset. The package is on its way from Iran. . . . Allah be praised," the excited mullah exclaimed to his fellow Hezbollah followers. A loud cheer followed from the band of religious zealots sweltering in the confines of the small room.

The mullah continued, "No longer will the Jews be so quick to steal our homes and land, once they realize that we have the capability to do what we will do to the Knesset. They will learn then, that we have the potential for doing even more damage to the whole population of Israel! They will know that we could have decimated the whole country instead of just teaching them a lesson for Allah. Our two agents, when in the Knesset, will become martyrs if necessary. There will be no protection from this virus.

"Allah is great and Muhammad is his messenger!" the mullah shouted.

The audience loudly repeated, "Allah is great and Muhammad is his messenger!"

"This weapon will be better than an atomic bomb," said the mullah. "Those few that recover will know what could have happened and tell others. The world will know also that we used restraint. We will announce that we confined our weapon only to the Knesset. We did not obliterate whole cities and their populations like the Americans did to the Japanese. We did not have to destroy homes, hospitals, farms or the infrastructure of the country.

"The Likud and Herut parties of Zionists will pay the biggest price for their crimes against Allah's people. Jews all over the world, including the U.S., who have listened with contempt to the warnings of the Hezbollah, will be forced to hear Allah's message. Islam's effort to proselytize people to the party of Allah will be accepted because of our judicious use of power."

The prospect of disabling the majority of the 120 members of the Knesset while they were unaware of their vulnerability, delighted the band of terrorists. Even though most would have preferred to kill all of them, they had to agree with the logic of the mullah and the Ayatollah Khouni. The psychological impact would be felt throughout all of Israel and the world when they realized what had happened.

"If we Moslems are to effect change, we need to get the Knesset's recalcitrant infidels replaced by reasonable Jews who can change their mindset. Dead men can't reconsider." The mullah knew he was right. Hitler had tried and failed to obliterate all Jews. True victory would come only when Moslems were able to change men's minds and hearts.

He went on with his tirade. "The proper use of bacteriological warfare will be like the use of America's atomic bomb; it can be a deterrent to anti-Islamic decisions in the future. Many will know, very personally, how they all could have been killed with any number of different lethal organisms. The calculated restraint would also send a message to the rest of the world that the Hezbollah are willing to sacrifice their lives for Allah. If the Israeli secret service, the Mossad, discovers our plot, we all may be killed. But, we will be remembered as martyrs by our friends and loved ones in this life. We will receive the highest esteem from Allah in the next life."

The leader stopped for effect and raised his arms anticipating the traditional response from the crowd, "There is only one god, Allah, and Muhammad is his messenger!" The group yelled in unison.

Small task groups of two or three formed to focus on certain goals. The leader, Mohammad Homani, talked on a cell phone to a source that claimed to have the ear of Ussama bin Laden, a billionaire Saudi Arabian Moslem. The very expensive delivery mechanisms for the virus aerosol bomb would not be delivered until the necessary funds were deposited in an unnumbered bank account in Zurich, Switzerland.

The two clandestine moles that had obtained jobs as custodians inside the Knesset building were Barry and Miriam Metz, brother and sister. Their hatred of the government began six years previously, but they had delayed their vengeance.

It all started when their mother and father committed joint suicide after certain members of the Knesset made false charges against them. The disgrace their parents felt had ostracized them from almost everyone they knew. The family had become bankrupt and the two siblings were forced to live in foster homes in their midteens. When the error was finally discovered, it was too late. The misappropriation of funds was proven to involve "parties unknown" within the Knesset. The Knesset never formally charged them by name, only by innuendo.

The public clearing of their parents' reputation never got adequate media coverage. Their tainted reputation remained for the surviving brother and sister, Barry and Miriam. They were ripe for becoming traitors to their country.

The siblings' first contact was a Hamas agent who came to them posing as a disgruntled Jew who not only sympathized with their grief and anger, but also expressed his opinion that the government should have to pay for their suffering. They didn't know that he was really Shaikh Mohammed Homani, an Islamic spiritual leader. He subsequently supplied them with money and housing which enabled them to become independent in their late teens and early twenties.

Mohammed Homani eventually advised them to get employed as custodians for the Knesset. Custodians were often given access to a number of areas, and they often seemed to be invisible. Periodically he found ways to fan their fires of paranoia and keep them hostile to their mother country. He encouraged them to learn all that they could about the inner workings of the large building, and he counseled them to wait for the right time to seek revenge.

Homani embellished his plot by saying the government betrayed him also. He assured them that he would tell them when it was the right time to render their revenge. He had informed them that the time was not far off.

Barry and Miriam felt that they had been offered their jobs as some sort of compensation, that powerful people's guilty consciences had found a way to give the two bright youths jobs normally reserved for others. They felt that their financial status and their parents' questionable reputation prevented them from getting state scholarships and going on to higher educationed opportunities. They were bitter for many reasons.

Every day Barry and Miriam walked by the massive menorah that stood across the street from the Palombo Gate to the Knesset. The menorah had reliefs of events and personalities sculpted into each of the seven branches. It was made by Benno Elkan and dedicated on April 15, 1956. The artist, David Palombo, had designed the three bronze gates that are known collectively as the Palombo Gate of the Knesset. A maze of bramble-looking projections at the entrance gave the two an idea of what a briar must look like to a hare or quail.

They always felt relieved when they had passed through the

324

gates into the inner courtyard and viewed the Court Gates of the House of Representatives. When they approached the front of the building, they could always count on seeing the Eternal Flame of the Burning Bush sculpture. The long, rectangular building, with its flat roof, framed the home of the Knesset, its ten pillars fronting the entrance. It made an imposing presence. Walking up the series of stairs to the elevated prominence, reminded them of approaching the Parthenon on the Acropolis in Greece.

The Chagall State Hall in the massive building, with its three extensive tapestries and twelve mosaics, was an impressive introduction to visitors. The Knesset Plenum on the first floor was always very busy on Mondays, Tuesdays and Wednesdays when the Knesset was in session. Workers learned to come early to work on those days.

Barry and Miriam had found a way to view the legislative process by sitting in the visitors' gallery. They learned that visitors in the upper balcony must sit behind bulletproof glass in the back section. The VIPs and president's entourage were always seated in the balcony's front left section, the news media on the right side.

Electronic voting charts hung from the ceiling above the 116 seats of the Knesset members. In order for each member to vote, two hands were necessary—one hand to push the attendance button, and the other to push one of the three voting buttons—the green in favor, the red opposed and the yellow in abstention.

In the center of the rectangular plenum sat a horseshoe-shaped table. The members of the government also sat at this lower area below the balcony. Protocol dictated that the largest political party group sat to the left of the Speaker and the second largest to the right of the Speaker. The Secretary General and the Sergeant-at-Arms also sat to the left of the Speaker. The Speaker and deputies were located at the Presidium. Nine of the eleven permanent committees also had offices on the first floor.

Barry and Miriam became familiar with them all.

On the second floor was the Prime Minister's Office and a large government room with a very large, donut-shaped table. When cleaning these areas, they would often find revealing doodles on scraps of paper. However, all trash was considered a security problem. It had to be shredded and burned in a special furnace. But sometimes just a glance at a single word on a scrap of paper could be useful information.

Barry confided to Miriam, "I don't believe we have been able to hear or see anything of great significance. I don't see how we can ever get retribution doing these menial chores. I wonder if Homani will ever give us an assignment?"

But Homani, their benefactor, had recently suggested that their chance was coming. He instructed them to become as familiar as possible with the air-conditioning system of the Knesset plenum. He told them to learn where access panels, heat pumps for air-conditioning, and the electric breaker boxes were located. They discovered that all of the air-conditioning air ducts had security sensors and closed circuit TV cameras focusing on key hallways. They found a way to neutralize the sensors if they needed to do so. The cameras would require help.

Homani had long ago decided that the best possibility for penetrating the security system of the Knesset would be through someone who worked in the building. He had the pair concentrate on the two large incoming vents positioned on opposite sides of the huge room of the plenum.

The bottom area of the plenum could be accessed quickly through conventional doors that were normally locked. The two became well-trained in lock-picking skills, and practiced with the two doors. Soon they could open them within seconds.

Knowing that the security people would always delegate at least one person to watch the multiple monitors, the two determined that they would also need a diversion outside the building when they were given a mission.

Homani decided that two Palestinian martyrs would stage a

demonstration directly across the street in front of the Knesset building at the monolithic menorah. They would ignite fuel oil at the base of the menorah and simultaneously explode concussion grenades and smoke bombs. Each man would chain himself to the large menorah while wearing a flak jacket with explosives taped to the outside. A third martyr would display a placard, throw leaflets from his pockets, and shout slogans from a bullhorn while standing in the middle of the street. All would be unarmed.

"Timing will be critical. Risks must be taken," Mohammed Homani said. "The first phase needs to happen on a day when the Knesset is not in session. Friday would be the best. The level of security should be at its lowest.

"We should be able to sneak the necessary devices into position on Friday. Then on Monday, a remote control will activate the release device so that it can aerosolize the thawed virus into the flowing air in the air conditioning ducts." However, when they hurried to alter the plan, an informer told them of new security policies on Fridays. They decided they would have to install the units and activate them on Monday. It forced them to rush. Tomorrow was the day.

The aerosolizers looked like inhalers for asthmatic patients. The modified aerosolizers were made of plastic. The accompanying, mislabeled vials would contain the deadly virus instead of asthma medication. Miriam and Barry would bring just the correct amount of dry ice necessary to keep the virus stable and inactive until it was time for it to thaw.

"The plan centers on the Knesset's peak activity at 11 A.M. just before the lunch break tomorrow. While most government people are in the plenum, the electronic signal will be sent to two remote release devices on the vials," Homani said.

One of the vials of Iranian influenza A virus that Laleh had produced before she left had been hidden by a lab custodian who was a Hamas spy. He had appeared to be slightly retarded, but functional. Laleh had befriended him when the hospital administration

327

suggested she might employ him in her lab. In reality, he was an intelligent and dedicated Islamic Palestinian. The spy with the missing vial arrived on a Saudi Arabian sheikh's private plane in the middle of the night from Iran. When Mohammad Homani was given the package, no forms or papers were exchanged. Homani was back to the Palestinian meeting place before dawn.

The small Styrofoam and plastic box seemed to be insignificant compared to all of the care and trouble it took to deliver it. Mohammad Homani raised the package high as he entered the cloistered gathering of anxious men.

Cheering acted as a release for the zealots, and from the prolonged sound, one might conclude that the men were indeed tense. Shouts of "Death to the Zionists" and "Kill the Jewish infidels" rang from the walls, along with praise of Allah. The group obediently quieted when Homani raised both of his hands.

Standing upon the large stone that gave his average stature dominance, Homani began reciting a popular sermon that could not be found by reading the Sura from the Qur'an. It seemed he began reconstructing the teachings to fit modern political doctrine.

"Jihad against unbelief and unbelievers is a religious duty. Therefore, all true believers are obliged to combat such governments and their supporters, whether individuals or foreign governments. Like the Kharijites in early Islam, we demand total commitment and obedience. You are a true believer or an infidel, saved or damned, a friend or an enemy of God. The army of God is now at battle with the followers of Satan. Zionism is the army of Satan!"

However, Homani knew that the two misdirected Jews, Barry and Miriam, would never have been accepted at this morning's emotional shouting frenzy, no matter how valuable they were to the mission. They were still Jews. Even though the Qur'an had a Sura that quoted Mohammed regarding the Jews and Christians as "People of the Book," he doubted if his fellow zealots knew of the Great Messenger's quote. There seemed to be few followers who didn't condemn all Jews and Christians as partners of the Judeo-Christian conspiracy—as enemies of Islam and the Muslim world. Homani, however, regarded Barry and Miriam as unique. They were special exceptions to the stereotypical Jew. He had grown to respect their commitment.

Homani telephoned Barry and Miriam from a public phone. "Meet me at the Minaret Oriental Restaurant in Jerusalem in one hour. I have your orders."

Across the entire front of the restaurant was a white ornate wrought-iron security grillwork. Though precautions had been carefully taken here as in other precarious areas of the world, hostilities had still erupted many times. Mohammed Homani chose to stay within sight of his vehicle while standing outside of the restaurant, knowing that the valuable box was locked in the trunk of his Fiat.

Barry and Miriam walked casually to the steps of the restaurant where Homani inconspicuously exchanged car keys with the couple. They all turned and briefly went inside the front of the restaurant.

After hushed conversations, Barry and Miriam feigned getting a cellular phone call and left. They went to Homani's car and drove away. Homani waited briefly for them to leave, then he left driving Barry and Miriam's old Ford sedan. He knew he could trust them with this critical mission. He was relieved that none of the Moslem members had questioned him, wondering why they had not been able to meet the mysterious "moles." Homani knew they trusted him implicitly. His plan was in action.

Barry and Miriam left at the usual time for work, wearing their usual attire, driving their usual route, and carrying their usual brown paper sack lunches with their usual Thermos vacuum bottles. Today, however, was going to be anything but usual. Barry drove and Miriam sat with their precious bottles and "special" lunches. No matter how it turned out, they would never forget this day.

Barry never had stomach trouble. He did this day. Miriam never had headaches. She did this day. Even though most employees entered the building from the employees' parking lot, Barry and Miriam had rarely done so because they usually started their workday in the front of the building. They usually parked on a friend's vacant property closer to the main Palombo gate. It was a typically warm day, but both wore long clothes—Barry pants and Miriam a long skirt.

Their uniform shirts were part of the dress code. Their picture ID tags were visible to the security people at each checkpoint. The two were familiar to the guards as each bid one another a good day.

As they walked toward the main building, the shadow cast by the large cantilevered roof reminded Barry of the Hasidic custom of men wearing large, black-rimmed hats that shaded their faces. It gave him a peculiar foreboding feeling, as if his ancestors were watching him.

Barry stumbled suddenly on a step and gyrated awkwardly, trying to catch his balance without dropping either the bottle or the sack. He struck the concrete with his right shoulder and scraped his face, making it look like someone had scratched him. Miriam was unprepared for his accident. She did not immediately want to put either her lunch or bottle down to assist her brother. She had to force herself to become focused on Barry and not the task of her revenge.

"Barry! Are you all right?" She struggled to find a handkerchief to stop the profuse bleeding on his cheek. Barry was stunned for a moment while he sought his composure.

"Thanks, I'm all right," he said as he held the cloth with his right hand. She gathered both lunches and left his bottle. Barry held his face. Two other people stopped to assist him.

He thanked them and told his sister, "You go on, I'll be there in a minute. Leave my lunch, I can carry it in a minute."

In that instant, Miriam knew it was best for her to enter alone, anyway—to allay suspicions why two asthmatics with similar medications would be entering the building at the same time. It would be too coincidental. She replied, "I'll run along then, if you are all right. I am going to be late otherwise."

Barry watched which security person Miriam checked in with and chose another one. Slowly he approached the security woman who had just arrived. The empathetic woman asked if she could help him as he handed her his lunch and Thermos. Barry put the handkerchief in his pocket and he decided to take advantage of his misfortune. "Oh, thanks, if you could spare a tissue. . . ."

The guard placed Barry's lunch and bottle on the secured side of the entrance, then handed him a tissue to staunch his bleeding. Barry managed to act unconcerned about his bottle and lunch, and began to leave without either. "Don't forget your lunch," she called.

"Oh! Yes!" Barry responded after first checking the tissue to determine how much he was bleeding. He thanked the guard and walked slowly toward his first workstation of the day.

He put his lunch in an area that was practical, even though it was not in the authorized employee locker area. He locked it in a cabinet with cleaning compounds. Only he had a key.

Miriam stashed her lunch in the wheeled cleaning cart that she pushed to different work assignments.

The people who came in contact with them during the morning found them emotionally distant and moody. Both Miriam and Barry constantly glanced at their watches. They worked extra fast, stopping occasionally to check their metal hole puncher, and aerosolizer with adapter and pressurized can of air. It was as though they thought some part might fly away even though they kept the packages secure constantly. The two were working on opposite sides of the Knesset plenum area, and each worried how the other was holding up.

Neither Barry nor Miriam had been able to sustain relationships with the opposite sex. They seemed inseparable to casual observers. One of Miriam's casual acquaintances even questioned her about the emotional atmosphere she had chosen. The acquaintance had warned her that some prospective male suitor might be put off, suspecting an incestuous relationship. Miriam had become enraged and had avoided the individual since that time.

At precisely 10:00 A.M., when many employees were taking a break from their morning's work, Miriam and Barry were escalating their level of activity.

On opposite sides of the very large conference area, each took lunch sacks and Thermos bottles into separate closet-like, air-conditioning access rooms. They locked the doors behind them.

Barry looked at his watch. They had five minutes to go before the diversion demonstration outside was due to start across the street from the Knesset security fence. Two Hamas—potential martyrs—had managed to stash the containers of fuel oil during the night under leaves in the shrubbery surrounding the gigantic menorah.

The two men quickly emptied their containers at the base of the fenced menorah and set a match to the oil. Black smoke erupted immediately from the flames. Simultaneously they threw concussion grenades and smoke bombs. Within seconds they chained themselves to the fence and had removed their light zippered jackets to expose what looked like flak jackets with explosives taped on the outside.

The third martyr then stalled his small pickup truck against the red and white painted curb and jumped into the bed of it. With a bull horn and boxes of leaflets, he propelled the leaflets with one hand and with the other held his horn to his lips as he shouted pro-Palestinian slogans.

The warm breeze blowing in from the Mediterranean quickly propelled the pamphlets down the street. Only the tourists seemed willing to pick them up and observe what was happening. Most natives sought cover, fearing a bomb attack any second. In less than two minutes, the entire area was cordoned off by hosts of military men and women with automatic weapons. They just materialized out of thin air. A team in riot gear quickly silenced the man with the bullhorn, but the wind continued to distribute his leaflets.

A discrete distance was maintained from the chained men and a bomb squad was called to neutralize their threat. A stalemate ensued; the pair continued to yell, clutching their dead-man switches. If they released them, they would explode.

Barry and Miriam, each with hearts pounding and both with trembling hands, began to use their screwdriver-looking metal hole punchers on the air conditioning ducts.

They had barely started when they heard an alarm sounding somewhere. Because they could hear various sounds from a multitude of locations through the ducts, they could not be sure whether they had activated an alarm with their drilling, or if the diversion outside in the street was at fault. But they had studied schematic architectural charts and felt sure that they hadn't deactivated anything associated with their ducts. Still, Miriam's head had started pounding so loud that she felt its banging must be echoing through the metal duct. Barry had to vomit in his empty plastic lunch sack. Both stopped briefly to evaluate their situation.

Despite the heavy fire doors on each of the small airconditioner rooms, both could hear running foot sounds and each expected their individual doors to be thrust open and their lives taken. Then there was absolute quiet. . . . After the longest five-minute wait in their lives, they finished drilling. Quickly they each screwed the adapters into the holes. Then they tried to attach the aerosolizers to the adapters with the vials that had dry ice in plastic bags taped to them. Each person had trouble screwing the threads of the pressure cans onto the aerosolizers. Their hands shook as they tried again and again.

"It just won't work!" cried Miriam. "It won't work!"

In the room on the opposite side of the building Barry also cursed. "What's wrong? It worked fine when we practiced last night. What . . . ?" Then it struck Barry. "The dry ice, the dry ice!" He realized that the dry ice had made the aerosolizer plastic port shrink. Quickly he untaped the plastic bag and warmed the port with his bare hands. When he tried to screw the pressure can in again, it worked.

"Yes!" Barry said to himself out loud. He quickly discarded the dry ice and finished anchoring everything with duct tape. The virus hissed into the plenum's air supply.

It was 10:50 A.M.; Barry thought, "Miriam probably has encountered the same problem with the dry ice. There is no other choice. I'd better go help her."

He started pushing his cart rapidly down the hallways. Normally he was supposed to stay in his designated area of the building. Stenciled instructions on the side of his cart advised, "Cart Must Remain on First Floor-East Side." Miriam worked in the west. His cart was painted yellow, a color code of the area. Her area was blue.

Barry thought, "I know I can't abandon this cart because of security rules. No package, luggage or cart can be left unattended. And if I'm lucky, no supervisor or security person will notice me pushing through visiting guests and VIPs with my yellow-colored cart. I must get to her before she panics and abandons her task. I can't risk jogging or running. . . ."

Barry's pants and shirt bore the evidence of heavy perspiration. The wet material stuck to his skin. As he pushed his cart, he was reminded of the electric carts in air terminals that delivered racing passengers to their airplanes.

When he was just a little way from Miriam's station, he caught sight of a blue cleaning cart coming his way with the same urgency. It was Miriam!

The two stopped side by side.

"Miriam, did you have any problems with . . . ?" Barry started to inquire, but she interrupted.

"I had to remove the dry ice to allow the plastic hole to expand," said Miriam. "It was working well when I left. Did yours work?"

"Same problem—same solution," answered Barry with relief. "Now we've got to remove these carts fast. If we're here at lunch time, we could arouse suspicions," he said.

Miriam and Barry each turned in opposite directions to beat the lunchtime surge. Everything was set. Their day of retribution was at hand.

Both Barry and Miriam pushed their carts to their proper spaces. Because of the disturbance outside, security inside the Knesset quickly stopped anyone from entering or leaving the building or grounds. Doors were locked electronically and surveillance became acute. Barry and Miriam inconspicuously began cleaning while they tried to determine if they could detect any awareness of the people in the plenum.

Miriam's supervisor rounded a corner to find her standing idly staring at the closed plenum doors. "Can't you find your work schedule?" he chided. "This isn't where you should be." The supervisor then cautioned, "Be careful, Miriam, there is a demonstration outside. Someone may try to make trouble in here also."

"Yes—yes, I will," Miriam stammered. She moved toward her next work assignment, but not before she noticed that there did not seem to be any change in the demeanor of the people coming and going into the chambers of the lawmakers. Even though she and Barry were outside the chambers, she did not relish exposing herself to the dangerous virus. Every minute they stayed in the building, the odds of breathing the contaminated air increased. She forced herself to finish her work assignment, constantly aware that ambient air currents might carry out of the plenum. As the time passed, she wondered how her act could go unnoticed.

She thought to herself, "It is a dichotomy; on the one hand I fear for my safety but on the other I yearn for recognition of my revenge." She felt totally unfulfilled. Here, she risked her life to achieve her revenge, and now no one seemed to know or care. Not until this very moment did she realize that she hoped to be discovered. The notoriety would have immediately descended upon her. It was all so anticlimactic that she felt depressed. She wanted to hurt those who had hurt her father and mother. "An eye for an eye, a tooth for a tooth." She started crying.

Barry, in a different area, also felt uneasy and unsatisfied.

Everything had gone like clockwork, but it was all so insidious and unremarkable.

"Now," he thought, "I know how it must feel to be a bomber pilot, silently releasing my bombs from tens of thousands of feet above my enemy in the dark. You can't hear or see the results when flying faster than the speed of sound. I want to shout my revenge and defy the rulers that abused my family and caused my parents' death." His hatred had not been vented. He wished he had shot someone instead.

Then he saw one of the pretty young women whose job it was to carry messages in and out of the Knesset when in session. She seemed to be stifling a cough in her handkerchief. He tried to slough the feeling of guilt that her image gave him. Was she going to be the only victim of his efforts?" he wondered.

Before her shift was over, Miriam's supervisor asked her to go up to the second level and retrieve some supplies near where the gallery of visitors went in and out. Miriam then noticed several schoolchildren who had visited the Knesset session that morning and were just leaving the session. It suddenly occurred to Miriam that even though bulletproof glass separated the lawmakers from the gallery, the air conditioning was probably shared with the gallery. A little boy smiled at her as he left. Miriam shuddered. Several of the children were coughing or sneezing as they left with their teacher.

The rest of the day passed. People finished their day's work and prepared to go home in the usual manner. Barry thought, "There is no evidence of our clever revenge. No packs of reporters asking us why we did such a vile act. No opportunity for us to tell the world about the injustice that we have suffered—or our revenge. What do we have to do?"

Barry and Miriam walked briskly in the warm breeze that had prevailed all day and got in the car, just as they had done for years. "But this should be different," each was thinking. The looks in each other's eyes told the tacit message. This was an empty victory.

Miriam spoke first as they headed for the planned rendezvous with Mohammed Homani. "I guess we just have to wait, now." The image of schoolchildren returning home to infect their entire families haunted her.

"Yes," mumbled Barry. He could see the pretty woman giving her lover a kiss of death at about that time. Barry avoided looking into Miriam's eyes, for reasons unknown to her. She couldn't look at him, either.

The plan was to wait in Homani's Fiat, which would be parked in a remote parking area. They had not thought about financial reward, until now. They both acknowledged that they would need the money to escape the country even with the promised false passports and other ID papers that were necessary for them to go to Canada.

They parked their car two hundred meters away and walked briskly to the Fiat. They had been seated only seconds before it exploded, sending them into oblivion.

Only a few secretaries and maintenance people reported to the plenum of the Knesset the following day. Many legislators and staff were too ill to work. A vibrating noise, heard in the relative quiet of the plenum, was cause for maintenance people to shut off the air-conditioning units and begin an inspection. The trained technicians discovered the two strange devices in two of the ducts. Security was called.

The bacterial bombs that had gone off in the air-conditioning system, blowing the virus into the plenum, had gone unnoticed—until it was too late. Ironically, the first deaths occurred to the youngest members of the government, not the old ones who had actually caused Barry and Miriam's parents to kill themselves. Later, some of the senior members would develop Parkinson's disease.

Panic burst out within Israel like wildfire. Many Jews called for an investigation and revenge against the assassins. The Israeli secret service, Mossad, could not believe that the plot could have evaded all of the security that had worked so well in the past.

The international press carried the story of the devastating plot on the Knesset. The Mossad could only guess that the labeled "asthma medicine" vials were really some deadly virus. The tests were not yet completed, they said, but most people felt that it was biological. The story that was released dealt with a bomb plot and did not even mention their suspicions about a bacterial warfare agent.

The Hamas waited to hear evidence of the deadly virus' effect upon the Knesset. At first the news was well managed and a spin was put on all reports. But eventually the truth became evident with the panic and rumors. The would-be martyrs of Hamas wished they had actually used their explosives during their demonstration. Now they couldn't escape the humiliation of being in jail and still alive.

The story told by Homani about the death of the two Jews who had acted with the conspirators only confused members of the Iranian Hezbollah and Palestinian Hamas. Mohammad Homani fell ill with some undiagnosed disease that left him depressed and bedridden.

Friends of Barry and Miriam who had escaped the flu epidemic attended their memorial service. Most people felt that some evil Palestinian Muslims, like the Izzedine al Qassam of the Hamas, were singularly responsible for their deaths. The Israeli secret service, Mossad, never suspected Miriam and Barry's complicity. No one knew why Barry and Miriam were murdered when they were, or why. It was filed as an unsolved case. No one suspected that the pair had a motive for complicity based on revenge for their parents' deaths.

Chapter 28
Afghanistan—Days 27–30

A staff member to General Abdul Malik of the Taliban Muslims was reading aloud from an International News report to the general and his staff: "KABUL, Afghanistan—The ousted government of President Burhanuddin Rabbani retreated, leaving the city in the hands of triumphant Taliban Muslim forces. Since that time, it has estimated that two-thirds of the country is in the hands of the Taliban.

"The weakened opposition forces are now operating out of the Hindu Kush mountain range. The base city of the opposition is in Mazar-i-Sharif of northern Afghanistan. The great leader Ahmed Shah Masood, who achieved legendary status in the ten-year war against the Soviet Red Army, is leading the opposition. Recent unconfirmed reports would indicate that they have introduced germ warfare on Taliban forces. There are scattered reports of whole villages being decimated by a flu-like disease that has caused numerous deaths and strange morbidity among the survivors, including central nervous system symptoms.

"The psychological effects have been notable in battles when ordinary smoke bombs have caused the Taliban troops to retreat in fear. Most are not equipped with gas masks. Ahmed Shah Masood denies that they would use such weapons on their own countrymen, and insists the stories are false. Despite his rejection of responsibility, the mysterious flu-like disease has gained the attention of the World Health Organization. The WHO is demanding to visit the afflicted areas and determine the potential danger. Neither the Taliban nor the opposition has been willing to allow outside investigators to enter the war zones. Recently, however, the Taliban was rumored to be considering some sort of limited access to confirm or deny biological warfare."

The Taliban staff member for General Malik glanced around the group as he continued to read.

"Masood is reported to have said, 'If they identify some disease, the international press will blame us even if it's a natural epidemic. We can not benefit from such risky speculation.'"

The general's staff member concluded, "In my opinion, we would benefit by allowing the World Health Organization to send in their scientists. It will prove that we have nothing to hide, and perhaps we can find out some way to convince our people that we will protect them. I suggest that we consider requesting the WHO's immediate help."

Another aide to General Malik then spoke. "To complicate matters, we have unconfirmed reports that Iran has been supplying some support to the opposition. However, our intelligence people don't think Iranian Hezbollah supplied the flu virus. They feel that it was originally given the opposition by the American CIA. And though the opposition did not have much virus to use, the disease is being spread. Medical people tell us infected villagers are the cause.

"The point is, we need to stop it, irrespective of who supplied it! We should also not become embroiled in accusing our Iranian neighbors. Given the pro-Zionist history of the American CIA, we would be better served if suspicion were focused in their direction. As a matter of fact, we are assisting the International Party of God, the Hezbollah and our Iranian brothers, in special anti-Zionist projects. Allowing the WHO to investigate will not compromise our goals. I, also, encourage you to allow the World Health Organization to do this. We need to protect our people from this disease as quickly as possible."

A consensus was quickly confirmed and the request was sent to the WHO.

The World Health Organization team arriving shortly after the request had been received, were shocked at what they found. The influenza virus that they found was their worst fear. The virus acted like the 1918–19 pandemic influenza—only with greater mortality and morbidity.

Reports showed that Pneumonia was decimating the wartorn villages' populations. The few pneumonia survivors were exhibiting early, clinical signs of Parkinson's disease. The virus was an obvious example of an antigenic shift. Serum collection stations were set up anywhere the local authorities would allow them, most often in undesirable locations. Usually a lack of electricity for refrigeration, and primitive sanitary conditions prevailed. Sand was often used as toilet paper—in the left hand.

The World Health Organization also had just been alerted by phone about a possible epidemic in the Hayden Lake area of Idaho. The initial reports were suggestive of a similar type of virus. The probability of two distant sites coming up with the same virus almost simultaneously suggested that some common vector or nidus was responsible. The state public health agencies and the U.S. National Institutes of Health and many other related worldwide agencies were suddenly concerned.

In the next few hours, news agencies of various countries began converging on the area in question and were offering to pay very handsome rewards to anyone who could provide reliable information from Afghanistan or the quarantined area of Sun Valley, Idaho. Freelance photojournalists converged on Idaho like locusts. Only the media with deep pockets could afford to send people to Afghanistan. Rumors of bribed security personnel and government employees hinted that thousands of dollars were being offered for photos or documented stories.

Various epidemiologists who collaborated worldwide to forecast epidemics, like the Diversity Biotechnology Consortium, were totally surprised by the events and could offer no explanations.

Health authorities around the world were all giving controlled spin stories to the news media to ease panic and needless fear. Most people didn't feel that the Ebola virus was a realistic concern. But they all knew about influenza. Stories that this could be worse than any flu yet seen by man, precipitated the purchase of cartons of remedies before hoarders could deplete supplies. Every case of the sniffles caused hypochondria in normally stable individuals. No one believed they had a simple common cold—they all believed that they had the dreaded new flu. Pharmaceutical companies everywhere competed for the opportunity to produce a vaccine from the first virus that could be isolated and identified.

The President of the United States appointed an oversight committee to monitor all of the activity relative to the threat of the new virus. The Senate and House of Representatives also discussed becoming independently involved aside from the executive branch of government. The United Nations discussed possible plans for nations to formulate various situations involving travelers and disease prevention. TV talk-show hosts competed to offer the latest information on the virus.

Afghanistan authorities projected the image of a country under siege. It seemed that the official government of the country did not have any power without the sanction of the Taliban. The WHO doctors became totally frustrated. It appeared that it would be weeks, not days, before they could ship anything in or out of the country. All of their conventional telephone communications were censored. The WHO had access to only one cell-phone tower in the country and radio communications were difficult because of the mountains.

Neighboring countries Iran, Turkmenistan, Uzbekistan, Tadzhk, China and Pakistan all restricted travel from Afghanistan. Only those people with current health-exam vouchers and special visas could pass over the borders. Movement of essential goods of all kinds slowed as nations became paranoid. Food riots started breaking out in various cities in Afghanistan. The nation was close to total anarchy. Educated leaders from medical, religious and political backgrounds were becoming sick and dying. The result was chaos.

The late CNN Television News was the first to report that "Alpha Omega Pharmaceutical in Palo Alto, CA, had an outbreak of the mysterious virus in their United States laboratory and one man is already near death. He was identified as Dr. William Balencamp. Apparently, he had been in the Sun Valley, Idaho, outbreak and had left before he knew that he had been exposed. It is unknown how many people he may have infected en route back to his home in Palo Alto."

Alpha Omega had secured its gates and deployed extra security people. The California state governmental agencies would not reveal what steps the pharmaceutical giant had taken to safeguard the rest of the plant's population. CNN's news staff had also obtained information that the virus had been definitely identified by the scientists at Alpha Omega. The virus was labeled Influenza A/Tehran 5/97(H7N4). The CDC, Centers for Disease Control and Prevention, in Atlanta could not confirm the designation. Public information officials at the World Health Organization and other organizations refused to confirm or deny the designation.

Before twenty-four hours passed, other TV networks and print media were repeating an official press release from Alpha Omega that complemented the CNN report. It said, "Alpha Omega has in their possession a preliminary nasal vaccine prototype under study for mass production." The release left the scientific community in shock. Many scientists said there simply had not been enough time to develop a vaccine from a new virus. Responses included words like: unbelievable, incredulous, ridiculous, preposterous, intriguing and suspicious. Infectious disease specialist Dr. Lewis Garfunkel of the National Virus Research Labs said, "It's impossible to produce a vaccine in such a short time without preexisting knowledge and techniques. There has to be some other explanation."

Chapter 29
Palo Alto-Days 29-32

Jim returned to Alpha Omega's Vaccine Production Facility after his brief jog. He was waiting for the security officers to okay his advance through the "Red Area." Red tape placed on the floor and a suspended red plastic cordoning strip labeled CONTAMINATED AREA roped off the section, designating limited access to any visitors without masks, gloves, slippers and gowns. Most of the security people had been deputized by the Sheriff to enforce not only company rules, but also the laws of the state.

Jim was very familiar with intensive care units in hospitals and accepted the protocol without question. Some family members had mistakenly believed that they could join their loved ones. They complained that the glass window between them and their loved ones should have given adequate protection, without the requirement of donning such apparel just to talk on a phone. Jim understood the buffer zone was a bit excessive, but understandable regarding the potential legal liability these circumstances could develop.

He awaited his turn and finally picked up a phone to talk to Laleh who was waiting for him on the other side of the glass. She looked exhausted and her bloodshot eyes caused Jim to be very concerned. "Laleh, you look terrible. How do you feel?"

"I know I feel better than most of the others in here," she replied.

"What do you mean by that?" Jim inquired.

"Jim, I am worried. Six people who worked closely with me trying to resuscitate Dr. Balencamp are sick with what I believe is the same illness that he had. They have all taken Tylenol because of their headaches and fever. They are also coughing a lot. It's only been twelve hours since the initial exposure!"

"My God, Laleh, do you think you should start taking some Rimantadine? No, on second thought, Amantadine would be better. The acetaminophen could interact with the Rimantadine. . . . Amantadine one hundred milligrams—you should start it right now!"

"I'm not sure of a diagnosis yet, Jim. Also, I'm not well enough informed about the other peoples' medical history to take that responsibility. Besides, they haven't asked me for any advice. I don't think that they trust a strange Persian woman who claims to be a physician," Laleh responded.

"Well, Laleh! At least think of yourself and start taking it for my sake!" Jim exploded.

"What are the side effects of Amantadine besides dizziness and constipation?" Laleh inquired.

"The only other side effects are very mild and well worth the risk," Jim added.

"I don't know that this is an Amantadine-responsive influenza A virus. It could be even some other virus entirely. It could be bacterial," she protested mildly.

"Laleh—it's worth the gamble!"

"Okay, I'll take it for you, my love. But I won't prescribe it for the others; I am not licensed in this country—remember."

"Thank you—I understand. Tell the others to get their own doc's advice," Jim said, looking somewhat relieved.

"Laleh, I got a fax from Ed and Claire at the hotel. I'll hold it up to the glass so you can read it." Jim pressed the page to the window. He could see perspiration on Laleh's forehead as she squinted to read.

Her jaw dropped and her mouth opened in amazement. "The FBI told them that the STRIKE summer camp in Idaho is now quarantined because of influenza A! Jim, Bill Balencamp has the word STRIKE tattooed on his arm with some other symbol I had never seen before!"

"Laleh, that clinches it. Somehow this is all related. This is the statistical straw that breaks the conspiracy's back. I am now of the opinion the virus you identified in Iran is somehow the same as the one causing this problem. Someone in STRIKE did it. All the more reason for you to take the Amantadine."

"I'm not sure that I comprehend the worldwide expanse of this conspiracy—but I know that you trust your friends in Salt Lake. If they and you are right, we must be very careful. I don't know who to trust here, besides you. And you should be careful, too," Laleh responded, and promptly started coughing.

"Laleh!" Jim reacted to her cough with obvious concern. "I'll go to the company dispensary here at Alpha Omega's administration building and wait for your prescription to be called in to the pharmacist. Get the staff doc in there to phone it in. I'll run it back to you. Bye love, see you soon." The two blew each other a kiss and Jim was shedding his protective garb as he departed. He dunked the used garments in the large suspended cloth bags for that purpose, and bounded out of the area. He still clutched Ed and Claire's fax that gave their story of the FBI report and their fear that Alpha Omega had dangerous people working there.

Jim arrived breathless at the outpatient pharmacy window. The pharmacist acknowledged that she had received the telephoned prescription and that it would be filled as soon as she finished with the urgent orders ahead of Laleh's Amantadine.

"I'm a licensed pharmacist and have reason to believe that Dr. Bazargan's prescription is a stat-order!" Jim's impatience with the stoic pharmacist was all too obvious and typical of anyone who feels medical need supersedes anyone else's desire.

The woman pharmacist reminded him, "Triage applies to any patients who need pain relievers for fractures, nitroglycerin for angina or medication for asthma attacks. It's my judgment that Amantadine is not in that category. You should also know that if you are a pharmacist."

Jim might have continued his argument, but he knew she was not going to change her mind. He paced until she finally asked him to sign the registry.

He put the fax on the counter when she handed him the prescription for the Amantadine and scribbled his signature. He grabbed the medication and ran out the door, absentmindedly forgetting the fax on the counter.

"At least," Jim thought, "I am getting my exercise."

The dispensary was quite a sprint for most people, but Jim was in good condition. The way he negotiated the obstacles reminded Jim of an old television commercial involving an airport terminal where O.J. Simpson vaulted over suitcases and obstacles. Jim loved finally being able to do something.

However, again he had to wait his turn to see Laleh when he returned to the production area. The access to the window was limited to one person or family at a time. Some company business tasks had to be conducted by this system. It was as frustrating as being gridlocked on a highway. Jim paced back and forth clutching the precious bottle of tablets.

Behind Jim a figure came out of Bill Balencamp's small office. It was the new CEO, Dr. Reichstadt. "Dr. Schriver. Dr. Schriver. . . . Please, can I talk to you in here?"

Jim was surprised that he was there at that time of night. "I was going to give Dr. Bazargan this medication," Jim said, holding the bottle for Dr. Reichstadt to see.

Dr. Reichstadt signaled to an individual in a protective suit to take the bottle. He instructed the person to take it in and then turned toward Jim. "Can we talk now?"

Jim looked uncomfortably toward Laleh's area and then turned to Dr. Reichstadt. "Yes, I guess I can't do her any other good right now."

"Jim, I have some disturbing information to share with you." As the two went into the small office alone, Jim saw a copy of his fax from Ed and Claire lying on the desk. "The pharmacist telephoned me to inquire what to do with your fax that you left. I told her to fax a copy to me here and that I would give it to you. She will send the original over by interoffice mail tomorrow.

"Jim, I had no idea of the extent and the magnitude of the relationships that you and your friends have discovered concerning a possible conspiracy connection with the Salt Lake virus and Alpha Omega."

Jim hesitated. "I guess I don't know where to start. It all sounded so unbelievable to begin with, and yet as you can see now, there is smoke. I have to ask you—is there any fire? What can you tell me?" he inquired.

Martin Reichstadt looked old beyond his years as his serious frown and depressed look spoke of defeat instead of hostility.

"Please sit down," he said, motioning to the only other chair besides his in the small quarters. " I must admit that I had repressed my worst fears for months. I refused to believe what I now feel are unrefutable facts. What I am about to tell you could ruin a great company. My reputation is also vulnerable, as it probably should be. I made a bad ethical decision years ago when I allowed a CIA operative to have unrestricted access to my laboratory when I worked in academia. . . . I know it is no excuse, but I had considered him to be a responsible scientist and that he would exercise a sense of propriety. I was mistaken about him, or someone else who stole it from him.

"I guess I should start at the beginning. Several years ago I recovered virus cultures of organisms obtained from two patients who had died mysteriously from what we now know was an influenza A virus capable of great morbidity and mortality. I was only concentrating then on the tissue damage to their brains that had caused the Parkinson's disease syndrome. I was hoping to find a cure for what I thought, at that time, might have been the universal cause of Parkinson's Disease. Doctor Stanley B. Prusiner has since discovered that prions are the problem. They are tiny inanimate proteins that somehow transform into rogue animate acting agents. They are not viruses, fungi, bacteria or protozoa, but are believed by many to be the possible cause. I still believe that viruses could be a trigger causing the folding of the protein—but that is beside the point now. I had felt that my virus could have been cloned on human fetal brain tissue to produce enough viruses to do a study. Then my funding was cut off and my position at the university was terminated. Before I could prove any relationship with the virus, my research was stalled. . . ." Dr. Reichstadt looked at Jim to evaluate his response.

Jim sat on the edge of his chair looking pensively at Martin—saying nothing.

"Then, I obtained a position here at Alpha Omega, thanks to 'Rock' Granite.

"I brought some of my isolates obtained from my research here with the hope that perhaps Alpha Omega might eventually develop a universal vaccine for Parkinson's disease prevention. It got put on hold when we became aware of data that showed there were many other factors that had to be considered, such as prions and new hereditary predisposition factors."

Jim still sat, contemplating the many aspects of what he had just heard from Martin.

"Since Bill Balencamp became ill, I have completed some initial tests on Dr. Bazargan's virus to see if my old isolates could possibly be the same. Even though it is premature to say conclusively, I am, unfortunately, now convinced that there is enough similarity to make an educated guess. If both the CIA and STRIKE used my virus, they probably are also the same as Dr. Bazargan's. I don't know how I could have been so blind," Martin added.

"Unbelievable! Then is it true, the disease that killed my wife originally came from your laboratory?" accused Jim as he stood in rage with his fists clenched.

Dr. Martin Reichstadt lowered his eyes. "It certainly is possible."

349

"Your virus was responsible for killing my wife and unleashing a pandemic on the world. And now all you can say is, 'It might be!' How incredulous! How ludicrous!"

"I know," said Dr. Reichstadt with his beard moist and reflecting the light.

"You should have known. Why didn't you?" Jim quickly swept his hand and arm across the desk spewing the documents, pen and other papers onto the floor. Shouting at the cowering man behind the small desk, he swore. "Now Laleh is sick as are countless others! What are you going to do now?" he demanded.

"I don't know. I don't know," Dr. Reichstadt responded. He looked into Jim's eyes pathetically and asked, "What would you do if you were in my shoes now? Because, in a way, you are—considering Dr. Bazargan's illness and your possible possession of a key computer disk that had been in Ben Carlson's possession. You too are involved. Ben's secretary confirmed that he took a key disk with him on the Caribbean trip and she feels that you may have inadvertently failed to return it with Ben's other possessions."

Jim stared at the broken man in disbelief. He looked away and slapped the wall, stinging his hand so hard that it tingled. He then shook it to regain sensation from the trauma. "Now you want me to clean up your mess? I can't believe it." Jim stood waiting for an answer that never came. So he continued in a defensive tone. "I retained the disk because of the suspicious circumstances of Ben's death." He stood with his hands on his hips. Then he placed his hands flat on the desk and cocked his head at Martin fully expecting a response. The man just sat with his chin braced in his right hand and his left arm across his middle.

Eventually Jim crashed onto a chair, frustrated and contemplative. Martin crossed his arms waiting for Jim's answer.

"I feel like knocking you senseless. But, I don't have a choice, do I, Martin?" said Jim in frustration. "What do you expect me to say? 'No, I won't be involved in saving the life of the woman I love and the lives of who knows how many'?"

At that moment, a knock on the door was simultaneously accompanied by an anxious voice. "Dr. Reichstadt? Dr. Reichstadt?"

"Yes—yes, come in," answered Martin.

"Oh! Dr. Schriver—good—you're here also. Dr. Bazargan has collapsed—she's unconscious. Just now she sat down in a chair and toppled onto the floor," the security woman announced.

Jim bounded out ahead of everyone and ran into the back of an armed security guard who stood between him and the door. Jim knocked the guard sprawling out of the way and broke the red warning cord. A woman security agent threw herself at Jim's feet and tripped him like a football block. Other agents came to her assistance and restrained him. Jim was dragged away as he clutched at his restrainers, calling, "Laleh—Laleh—Laleh!"

Everyone outside looked stunned. Only one person who had been wearing a decontamination suit had remained on duty during the very late hours. That man had just gone into a storage room when he was summoned to help Dr. Bazargan.

Dr. Reichstadt had regained his composure and began ordering people into action. He informed them to leave Jim locked in a room next to the contaminated area. He ordered a physical security barrier constructed to prevent similar escapades. The entire area was then sealed off until additional measures could be instituted. Jim eventually regained his composure and promised to "suit up" before going to her side. He was released to go to her.

Laleh had a fever of 105 degrees Fahrenheit and was delirious. Jim was relieved that she was still alive. A nurse in a special suit came in to assist. Jim told the nurse that Laleh needed to take her prescription for Amantadine and some Tylenol. Jim answered numerous questions of the nurse who had been summoned to the area to assist.

One question was quick and to the point. "Were you nuts—trying to force your way in here? You could have given yourself a death sentence. Not everyone responds to Amantadine, you know."

Jim responded. "I know. I lost my head for a minute."

Jim held Laleh's head on his shoulder while she dozed. His protective garment made him look like an alien from another world. Jim remembered the first praying mantis he had ever seen. It had held a morsel in its folded arm that it eventually devoured.

"This is a cotton-pickin', gosh-awful nightmare!" Jim exclaimed.

Laleh regained consciousness. "I must have fainted. I'm awfully tired," She said with her eyes half open.

"Just rest, my love," Jim replied, barely masking his anxiety.

The telephone rang. Jim punched the speakerphone button to allow both him and Laleh to respond. It was Dr. Reichstadt peering through the glass with his gown and mask on. Martin asked one question. "What do you want me to do?" He was obviously sincere.

"Martin, I wish to apologize again," Jim said. "The stress we've been through got to me. I'm sorry. When Laleh is feeling better we can discuss the legal considerations. But right now, I can only suggest you start the production process with Laleh's virus to make some vaccine." Jim looked to Laleh for her confirmation. She nodded her approval.

"It will be much more expeditious to have you two manage the questions and make the decisions directly from the very start. Much will be coming your way," Martin said.

"I don't know your operation well enough to do that yet, and neither does Laleh. Besides, she is not well enough to do that," Jim responded.

"Just remember, you can't do any worse than I have so far," said Dr. Reichstadt with a slight smile on his face.

"You make a point." Jim responded critically.

"You may need to do Dr. Bazargan's work until she has recovered. I will help. Fortunately, Dr. Bazargan does not appear to have any pneumonia yet and we do have sufficient Amantadine to protect you both. Concerning the job descriptions, each of you will have the best staffs in the world to work with. Ask them to help you. You will be mainly administrators. Your staffs can attend to the tasks that need to be done. Just trust them for now and ask them what they think needs to be done. Then make decisions accordingly," Dr. Reichstadt counseled.

"Everything is happening too fast," said Jim.

Jim looked at him in amazement and thought to himself. Had Martin suspected that he had the missing disk because of some secret security system or had Ben's secretary just been guessing? Here is a man who had risked everything by being candid. Jim hadn't been so candid. Martin freely admitted committing an error that had allowed an agent of the government to misuse a dangerous virus, plus he had also been oblivious to Bill Ballencamp's crimes. . . . Jim still could ruin him. Yet, he felt that Martin was basically an honest man, naive perhaps, but relatively honest. Martin also had a point about his own honesty concerning Ben's computer disk.

Jim decided to rationalize quietly to Laleh. "To err is human. I also know that academia could never meet this industrial pay scale. I can work for such a man, if he can work with me. Can you?"

He then looked into Laleh's eyes. She understood Martin's suggestions. She slightly closed her eyes and nodded weakly as she whispered, "Yes."

The nurse was ready to assist with Laleh's care. "I can take over now, Dr. Schriver."

Jim surprised himself when he answered Martin, " Well let's get busy. We have lives to save!" He comforted Laleh and told her, "I'll check on you every few minutes, Love. I've got to discuss a few things with Martin now. I'll be back soon."

Jim knew that because of her fever she had some difficulty grasping everything Martin had told them about his and her new potential positions.

Before he left, he said, "Darling, force yourself to drink all the fluids you can. Then try and get some sleep. We'll talk about this again—later."

She slept soundly for a few hours while Jim formulated an action plan with Martin. Jim checked in on her just when Laleh seemed to start hallucinating. She mumbled as he tried to make sense of her whispering.

"I was wondering why humans have spiritual needs. Why they search for a source of relaxation for their minds. . . . It seems to me they take primitive mind altering drugs to pacify themselves. . . . Religion is the opium of society . . . Karl Marx. . . ." Her hand rose slightly off the bed as if she were trying to add emphasis to a speech.

The lobby TV was on and a commentator for CNN was reporting. "The President of the United States has requested that the Federal Interagency Group on Pandemic Preparedness include the Federal Drug Administration, the National Institutes of Health, the Centers For Disease Control and the World Health Organization. They will dispatch representatives to confer with the scientists at Alpha Omega as soon as possible. Alpha Omega invited the American representatives and selected foreign representatives, including Afghanistan scientists, to the conference to be held today. They cited a need for confidentiality, 'to protect the common good,' as the reason to exclude the press. Access was promised immediately after the conference."

Jim had heard that the board and legal staff were going to do something. "This must be it," He thought.

He left Laleh's side to arrange a closed-circuit TV conference with a company task force. It was morning already.

"Folks, I know all of you have been anxious about the news reports you have been getting about the epidemics here in the plant, in Idaho, Israel, and Afghanistan. Dr. Reichstadt and I will try to answer your questions. Let's hear from area one first. What is your first question?"

"We're area one. Our first question is, how can we protect our families and continue to work here? We heard that all of our nation's Amantadine and Rimantadine has been purchased by the Israeli government."

"That is not true. A considerable amount has been reserved for our nation's essential industry and other special groups. You and your families will be some of the lucky ones in this country. There is a worldwide shortage—that is true," Martin answered.

"Area two," Martin directed.

"This is area two." The TV monitor's image changed to a different conference room in Alpha Omega. "We are curious about how you believe we can make a vaccine more quickly than ever before? We've heard the rumor that there's a plan."

"Alpha Omega does have a plan. By this time next week we will be in full production!" Dr. Reichstadt announced. "We will utilize duck eggs instead of chicken eggs. Experience in Iran has shown that the yield will be increased almost one hundred times using duck eggs. In addition, the late Dr. Ben Carlson left us a treasure on a computer disk revealing an Alpha Omega proprietary system for enhancing vaccine production. It's based on a formula developed from human/swine spliced and cloned media. It incorporates a special temperature, humidity and pressure variance control. We will need to produce only one ten-thousandth of the volume that we have required in the past with other virus strains and can do so in only a tenth of the time. We will market the first nasal vaccine spray ever made in the United States and do so in one week! It will give long-lasting immunity more quickly.

"Starting in eight hours from right now, we will work three shifts every twenty-four hours, day and night. Alpha Omega is insisting on a rigid chain of command. Most of you will not hear directly from any of these visiting experts. You should report only to your usual supervisor," Dr. Reichstadt said with authority.

The conference lasted for two hours and was finally terminated with a promise of future short daily conferences prior to each shift.

"Action plans will be distributed electronically to each work station," Jim promised.

Jim then returned to Laleh's side to find her almost comatose

355

and unresponsive. He knelt beside her, the nurse's sympathetic hand on his shoulder. His bulky costume restrained most of his instincts. He managed to hug her and wipe her brow.

Seeming to respond to his caresses, she opened her eyes slightly again but then mumbled unintelligibly.

Jim responded in pity.

There was no further response from Laleh. The nurse patted his arm and Jim left depressed and anxious.

Jim returned to Ben's old office and plunged himself into his new position. Two secretaries stood at the fax machines, opened written letters and notes, and took phone mail messages. They told him that his e-mail was overloaded.

"PLEASE! Prioritize, prioritize and prioritize!" Jim commanded angrily.

Everyone in the plant seemed to be rising to the task. . . . Because of the turmoil of getting into and out of the plant, it was easier to just stay within the plant's confines. Many workers were sleeping in their offices a few hours at a time and then returning to their work.

It was a wartime mentality. The governor ordered the National Guard to back up the police and security at the Alpha Omega plant. It was declared an essential industry, and martial law was in effect. The National Guard was ordered into duty because of the multitude of threats from various international groups. Some wanted revenge on the company for all sorts of contrived reasons. Some claimed that the Islamic woman doctor stole the Iranian virus and took it to the U.S. to start an epidemic. American militia groups were threatening the plant because they believed that the STRIKE members had been poisoned with a virus obtained from the United Nations' military conspiracy.

A five-mile diameter containment line had been formed around the neighborhood limiting vehicle traffic in and out. Still, hundreds of people on foot were protesting and harassing anyone coming or going. Power lines had been sabotaged twice and auxiliary power had to be used. Water was constantly monitored and filtered. Terrified neighbors of the plant were on talk shows complaining about real and imaginary conditions.

Jim became more concerned each time he sat at Laleh's side. Though her fever had been reduced, she was still not lucid. Jim tried to listen to her despite her whispered ramblings.

Jim could tell she was holding her own, but he insisted that she take her next dose of Amantadine while he watched her.

"Don't worry so much, Dear. I'll take the medication. I'll be okay. . . . You need to take your Amantadine also. Remember, you have to get them busy making vaccine some day, " said Laleh. She coughed violently and commenced to shake uncontrollably.

"NURSE!" Jim called frantically. "SHE'S CONVULSING!"

"She needs oxygen," the nurse said as she adjusted the nasal cannula to Laleh's face. "Dr. Jamison, would you please come to Dr. Bazargan, we're having some difficulty stabilizing her," she said over her hand-held radio. "Dr. Schriver, would you please wait outside for a little bit?"

"But," Jim protested.

"Please!" The nurse stared in Jim's eyes.

He retreated sullenly and again felt useless, but crept back into Laleh's room as the team worked over her. "Would you please call me in my office, Ben Carlson's old office, when she is again stable enough for me to see her?"

"Yes—certainly," the nurse said curtly while snapping a glance back at Jim. Dr. Jamison didn't even look up.

Jim surmised that whatever they were doing was quite stressful for them both. "I wonder what the hell they are doing to her," he said to himself as he walked toward his office. Jim went in his back office door and collapsed on the sofa—exhausted and depressed.

"Dr. Schriver! Dr. Schriver! JIM!" Mary Whiting, his secretary called. "There you are! I have been hunting all over the plant for you!"

Jim had been sleeping so soundly that he couldn't remember where he was or what day it was. "Whaaa. Who . . . Yeah?"

"You must go to Dr. Reichstadt's office immediately. Rock Granite is back in the plant in his wheelchair and is creating chaos! He is demanding that Martin—uh—Dr. Reichstadt get out of his office and he's trying to order everyone else around. We have been trying to contact some of the Alpha Omega board members to talk to him. We've called Security—but you've got to do something until we get help!"

"What?" Jim said as he straightened his clothes and bolted down the hall toward the C.E.O.'s office. He could hear Rock clear down the hall.

"I SAID GET OUT OF MY OFFICE—NOW!"

"Rock—calm down. Listen to reason," Martin's restrained voice responded.

Jim burst into the office. "What seems to be the problem?" He said in a controlled tone.

"WHO THE HELL DO YOU THINK YOU ARE, BARGING IN HERE?" Rock shouted while rising from his wheel chair with his fists clenched while supporting his weak legs.

"I'm Dr. James Schriver, the new director of marketing."

"BULLSHIT! I NEVER AUTHORIZED YOU TO BE ANY-THING HERE. GET OUT BEFORE I KICK YOUR BUTT OUT OF HERE!"

"I'm sorry, Mr. Granite, but we'll have to wait until some of the board members get here for you to make that request. They are on the way," Jim calmly responded.

"You're that crazy Muslim-lover—aren't you? You are the traitor who's responsible for everything! You and this little Jew-boy think you can steal my company. Well, think again! Rock grabbed a forty-five caliber automatic pistol that had been hidden in his wheel-chair and pointed it at Jim. He squeezed the trigger.

BAM! The first shot barely missed Jim as he dived behind a

low couch. It blew a hole in the office wall, imbedding itself in a secretary's desk in the outside office. BAM! He fired again at Jim, grazing his hip.

"I'M HIT! I'M HIT!" Jim yelled.

Rock steadied himself with his legs against the bookcase; the next two-handed shot was aimed lower in the couch. Rock knew the power of his weapon. His bullets were hollow points designed to expand.

"YOU BASTARD!" BAM! The couch split and collapsed as the dumdum slug hit a main support.

A large, solid-brass cuckoo bird that had always sat on Martin's desk flew straight into Rock's temple just as he turned to fire at Dr. Reichstadt. Martin had never been an athlete—but today he could have thrown a strike in the National or the American Baseball Leagues. His family's brass gift of years past just saved his life.

"DUMBKOPF!" Martin shouted just after he released his pitch.

BAM! The shot blew a two-foot diameter hole in the desk in front of Martin.

Everyone was on the floor when the security men burst into the office. Rock Granite was bleeding profusely from the head wound caused by the brass cuckoo bird. Jim was bleeding from a flesh wound on his hip. Martin had been thrown off-balance when he had pitched the brass bird and he had bumped his head on a table. He was suffering from a minor concussion.

Rock Granite was taken to the county hospital under guard. Charges were pending, and his condition was critical. The medical staff on duty at the plant treated Martin and Jim. Dr. Reichstadt was exhausted by the experience and was given a short-acting sedative to get some much-needed rest.

Because the medical team had cut Jim's pants off him to treat his hip, he borrowed some company-supplied blue work pants to wear. Anxious to tell Laleh that he was okay, he went to her area to visit her. Finally, he changed into a bunny suit and went to the place that he had last seen Laleh.

359

She was gone!

"Where is Dr. Bazargan?" Jim shouted in panic.

"Dr. Schriver, we felt it best to transfer her to the teaching hospital nearest us. They have a full infectious-disease staff there. Frankly, she wasn't doing well."

"Get them on the phone—PLEASE!"

Jim was informed that Laleh had been stabilized and was resting comfortably by the I.D. physician. Jim was advised not to visit for a few hours. They would call him if there were any changes—good or bad.

"Any time, day or night," Jim insisted. "Without fail?"

"I assure you, without fail."

Jim could hardly concentrate, but he knew he had a lot of work to do to discharge his new responsibilities. The weight of the world seemed to descend upon him. Day turned into night and back again. He was constantly looking to his watch to determine what day it was, as well as what time it might be. News about Laleh didn't vary.

"She is still comatose and she hasn't said anything to anybody, I'm sorry to report," the physician told Jim.

Jim had been asleep in his office for two hours when Martin came into his office and turned on the lights. "Oh, I'm sorry—I didn't realize."

"That's okay," Jim said. "What's going on?"

"The other folks in the infirmary here were transferred to the hospital. The medical staff started them on the Amantadine, but they weren't doing well. They are still hanging on—even though some have pneumonia. Unfortunately, however, we did hear that several militants have died in the Idaho STRIKE camp. They rushed some Amantadine up there and hoped it got there in time to help. The Idaho National Guard and the law enforcement agencies have had their hands full keeping the STRIKE Militia quarantined. Possible contacts, including Bill's family, have been started on treatment. Unfortunately, one remote convenience-store clerk that Bill met enroute has died. Others are sick along his route, but those who were lucky to seek treatment in time are getting by with therapy," said Martin.

"What about Iran, Afghanistan, Israel, and people in the rest of the world? What about the third world countries? Are they surviving the virus?" Jim asked in a concerned tone.

"Unfortunately," Martin continued, "The supplies of the tablets are very limited now and the distribution in the remote parts of the third world is impossible. There have been several failures of the drugs. Also, the cost is prohibitive for poor countries. The disease has been reported in Afghanistan, Pakistan, India and certain areas of China. The only real hope is to make enough vaccine in this country and abroad to protect people before they are exposed. Then, as you know, we must get it distributed—before the disease kills millions of people.

"Most of the news now is coming in by fax and Internet. News on television, radio and telephone has been restricted in most areas. We are hearing rumors about mass graves already. Usually, the weak and the old are being taken down the most quickly, but there is a demographic change emerging where the peak rates of death now are in the nineteen to twenty-nine age bracket." Martin paused to confirm that Jim was coping.

"The World Health Organization reported that patients develop discoloration of the skin. First, dark reddish brown spots appear over the cheeks, then in a few hours the ears and the rest of the face blotch until the whole body is discolored. Bloody fluid from the mouths and noses of victims soaks their clothing or bedding before death. People in triage are being abandoned as hopeless if their feet are black. One documented autopsy report paradoxically described very red and firm lungs due to the hemoglobin from ruptured red blood cells pooling in the air spaces of the lungs of victims. The disease is moving uncharacteristically fast for common influenza. It is more like cholera or Ebola in its speed."

"Martin, what about Rock?"

"He's near death from his head injury. He had been on blood thinners because of his stroke and this injury caused a major bleed into his brain."

"Have we heard anything from Iran or Laleh's family? What can you tell me?" Jim inquired.

"They are being very guarded in Iran about reporting anything relative to the epidemic. Only one Iranian physician, a member of the World Health Organization, has been candid. Even he can't seem to get complete critical information on the estimated deaths or morbidity from the government. It would appear that there is some sort of a political struggle developing because of the epidemic.

"Iranian authorities have failed to successfully make vaccine from Laleh's notes that she left in her hospital computer in Tehran. None of our friends in Iran have been able to communicate during the past few days. Distribution of food and medical supplies had overloaded an already poor service system. There have been undocumented reports of some new virulent cases of flu in Turkey, Iraq, Kuwait, Turkmenistan and Baluchistan. They may have several cases in Israel—but it might be stabilized now. They started drug therapy early. But I would bet they, too, will be a part of the pandemic if we can't get vaccine to them soon."

"Tell me some good news," Jim requested.

Martin continued. "You will be encouraged to know that Alpha Omega has agreed to allow all of the rest of the world's vaccine manufacturers to share their proprietary knowledge necessary to make the nasal vaccine, if they ask for our help. The White House Commission has prepared a press release for the five o'clock news. I just found out that they decided—since your data has not been published in a refereed American scientific journal—that U.S. manufacturers will be advised to stick with their fertile chicken eggs and make an injectable vaccine. They are not recommending production, for domestic U.S. use, of nasal vaccine made from duck-egg media. However, they were charitable enough to allow Alpha Omega or others to market our prototype nasal vaccine for export only," said Martin.

"I can't believe that! I can't believe that they can't understand basic science and are taking the ultraconservative route in a pandemic!" Jim fumed.

"Politics rules everywhere; we just have to live with it, Jim. I would like to have considered evaluating gene splicing of the virus with an E-coli from a pig or duck to see if we couldn't produce the virus faster and in even greater quantity. But, that would take more time and money. Splicing of E-coli and hepatitis-B virus was the key, of course, for the first hepatitis-B vaccine." Martin paused. "Do you think we can produce enough virus fast enough to make the adequate vaccine?" he inquired.

"Of course I do," Jim said." Alpha Omega had a little lead-time because of Laleh's work. The use of fertilized duck eggs instead of chicken eggs as a growth medium was a great boost to the yield of virus. Our competition, who use 150,000 chicken eggs to produce 250 gallons of pure virus, will probably find out that we are able to do it with a fraction of that many duck eggs."

"The board decided that we should focus only on the foreign market, because of politics," Martin announced. "Consequently, your goal to get a contract with every reputable duck-egg producer was a good strategy. I feel we will have all of the fertile duck eggs that we can use with our finite production capabilities, now. But we wouldn't have had enough for the U.S. market also."

"Any other news?" Jim asked.

"One more thing that was very important legally. Information obtained with the Freedom of Information Act about some flu epidemic that caused the *USS Arkansas* to return to port in February 1997. That established a legal precedence used by our legal department to establish a protocol for dealing with the virus' liability. The government has legislated liability immunity for this epidemic. Also, the FDA has been instructed to set aside most of the required testing protocol for foreign distribution. Our armed forces off the continental

United States can also be immunized with our nasal vaccine. Instead of the usual six months required to get a flu vaccine to market, we can do it in a fraction of the time, if we continue working around the clock. How we can ethically do this is a mystery. But in this emergency, I believe that it is necessary," Martin said.

"Jim, It would appear that everything your friends in Utah suggested is turning out to be true. Even though the evidence has been scant, I now believe the shipment to Utah of the virus that killed your wife must have come from here. The circumstantial evidence, the type of packaging and labels, were the kind we were using then. There is no computer or paper trail to confirm anything. The company's legal counsel objected to any of my admissions. But I felt that I owed you my opinion—whatever it is worth now," Martin admitted.

He looked apprehensively at Jim, wondering what sort of reaction he might have to such a frank admission.

Jim's jaw set and he took a deep breath, saying nothing. Tears welled in his eyes. Then he simply said softly, "Thanks, Martin."

Martin Reichstadt quietly left. As a youth, he had learned the concept of "an eye for an eye." He wondered what it would have been like to be raised as a Christian. He couldn't comprehend it.

Martin considered the need to increase production as he walked back to his office. He was well aware of the four hundred or so years of record keeping on influenza outbreaks and knew that pandemics from natural mutating virus had killed countless millions. In just three months in the fall of 1918 during September and November, between twenty-one and thirty-nine million people died. More Americans had died from the flu during the epidemic than from the First World War, the Second World War, the Korean War and the Vietnam War combined.

This would be the test of monumental proportions.

Chapter 30
Palo Alto and Salt Lake City—Days 33–40

The horrible influenza pandemic started to sweep the globe inflicting chaos among the poor people of the Third World. Jim worked day and night struggling to meet the insatiable demand for the nasal vaccine, in spite of his constant worry about Laleh's condition. Everyone at Alpha Omega looked like zombies with their sleep-deprived, sunken eyes. That week Alpha Omega shipped to the four corners of the planet, the largest quantities of vaccine ever shipped by any pharmaceutical company in the world.

Jim stopped to down his tenth cup of coffee of the morning. He reflected to himself that he'd had a routine of checking on Laleh. But, it wasn't enough. The office staff no longer felt pity for him and he'd evolved into a tyrant. Since his forced departure from academia at the University of Utah this week, he'd been feeling down. But under the circumstances, he felt he had no choice.

Jim went into the large conference room to hear the latest update from the International Task Force on the Influenza Epidemic. It was being broadcast in English by satellite from Saudi Arabia.

"For the first time we have some good news today. The world's vaccine producers—those who started later than the Alpha Omega Company in the U.S.—have all last week been functioning at maximum capacity to make their injectable vaccine available to America.

"The numbers of new cases had continued to climb every hour until just this week in the Mideast. With the exception of Iran and Iraq, governments have deployed the vaccine-like weapons in a military campaign. They have tried to anticipate which direction the

365

disease was moving and then sought to leapfrog ahead of it to establish a line of defense. For the first time since it began, hope is born that we might be able to stem the geometric progression of the disease.

"The slope of the growth curve has eased downward, thanks largely to Alpha Omega's nasal vaccine, used in much of this part of the world. Iran and Iraq are the exceptions because religious and political problems have prevented them from accepting American help."

It had become the habit of most AO employees to watch the Monday report. When they heard the news, a cheer went up that could be heard all over the plant. In the boardroom, the production areas and other offices, shouts of pride echoed.

Jim's spirits should have been raised, but they weren't. He had no excuse now to shirk away from Laleh's bedside; he had to face his own reality. The intensity of his work commitment could be relaxed. At least he should feel free to spend more time with her. Guilt was now his constant companion. When his cell phone rang, he ran to answer it in the privacy of his office. He feared it was probably the hospital with more bad news.

"Jim Schriver," he answered.

"Dr. Schriver, this is nurse Kay Smith, and I've been asked by Laleh Bazargan's doctor to inform you that it is time to come over ASAP."

"Is that it? Is that the only message?" Jim inquired.

"I'm sorry, but I just have a fistful of patient phone messages and that's all that it said. No new patient condition report has been posted on the computer record."

"I'll be there right now!" Jim shouted.

"I'll tell the doctor what you intend to do."

Jim left immediately with his heart pounding and his imagination speeding to the worst conclusions. He drove the rental car with abandon.

"If Laleh dies—so will I!" Jim threatened fate.

He parked the vehicle and ran all the way to Laleh's floor. He stopped dead in his tracks when he entered the hall where her room was located. The "Caution—Oxygen in Use" signs were removed as orderlies were moving equipment out of her room. Just then, Jim forced himself to walk to the room's entrance and look in. A person from housekeeping was removing the bedding and sheets. Laleh wasn't there!

"Where? Where is the patient that was in here—Laleh Bazargan?" Jim asked the woman from housekeeping.

"Senora gone," she answered and proceeded to remake the bed with clean linen.

"Hello Darling! How fast did you drive?" A voice greeted Jim. Jim spun on his heel and almost fainted.

"LALEH!" Jim couldn't speak another word. He grabbed her from the nurse's supporting arm and pressed her in his arms with abandon. Her stifled protest was dissolved with a kiss.

"Darling, I didn't tell you. I didn't want anyone to worry, but before I left Iran, I gave myself the first dose of the vaccine that I made there. I had no time for all of the animal studies I had planned. We were pressed for time. And, I wanted to make sure that it was safe before we gave it to anyone else. In spite of inadequate time to develop adequate immunity from the vaccine, and the large dose of virus I got from Bill Balencamp—it saved my life," Laleh revealed.

"You didn't tell me. Oh, that's quite a relief. . . . You gave yourself the first dose. Wow, you and Jonas E. Salk. He gave himself one of the first doses of polio vaccine," Jim said.

"Oh, I know how this must sound to you now. I'm so sorry—I had wanted to surprise you for happiness."

"I thought that you had taken a turn for the worse."

"I'm so sorry. My fever broke last night and all of my symptoms left this morning. I feel weak—but fine. I prayed that my vaccine would work in spite of the huge inoculum I got from Bill Balencamp. I just wanted to give you a good surprise."

"That you did. Oh, you don't know what a relief . . ." Jim's eyes filled with tears as he again held her tight. Both cried tears of joy.

After a few more days, they decided that it was safe for both to get away for a needed retreat. She needed more rehabilitation and Jim needed a rest. They booked a flight for Salt Lake City.

When Jim and Laleh arrived on the morning flight from Palo Alto to Salt Lake City. Eddie and Claire met them in the terminal building.

"Over here! Over here!" Claire yelled excitedly as she spotted Jim and Laleh exiting their portal. Ebullient voices from the entourage caused smiles on some passengers waiting for their flights.

Claire and Eddie had a small bouquet of flowers for Laleh plus a balloon that said, "Welcome Home." Many passengers and all of the airline employees wore surgical masks, but some people who had received their immunizations felt protected and had chosen not to wear them. The celebrating party did not wear any.

Despite the fact that they had all communicated on the phone and e-mail the day before, they all squawked like magpies. To some they sounded like children just leaving on a holiday. Most people had someone that they loved or knew who had been affected by the pandemic flu virus. As they left the terminal building they hardly noticed the government signs warning travelers of the need to be aware of the risks of travel during the epidemic and the regulations imposed on them.

Ed filled champagne glasses to toast what he had assumed would be a formal announcement by Jim and Laleh of their marriage. The shaded deck looked out over the Salt Lake Valley with the view of a city that looked just like it always had, despite the trauma of the disease that had occupied everyone's attention for so long.

Ed handed Laleh and Claire the first glasses and when he handed Jim his glass he asked, "Jim, would you like to give us a toast first?"

Reggae music played quietly.

368

Jim tilted his glass toward Laleh. "I invite you to raise your glasses to honor my best friend and the love of my life—to you, Laleh." The others joined.

She responded by blushing and instinctively avoiding eye contact, but smiling modestly. She also clandestinely avoided drinking from the glass; she could not shed her religious traditions. It never occurred to her that some women in America might have responded with a toast of their own.

The party evolved into a victory celebration over the pandemic. After a few sobering hours passed, Laleh was happy when Jim finally thanked Claire and Ed for the party and announced that they were going to drive up Big Cottonwood Canyon to be alone for a while.

As Jim, the newly-sober designated driver, drove up the Big Cottonwood canyon east of Salt Lake City, Laleh commented, "Nature seems to have reached her puberty and blossomed for all to see."

The sound of the creek and the sight of aspen, western maple, gambel oak and Douglas fir combined with the fresh aroma took Laleh into an imaginary world. She laid her head on Jim's shoulder and closed her eyes.

The tension and anxiety that had floated within her in the past was beginning to abate. She realized that Jim had become her source of relaxation. Thinking of him, touching him, being with him, always gave her a sense of security. His presence was better than any of the newest tranquilizers. "I believe that he is my nidus of love," Laleh thought to herself.

Jim looked at Laleh and demurely asked," Penny for your thoughts?"

"Did you know that my thoughts could be very expensive?" Laleh replied as she smiled facetiously.

Jim grinned at her. He hoped that she had some sensuous thoughts on her mind that would involve him.

The open windows of the vehicle caressed Laleh's long, beautiful, black tresses.

"Well, tell me," demanded Jim.

Laleh continued, "If you really want to know what I was thinking you may be shocked."

"I am all ears," replied Jim.

"I think I might be happy living in America."

"Great!" He glanced in her eyes. "Hey, we're almost there. Hidden Falls is at the top of this 'S' curve."

"This is the place where I thought we could get married," Jim announced pensively.

"Are you sure, Jim, that we shouldn't choose a holy place? A mosque or church?" inquired Laleh.

Out of respect to tradition and trepidation of such a commitment, uncertainty hung in the air like impending gloom.

Jim responded. "Laleh, even though you Moslems may not have Mohammed's physical presence, you still have his message from Allah. Jews also learned that they could worship Yahweh without a temple. Christians do not have Christ's physical presence, but they can feel his spirit both in and out of church."

The two parked at the tiny parking lot just below the side canyon known as Hidden Falls Canyon. Jim took Laleh's hand in his as they entered the narrow seclusion and followed the damp trail into the glowing natural sanctuary. He could feel her sweaty palm was just like his. They didn't talk much. They just walked the trail and surveyed the beauty.

Midday was the only time that this refuge from the heat was illuminated. When they reached the end of the short side canyon, the small waterfall cascaded down in front of them, reflected light sparkling from every drop. It seemed to radiate its rays from Laleh in every direction as she stepped in the middle of the shallow creek onto a big flat rock. As Jim started to join her he was fixed in awe as the sunlight caressed her.

Suddenly, as the two stood on the flat rock, Jim decided to risk it all. He kissed Laleh more passionately than ever before.

"Laleh, will you marry me now?"

Laleh simply smiled and said nothing.

"Laleh, will you marry me?"

She remained silent.

"Laleh?" Jim repeated with alarm in his voice.

"Of course I will—some day," she finally announced.

"Are you sure? I had to repeat myself three times," Jim said still concerned.

"I'm sorry, Darling, but it is an old wedding custom in Iran. When a bride is asked if she will marry a man, he always is expected to ask three times in a wedding ceremony."

From that moment, their passion started to grow uncontrollable. They both felt the repressed nidus of their love for one another. Their love was hidden from others in this microcosm of Hidden Canyon, with only the waterfall's music and the bird's chorus gracing the flickering soft yellow light dancing to the rhythm of the wind.

"Darling, I can't! I can't right now." She began to weep uncontrollably."

Then the muted sound of voices of rock climbers and their jingling metal met Jim's ears. "I understand, Laleh. I didn't know this area would be popular with climbers."

"You don't understand, my love. I haven't understood until—right now." Her river of tears continued.

"What's wrong, what do you mean? We can go somewhere—more private."

"My family. My people. My country. I've abandoned them all!"

"Oh Laleh—YOU HAVEN'T! You almost gave your life for them. You owe it to yourself to live your own life."

"Please don't make it any more difficult than it is for me now."

"We can both go back to Iran together as a married couple. With the new moderate president and moderate local councils gaining power, it will be easier. After the epidemic has been conquered," Jim reasoned.

"Oh, sweet Jim, you just don't understand. That one terse government fax that said my family was okay—is not enough for me. I don't trust the beaurocrats, I've got to go do what I can for my family and my countrymen. The news reports tell of Iran's troubles producing their own vaccine. The immunization program in Iran seems to be faltering because of a lack of good technical knowledge. With world opinion as my protection and my advantage of being well-known now—I feel certain that I can return to Tehran. With my experience and rapport with Alpha Omega, I can make a difference in my country. If I can show courage to them by doing it as a single woman, it will be a sign of hope for all women in Iran."

"Laleh, they might put you in prison again. If I go with you as your husband, you would also be an American citizen as well as Iranian. We would have a certain amount of combined world public opinion as protection."

"Jim, that isn't a risk that you should take just to be my husband. As I said before, I think I have some new immunity on my own."

Jim grasped for a compromise. "Maybe we could convince Alpha Omega to consider locating a cooperative plant there and work together as Iran did with the oil industry—years ago."

"Love, you don't understand the political realities there. A bad history with the Shah and America is still too predominant in most radical leaders' minds. I need to go there and try to make things better. I also need to be with my mother. My sister and brother need help politically to get an education. I also need to work through my guilt of Sonbol's death."

"Laleh, there must be a way that we can stay together through these new challenges. We have already been through more problems than some couples encounter in a lifetime. We can face the future in Iran together better than you can by yourself." Jim insisted.

"I've repressed these feelings too long, Jim dear. I know for us to be truly happy in the future, I must try to deal with the shadows of the past. This peaceful place has allowed me, and your love has helped me realize, what my true destiny must be. It's perfectly clear. It is my calling in life at this time. It's what I must do—alone."

"What about Alpha Omega? What about our plans? What about our lives together?" Still searching, Jim made his last try. After a long exhausting debate, Jim realized that he could not capitulate. He became silent. . . . Then he exploded. "As difficult as it seems for us now, I can see no other solution because our future together can't be sidetracked! We must have faith in each other and our ability together! The time for us and our need for commitment is now!" Jim concluded.

Laleh collapsed in Jim's embrace without further dissent.

Their walk out of the canyon was like awakening from a dream for them both. They held hands as they emerged into the harsh light of the midday sun. It was their first day of really being together—for now—but perhaps forever—soon.

THE END

Bibliography

Al-Khalil, Samir. *Republic of Fear: The Politics of Modern Iraq.* Berkley,Calif.: University of California Press, 1989.

Baraheni, Reza. *The Crowned Canibals: Writings on Repression in Iran.* New York: Random House, Inc.

Beizai, Bahram. *Bashu: The Little Stranger.* International Home Cinema, 1992 [video].

Brooks, Geraldine. *Nine Parts of Desire: The Hidden World of Islamic Women.* New York: Anchor Books, Doubleday, 1995.

Cavendish, Marshall. *Iran.* Cultures of the World series. New York: Time Books International, 1995.

Craig, Harry and Moustapha Akkad. *The Message: Mohammad— Messenger of God.* 1976 [video].

Draper, Theodore. *A Very Thin Line: The Iran-Contra Affairs.* New York: Touchstone, 1991.

Dudley, William. *The Middle East: Opposing Viewpoints.* San Diego, Calif.: Greenhaven Press, 1992.

Esposito, John L. *The Islamic Threat: Myth or Reality?* New York: University Press, 1995.

Geyer, Alan, and Barbara G. Green. *Lines in the Sand: Justice and the Gulf War.* Louisville, Ken.: Westminster/John Knox Press, 1992.

Goldschmidt, Arthur, Jr. *A Concise History of the Middle East.* Boulder, Colo.: Westview Press, 1991.

Jaan-E-Jam Television. *Radif-E Raqs, Collection of Dance Sequences of the Persian Tradition.* Iran [video].

Kritzek, James. *Anthology of Islamic Literature: From the Rise of Islam to Modern Times.* New York: Penguin Books, 1964.

Mahmoody, Betty. *Not without My Daughter.* New York: St. Martin's Press, 1987.

Mandell, Douglas and Bennett. *Principles and Practice of Infectious Diseases*. 4th ed. Vol. 2. New York: Churchill Livingstone Inc., 1995.

Maslow, Jonathan. *Sacred Horses: The Memoirs of a Turkmen Cowboy*. New York: Random House, 1994.

Mehrjui, Dariush. *The Tenants, a Comedy*. International Home Cinema, Inc., 1991 [video].

Moody, Sid. *444 Days: The American Hostage Story*. New York: Rutledge Press, 1981.

Morgan, Marlo. *Mutant Message: Down Under*. New York: Harper Collins Publishers, 1991.

Persia: Past-Present-Future. [video].

Pintak, Larry. *Beirut Outtakes: A TV Correspondent's Portrait of America's Encounter with Terror*. Lexington, Mass.: Lexington Books, 1988.

Ramazani, R. K., editor. *Iran's Revolution: The Search for Consensus*. Washington, D.C.: Indiana University Press, in association with the Middle East Institute, 1990.

Sanders, Renfield. *Iran*. Places and People of the World series. New York: Chelsea House Publishers, 1990.

Sasson, Jean P. *The Rape of Kuwait: The True Story of Iraqi Atrocities against a Civilian Population*. New York: Knightsbridge, 1991.

Sharkir, M. H., trans. *The Qur'an Translation*. Elmhurst, N.Y.: Tahrike Tarsile Qur'an, Inc., 1995.

Speight, R. Marston. *God Is One: The Way of Islam*. New York: Friendship Press, 1989.

St. Vincent, David. *Iran: A Travel Survival Kit*. Oakland, Calif.: Lonely Planet Publications, 1992.

GLOSSARY

Aba: A black or white cloak with slits for arms. Islamic dress for Mullahs.

Ammameh: Turban

Ali: Ali ibn Abu Taleb, husband of Fatima (daughter of Mohammad) founder of Shi'ite sect of Islam.

Allah: Arabic word for God.

Allah-O-Akbar: God is great!

Andarun: Quarters where females live away from the outside world and isolated from views of non-family males. Often an inner section of a traditional Islamic home.

Anfal: A chapter or sura of the Koran. It also can mean "spoils of war."

Aqd: A wedding contract or agreement.

Ayatollah: Shi'ite Islamic religious instructors and translators of the law. Known also as a single word meaning "Reflection of God."

Bazaar-e-bozorg: The great bazaar.

Bismillah al rahman alrahim: In the name of God, the compassionate, the merciful.

Caliph: Leaders who "came after" Mohammad in the initial Muslim nation.

Chador: A type of hijah or Islamic dress code. A square, usually very dark, fabric covering of an Iranian or Lebanese Shi'ite woman from the top of her head to the ankles. It is fastened under the chin.

Farsi: Persian Language.

Fatwa: The legal opinion (or decision) of a religious leader concerning religious law. Death or imprisonment can be the sentence of such action.

Feast of the Sacrifice: A feast following the three day holiday of Ramadan. A sheep is often slaughtered and the meat given to the poor. Muslims and pilgrims worldwide participate.

Fitna: An Arabian slang term for beautiful woman. It also can mean civil war and chaos.

Hadith: The teachings of the Prophet Mohammad may be quoted or interpreted to mean something relative to contemporary considerations.

Hajj: The pilgrimage to Mecca that all Muslims endeavor to make once or more in their lives. It is considered a process of purification. The pilgrimage should coincide with the Islamic calendar designation.

Halal: Permitted relative to religious law.

Hammam: Bathhouses.

Haram: .Abstention from drinking alcohol or eating pork because it is religiously forbidden. Violations may cause the perpetrator to face Islamic court.

The private quarters of the women in a family or the women themselves.

A religious shrine.

Hezbollah: "The Party of God." A political and religious organization popular with Lebanese Shi'ites as well as Iranians.

Hijab: Islamic women's proper dress.

Hijrah: Mohammad and his followers' escape from Mecca to Medina, July 16, 622 (Christian calendar). This is the starting date for the Muslim calendar.

Hussein: Mohammed's grandson.

Husseiniya: A center for Shi'ite study and prayer.

Imam: The first twelve leaders of the Shi'ite community.

Insha' Allah: As God wills it.

Islam: The submission.

Jihad: Holy war or struggle to defend Islam.

Khadija: Mohammed's first wife for twenty-four years.

Komiteh: Islamic disciple group.

Koran: Muslims' holy book containing the revelations of Mohammad. The word means literally, "Recitation."

Kurd: People who live in the mountains between Iran, Syria, Iraq, Turkey and Turkmenistan.

Lapidations: Stoning. Omar, the second Caliph, instituted the Jewish custom of punishment for adultery.

Lavosh: Thin bread.

Madresse: School.

Magneh: An Iranian head covering worn by women similar to Catholic wimples.

Majlis: Gathering. A room for receptions. A parliamentary type council.

Makruh: A religiously undesirable act that is discouraged. Those who refrain from such acts may be rewarded.

Marg bar America: Death to America.

Mecca Pilgrimage Ritual: Orbiting the Kaaba (large black stone structure) on the Plain of Arafat while praying for forgiveness.

Moazzin: A man who sings his call to prayer from a minaret.

Minaret: A narrow columnar structure forming the spire of a mosque from which a Moazzin (or a recording) sounds the call to worship.